For all miserable, sullen libras everywhere. Especially my husband.

To chat to me about permission please email me
jemmacroftauthor@gmail.com

If you bear more than a striking resemblance to the MMC, I am going to need photographic evidence.

Note from the author

I have really loved writing this book. It has been my catharsis over a few pretty shitty years, I'll spare the details. I hope you enjoy reading it as much, but I also want you to feel safe in the knowledge you won't stumble on something that isn't right for you.

With that in mind, here are a list of content/trigger warnings.

Explicit scenes of a sexual nature

Profanity

Mild threat of violence

Themes of discrimination

Casual drug use

Also, please note this book is written in **British English**, please do not give me a bad review because I'm generous with the U's.

Cheers, mate.

By the Horns

by

Jemma Croft

Fantasy Flatmates Book 1

THE EIGHT AND A HALF KINGDOMS
THE MYTHIC REALMS
EAST WINTERLANDS
BORDERLANDS
ST. CLOUDS
REMY
BORDALIS
THE HUMAN REALMS
PANNOR
D.I.NLOW

Chapter 1

Joey

Every course at The University of Remy began at nine pm sharp, on account of all the vampires.

And no, he wasn't a vampire.

Thank the gods for small mercies.

The dash clock read nine-fifteen. My foot nudged at the gas. The muscles, not used to holding back, sent cramps up the length of my calf. It was like fighting to keep two magnets from snapping together. Sweat beaded at my temples. My armpits, for want of a better word, gushed. I felt sorry for the poor chump who'd end up seated next to me in class.

Either I could be late on my first day or risk another ticket. Considering I was due to start a course titled Compulsory Corrective Control for Apprehended Acceleration Addicts, it was a no-brainer. Long story short, I'd been caught speeding at least eight times too many, and if I didn't pass this bloody course, they would impound Little Red and remove my license. And if I didn't have a car or a license, I didn't have a job, and I'd have no way to pay Hell-Bitch Christie the multiple back payments of rent I owed her, and she'd kick me out of her flat.

And call me old-fashioned, but I rather liked having a roof over my head while I slept. Not to mention the snuggles from Hell-Bitch's adorable ginger tomcat, Ludo.

At nine-twenty I pulled into the carpark, sweating more, if possible. At nine-twenty-two I collided into the university's reception desk and the leaflet stand, party-cannoning approximately eleventy-thousand pamphlets around the cathedral-like entrance hall.

"Miss Joey"—gasp—"Silver. Here to start"—gasp—"speed school," I said between thumping down handfuls of *'Apply for a Student Loan in Three Simple Steps'*, and *'Mo' Magic, Mo' Problems: Why UR Doesn't Allow Any Weapons on Campus'*, and *'Pound A Pint Nite at Tallywhacker's'* onto the counter-top. I massaged the stitch developing in my side.

The receptionist, an ethereally beautiful, thirty-something merman with skin made of sunshine and hair the colour of a rose chafer, assessed me over the top of his yellow plastic spectacles. He sucked at his teeth and proceeded to spew a heck-ton of directions at me. "Right-down-the-corridor-first-left-second-floor-second-right-left-again-round-the-bend-room-number-should-be-forty-six-F."

Having registered only the first and last words, and nothing in between, I said, "Ha, that's my bra-size." To which he did not laugh, didn't even raise an eyebrow. How Mermish of him. I scooped up the remaining debris as nonchalantly as possible and made my way further into UR's intestines.

Another ten minutes, and I was ready to send for a search party. I didn't remember any of the merman's words being elevator, yet every single corridor I turned down ended with a set of elevators. I was about to give up, shoot up a flare or smash the fire alarm and let myself become swept out with the rush of bodies, when I spotted the room.

There it was. Room number thirty-six-F. Same as the girls.

I knocked on the door and smoothed down my strappy red summer dress. Chosen specifically for today because, of all my strappy red summer dresses, this one was the most mature, most capable, least . . . cleavagey. Even if it did have tiny, embroidered peaches all over it.

Wait.

It was thirty-six-F, right?

The door opened inwards, and framed in the jamb stood a creature with a man's body — gleaming ebony six-pack, threaded muscular arms, and a cotton-soft white kilt — and the head of a falcon — curved golden beak, black-rimmed eyes, and a plume of navy feathers fanning from his brow ending around the middle of his back.

"New girl?" he said, his cadence unexpectedly smooth and warm. He sounded like the man that did voice-overs for movie trailers. It was the voice of someone with decades, centuries even, of seniority. It was the voice of omnipotence and exorbitantly expensive education, and maybe a cartoon unicorn I remembered from a kids' programme I used to watch.

I shook the thought from my head. "I'm so sorry I'm late. I was really trying to keep to the speed limit—Below the speed limit, actually. Well below it. There were, like, all these red lights. And—"

"Okay, kid. Let's take a quick breather, shall we? Name?"

"Joey Silver."

"Human?"

I nodded.

Never assume someone's species. Borderlands' rule number one. Though sometimes assumption wasn't necessary. Take, for example, the fae with their pointy ears, or the sirens and their clacky bird feet, or the werewolves and their moon worshiping and general wet dog stink. In my case, rounded ears, pink doughy flesh, typical human imperfections such as stretchmarks and pimples. Safe to say, me, human through-and-through.

He stood aside, peered down at the paperwork on his desk, and I got my first proper look into the classroom.

My initial thoughts. It was busy. There weren't any free seats. Maybe I'd have to perch on the end of a table. The students were an almost fifty-fifty mix of humans on the left side, and mythics or legends, whatever you call them, on the right. We're not supposed to use the term 'monsters' anymore, but old habits die hard. Especially with some folk. Folk who I happily left behind in the Human Realms a decade ago. I spotted a handful of humans mixed in with the mythics, and a couple of gargoyles who'd elected to sit behind two jittery-looking human women. The tables ended at waist height, and most people sat on bar stools, while some (namely the vampires) preferred to stand.

The teacher narrowed his eyes at me. "You're not on the list. When did you enrol?"

"About two days ago. They told me if I didn't do the course, they'd take my car away." I pulled an *eeeek* face, and the classroom collectively laughed.

"Very well, very well," said the falcon-headed shirtless guy with a chuckle. "It's likely your forms haven't come through yet. Where to seat you?" He glanced around the room and gulped.

In the back row, a gigantic . . . man (?) — might have to pop a question mark on that one and circle back to his species — pulled his sweater hood up over his head, leaving a mass of bronze-coloured hair poking out either side of his face and two enormous white horns escaping at his forehead. My guess? He was going for inconspicuousness. Perhaps in a bid not to be noticed by the tutor. Fat chance of that, considering he was getting on for seven-foot and his shoulders were as wide as . . . Well, put it this way, he'd probably have to turn sideways to fit through doors.

Yet, beside him, revealed the only free seat. Or, at least, part of a seat. It would be a squash for sure. What, with those aggressively abundant biceps encroaching on all the available space.

Eh, I'll live.

"Looks like I'll have to sit you in the back, next to Taurin." The gasps came from students on both sides of the room, and the horned man in the sweater hood stiffened. "That okay with you, Taurin?"

The giant man, Taurin, shrugged, and then rolled his eyes up to the gods, in a gesture that told me it was, emphatically, not okay with him. I nodded to the semi-naked falcon-fella and began my walk to the back of the classroom to claim the few remaining inches left on Taurin's desk. All gazes followed me. Mouths hung open as though my new classmates were witnessing a ghost. Even the ghost in row three had clamped her hands over her cheeks in an eerily similar recreation of a painting I once saw on a class trip to Pannor Museum.

"Hi, alright? I'm Joey," I said to Taurin in a somewhat pared down version of my usual over exuberant greeting.

He responded with an almost inaudible, "Shit." Then, he reached inside the front of his hoodie, seized a hidden scarf-bandana-thing, and pulled it up over his nose.

I discreetly sniffed my armpits, choking down my cough of disgust. "I'm so sorry, I ran from the carpark."

Everyone turned to stare at us. At me. Whispers, covered by palms, filled the classroom, though I couldn't make out anything said. I'd never minded being the centre of attention, enjoyed it sometimes, but this felt another level of weird.

"Okay kids, settle down," said the bare-chested falcon-dude. I really ought to find out his name. "Please set up your kits as usual. I'm going to have a quick chat with our resident new girl."

A cacophony of clattering rang out as people hoisted bags onto tables and began pulling things out.

"So nice of you to join us," came the honeyed tones of falcon-bro, appearing beside the desk. "Now, we're a few weeks into the course already, so you'll have a bit of catching up to do. Taurin can fill you in." Beside me, Taurin shook his head, eyes narrowed. Falcon-chap gave him A Look which I had no hope of deciphering considering all the feathers, and Taurin lowered his scarf like a reprimanded child. "He's a good lad. I have a feeling it might benefit both of you."

At this, Taurin snorted. I swear a cloud of steam billowed in front of his face. Falcon-man simply laughed.

"You'll need to order your kit," he said to me. "This can be done online through the student website."

"Kit?"

"For today," he placed a hand on Taurin's hirsute one in a fatherly sort of way, "you can borrow Taurin's?"

The colossal chest level with my face rose and fell with exaggerated whooshes. It seemed, though I couldn't be sure, that the mountainous man next to me was taking measured breaths.

"Fine, whatever," Taurin said pedantically, yet in a voice gruffer than my forty-a-day grandmother.

Falcon-guy beamed, simultaneously proud and smug. I wouldn't have been surprised if he'd said, "See now, that wasn't so difficult, was it?"

"So, what brings you to my class?" he said, returning his attention to me.

"My, uh, probation officer told me I had to."

"Ah. Well, at least you'll be in good company." He patted my new miserable friend on the arm. "I'll get you started on your paperwork and your student lanyard." And then he turned away, leaving me feeling as though I'd missed a large chunk of vital information.

As soon as the tutor's back was turned, and before I could get a decent peek at Taurin's face, he pulled his scarf back up. *Wow, I must really stink.*

"Sorry, excuse me," I said, before I could ruminate on my body odours. Falcon-man's head spun one-eighty. It made the same sound as rearranging naked limbs on a leather sofa would. Okay, unnerving as heck, but whatever. "Uh, I don't know your name."

I think he smiled, difficult to tell with the beak. "It's Horus. My students call me Russ."

Right. Horus. As in *the* Horus. As in the ancient Egyptian god of kings. Teaching a speed control class. To a bunch of delinquents. And likes to be called Russ.

I chanced a side peek at my huge neighbour. Were his eyes crinkling at the corners?

Horus—Russ returned to the front of the room. "Okay folks, today we're picking up where we left off last week. If you take out your paste"—paste?—"and using the method we talked about, I'd like you each to make a sugar rose."

"What?!" Did I say that out loud?

Beside me, and without turning his head, Taurin pushed a piece of torn-off greaseproof against my hand. In the centre of the paper lay a tear-drop shaped cookie-cutter, a tiny white twig-like wire, and what looked to be a pink ball of dough. I glared at him.

"And guys, let's not forget our hairnets this time. There are hairnets, beard-nets, and for our furrier friends," Russ shot a look at a pair of giggling werewolves, "Knuckle-nets."

What in the Eight and a Half Kingdoms were knuckle nets?

I let my eyes rove over the classroom, taking in details I failed to notice until that point. Such as the cabinets with labels that read things like '*Baking Tins 6" - 14"*' and '*Icing Bags*', the row of sinks in the corner, the black and white homemade ink-jet posters reading '*Hand Washing is for Heroes*' and '*Only Losers Lick Their Nozzles*'. And the biggest clue of all: the sign above the whiteboard, spelling out, in ten-inch letters . . .

Cake Decorating 101.

Well, shit.

Taurin stomped away from our desk and returned. He passed me a net, again silently, and began placing his own on himself. First the knuckle-nets. Boy, his hands were downy. Then he pulled down his scarf, revealing a glossy bronze two-week-old beard, which he netted. He took a shuddering sigh before removing his hood and exposing his shiny mane of hair. Mane really was the right word for it. It reached all the way down his neck and disappeared behind his collar. The same rich, silky bronze as his beard. It looked invitingly soft. Unbidden, my fingers twitched with the need to sink themselves into it. He tied it up into a topknot — noooo, topknots were the ruin of me — and pulled a net right the way over his head, including the horns, which defiantly sliced their way through the electric-blue web.

The face that lay underneath all that hair and beard, and the small silver septum ring, was even more inviting. The most accurate descriptor I could summon would be coochie-twingingly-hot. Tanned, weather-aged skin (outdoorsy type?), thick expressive brows, perfect full cupid's-bow lips, and the most piercing blue irises I'd seen on anyone, human or mythic. The word that came to mind was cerulean, and I did not do fancy words. His face was almost painful to look at, like someone was reaching in through my eyes and gripping at something in my chest with clawed fingers.

I wanted to ride it.

Joey, behave yourself.

I tore my gaze from him, but not before he caught me staring, raised a perfect eyebrow, and pulled his hood back up.

What was he?

"Alright, let's pop our tails and phones away, and any wands or amulets or whatever else it is you kids use these days, and get to it," said Russ, who'd now, somewhat disappointingly, donned a white apron. He pressed a button on a palm-sized remote, and the classroom filled with the morose acoustic thrumming of folksy disco covers.

I had two choices. Put my hand in the air, admit I'd got the wrong room, and ask to join the speed control group. Hopefully, it wouldn't be too late for me to sit the course, and hopefully, I'd get to keep my car, and my job, and my home.

Ooooooor . . . I could stick it out here next to the cantankerous hunk and bluff my way through the rest of the evening. Call my probation officer tomorrow and grovel for a resit. Maybe lose the car, the job . . . Gods, I hope Christie will let me keep my room.

Beside me, Grouchy McGroucherson made a noise similar to a horse's blow and pushed the greaseproof closer still. In his hand, he held another white wire, identical to the one he'd placed in front of me. It looked ridiculous in his massive paws, like a sewing needle. From his own lump of pink dough, he pinched off a small amount, rolled it into a ball and squished it into a point on the end of the wire.

He watched me from the corner of his peripherals, just long enough to satisfy himself that I would follow his lead.

I swallowed, closed my eyes for half a beat. Dammit, if I end up losing my car because of this gorgeous curmudgeon, I will be so pissed.

I leant forward, pinched a piece of dough free, and copied what he did. He didn't turn his head to look at me, but the one visible corner of his mouth twitched upwards.

In that moment, I guessed I was seeing the night through here.

After a couple of hours, I had the beginnings of a pretty decent looking rose. Nowhere near as accomplished as The Misery Man's, but he turned out to be a surprisingly patient, albeit painfully taciturn, teacher. And although he didn't speak, or look at me, or even turn his body an extra degree towards me, he demonstrated how to cut each petal, how to shape the top to make it appear realistic, and how to attach it to the bud. And I watched as a flower bloomed from nothing. All the while, I tried to figure him out.

I wanted to ask him. I wanted to know more than anything. *What are you?* But most considered the question rude. It could even be dangerous with some mythics. Sure, it was one thing for a three-thousand-year-old God to take a, quite frankly, obvious leap at my species, but it was entirely another for a human to assume a non-human's species. At the very least you risk offending someone. At the worst, I'd heard the Four-Hundred Years War was started because a human mistook a hippocampus for a kelpie.

I couldn't ask Taurin. I'd have to work it out.

He wasn't fae. That much, I was sure of. His ears weren't pointed. Not sea-dweller. No scales or gills. Not dragon or demon, no wings. Not undead. I could hear his deep, unsteady breaths, could feel the warmth that radiated from him.

The silence was excruciating. I didn't think I'd been this quiet since I was in utero. I had to break it.

"Come here often?" I said.

Nothing. Not a smile, or a raised eyebrow. Not even an eye roll.

I continued, "Gosh, I'm so glad we've had all this time to get to know one another." A few heads in the classroom turned towards us.

He took a breath, pinched the bridge of his nose, and exhaled so long and loud it sounded like he was peeing. He must have a massive . . . lung capacity. More heads shot up in our direction.

"What do you want to know?" he said, his voice like waves crashing against pebbles.

I started simple. "What do you do for a living?"

A pause. "I work in a timber yard."

Big, hulking arms. Yep, I could totally picture that. Would be later, in fact.

"Well, thanks for the reciprocal question," I said, when it became obvious it would never arrive. "I'm a delivery driver—Hopefully still a delivery driver. Mostly for takeaway food. You know Goblin Grub? Or Siren Scran? Wet 'n' Waffles? Mermish 'n' Chips? The merpeople place?"

Nothing.

"You from Borderlands?" More heads.

Another pause, then a solitary, "No."

So definitely not human, not that you'd find huge curving horns on a human, but we humans couldn't easily travel to the five kingdoms north of Borderlands. Species tended to stick to their own patches.

"Yeah, me neither. I'm from the Human Realms. Pannor, actually. But my parents live in Dinlow now if you've heard of it?"

He nodded. Once. But he nodded. I was finally getting somewhere.

"How old are you?"

"Thirty-eight."

"In human years?"

"Also, thirty-eight."

So not a demigod, or a legend. I was well and truly flummoxed, my curiosity peaked, and somewhere deep in the cavities of my chest, something new was blossoming. Something akin to . . .

No, it couldn't be.

"I'm thirty-four," I offered. A time-honoured habit of mine; over sharing when nobody asked. No response, but what did I honestly expect?

Okay, in for a penny. "You're so tall. What are you? Six-ten, no eleven?" That would make him an entire foot taller than me.

It was at that moment I realised the class had gone deathly silent, and everyone had paused their sugar-paste sculpting to gawk at us. Even the music had stopped.

"In my human form," was his answer.

As enthusiastic as I was, I wasn't stupid. I chose my next words carefully. Ish. "So, how tall are you when you're not in your human form?"

The class was so quiet you could have heard one of those flimsy white wires drop.

"Almost nine feet," he said eventually, his voice rolling through the room like distant thunder. "Not including the horns."

I didn't even care who was listening in anymore. I needed to find out more, and if they wanted a show, I guess I was going to give them one.

"And," — *Don't do it, Joey. Don't ask him.* — "Do they get bigger as well?"

I *felt* the collective intake of breath. It could have snuffed out a hundred candles.

He turned to me, his movements stiff and strained. His eyes swept from the top of my head all the way down to my red high-tops, and back up again. Slowly, so excruciatingly slowly, the corners of his mouth twitched upwards into a smile.

I won. At least, it felt like I won.

"Okay then kids!" called Russ from somewhere near the front, causing everyone to startle. "Five minutes left. Let's pack up. Don't forget to wash up any UR equipment and put it away in its proper place. I don't want a repeat of last week."

The same cacophonous chorus broke out once again as people began shoving equipment inside bags and cupboards and discussing their plans for the rest of the week. A few moments went by as Taurin and I stared at each other. Silently, of course. His chest rising and falling, his fingers twitching on the edge of the desk, his lips ever so slightly parted.

It was then that I realised I wanted not only to know *what* he was and how big his horns got when he shifted, but I also, maybe, just a teensy bit, wanted him. Just for a day or two. If he opened up a little, we could have some fun together. I wanted some fun.

I was a Some Fun kind of girl.

I wanted to add him to my ever-growing collection of Men Who'd Inevitably Want More From a Relationship Than I Could Offer Them.

"Here, I'll do this." He took the equipment from my hand and hoisted his kit bag onto the table. And I just watched him like I was incapable of movement. I watched the muscles in his back flex underneath his sweater. I tried not to notice the curvature of his thighs, or his woodsy, earthy, immoderately male scent, or the strip of tattooed skin revealed at his hips when he lifted his arms, or the thick swirling shadow of a tail, coiled in the seat of his jeans extending down the back of his leg.

Gods.

Why was my mouth so dry?

"It was nice to meet you, Joey," he mumbled, his bag slung over his shoulder. And then he left. And for the first time in my entire life, I felt speechless.

I turned back to the desk and grabbed my backpack from underneath it. And that's when I noticed he'd left his sugar paste rose. And taken the one I'd made.

Chapter 2

Joey

Ash answered the door as he always did, gilt housecoat and slippers, oiled brown skin peeking out, his long silver hair braided and pinned up and his silver beard and moustache clipped with ardent precision. He had a butler, and a full staff of around a dozen servants, but the two-thousand-year-old fae preferred to answer his own front door. At least to me.

"Good morning, stranger," he said, his voice singsong and effeminate. "Is it Thursday already?" It was always stranger, or my lover, nothing in between.

"I thought I'd come early this week. Pretty sure they're going to take Little Red away from me."

He looked over at my car parked on his drive. A hand painted sign indicated to a space allotted exclusively for me. The middle of which had been planted with grass so Little Red's oil leak wouldn't damage the cobblestones.

Despite the leak, she was beautiful. My baby. My livelihood. Red, obviously. A classic, sort of, only a few years short of being tax-free. I'd given her power steering, and replaced the heating system, and had her turbo super-charged. Also, her interiors reupholstered, her rust patches filled in and sanded down, and all her sleek, sexy-as-hell curves resprayed. She shone. I could spend hours upon hours staring out the living room window, drinking her in, and I'd never get bored. The leak was next on my list. And then the emissions.

"You failed the course?" I shook my head. "You didn't do the course? Oh, this is going to be good. Come in." He turned to his housekeeper. "Lauren, espresso martinis for my lover and myself and some of the fancy coconut biscuits." Like Ash would eat anything other than fancy biscuits.

"I've brought a book," I said, as I followed him into Lavandou Hall, his Eastside mansion.

I met Ash the same way I met most men. At a bar. Christie, who at the time didn't hate my guts, snagged us tickets to Abysm, the most exclusive club in Remy, with the sole purpose of locating some decent, preferably non-human, D. What she failed to grasp was that I already had mine in my handbag, in the guise of the most recent Nikki Star novel, and had become rather single-minded about consuming it.

After a few hours of rebuffing real-life men, one guy in particular, a rather too persistent (read predatory) satyr, I found a quiet booth, tucked my legs up on the bench and got stuck into my book.

"Is it good?" came a voice from across the table once I'd reached about ten pages in.

I had been about to tell Mr Persistent to fuck off when I looked up and instead, saw an elderly fae perched opposite me.

"Nikki Star. She's my favourite," the old fae said.

"You like Nikki Star?" I blinked at him, awestruck.

Nikki Star was a human author, living in the Human Realms, writing smutty romance novels about ordinary, yet well-endowed, humans. Therefore, she wasn't known in Borderlands. At all. And not well stocked in any of the bookshops. Even ordering her books online was near impossible. I had to get my sister to ship this one to me as soon as it had been released.

"*The Cowboy's Secret Baby* is . . ." He brought his thumb and fingers to his lips and did a chef's kiss gesture.

"I love that one! Have you read *The Billionaire's Fake Fiancée*?"

"Oh, Ryan. Be still my heart. My forever book boyfriend. How can a man inside my head be so hot?"

"I know right!" I found a napkin and shoved it into the book to mark my page. "I'm Joey." Wow, I really just gave him my real name.

"Joey." He smiled. "Hi, I'm unpronounceable, but you can call me Ash."

"Try me."

He growled, at least, I think he growled, he didn't open his mouth, but a low rumbling sound emitted from his chest . . . vicinity.

"Nice to meet you, Ash." I held my arm out for him to shake. He took my hand and kissed my knuckles.

"So, it's good? I haven't been able to get my mitts on that one yet."

"Our hero is called Daniel. He's a mechanic. With a ten-inch wrench," I said with a wink. "You can borrow it when I'm finished."

"I've got an even better idea. How do you fancy calling it a night and coming home with a handsome stranger?"

"I don't know. You're not an axe murderer, are you?"

"Not done that for a few centuries," he said. He raised his hand by an inch, and a server was instantly at his side. "Place this gorgeous creature's bill on my tab and bring the car around."

And that was that. I've been reading to Ash, in his one-room-fewer-than-a-castle home every Thursday for the past three years.

"You got your hands on the new Nikki Star," said Ash, as he led me through Lavandou Hall. "Your sister mail it to you? Are you two on speaking terms again?"

"No, still not speaking to Ottilie. I don't know why she can't see things from my point of view."

Ash gave me a pointed but patient look, as though suggesting I should be the one to change my mind and not my sister. I ignored this, as I always did.

"So, tell me about this course. What kept you from attending? Or should I ask, who kept you from attending?"

"Ah, you know me too well." I sat with a sigh on the red tweed armchair. Even though it was twenty-six degrees outside, and Ash liked to keep his air conditioning on the slightly warmer side, I pulled the patchwork blanket across my legs. Immediately Four-Feet, Ash's tabby, jumped onto my lap.

"So . . .?" he said, making himself comfortable on the chaise longue opposite me. This is how we always sat. Me on the chair Ash purchased on a whim because he said it reminded him of me, and him on the chaise, matching blankets, and mismatched cats. His was a yellow-eyed calico named, for obvious reasons, Three-Feet. Lauren brought in a tray of drinks and placed them on the table between us.

I told him about the course. How I had every intention of going to speed school, how I'd arrived late, how I'd gotten the room numbers mixed up, how I'd somehow found myself in cake decorating class instead, and how I'd been unable to admit the truth and leave.

"Is he human?" I hated that Ash already knew the reason I stuck it out and bluffed my way through the nonsense was a *he*. It was always a *he*. Not that I was a relationship type of girl. I liked the challenge and the chase, and I loved the happy endings. And then I could move onto the next one before either of us got burned.

"Nope, not human."

"Ooh, I have to guess, do I?" His eyes lit up.

"No, that's the thing. I don't know what he is."

He clapped his hands together. "My favourite type of puzzle! Describe him," he demanded, flourishing a hand. "Start at the feet and work your way up."

"Human feet, big though, but no talons. Jeans. Tail, not quite sure what kind, he'd tucked it away. Human legs, human body, big, sexy as fuck human arms. Gorgeous face, like"—I made a pained expression—"that gorgeous. Summer-sky-blue eyes. Hairy. So hairy. All the way down to his shoulders. Horns. About seven-feet tall. He said in his non-human form he's nine-feet."

Ash brought his hand to his chin. "Hmm. Shifter?"

"I guess so."

"Any other defining features? What were his hands like?"

"Normal. Hairy, but normal. No claws."

"His voice?"

"Gruff. Like post week-long bender."

"Ears?"

"Rounded."

"Horns? Did they go up or out or back? Curly or straight? Colour? How big were they?"

"Massive. White. They curled up and out like this at the front." I made C's with my hands and demonstrated the size and approximate trajectory of Taurin's horns.

"Man's got some girth." He nodded in approval. "Age?"

"Thirty-eight, in human years too, I already asked him."

He stood and began pacing, massaging his jaw, talking to himself, eliminating all the species as I did during the class. "Not fae, not dragon . . ."

Four-Feet stretched out her front legs and kneaded my thighs.

"We might have to cheat on this one," said Ash. He picked up his eSlate. "What's his name? I'll look him up on social media."

I considered how surly and taciturn Taurin had been. "I doubt you'll find him on social media. He didn't exactly seem the social sort."

"It's worth a shot."

"His name is Taurin. I don't know his last name."

"Taurin?! His name is Taurin?"

"Yes . . . Why?"

He frowned at me and pressed some buttons on his eSlate. My heartbeat kicked up a few gears. "Is this him?" He handed it to me.

There, staring at me, was a colour photo of a scowling Taurin. So on-brand for him. He stood in front of a white background with thin black lines and height indicators, and in his hand, he held a black sign with a bunch of white push pin numbers and letters that read REMY CITY GAOL.

Dammit, a mugshot. And damn him for still looking incredible in it. So, he was a criminal. Technically, so was I. That's why I was at the bloody course in the first place. Horus had said, *Ah. Well, you're in good company then,* and patted Taurin on the arm. I should have put the two together quicker.

"What did he do?" I asked.

"He demolished an Ichor. To smithereens, as they say."

"Oh," I said, and I found myself, for some absurd reason, laughing.

"My local Ichor actually, not that I drink coffee these days." I side-eyed his empty espresso martini glass. "And, in any case, there are far too many of those blasted café chains about. Do you know what he is?" Ash asked, his features having adopted an uncharacteristic sobriety.

I shook my head.

"He's a minotaur."

"Oh," I said again, because all other words had vanished from my mind.

"The body of a man and the head of a bull—"

"Yes, I know what minotaurs are."

"They're extremely aggressive."

I let out a sigh and sank lower into the armchair.

"Listen, I'm not saying there can't be anything between you. But you need to be aware that the smallest things can trigger them. You've heard the term See Red before?" I nodded. "They have bouts of rage wherein the rest of the world dissolves and the only thing they are capable of focusing on is destroying whatever, or whomever, has upset them. They can't control themselves, and you wouldn't be able to either. I don't want you to become one of those women who's convinced she can change a man, and then gets caught in the backfire."

"Yeah, I understand," I said, unable to stop the unwarranted sinking feeling in my chest.

Ash pressed on with his lecture. "Back in the day, when Borderlands was formed, minotaurs were highly regulated. They weren't allowed outside of the Mythic Realms unless they had all the correct paperwork, and an escort. Much the same way humans today travel into the Mythic Realms and mythics into the Human Realms."

"You're joking?"

He shook his head. "They weren't even allowed to live in Borderlands until about fifty-years ago. Most of the ones that came were forced to leave. To go back up north. And the ones that stayed faced a daily battle. There are still many today that would prefer Borderlands to be minotaur-free."

"That's unfair," I said, though my voice was quiet.

Ash showed me the page on his eSlate again. "I want to agree with you. I really do. But the evidence speaks for itself. I'm sorry, my lover." He placed his hand on my shoulder and gave it a comforting squeeze.

"No, don't be. I'm glad you told me. It's not like I do relationships, anyway."

It was probably for the best that I try to get him out of my head. I should stop thinking about those huge arms, and that silky bronze hair, and those bottomless blue eyes. And I should definitely, definitely stop thinking about doing the no-pants-dance with him.

Or . . . Oh, shit, the monster mash! I'll have to save that one for when Ash was in a better mood.

Acid flared in my stomach. Damn it, now I was getting indigestion too. I needed to forget about him. And, if I ever saw him again, which I had no reason to since I didn't plan on attending the cake class anymore, I would tell him where he and his massive lung capacity can go.

I tried to rearrange my face and voice into something more cheerful, more Joey. "Shall we get our Nikki Star on?"

"That's a wonderful idea. What's this one about?" he asked, curling onto the chaise again.

"Amy is a big city girl that has to go home for the holidays because her parents are getting a messy divorce, and Kent is the handsome, three-legged surf instructor she takes her frustrations out on."

"Excellent," he said, picking up his espresso glass and huffing to find it drained. "So, it's set by the seaside. I do love the seaside. Did I ever tell you about my house by the beach?"

"Yes, often."

And then we both said in unison, "It's in the Human Realms."

He sighed a memory and dopamine laced sigh. "One day."

"You want me to read this or not? It took me ages to track down this copy. I had to physically fight another woman in The Biblio Jungle for this. She almost scratched my eye out."

He made a zipping-mouth gesture and tossed an invisible key over his shoulder.

I cleared my throat and opened the book to the first page. "Of all the times Amy D'Luca pictured herself on her back spread naked in front of Kent Ryder, she never imagined there would be a two-sizes-two-small wetsuit twisted around her ankles and the contents of a random child's castle-shaped bucket dumped over her head. Thank the gods she remembered to shave. In her defence, she'd tripped, and Kent, ever the gentleman, was valiantly, albeit unsuccessfully, attempting to shield her from the horrified gazes of the approximately one-thousand families who'd also ventured onto the beach that sunny, summer's morning . . ."

But the more I read, the more I realised I was merely saying the words. Somewhere between my brain and my mouth and my ears, they got lost. My mind still whirred over the gigantic man I'd met yesterday. He was grumpy for sure, but I found it difficult to believe he was the brute Ash claimed him to be. I know, I know. The proof was there in black and white. But evidence, schmevidence, all I saw was gentleness. He'd held a delicate material in his massive hands and fashioned something even more delicate from it. I thought back to the sugar-paste rose he'd created, which now sat on a shelf in my bedroom inside its Tupperware cloche. Not only had he made his own perfect flower, but without speaking, he'd taught me how to craft one. Me. Joey. That in itself should come with its own awards ceremony.

This man wasn't the coffee-shop smashing aggressor pictured on Ash's tablet. This man was patient, deliberate, benevolent.

At some point, I'd stopped reading. Ash assessed me thoughtfully.

"You like him?"

I shrugged. "Not likely. I've only just met him."

He said nothing and watched me.

"It's . . . I . . . I can't explain it. I have a weird feeling about him. I *get* this weird feeling when I'm near him, like in my chest."

"What kind of feeling?"

"I don't know, excitement maybe. A buzzing or something, like indigestion. I've got it now, thinking about him." I laughed.

Ash didn't. He narrowed his eyes at me. "Goodness, okay! I think we're done with reading today." He rang his bell. "Let's get drunk instead."

Chapter 3

Taurin

Three months ago

"They're not gonna fit," I told the human police-officer fruitlessly slapping human-sized handcuffs on me. His hands shook, in fact, his whole body shook, as he accidentally ripped out all my wrist fur on the metal clips. It fucking stung. "Here." I opened the side of his van, pulled on the relevant drawer catch, and selected the correct sized handcuffs. Size zero-zero-A. I dropped them into his palms and held my wrists aloft.

"S-sorry." He clipped them down onto me and stared, blinking, up. "Uh, Gods, what do I do now?" he asked. He swallowed audibly.

"First day on the job?"

He ran his palms over his trousers and pulled his eyebrows together in one thick black cable. "Summat like that."

I considered shifting and releasing my full beast, letting the poor bastard shit his pants, and then casually walking off into the night. But what would the point be? They had me on CCTV. And as far as I was aware, I was the only one of my kind in Borderlands. They'd know it was me. My best hope was that the quivering human before me would fuck up the arrest somehow, and Elektra could fight it on a 'technicality'.

"You read me my rights. For argument's sake, let's say you already have. Then you fill out an MB62 form . . . A Mythical Beast Arrest Certificate," I clarified, because he looked like he was having difficulty keeping up. "And then you take me back to the station. You might need a bigger van to transport me. Confined spaces can make me a bit twitchy."

He smacked his lips together as though his mouth had dried up, and with trembling fingers, he took out his electronic-slate and unclipped the stylus.

Bullseye.

He never even noticed his slip up.

"Do you want to sit down?" I offered.

"Yes, please." He dropped to the curb, still shaking. Perhaps I should've handed him his anti-hypothermia blanket too. I sat next to him, invading his personal space a little too much. I knew I was being an asshole, but I wanted to keep him this side of intimidated. "Uh, name?"

"Taurin."

He made a note. "Surname?"

"Don't have one. Don't need one."

He wiped the sweat from his brow. "Date of birth?"

I told him my birthdate.

He looked up at me and caught my eye for a second before fixing it onto his eSlate. "Gods," he said under his breath. "Uh, species?"

Ah, here we go. This is the question I dreaded answering. He already knew what I was. He would have been told over his radio what to expect at the scene, and yet, he was still shaking like a seismograph needle during a Richter-scale eight quake. Everyone was the same — no matter the species — no one wanted to hear the next word that would drop from my mouth. As though, until that point, they could pretend I wasn't what they already knew me to be.

"Minotaur."

He almost dropped his tablet. The scent of urine hit my nose, and I decided to go easy on him since I already got my 'technicality'.

"What's your name?" I asked him.

"My—my name? It's Oz."

"Oz, okay. First of all, you need to calm the fuck down. I've smashed up the coffee shop once. I can't do it again." I shot a look over my shoulder at the Eastside branch of Ichor smouldering across the highway, and I had to admit, I'd done a pretty thorough job. All the windows shattered, roof blown off, tables and chairs scattered to the winds, columns of black smoke rising like the pillars of Parthenon. In the distance, sirens wailed, and blue and red lights painted the night sky.

"It's out of my system now. Seeing Red takes a lot out of me. I'm pretty tired."

He didn't reply, just stared at me, holding his tablet as though it were a shield.

"Listen, Oz, I'm not going beast mode again tonight. Okay? And I'm not mad at you. Blame that fucking barista, George. Antagonistic little prick. I hate to generalise, but fuck dragons, man."

He nodded.

"You don't need to worry about me tearing your face off. I'm spent. Actually, I need a nap. I'm getting way too old for this shit. So, here's what's going to happen. You're going to change your trousers, and then you're going to take me to the station. And I'm gonna ride in the front with you, because,"—I stretched out my legs into the road and rolled my neck with an echoing crack—"I've been known to get a tad claustrophobic."

I let my head fall back against the headrest and pushed all thoughts of what I'd done from my mind. How many thousands of silvers damage had I caused? No injuries this time, which I supposed I should be grateful for, though I would've liked that dragon to be down a wing, or two.

I was already on my last chance.

And I had well and truly fucked it up.

"I . . ." began Oz, in a tentative whisper, his eyes fixed on the road ahead. "I'm a transfer. From Pannor. You're my first mon—uh, mythic arrest."

"Deep end."

"Yeah."

I took a deep breath. "You know, life, living, it's like money. The more people have, the more they want. You'll find vampires and fae and demigods that are thousands of years old. You think they'd be bored with it all by now, but they're the ones clinging on like parasites. They won't jeopardise centuries of everything they've built up. Every monster"—even though he'd almost used the word himself, he flinched when I said it—"knows that harming a human is an instant death-sentence. You'll be safe . . . ish, around them. It's the humans you want to watch out for. Living such brief lives makes them feel as though they have to cram it all in at once. It makes them irrational and impulsive."

He nodded, apparently satisfied. I failed to mention that my expected lifespan was the same as a human's. I didn't want him pissing through another pair of trousers.

I let Oz lead me into the station through the front doors. I figured he could do with the ego boost. I could still smell the uric fear leaking from every pore, and likely the other officers would too, in particular the non-humans, but there was only so much image massaging I could manage. Especially since I was prepared to tear it all down the moment Elektra visited me.

"Well, well, well," came the vicious hiss of Commissioner Pounder. He moved from behind the desk, filling most of the space with his hideous, eight-foot form. Crimson skin, crest of horns, leathery wings barely concealed. Whoever's idea it was to put a dragon in charge of Remy's police-force needs redeployment, preferably to the East Winterlands.

"Nice work, officer Ozwald. Very nice work." He slapped the human on the shoulder, who, in that moment, sandwiched between a minotaur and a dragon, seemed like a child. Other officers watched on, not one of them remarked on Oz's little accident. They'd at least wait until I'd been locked in my cell.

Without waiting to be told, I placed my hands on the perspex board so that Oz could turn out my pockets into an orange plastic tray.

Pounder circled us, clicking his tongue, touching my possessions as the human officer dropped them down. My phone, my lighter, my Grizlas™, an empty baggie.

"Get a drugs test done on him," Pounder said to the tiny Oz.

"Yes, chief," Oz said with wide eyes.

The dragon turned to me. "I do believe you're on your final warning, young Taurin. What will become of you now? What do we think? Twenty-percent term? Twenty-five?"

"Shall I take him to the cell, Chief?"

Pounder nodded. "Cell sixteen." The smallest cell.

I rolled my shoulders back, took a deep breath, and let my bullhead rip through. I'd already shredded my shirt clean off earlier, so it wasn't as though I'd be ruining another one. Pounder's smug face didn't waiver an inch. Even when I grew an entire foot taller than him. Oz placed his still quaking hand on my arm. I turned to Commissioner Pounder and flipped him both fingers.

Fucking dragons.

"Taur, I'm at a loss. You cannot keep repeating the same behaviours." My lawyer, Elektra, an orc, paced her compact office. I had my human head on again, though since she brought me there straight from the station, I was also shirtless, exhausted, and filthy. She sat down in front of me, choosing to place her chair not behind the desk but to the side, so that our knees were almost touching.

"You're going to be the death of me." She took another deep breath. "You can't keep relying on technicalities to get you out of these things. Tricking officers into not reading your rights—"

"It was too easy," I said, secretly pleased with my resourcefulness.

"They've come to expect it from you now. Next time you won't get the new guy. You can't keep frightening the officers into submission."

"Pounder does."

At the mention of the Commissioner's name, she stiffened. Everyone knows Pounder hated me. Had always hated me. From the moment I moved to Remy with my sister, Tina. He managed to drive her back North. She never told me what he had done to achieve that, but as soon as she had left, he'd fixed his obsession on me. Since then, he's had a hard-on for seeing me behind bars.

"Pounder is . . . He's claiming you put the officer under duress. The same technicalities don't apply. He's pressing ahead with a case."

"Shit."

Fuck, and I cannot emphasise this enough, dragons.

"When's the trial? And how long is the sentence?"

Gaol sentences were calculated based on a percentage of a person's lifespan rather than years. Seemed fair to me. Ten years is an age for a human, but a good nap for some monsters.

"Taurin, there won't be a trial."

"The fuck?! They can't do that, it's illegal—"

"Calm down. There won't be a trial because I've wangled you one more final, final chance."

I could have cried. Or done a jig. And I do not dance. I really didn't want to go to prison. Especially not Remy City Gaol. My flatmate Dima went there once. Said it was the worst century of his life.

"Can I kiss you?" I said. Elektra laughed, her cheeks flushing as pink as green orc skin could get.

"This is your new rehabilitation plan." She placed a manilla folder in my hand. "You'll need weekly therapy sessions with Dr Landyn. She's very good. You must attend these. But remember, because of what you've done and, ah, what you are, they've placed a Red-Alert on you. So, be aware that while most of what you say to her will be confidential, if you mention anything that she feels might represent a threat to society, she's legally obligated to share this information with Commissioner Pounder." She waited for me to nod my understanding before continuing. "Taur, I hate to say this, but Pounder seems to have made it his personal mission to bring you down. Any wrong move and he'll be waiting for you. Please do not give him the opportunity."

"Yeah." I took a steadying breath. Even thinking about that big red bastard made the blood pound against my eardrums.

"You'll need to pay the damages on the café. Eighty-thousand silvers."

Crap, crap, crap. I'd have to ask Mal for another loan.

"And you need to take a measurable step to prove you can control your temper around other beings—"

"It's only dragons."

She held up a hand. "You need to go to night school."

"Night school? To, what, like anger management class or something?"

She shook her head. "The courts need evidence that you can integrate into society, that you can make friends."

"I've got friends. I've got three flatmates."

"And that's a great start, but they want more. They want paperwork and reports. They want to know that you're making a change. They want you to integrate with humans. To prove you're not a threat to them." Her voice was much softer now. "Taurin, if you break the terms — miss class, fail to report, fail to see your therapist — you'll be looking at a fifteen-percent term. Ten with good behaviour."

I let out a grunt and ran my hands through my hair. "I'm fine with humans." And generally, I was. Humans have a habit of winding you up only when behind the safety of their online anonymities. They're never stupid enough to try it out in person. "What's the course?"

"You can choose." She handed me a UR prospectus. "I've highlighted the ones available to you. The cake decorating course, in particular, looks fantastic. They have an incredible teacher."

"Cake decorating?" Was she serious? I was a seven-foot minotaur, and she wanted me grappling with . . . fondant? Frosting? Weren't they the same thing? Who the fuck knew?

"I think the change of pace will be good for you."

Dima's voice rang through my head. *They tried to stake me in my sleep, sixteen times. The food's awful. And I only drink blood. Go figure. None of them can piss in the bowl. The smell was unreal.*

"Fine, yep, sign me up," I said, getting to my feet and tossing the brochure onto her desk without looking through it.

She nodded. "Before you go, Taur. If you can't control your temper, if you raze another coffee-shop or off-license or . . ."

"Police station?" I offered, not even pretending I didn't remember that one with nostalgia.

"Anywhere. Look, if you do it again, smash up anywhere, it's a fifty-percent term. Got that? Five, zero. No exclusions, no reductions."

Chapter 4

Joey

Also three months ago

The night sky filled with an eye-gouging flash of blue, followed by the attention seeking *bloop bloop* of a siren.

"Fuck. No. No, no, no, no. Not again."

I pulled Little Red to the side of the road. The Goblin' Grub takeaway on the back seat wafted its mushroomy, gravy scent under my nose. Goblins were fantastic cooks, but lousy at wrapping the actual cartons, meaning by the time I was through with this officer, and I got to the intended recipient, guaranteed the food would be stone cold. As if by coincidence, my phone buzzed. I glanced at the screen.

Message from customer: Where's our order?

Great, another one-star rating for me.

I looked up to the sky and prayed for forgiveness from the goddesses of feminism, but desperate times. I shimmied my vest top down by an inch, ran my teeth along my lips to pink them up, and pushed my hair over one shoulder. The vampire cops were suckers for a bit of neck.

And the orcs never failed to go mushy for a full flash of tuskless teeth. I hated myself a little.

In my rear-view mirror, the silhouette of the officer emerged from their vehicle.

Shit, human.

The silhouette grew larger.

Shit, shit, shit. That *human.* How would I worm my way out this time?

He rapped on my window with a metallic sounding finger.

"Step out of the vehicle, please."

I did as instructed and followed him to the bank on the other side of my car. My phone buzzed again.

Message from customer: FOOD?!!!!!!

"Name?" he said. He rubbed his eye with the heel of his palm and yawned so wide I thought he might dislocate his jaw.

"Josephina Silver. Human." I added my date of birth too because it would be next in the line of questions. He tapped it into his eSlate.

He looked up at me. "Oh, it's you again."

"Officer Ozwald," I said, as though only just recognising him. "Fancy seeing you here."

"Do you know why I pulled you over?"

"Uh, I may have been going a smidgen too fast?"

"You were going seventy-eight in a thirty zone."

"Get in! New PB!" I held up my hand for a high-five. He didn't even laugh.

"Nothing against you, but I have to book you."

"Please—"

"Joey, I can't. This is my third time cautioning you. I've only been with this force for two weeks. And your records show at least seven other cautions from different officers—"

"I promise I won't—"

"Look," he said, placing one hand on his forehead and the other holding the tablet on my shoulder. "I've had an awful night so far. I had my first monster—fuck, mythic arrest today." He puffed out a long stream of air. "It was a bit of an ordeal. The guy was fine, actually pretty decent, considering . . . but I fucked up and chief is fuming with me. Literally. He's a dragon. Sorry, but I can't afford any more mistakes."

I nodded. I had pushed my luck and reached my limit. Any other officer would have done the same. I'd pushed it too far with all of them. "What will happen now? To me? And my car?"

"You'll get a letter and a fine. You'll have to do a speed awareness course within three months of receiving the fine. If not, they'll take her away." He aimed a kick at Little Red's wheel.

"Shit!" I buried my face in my hands.

My phone buzzed. *Cancelled Order.*

Another cancelled order. Fuck. My. Life. That'll be Goblin' Grub firing me then. Well, the Westside branch of Goblin' Grub. At least I still had the east branch, and the north, and the three Mermish 'n' Chips restaurants to deliver for.

Believe it or not, I enjoyed my job, jobs. Most people couldn't wrap their heads around it. They used words like 'only' and 'proper' to ebb away at my happiness. *But you're* only *a delivery driver*, they'd say or, *don't you want a* proper *career?* And the answer to that was *Meh*. I didn't know. Delivering takeaway food allowed me to drive my own car, which I loved, work my own hours, which I loved, listen to audiobooks, earn shitloads of tips, and there were leftovers. It really didn't get any better than leftovers. Did doctors get leftovers? Or teachers, or lawyers? I rest my case.

It sucked when I lost a job, but there would always be more. New eateries opening everyday across the city. New species finding their niche. Dwarves, gnomes, elves, centaurs, hell, even zombies. Though I could probably do without the leftovers from Braaaiiiiins.

I could buffer the loss of one restaurant.

"How long left have you got on your shift?" I asked Ozwald.

His eyebrows knotted together. Man, they were huge. "Uh, about thirty-five minutes. After the disaster of earlier they put me on traffic duty. I'm probably going to be on traffic duty for the rest of my career. I had planned to spend the night sitting in my car, but then you came along."

"You like Goblin food? My order just got cancelled again. Wanna talk about your awful evening and stuff our faces with mushroom knucktak? I feel like I need to hear about someone else fucking things up worse than me."

He took a deep breath in. "Yeah, fuck it, why not?"

I opened Little Red's door and retrieved the takeaway. I gave Ozwald a biodegradable bamboo fork. He sat on the bank.

"Knucktak, rabbit broth, squirrel fritters? What're you having?"

"Knucktak. I'm still getting used to all this non-human food."

I handed him the carton. "So, tell me about this guy. What happened? And why is chief pissed at you?"

He dug his fork into the dish. "Minotaur he was. My first mythic arrest, and he was a fucking minotaur." He shook his head and finally relented into laughter.

Chapter 5

Taurin

Present day

By the smell of it — citrus cologne, semen and weed — only Goldie was home. I debated going straight up to my bedroom. Goldie wouldn't care, too used to my sullenness to expect anything else. Besides, it was Mal I really wanted to speak with. Instead, I chucked my keys on the side, dumped my kit bag in the hall, and made my way to the living room.

He was playing on his FaeStation. Elvish food takeaway wrappers littered the space, and a half-smoked joint nestled on an antique trinket tray. He'd propped his feet up on the table and pushed his short, golden, so-shiny-it-always-appeared-wet hair behind his pointed ears. As per, he was shirtless.

"Not got work?" I asked.

"This is work," he replied.

He worked for one of the leading fae games design companies, so in theory, if he really wanted to stretch the truth, he probably had been working. Though, just how much of Goldie's workday comprised of staring up into space, high as a pegasus on coke, would likely have his boss spitting blood.

"Is Mal about?"

"On his medicine rounds. You not seeing Clair tonight?"

"No."

"Then why are you wearing that ridiculous human head?" I accepted his question for what it was, an invitation for me to strip off.

I'd only ever let a handful of people see me with my bullhead. My flatmates (Goldie, Mal and Dima) a couple of guys from work (because I'm significantly stronger in bull form than human form, which comes in handy when your job is lugging about tree trunks), and those who already expected the worst from me. Like the police. The general public did not want to witness my bullhead. Definitively bullhead averse. It always put them on extreme edge. As though shifting and Seeing Red were inextricable. They weren't. In my shifted form I was still in control of my actions. Two feet taller and a foot wider, but still very much in control. Seeing Red was something completely different. My flatmates were the only ones that didn't give a shit what I looked like, man or bull.

"Come splat some humans with me."

I lifted my arms behind my head and pulled my hoodie and t-shirt off. I only had a finite number of them and there was no point shredding another if it was avoidable. Most shops tended to stock only human-sized clothing. There was a time in the past when I bulk ordered t-shirts and sweaters online, but I haven't needed to recently. Have been doing a much better job of controlling my outbursts. For the most part.

Goldie's eyes flashed over my stomach before returning steadfastly to his game. He was an Oread. Also known as an Oros, or mountain-nymph, or even fertility-fae. His hobbies were prohibitively limited. He liked fucking, thinking about fucking, and talking about it. Sometimes when he got high, the topic might stray to more philosophical matters like the imagined war against humans, but generally he spoke of little else besides who, where, how, how many times, and which holes were utilised.

With my hoodie and t-shirt folded over the arm of the sofa, I rolled my shoulders back, stood to my full height and let the bullhead burst through. Thank Gods Mal's ceilings were super high. It didn't hurt to change form, but it was a relief to get out of my human head. Like releasing a breath after you've been holding it. I imagined it was what those in possession of breasts felt like after taking off a bra or corset for the day. I sat next to Goldie, and he handed me the spare controller.

"You smell . . . different, weird," he said.

A jolt of panic shot through my entire body. Could he scent what had happened to me today? What happened when *she* walked in and stood at my desk? "Uh, I've been fondling sugar paste all evening."

"Sugar Paste? Is that your new girlfriend?"

On the screen, Goldie's character shot a human between the eyes with a rifle at point blank range. Technically, you weren't meant to shoot the humans, but it was one of those games where you could walk about and do whatever you wanted. Which, in Goldie's case, and for most of the monsters I'd met, was, in fact, murdering humans with impunity.

I didn't reply. Didn't know what to say. Hadn't fully processed the gravity of it all. And it was . . . gravitous? Gravitacious? Gravit—It was heavy as fuck.

"There *is* a girl!" Goldie said, like a detective uncovering a murder weapon. He put his controller on the coffee table, tucked his legs underneath himself, and turned to me. The thirst for every sordid detail written all over his face. A few times in the past, he'd invited me into his bed, but aside from the occasional suggestive comment, he never pushed it after I rejected him. Still, it didn't escape my notice how his gaze often fleetingly shot down to the waistband of my jeans.

"She's no one," I said, hoping his over sensitive fae hearing couldn't detect my heart trying to jackhammer its way through my ribcage. "They sat her next to me on my course."

He narrowed his eyes. "Bang or fang?" A game our flatmate Dima, a queer vampire, invented. Basically, would you rather fuck her, or eat her? Sometimes referred to as 'fuck or suck'. I think humans call it 'smash or pass'. Same deal, less cannibalism. "So, what does Sugar Paste look like?" he added when I didn't respond.

I shook my head. I wouldn't play his weird spank-bank games, so I said the one thing I knew would shut him up, "She's human."

"Urgh." He freed his legs, retrieved his controller, and began playing again. Background gunfire immediately filled the room. "You fucked her?"

"Of course not, I've only just met her."

He shrugged, picked up the joint, re-lit it, took a drag, and then passed it to me. I sucked it to my fingers in one.

We were silent for a few moments while Goldie's on screen character wandered about 'sploding humans. Ironic, since his character was human. An origin story type thing. At least that's what he'd told me when he designed the third one. I think he was on iteration five or six now. You're a human named Colin. You have only human weapons and transport, and you have to travel across the eight kingdoms — he conveniently left out Borderlands — and steal magic from all the other species.

"Are you gonna play?" The split screen showed my character attempting to walk through a wall, his legs windmilling around, his body bouncing off the bricks. "Sugar Paste has really got into your head?"

"Hmm?" His words, the game, seemed to register half a second too slow.

"You want my advice?"

"Literally never."

"She's not worth this much thought. And not just because she's human," he added before I could call him out on it. "Mate, this is your last chance to stay out of gaol. You can't afford the distraction. I say hit it and quit it. Tap and tap out. Get her out of your head. And if you can't, ask your tutor to move her, and forget about her. Stop thinking about your dick for five minutes and try to think of your future."

I laughed. Oddly profound words from my sex-addict flatmate. "You're the one thinking about my dick."

He smiled and shot another two humans in the face. "The things I could do to those eleven inches."

I ignored him. "Besides, I don't need to worry too much. I doubt I'll see her again."

Goldie turned to me.

"I'm pretty sure she was in the wrong class."

Chapter 6

Taurin

"They put someone else on my desk. A human woman. Elektra told me I'd have a desk to myself."

"I'll make a note of it and get a message to Elektra. See if she can have a word with Russ."

Dr Landyn's office was exactly as you'd imagine a therapist's office to look. Banal decor, offensively inoffensive motivational posters, a bookcase filled with volumes so tedious in their appearance, I could barely bring myself to glance at the spines. It was comfortable, sure, but with that weird semi-corporate edge. Like the peeling vinyl on the corner of the coffee table, the constant drip-drip-drip of the water cooler, the shallow layer of dust on all the picture frames, or the couch, that had definitely not been designed with a six-foot-eleven minotaur in mind.

Dr Landyn herself, was nothing I'd imagined a therapist to be. A three-foot, pink-haired gnome, with an unusual and fucking irritating habit of waiting approximately seven years before answering a question. She knew I was on the metre, and I respected that about her. Even if it did make me grind my teeth to powder.

"What's she like? This human woman," Dr Landyn asked.

"Loquacious."

"Oh, dear." She leaned forward and perched her chin on steepled fingers. She waited for me to say more.

"She's . . . I . . ."

I imprinted on her.

That's what I wanted to say. I fucking imprinted on her. Like fated mates. The whole shebang. I didn't even know minotaurs could imprint. Yet the moment it happened, the moment I scented her, I knew what it was. I felt it in my chest, like I had swallowed molten lava. I didn't tell Dr Landyn this. Fear had stopped me. Though, fear of what, I wasn't sure.

"I'm attracted to her. Sexually." Was about as much as I was prepared to admit.

Clair remained silent for a few moments. "Is it reciprocal?"

"I doubt it!" I accidentally shouted. "I'm a minotaur and she's . . ." Absolutely gorgeous. I finished the sentence in my head. Atomic-red hair, lush, pouting lips, honey-coloured eyes, sexy kitten-purr voice, and curves every-damned-where, barely hidden under that flappy red dress with the tiny peaches. I didn't know what the correct term for her body type was. Curvy? Plus sized? Goddess? All I knew was she was . . . mouth-watering, hot as hellfire, made my jeans too tight. There was no part of her I didn't want to squeeze, or bite until it smarted, and then suck the sting away.

Dr Landyn gave a pitying tilt of the head.

"Do you think being near her might trigger me?" I asked.

The thing I'd been fearing since the moment she sniffed her pits. As endearingly gross as it was, it pushed all her raw scent up my nostrils. Sent off little fireworks in my brain. What if having a woman who I'd imprinted on close by is enough to set me back? Draw the animal instincts out of me.

She peered at me over her finger-palace. Quiet again for the longest time. Man, I hated these silences. It would be so much easier if I were Dima, and I could force my way into her mind.

"It's a possibility," she said. My stomachs dropped. I knew, *knew* that would be the case. It didn't stop the ensuing disappointment. "Have you spoken to any of your friends about her?"

"Only Goldie."

She pulled a face which I could only describe as unprofessional, her mouth turning down at the corners, like a bit of sick had come up. I'd spoken about all my flatmates — or as she liked to call them, my network — since I started seeing her three months ago, and had been, shall we say, frugal in my descriptions. She still managed to develop a distaste for Goldie and Dima in particular. I don't know why it bothered me so much, but it did.

"Okay." She drew out the word in predictive scepticism. "And what did he say?"

I puffed out my cheeks. "He said . . . I should get it, I mean her, out of my system." I hoped she understood what I meant.

She held out a hand for me to continue.

"He told me to fuck her and then forget her."

In the twelve hours it took her to answer, I could have driven right the way round the Eight and a Half Kingdoms, and been back in enough time to found my own indie gin-distillery.

"I can't tell you what to do in this situation. You need to look internally. Morally, do you think it's the answer you're looking for?" *Surprise, surprise.* "I think perhaps the best thing to do is to prioritise finishing the course. Get in the court's favours. And then, if you're still interested in copulation"—*good Gods*—"perhaps you can pursue her once you graduate."

"And in the meantime, what do I do? Ignore her?"

"Do you want to risk it? Do you feel it's worth the risk? You could be inadvertently putting both her, and your future prospects in danger."

I said nothing. No, I didn't want either of those things. I couldn't give Pounder any more ammo. Another excuse to lock me up. And I definitely couldn't risk anything happening to her. I imprinted on her. We were tied by an invisible bond. Fated. Whether or not she wanted to be. I already knew that the pull on me would be too strong to ignore her. There would be too much temptation to touch her, to claim her mouth with mine, her body with my hands, to fit myself inside her. Would I be able to stop myself around her? Surely, I wouldn't See Red.

Would I?

Maybe Clair was right. Maybe I should wait until next year, until I've completed the course and temporarily gotten Pounder off my back. Then I could find her again, somehow. Use Goldie's FaeBook account. She seemed like the type to have a social presence. Failing that, I could probably just step outside and stiff the air, let the bull take over, and track her down that way. And if she's single in nine months' time when the course is completed, I will ask her out on a proper date. With food. And flowers. And . . . Gods, it was more than half a year away and my palms were already sweating.

"Okay," I said. "I can wait to . . . pursue her." The words sounded robotic.

I was in control of this. I could control this.

Clair fucking paused again. "I'll get a message to Elektra and have the human woman moved."

I didn't bother to mention that there'd be no need. That I was certain she'd found herself in the wrong classroom. I could do with the back-up, in case she showed up in Russ' class again.

A nagging feeling in my stomachs developed. I twisted my septum ring. So, she wasn't meant to be in Russ' class. She made a mistake. We've all made mistakes. But what I couldn't figure out, the question that had been bouncing around relentlessly in my mind since Monday night, was why didn't she admit she was in the wrong room?

Why did she stay?

Chapter 7

Joey

Ripped straight from my nightmares, the noises rang through Christie's tiny living-room-cum-kitchenette-cum-breakfast nook like the director's cut of the scariest horror movie of all time. A panicked, screeching alarm. The monstrous growl of an immense beast. The leaden clanging of fat iron chains against concrete. My own sobs bouncing limply against the windowpane.

"No, no, no, no, no. My baby. Please," I pleaded.

But the banana-yellow monster continued to emit its callous cry as it crept closer.

BEEP BEEP BEEP BEEP Vehicle reversing. Stand clear. BEEP BEEP BEEP BEEP

A Remy City grunt, this time an Orc, jumped down and jimmied a hook under Little Red. I could do nothing but weep as he yanked her from her peaceful slumber onto the back of a scuffed, filth-crusted flatbed marked Highway Dept.

"My baby. My beautiful baby. My livelihood."

I pushed away from the window after realising I'd been staring at the dark circle of oil-ruined road for twenty minutes. Two greasy handprints on the glass, the only evidence of my ordeal.

Steadying my sobs, I pulled up the number of the Highway Dept and rang them. The call handler told me I could come and collect my car. Just as soon as I'd passed my speed probation course. I called the uni straight afterwards.

"Sure, I understand," said the person on the other end. "Our next availability is in two weeks. Shall I book you in?"

"Yes! Yes, please."

"Great, you'll need to go to UR and pay the course fees."

My heart fell out of my bum. "I'm sorry, what?"

"It'll be five-hundred silvers. The balance must be paid today, otherwise we can't guarantee your spot."

"Shit, yeah, okay." That was my rent money gone. For the—ahem—fourth month in a row. I grabbed my phone and backpack and headed out of the flat, texting Hell-Bitch as I went.

Hey Christie, don't hate me, I can't make rent this month. I'll get it to you as soon as possible. Promise.

I shot off another few texts, copied and pasted to each one of my bosses.

Family emergency. Can't come to work for a few weeks. Will text when I'm back.

Two whole weeks of missed jobs. Of missed pay and missed tips. This was really going to hurt. I'll be living off those out-of-date macaroni-cheese tins Christie refuses to throw out.

I called home when I got on the bus. "Hi, Mum."

"Ottilie! Hi!" came mum's buoyant voice.

"It's Joey."

"Oh, hi Joey." I didn't fail to notice the subtle decrease in excitement. Though mum never had favourites with her daughters, Tilly hadn't been the one to move three-hours away to a different realm. Tilly was also the daughter with the perfect life and husband, and Mum had been on tenterhooks for nearly a decade now waiting for news on the pitter-patter of tiny feet. Or claws.

"Everything okay? What's the matter?" It spoke volumes her go-to reaction with me was *what's wrong*.

"Nothing, I'm on my way to uni." I put on my breeziest tone.

I had intended to ask for help, a loan maybe, but for some reason my mouth changed the words as they came out. Did I really want my parents to see that side of me? Again.

"I thought you already did your speed course?"

"I made a mistake. It's not for another fortnight. I'm just going in to, uh, sign some paperwork. Anyway, how are you? How's dad?"

"We're fine, pudding. I've been thinking about joining Jen From The Farm Shop's" – her full name – "book club, but she wants the group to get together on a Sunday evening, and you know I like my lazy Sundays in the garden. Your dad's off at one of his meetings."

I groaned. For a while now, my father had been not involved per se, more like swept along by the alt right anti-monster crowd. He'd read too many billionaire owned news outlets, and parroted opinions like they were running out. It was one of the main reasons I moved to Borderlands. Well, that and escaping my first boyfriend. The Human Realms had become stifling. A prison for an adventurous twenty-four-year-old like me. I needed to see more of the world. More of its people. Needed to know that the newspapers were wrong. Ten years down the line, I'm happy to say, for the most part, they were. Most species didn't hate humans. You always get the odd individual now and then, faes and warlocks in particular, but on the whole, Borderlands was a vibrant melting pot of interspecies. And I loved it.

I could walk down the road and, depending on the time of day or night, see dwarfs, fae, vampires, werewolves, gorgons, demigods, actual gods, or mythological beings. My mind wandered to the beautiful, miserable minotaur I met last week, and a tiny fire ignited in my chest.

Did I just sigh out loud?

"No, no, pudding, your father doesn't go to those meetings anymore. He goes to a different pub now. With Nige From The Farm Shop. He's . . . trying. He wants to be there for you girls."

"Oh," I said, because there were no other words. Was I hopeful? Sceptical? I wasn't sure.

"It's all because of Wyn. They've been spending a lot of time together. Wyn's been brilliant, helping your father realise he was wrong. Earning his forgiveness."

Gods, that was rich. It should be Wyn trying to earn my forgiveness, but whatever, I'd never give it to him.

"Oh, that was what I wanted to ask you," Mum said. I was grateful for the change in topic. "We're thinking of having a nice cosy family dinner for Harvest Festival next month and we were wondering if you'd like to visit for the weekend?"

"Will Tilly be there?"

"No, just us three, pudding. Unless you have a fella?" So typical of mum, always asking after my love life, or lack thereof. I'd only ever taken one guy home to meet my parents, and that ended in me packing my bags and legging it to Remy.

Once again, my thoughts drifted to the hunky minotaur. My belly filled with a comfortable warmth, like I had taken a huge bite of chocolate-fudge cake, but my chest did that weird indigestion buzz.

"I hate to disappoint you, Mum, but there's no one. It'll just be me."

"So, you'll come?" She sounded genuinely excited, and a gnawing guilt replaced the chocolate cake warmth. I didn't go home often enough. Not even a fraction of what I'd promised them when I left for Borderlands.

"Of course, I can't wait." And I supposed, if I didn't have to listen to six hours of my father's bigoted diatribes, I might enjoy myself this time. For everyone's sake, especially Tilly's, I hoped he had changed.

The bus pulled up outside of UR. Right outside of the main doors. Sometimes I wondered why I always drove everywhere when Remy's public transport system was actually pretty decent. But then I imagined Little Red all alone at the impound centre and I wanted to weep again.

The beautiful green-haired merman sat behind the reception desk. A one-person-sized water tank his chair which, in my haste last time, I'd failed to notice.

"Not knocking over my leaflet stand today?" he said, deadpan.

"Aw, you remembered me."

"How could I ever forget you?" He said it so flat, so emotionless, it was impossible to tell if he was kidding, flirting, or being cutting. But this was what Merpeople were like. For a people borne from water, they were exceptionally dry humoured.

I peered down at his lanyard. "Ben."

"That's my human name." No hint of a smile.

"Yeah, I got that. I'm—"

"My Mermish name is"—he screamed at me, lolling his tongue about in his mouth—"but you humans have difficulty pronouncing that."

I screamed back at him.

"Not bad. Not bad at all." He said it like I impressed him, but his face gave no indication.

"I dated a merman once," I replied. One of my first boyfriends in Borderlands, and my second longest relationship of all time, lasting an entire four weeks. He was a lovely guy, don't get me wrong, but it would never have worked. Every time I went round his place, I'd wind up shrivelled as a prune. "I'm here to pay the fees on a course."

He nodded, expressionless. "Name?"

"Joey Silver."

He typed it into his computer and sucked at his teeth. "Five-hundred silvers for a speed caution class?"

"Yeah," I said, pulling my bank card from my backpack. I paid the money and somehow contained my tears.

"Anything else I can help you with?" he said.

"No, just that. I—" I paused, remembering this time last week when I smashed into the leaflets, walked into Horus' classroom, and stood next to *him*. I put the rose he made on a shelf in my bedroom, and my insides gave a little jolt of electricity every time I glanced at it.

I really shouldn't. . . No, definitely shouldn't . . . But . . .

"Is it possible to join another course?"

"Depends on the availability. What one are you considering?"

"Cake Decorating."

He typed something on his keyboard. "Yep, one spot left. Shall I sign you up?"

"Uh."

This was a stupid idea. He was a minotaur. Sullen, temperamental, often violent, proven violent, and yet, so fuckable. Was I honestly contemplating committing one night every week to making fondant flowers because there was an off chance to have a fumble with this cantankerous mountain?

Oh, Joey, when will you ever change?

"Yeah, sure."

Never, apparently.

He typed some more. "Okay, that'll be five-hundred silvers."

"What?"

"For the course fees."

I didn't know what part of me assumed it would be free. "I don't have that money. I already gave you my last five-hundred so that I can get my car back."

"I can transfer the fees to this course if you'd like to change?"

I didn't need to think about it. I couldn't throw away my revenue stream because I was curious about a huge grumpy man who probably hated me anyway.

"No, it's fine. Thanks," I screamed Ben's Mermish name at him, and headed back to the bus stop. Internally trying to convince myself that keeping my jobs was more important than a casual shag.

Of course it was . . .

"Hey, Joey Silver. You're going the wrong way," came an otherworldly, silky voice. Horus. He stood at the boot of his car, an enormous, glossy, black, cost-more-than-my-parent's-house type thing, lifting out large white boxes. "Help me with these, would you?" He deposited three into my arms. They were alarmingly heavy.

"Sure," I said, realising I had no better place to be. No jobs to get to, and the longer I could keep myself away from the flat, the longer I could postpone confronting Christie about the rent.

He took another three boxes from the car and kicked the boot shut, giving me a split-second eyeful of what lay under his kilt. *Holy salami*. That poultry was packing.

"I wanted to say well done, for last week," he said as we walked back inside the uni. "It must feel like we dropped you in at the deep end, but you've managed the rare feat of impressing me. That rose was fine work, considering it was your first ever go."

"Thank you," I said, not sure how to tell him I couldn't afford to attend any of the remaining sessions. We reached the elevators.

"And thank *you* for what you did with Taurin." I almost dropped my boxes. "He's . . . He hasn't made any friends since the start of term. People . . ." he continued, deliberate with his words. "People can be wary of him. You don't get many minotaurs these days. Heck, I've been around for millennia, and I've only ever met a handful. They're often regarded as rather tempestuous—bullish if you will. And unfortunately, people are not always wrong. You didn't show that same fear, and you didn't give up on him. And I wanted to tell you how much I appreciate that. He could do with a friend like you. I'm sure if you keep teasing, he'll eventually come out of his shell."

Great, now what should I do? I didn't bother to mention I was the way I was because I had no idea what he was. If I'd have known he was a minotaur, would I have spoken to him in the same manner? Would I have tried, deliberately, to push his buttons to garner any kind of reaction? Doubtful.

But then . . . I am me.

The elevator doors pinged open, and we stepped inside.

"So, what about you, Joey Silver? Let's hear more about you. Where are you from?"

"Pannor," I said.

"Nice. Big city girl."

"Suburbs, really."

He could do with a friend like you. His words bounced around my mind. In the mirrored walls, he watched me. In a way that only a man with the head of a falcon could.

"You've got a big decision to make?" It was a question. The words dripping like nectar from his mouth. Did he know what I was thinking? Or was it simply that he'd been alive for, like he'd said, millennia and had all the wisdom that came with it?

The doors opened, and we continued into the hall. Horus couldn't know I hadn't paid for the course. Nobody, except Ben, could know that. I could walk straight into his classroom right now and take up the place next to Taurin again, and no one would be any the wiser. Was it fair of me to sit a course I wasn't officially on? Potentially steal someone's rightful spot?

I swallowed. "Yeah, I guess." He remained quiet, didn't push for more, but more was brewing. "Thing is, I've always lived my life on the hoof"—pun not intended—"I never needed to make grown up decisions. I went with the flow. I see the thing I want to do, and I do it, you know? Only . . . now, I'm not so sure I should do the thing. Not even sure I truly want it. But it's calling out to me." I was babbling. "Or . . . something's calling out to me. Anyway, there are consequences, not terrible ones, just"—I puffed out a sigh—"just grown-up ones."

He assessed me for a few moments, didn't ask me to repeat myself in a more coherent way. His expensive-looking leather sandals made an incongruous clopping sound on the tiled hallway floor. Eventually he spoke, "The thing I envy most about humans is you don't have the luxury of time like we do."

That stumped me. "You're jealous of our short lifespans?"

He chuckled. "It takes away the safety net of knowing you'll have forever to ponder your terrible decisions. When you've only got eighty, a hundred years, you can't afford to waste any of them wondering if things would have been better this way or that. You simply have to take the leap and pray it's the right one."

"So, you're saying I should just do it? Do this thing? Even if it might be the wrong thing?"

"Living life on the hoof is a great motto," he said. "You've already lived in a way most cannot dream to hope for. Carpe diem, Joey Silver. Seize the day. Grab the bull by the horns." And then, I swear to Gods, he winked at me. "So, you coming in?" he said, kicking the door of his classroom open.

Chapter 8

Taurin

She won't be there. She won't be there. She was on the wrong course. There's no reason she will be there.

I repeated this mantra as I made my way into UR. I even asked Ben at reception to check the records, and once I described her, he was very adamant she had not enrolled. And yet I knew she would be there. I felt it in my chest, like a magnet pulling me. The closer I got to the classroom, the stronger the force. The more it tingled. This, whatever it was, this mating bond. Telling me to waste no time and get busy, floating incessant, and decidedly carnal, thoughts around in my head.

Sure enough, when I rounded the corner to the lesson, there she was, stood at my desk. Not wearing red today, but a variation of it. A curve skimming orange t-shirt, pink spray-on jeans, and those red high-tops she had on last week. She'd tied her hair up in a ponytail and pulled her lip-sticked lips into a pout as she copied something from the whiteboard on a notebook. She looked better than I remembered. *Fuck*. The bond in my chest gave a little thrill when she glanced up and caught my eye.

"Hey, Horns," she said.

Shit, nicknames already.

"Peaches?" It was out before I could stop myself. *What was that?* I'd never given anyone a cute nickname before, but Gods, it suited her. "I didn't expect you to be here this week. Since, you know, you're not technically enrolled on this course."

"Ssssh," she said, her mouth contorting into yet another kiss-me face, causing blood to rush south. "How do you know?"

She had me. I couldn't be honest. She would learn I'd been asking about her. Luckily, Russ saved me from having to conjure something up.

"Welcome kids. Hope you've all had a lovely weekend. Today we'll be practicing our piped flowers. So, when you're ready, I'd like you all to grab a pen and your notepads and come to the front for a demonstration."

Joey raced to Russ' desk. I followed her. The rest of the class parting like the red sea for me. Naivety, the imprint, and an irrepressible instinct to protect her kicked in, and I claimed the position directly behind her. I immediately realised what a colossal mistake I'd made.

It was impossible to concentrate on anything Russ showed us. He had a bag filled with . . . something, and a nozzle, and there was squeezing involved and some kind of spinny thing . . . I think. But she kept moving her head from left to right like a puppy waiting for treats, and every time she did, it wafted her scent right up my nostrils.

Our scent, my stupid brain reminded me. The scent of the bond.

After a few minutes, I tried to move away, put some distance between us, to stop these progressively filthier thoughts flitting uninvited through my mind, but I'd been hemmed in by a pair of acrimonious vampires, a ghoul, and this annoying-as-fuck gryphon named Clarke. He was such a preening bastard. Perhaps he assumed, because of the bird skull, Russ might show him some favouritism.

I considered my options. Listen to Goldie, hit it and quit it, and hope that it satiated my appetite enough to clear my head. Or listen to Clair, and stay away from her. The first option would definitely be more enjoyable. But would it work? Could I fuck her and then pretend like she didn't exist?

No. No way. I already knew that wouldn't be an option. That if we fucked once, I'd never be able to give her up. The bond wanted her, and it wanted to keep her.

Russ clapped his hands together, snapping me out of a fantasy in which I tore off her orange t-shirt with my horns, and buried my face in the valley between her tits.

"So, kids, what's the first thing we're going to do?"

"Royal-icing," thirty voices chimed in unison. *The fuck was royal-icing?*

"Yes, but before that?"

"Wash our hands. Hairnets," everyone said, this time a little more disjointed and with a little less enthusiasm.

"Excellent. Right, pop your tails away and hop to it."

There was mass exodus to the sinks, while I stood stock still, staring at the table on which an overlarge, plastic drawing pin now sat. Joey seized my elbow and gently guided me to our desk. *Our desk.* It took me a moment to snap back to reality.

She was real, and not a figment of my fantasies for the past week. As evidenced by the way her touch caused all the hairs along my arms stand to attention. It was a soft touch, feminine, from hands that saw lotion. Not the rough, calloused, splitting fingers of someone that worked in a timber yard. She'd painted her nails red, because of course she did. I bet those fingers would look and feel amazing wrapped around my—

I shook the thought away. Would I lose myself around her? It was always my biggest worry in any situation but Seeing Red was something that only happened when I'd been pushed to my absolute limits. It happened when I was angry. Enraged. But only ever then.

I would lose all control. *All control*. Lose all my senses. And usually end up obliterating whatever was close by. Homes, vehicles, buildings. A school. A cafe. A shopping centre. One time, a factory that made oversized, photo-op deckchairs for the leisure industry. I never hurt anybody, at least not on purpose. Sometimes a few people got caught in the crossfire. Never gravely injured, though. Shrapnel mostly, or a lungful of smoke.

Could she elicit that kind of emotion in me? I had no idea. I never once Saw Red because I'd been . . . aroused. Could it even happen? Could I get so consumed with passion that I posed a different danger?

Surely, it wasn't worth waiting to find out. I didn't mind being thought of as a violent menace to society, but I was no rapist. I squeezed my eyes shut, tried to clear the scent out of my nose, and the delicious, yet unbidden, images from my thoughts.

No. I absolutely would not risk any harm to her. Especially from me.

I spent the rest of the lesson trying to listen to what Joey was saying and showing me. But every time she spoke in that sexy purr, every time she caught my eye, every time our elbows brushed together, every time she swished that ponytail, the bond in my chest crackled, like electricity zapping through water.

I couldn't be around her, not with this constant drive to push her underneath me. Clair was right. I had to forget her. I'd have to stay as far away from her as possible. At least until I finished this course. After class, I would speak with Russ and get him to move her to a different seat, or maybe realm.

"Okay kids, five minutes left. Can we wash up our bowls and nozzles? And then return to your desks. I have an announcement to make. A rather exciting one."

We did as Russ instructed. I seized the opportunity to spend a few moments away from her and the persistent magnetic tugging in my chest and took the equipment to the sink while she tidied up the piping bags.

"We're going on a class trip!" said Russ once everyone had returned to their places. Heads shot up in excitement but remained quiet. "In almost four weeks we'll all be going to the Inter-Realm Cake Convention, also known as Cakecon, in the glorious city of St. Clouds." Some people whooped. Joey looked up at me. I determinately kept my eyes forward, though I caught her smile in my periphery.

"But the best news is, I've arranged for you all to participate in the student category. The theme this year is . . ." He looked down at his notes. "Unity. You're to bake a cake from scratch and decorate it with 'unity' in mind. I'll put all the T's and C's on your student app. There is prize money," he said, raising his voice infinitesimally. "Five-thousand silvers to the winning team."

Chatter broke out. Someone looked up and said, "Team?"

"Oh, yes. I nearly forgot. You'll be working in teams of two. Whoever is seated next to you now will be your new partner for the rest of term."

"Noooo!" The word escaped my lips before I could stop it. Joey shifted her weight to her other hip, away from me.

"And there's homework!" Russ said, calling everyone to silence again. "I want you, in your pairs, to come up with a concept for your design, and present it to me next week. Yes, yes, that means you'll have to meet up outside of class, or chat on the telephones, or video-call on FaeBook, or whatever technology you youngsters use."

Again, Joey looked at me. This time, I allowed myself to meet her eyes. Her brow creased, and, where she was chewing on the corner of her mouth, her lips puckered again. What was she thinking about? Gods, I was desperate to know. Me, miserable, minotaur Taurin wanted to know what someone, who I'd only met last week, was thinking.

Imprinting was really doing a number on me.

She offered me a shy smile, and the thing in my chest revved. I fought the sudden urge to seize her around the middle, perch her on the table, bite down on that fat bottom lip, and suck the thoughts from her head. The desk might have been waist-height for everyone else, but it was hip-height for me. The perfect height for—

No. See how quickly my mind went there? I couldn't do this. She had to go. I wasn't sure I could trust myself around her.

Russ dismissed the class, and I watched Joey leave with the rest. That rounded ass bouncing from side to side.

The enticing little Y at the apex of her pink jeans. The delectable flashes of skin revealed at each hip. When she reached the door, she turned and glanced over her shoulder at me, her expression unreadable, her smile absent. I already missed it. I realised, in that moment, she could have asked for the moons, and I would have been on my way to find a scaffolding company with enough resources to reach them.

Anything to see that smile again.

But . . .

Was she in danger? Was my future as a free man?

Was I really the monster everyone assumed I was?

I hung back until I was the last in the room. "Russ, can I have a word, please?"

"Sure thing. What do you need?" he said, hanging up his apron on a hook by the door, once again revealing his gleaming, jet six-pack.

"I . . . I need you to move Joey." I could have told him she wasn't enrolled on the course, and he'd likely have no choice except to kick her off. Only that seemed unnecessarily cruel. "I can't be her partner for this project."

"I'm sorry, Taurin, there's nowhere else for her to sit."

I scrubbed my palms down my face, took a controlled breath. "Can you swap her with someone?"

He placed his hand on my arm. I could still smell her, her perfume, the bond, like the scent was trapped in my nostrils. Taunting me.

"Please? I can't stand to be around her. She's driving me crazy."

"Have faith, Taurin. It won't be as bad as you are imagining."

"I can't be near her anymore. I'm going to lose my mind if I have to sit next to her every week," I said, snatching my arm away. "You don't understand!"

He cocked his head to the side. "Child, you're not giving me enough credit. You're forgetting I've been alive for millennia. I understand more than you can possibly comprehend. Much more."

Did he? Did he honestly realise that I'd imprinted on her? That just having her next to me was sending all my senses into a tailspin. This bond in my chest was telling me to bend her over his desk and pound her until I broke her, and then carry her home in my arms and feed her grapes until she recovered. And then repeat steps one and two until the end of time.

How long could I ignore it before my animal instincts kicked-in and I'd no longer have agency over my body, my actions. Every time I was near her, she was in danger.

Wasn't she?

I didn't see how I could explain myself without revealing the truth, the full nature of who I really was. Who I became.

I grabbed my kit bag and pushed past him out the door.

Chapter 9

Joey

Five-thousand silvers.

The prize money if we won. It was too good an opportunity to pass up. If I convinced him to get some lunch with me, we could get a head start on the homework.

Five-thousand silvers.

I could pay Hell-Bitch back. I could even afford the fee for this cake dec course and become officially enrolled. Obviously, we'd split the cash, but two and a half grand was still more than I needed to worm my way out of the Christie-sized hole I'd dug myself into.

Horns. Such a riddle of a man. So tense and standoffish around me, yet whenever I looked at him, he'd quickly avert his eyes, as though he'd been spying on me all along and didn't want to be caught looking. The vibe I got said he was into me, his actual words and body language, however, I had no clue.

I left the classroom and leaned my weight against the opposite wall. Now was as good a time as any to get the ball rolling on this project. *Five thousand silvers.*

While I waited, I pulled out my phone and texted Dad.

Mum told me about your new friends, and I wanted to let you know I'm proud of you. (Smiling face emoji).

If he could make the effort to be a better person, so could I.

Despite it being past midnight, his reply came immediately.

Hi Flower. Thank you. xx

Followed by:

I'm trying to do what's best for my girls. xx

Followed then by:

It's Dad, by the way. xx

I smiled and tucked my phone into my backpack, and that was when I heard it, rumbling out from inside the classroom. The unmistakable half-growl of Horns.

"I need you to move Joey. I can't be her partner for this project." My heart skipped one, three, five beats. Instinct kicked in, and I positioned myself closer to the crack in the door.

Then came the silken tones of Horus, though his words didn't carry the same way Horns' did and I couldn't make them out.

"Can you swap her with someone? Please? I can't stand to be around her. She's driving me crazy."

Oh Gods, he hated me. Truly hated me. I'd been way off the mark.

"I can't be near her anymore. I'm going to lose my mind if I have to sit next to her every week. You don't understand!"

Waaaaay off.

Horus spoke again, but I couldn't stay. I had to get out. I barely knew Horns—Taurin. Had said about twenty words to him. So there really was no justification for the tiny feather-like cracks snaking across my heart. How could I have gotten this so wrong? How could I have misjudged him by so much? Maybe Ash was right all along. I slung my bag over my shoulder, just as the door wrenched open and Taurin ducked into the corridor.

He froze when he caught sight of me. "Hi, shit, uh . . . How much of that did you hear?"

Heat prickled behind my eyes. Gods, was I crying? No, no actual tears, yet. This was so un-Joey of me. I wasn't this girl. The girl that almost cried over a man she only just met. I should confront him, ask him for clarification, demand he apologise and explain how I must have got the wrong end of the stick. That he'd been telling Russ about a different Joey he despised. I couldn't. The words became stuck.

Instead, like the masochist I was, I said, "How much of what?"

His shoulders dropped, relief tugging at the corners of his mouth and crinkling those unfairly gorgeous blue eyes.

Five-thousand silvers, Joey. Think of the ackers. "Are you hungry?" I forced as much brightness into my voice as I could muster.

We could do this. I could do this. We could work together, come up with a design, win that money. His sugar-paste rose was exquisite. He had the talent for this, and I . . . would also be present.

He cocked an eyebrow at me.

"Wanna join me in the canteen, and we can discuss our project?"

He took a deep breath and held it for so long I thought perhaps he'd made eye contact with a gorgon. "No," he finally said.

I could only attribute the sinking feeling in my chest to the potential loss of five-grand. It definitely had nothing to do with the belligerent beefcake rejecting me twice in the space of three minutes.

Beefcake, ha! At least I hadn't lost my sense of humour.

"No, not the canteen," he added, giving way to a tiny bubble of hope. How pathetic was I? "The food is shit. Unless you like scrambled locust."

"I do not," I said.

"We'll go to Tallywhacker's, the student bar. The food is surprisingly good, and they do table service until three am."

I pretended as though my insides weren't doing a happy jig. "Table service at a student bar? Things have changed since my day."

He offered me a half-smile — Gods, those lips — and I let him lead the way to the bar. I could do this. I mean, sure, there were a million reasons why I shouldn't. One, I wasn't enrolled on the course. If they found out, they'd kick me off and I'd be back to square one. Two, this man hated me. There was undeniable proof of his contempt, though his reasoning remained mysterious. Three, he was a highly dangerous minotaur, who recently flattened a local Ichor. Even dragons, *dragons*, are afraid of minotaurs. Four, did I mention he hates me and is extremely volatile?

And five, the most pressing reason. I was profoundly, deeply, sexually attracted to him.

"Restaurant or bar?" said the cycloptic, apron-clad server at Tallywhacker's.

"Restaurant," said Taurin.

We followed the server to a booth and took our seats. The space was enormous. I wasn't sure about square-footage, but there were at least two, maybe three-hundred tables. Yet it still had that cosy, Ye Olde Tavern feel. Stained-glass dividers depicting knights on horseback, princesses with pointed pink headgear, and phallic-shaped stone towers separated the booths. On the walls, and dangling from the ceiling, were silver tankards and patina shields and faux-ancient scrolls and decorative swords and triggerless blunderbusses. It was theme-parky, yet comfy. I sidled up the bench, closer to Horns.

I glanced over the menu. Horns didn't bother to pick his up.

I can't stand to be near her.

My stomach dropped as I remembered his words. I needed comfort food.

Can you swap her with someone? Please.

I never heard what Russ said. Did he agree to Horns' demands? Did he agree to move me?

"Wait, are we still working on this project together?" I said, making my voice as small as possible.

He spun his nose ring and side-eyed me.

"It's just that I overher—Got the impression you, uh, might want to work with someone else."

"Of course we are. Why would you say that?"

Gah, why was he being so hot and cold? It was my opportunity to ask him what the hell was going on. Why he loathed me so much. Why one minute he was yelling at the god of kings to move me and the next acting like I was an idiot for suggesting he wanted to work with someone else.

But . . . I wasn't sure if I was ready to hear the truth — whatever that might be — and I had no idea why.

"We should maybe talk about the cake. Our project . . . For the competition," I said. Gods, why did I find it so difficult to confront him on this?

His half-smile returned, and I made a concerted effort not to stare at that gorgeous mouth. "Sure."

The server reappeared, notepad in hand. "Have you guys decided what you want? Or do you need another minute?" He spoke the last question as though he might weep if we asked for more time.

"Uh," I said, eyes slipping over the list once again.

Taurin handed the server the menu he'd not once looked at. "Two tempeh salads, extra pickles, and two flagons of beer, please."

Urgh, I hated it when a man ordered for a woman. Also, salad, the fuck? Was he insinuating I needed to go on a diet? I was far too hungry for salad.

"And whatever she's having."

I laughed like he was kidding, but both Horns and the server narrowed their eyes at me.

"Oh, you're really having two salads, okay. I'll have the chicken burger, and cheese fries. And a bottle of beer. Please." The server left. I glanced at Horns. "You must be starving."

"Always. Though I usually just graze throughout the day."

A bark of laughter erupted from me, and I slapped a hand over my mouth before I caught the glint in his eye that told me he was, in fact, messing with me. Hold my not-yet-delivered beer. He made a joke?!

"In all seriousness, I am always hungry, and these salads are delicious. I could eat four. Normally do. This is me trying to show some restraint."

I laughed again. Oh no, this wasn't helping me quash the desire to smash my lips against his. Why couldn't he be a consistently miserable, sullen prick and let me hate him back?

"Wait, are you vegan?" I said.

He nodded. "Ungulates are almost always herbivores."

I understood none of that. "Ungulates?"

"It means 'being hoofed'."

"Wow, okay. We only just met, but sure. I'm open-minded. As long as we use protection, right?"

His laughter rumbled right through the furniture, shaking the pot of cutlery on the table. I felt it in my sternum, and in my fingertips. It pushed his scent towards me. Woods, like pine, made sense since he was practically a lumberjack. And something else, something earthier, like fresh, wet mud. Cologne? Or his natural thigh-clenching man aroma? I squirmed on the bench.

And then I remembered what I ordered. "Shit, are you alright with me eating meat?"

"You can eat whatever you like," he said. "Chicken's not too bad. Could have been worse. At least you didn't order the steak."

"Yeah, that would have been weird for you. I don't eat red meat, anyway. It gives me constipation." I thought I had said that last part in my head. Going by Taurin's snort of laughter, evidently not.

"Honestly, it's fine," he said. "I have a flatmate who's a vampire. Like I said, it could've been a lot more awkward."

It was as though the Eight and a Half Kingdoms had shifted on its axis. He'd begun to open up. He was smiling and joking. Like he'd started to trust me. Trust that he could let a bit of himself through that grumpy barricade he'd pulled up. I wasn't about to waste my chance to find out everything before he clammed up again. It could be my only opportunity.

"A vampire flatmate? That's unusual." Vampires often flocked together. I'd never heard of a vampire and a non-vampire sharing a living space before, besides familiars of course. "How did you meet?"

"Here, actually, about eleven, twelve years ago. You ever heard of the company Blooze?"

"Alcohol blood for vampires?"

"That's the one. My flatmate, Dima, founded it. Just a small indie brewery at the time. But it was his idea. When I was a student here, you could go to the bar and pay for your drinks, or you could go to Dima's bar, get drunk for free, and all he asked for in return was a pint of blood." He shrugged. "I started going every night. Because I'm so big, the blood loss never affected me the way it did others. Dima started to recognise me, and we became friends. He said another friend of theirs was looking for a fourth flatmate, and did I want to be it? He sold the company a few years ago, made an absolute killing. Now he just lives off the profits. But he still lives with us, not in some gothic Eastside mansion because, well, it's Dima, he's an absolute oddity."

"I have loads of questions. Firstly, I had no idea you were capable of placing so many words one in front of the other. So, thank you for that treat." He gave me a genuine smile. "Secondly, you went to uni here? What did you study? And when did you go because I went to uni here and I've never seen you before, and also, I really, really want to know more about your flatmates."

The rumble of his laugh echoed through the bench, right through my chest and down my spine. "I studied politics. I graduated . . ." He pinched his face into what I assumed was a thinking face and not a kiss-me-this-instant face. Shame. "About nine years ago."

"I graduated six years ago," I said. "So, we wouldn't have been here at the same time." I would definitely have remembered those muscles and that voice.

"What did you study?" he asked.

"Lots of things. I changed my degree about seven times. But in my final year, I managed to settle on drama.

Though, if you ask my dad, he'll tell you I studied dramatics."

At that moment, the server came over with our drinks. I took a sip of my beer, and Horns drank half a flagon in one swig.

"Sorry, just thirsty."

"You should see me with the bathroom tap at four am," I said, thankfully not spurting out the first response that popped up in my head. "We have an intimate acquaintance. Tell me more about your flatmates. How many people do you live with?" *Translation: please don't ever stop talking. I like this chatty version of you.*

"Three flatmates. Dima, the vampire. Goldie, he's a fae, and then there's Mal, our sort of live-in landlord. He's an incubus."

I almost projected my beer through my nostrils.

"A vampire, a fae, and an incubus? Wow, I guess that makes you the ugly one."

He laughed so hard and so loud the whole restaurant shook. Gods, had anyone ever become addicted to a laugh before? "That's one-hundred-percent accurate, unfortunately. But I am the tallest and youngest, so there's that."

"Any household that boasts you as the ugly one is definitely somewhere I want to be."

"Is that a compliment?"

Great, now I was outright flirting with him. And he was smiling, and oh my Gods, was he beautiful when he smiled. There were dimples. Dimples! Under all that stubble. The server arrived again, this time with our food.

"It's not somewhere I'd like you to be," he said, once the cyclops left.

The way he said it gave me a strange tingling sensation in my chest.

"One of my flatmates might try to eat you."

"The vampire?"

He nodded. "And one of them would try to fuck you."

"The incubus?"

"Mal? No, Mal's a good guy, but Goldie would. The fae. He likes to pretend he hates all humans, but honestly, he'd fuck anything with a pulse." Panic flashed behind those mesmeric eyes. "He's an Oread. A mountain-nymph. He's constantly trying to get into my pants."

I didn't know what to say. I wholeheartedly agreed with Goldie. I took a bite of my chicken-burger — satisfactorily mediocre — and tried not to glance at Horns' pants area.

"I'd tear their throats out before I let either of them near you, though," he said. He picked up his fork and started eating his salad as if he'd said nothing more than, *looks like it might rain tonight*, and not, *I'd murder my friends before I'd let them harm you.*

The temperature of the bar rose by at least ten degrees. I should not have found this unprompted and frankly bloodthirsty overprotectiveness arousing. I shifted on the bench, clamping my thighs together, while my eyes took their own tour of his biceps. His bare biceps. As in, no tattoos. I half wished his grey t-shirt was a little more see-through, if only to make sure I hadn't imagined the decoration on his hips.

Get a grip, Joey. He's a dangerous, miserable, hot-as-fuck bull-man.

I shook the thought away. "We should do a cake shaped like Borderlands," I said, spewed in fact. At the exact moment, he said, "So, what are your flatmates like?"

He pushed his empty salad plate to one side and pulled the full one in its place. "That's a great idea. I like it."

"Uh, thanks." I blinked a few times before remembering he'd asked a question, too. "Just the one flatmate." I set aside the conflicting emotions raging inside me. "Hell-Bitch Christie. She's horrible. A human."

"You don't get on?"

I let out a sigh. I didn't want to get into a discussion about Christie and all the ways I've failed at everything in life, and all the ways she insisted on reminding me.

"We used to, but . . ." *Like everyone else she always expects more*. "To her, I'm *just* a delivery driver. I don't have a proper job like she does, or a mortgage or a boyfriend, or any of the other things she tells me proper grown-ups have." I dug my fingernail under the label of my beer bottle. "She's also my landlord and I haven't been able to make rent for a couple of months. She hasn't been very . . . understanding."

"Oh," he said, and then, "*Oh.* That's why you're so keen to enter the competition. The prize money."

"Yeah." I couldn't be sure, but I thought I saw a flash of disappointment in those blue eyes.

I wasn't inexperienced with men. I'd had plenty of sexual partners and part-time, and very brief, boyfriends in the past, but I'd never before been so confused about a man's feelings towards me. His signals were so varied, so contradictory. One minute he told Horus he hated me, the next we chatted like old friends. Perhaps he should quit lumberjacking and take up mixology. Did he hate me? Did he want to fuck me? I couldn't work it out.

"But okay why are you being so weird with me?" I blurted out.

He paused, his flagon halfway to his lips. He sighed and placed it down. "What do you mean?"

"You hardly speak to me in class, and now you're like this." I gesticulated to the whole of him. He was leaning towards me, his arms were open, his palms face up, both feet pointing at me. His body language told me I was the most interesting person in Borderlands.

His eyes searched my face, as though he might read the answer on my forehead. After a while he said, "Do you know how acute monster hearing is?"

"What?" I said, genuinely confused. Of all the things I expected him to say, this wouldn't have made it to the top one-thousandth.

"There are too many people in that class watching what I'm doing, listening to what I'm saying."

"You sound paranoid."

He shrugged. "I feel very self-conscious in a big group. Like everyone's waiting for me to . . ."

"To what?"

He didn't answer.

"I'm more of a one-on-one kinda bloke. You know? I get crowded out when all three of my flatmates are home at the same time."

"Noted," I said, feeling like a minotaur sized weight had been lifted from my shoulders. Did he still hate me? I couldn't be sure. He'd been completely different this past hour. Chatty, comfortable, easy-going. There were no awkward silences, no overriding feelings of whatever the culinary equivalent of buyer's remorse was. No itchy feet. No moments of existential dread. It had been fun, exciting even. It had felt . . . natural. Like we were two people who would always be content in each other's company. Even if we weren't filling the quiet moments. Was that how a person behaved with someone they despised? I didn't think so. Though, I struggled to find another way to decipher *I'm going to lose my mind if I have to sit next to her every week*.

I chanced another peek at him. Again, he sharply averted his gaze, his mouth quirking up at the corner. I used the opportunity to get my visual fill of him. Part of me hoped to discover flaws. It would have assuaged the conflicting, squirming feelings in my gut. But who was I kidding?

Everything about him was too perfect. His hair, now beginning to tumble free from its top knot, perfect. His tanned face, with its perfect contours and perfect amount of weathering, perfect. Those eyes, those lips, that torso, those arms, Gods, those arms.

It wasn't as if I was a challenge-shy person. There was no reason we couldn't have a little fun together while we chased the prize money. Right? Ash had said he didn't want me to become one of those women who thought they could change a man. But I wasn't a relationship kinda girl. There'd be no need for me to change him. Not if I only wanted him for a little while.

Besides, maybe I liked that dangerous edge to him.

"Hey, give me your phone."

He pulled his eyebrows together, but handed over his phone, regardless. I opened up his contacts, pressed 'create new' and tapped out my number. When I came to add my name, I faltered. Usually when I did this, I'd write something outrageously flirty like *Best Shag Ever*, or *Future Wifey*, but I didn't do that this time. It felt too . . . risky. That buzzing feeling in my chest had returned. Was it heartburn? Instead, I simply wrote Joey from Cake Dec, but that seemed boring, so I added a surprise or two.

I gave him his phone back and placed my hand on the top of his. He jolted, but didn't move away. "Hey, would it be weird if I get a milkshake?"

Chapter 10

Taurin

I slung my kit bag into its rest-of-the-week nest and made my way into the living room. Goldie and Mal were offing humans on screen and Dima observed the game from his usual corner, his quilting hoop lay abandoned on the arm of the sofa.

Goldie lifted his eyes up to me. "Hey," he said, drawing out the word. "Where've you been?" He raised his brows. "Was she good?"

"She?" It was as though someone had flicked on Dima's power switch. I should have gone straight to my bedroom.

"Sugar Paste," my sex-obsessed flatmate clarified. "Human." He made an obscene gesture, his fisted hand moving towards his mouth, his tongue filling out his other cheek.

"You getting busy at cake class?" Dima said, surging forward in that creepy, motionless way vampires do.

"Fuck off. No, I wasn't."

Goldie's smirk vanished. "Taur, you're not gonna let her get to your head? Didn't we go over this? Fuck and forget, yeah?"

"What's going on?" asked Mal.

"Girl on his course," said Goldie, matter-of-factly. He turned to me, "I just don't want you relapsing."

"Why would he relapse?" asked Mal.

"I won't relapse," I said. "That is not what causes me to See Red. Besides, Dr Landyn told me to stay away from her and I'd be fine."

Both Goldie and Clair advised me to forget Peaches. Toss her aside like she meant nothing, like another shredded t-shirt, or disposable coffee cup. Not possible. Not now. Dinner with her had been . . . unexpected. Unexpectedly reassuring and highly flustering. I spent the entire hour and thirty with a semi and heart palpitations. She was different to what I'd imagined. No, scrap that, she was exactly as I'd dreamed. As I'd knew she'd be. Gorgeous, hilarious, easy to be around. She felt comfortable, like she was where I belonged. She felt like returning home from work after a long day of hauling logs. Like a hot shower, or a great movie that you've seen a hundred times, or a vegan jam-doughnut.

But *I* wasn't as I expected. Of course I wanted her, I couldn't stop imagining all the ways I wanted her. But no part of me wanted to take it without first making sure it was something she wanted too.

I felt . . . in control.

"Mmhmm, so how come you're late home?" said Goldie.

Dima answered, "Ooh! He went to the student bar with her! She's pretty."

"Get the fuck out of my head, Dima!" I said.

He gave me an apologetic smile. "You want me to eat her for you? Take her out of the picture?"

"I'm getting a beer," I said, marching straight past them to the kitchen. Mal handed Dima his controller and followed behind me.

Goldie yelled, "Taur, can you grab me one? And bring Dima a Blooze."

I chain emptied three cans and threw them into the recycling. When I turned around, Mal stood directly behind me. He came up to my cheeks, his ice blond hair tucked over his onyx horns. Today he deigned to wear clothes (a black vest) on the top half of his body, it was the same colour as his skin. He'd made some rudimentary design adjustments so that his wings could hang out freely. For a moment, he stared at me. His eyes narrowed, his tongue tracing his bottom lip. Then he leaned forward and sniffed me. And sniffed again.

Recognition slid across his features, his mouth forming a perfect O.

"Mal?" I said, panic now coursing through me. He'd figured me out. He knew.

He shut the kitchen door. "You imprinted?" he said, in the softest whisper.

I collapsed onto a dining chair. "What the fuck am I meant to do?"

Mal had always been the parental figure of our little motley crew. The oldest, only by a handful of decades, but by far the wisest. As an incubus, sex was his business, his life, it was him. He was bankrolled by roughly two dozen very wealthy older women who he 'visited' anywhere from monthly to once a decade. He called these visits his medicine rounds because, as a child, he'd wanted to become a nurse. But now, as a seven-hundred-year-old adult, he was more than his work, more than simply fucking. He understood things on a level neither Dima or Goldie, or I, could. He'd know exactly how I was feeling. How I felt about her. Peaches. He could probably tell me how she felt about me.

He sat opposite me. "Ignore Goldie. This won't go away. If you fuck her, you'll only seal the bond, strengthen it. And if you fuck her without a condom, there'll be no going back. But perhaps it's too late for that. Not sure there's any way to counter imprinting."

Nope, definitely too late.

"And you can't ignore *her*, either," he continued. "That sensation, that pull that you have in your chest, she'll have it too. Even if she doesn't understand what it is."

I already knew this. I had tried to ignore her. It didn't work. Tried to give her monosyllabic answers. That didn't work either. Somehow, against all my better judgement and against years and years of compacted, crusted-on sullenness, I found myself engaging. And not only engaging, but engaging and enjoying myself. She asked me questions. Though part of me screamed not to tell her anything or let her in, another, much larger and with decidedly more driving force, happily went along with it. I answered them with more than a yes or no. I let her in, and I wanted to be let in. And I had a great time. It felt natural, right, easy. Like we'd known each other for years.

"I . . ." I fiddled with my nose ring. "I don't act like myself when I'm with her. She makes me feel like, I don't know, social." I laughed through the sheer ridiculousness of it.

He brought a leg up over the other and crossed it at the ankle. "Perhaps she makes you feel more like yourself than you realise. Maybe the real you is chatty. Maybe the miserable prick that everyone else sees isn't who you're truly meant to be."

"Ha!"

"She's human, yeah?"

"Yeah."

"Mate, this is it. The moment everyone — almost everyone, probs not Goldie — lives for. You've found *it*." He smiled, and in his smile, I saw his genuine happiness, and something else too, which, over the years of knowing him, I'd come to realise was grief. The kind of grief that came woven into nostalgia and baked together like bread dough. The kind that was now impossible to separate. He knew all too well what I felt, what I was going through. More than I could comprehend.

One time, when I first moved in, Dima had been out at his bar, and Goldie had gotten so high he passed out face down on the living room rug, I asked Mal if he ever got bored with his work.

He'd shrugged, and said, "Sometimes you have to embrace what you are." As someone grappling so much with self-acceptance, I needed to hear that. Something even now I struggled to remember.

"Have you ever developed feelings for any of the women?" I'd asked.

"I care for them all," was his answer.

"You know what I mean. Have you ever been in love?"

He took a few minutes before saying, "Once. It was intense." He'd laughed. A sad sort of laugh. "Fated-mates, and all that."

"What happened?"

"Human. She . . . grew older. She didn't cope with the passing of time. I couldn't cope. She . . ."

But he never finished his tale, and I never found out what happened to her.

"You need to take it slow," Mal said, pulling me from my memory. "Just because you imprinted on her doesn't mean it *will* happen. You still have to make it happen. Like any other relationship. The only difference is that you already know you're sexually compatible. But you have to work on making the other pieces fit too." He placed his elbow on the table and his hand on his chin. "Actually, you'll need to work harder than any other relationship. You'll have to get to know her first, despite that burning urge to wet your dick. Because once you fuck, that's it, the bond will never give her up. She needs to be okay with this being a long-term thing. Like super long-term."

Inwardly, I groaned. That's exactly what the bond told me it needed. All of it. The sex and the forever. I knew she wanted the former, I could scent her arousal, feel it in the ways her gaze travelled over me. I guess they don't call it Mates for nothing. But what if she only wanted that one thing? A hook up. A fling. What happened when I've been flung?

"What if she's not okay with the super long-term thing?"

He looked at me for a few seconds, quirked his shoulders, and began laughing. "Gods, it's not funny. I don't know why I'm—Fuck, man," he wiped tears from his eyes. "You'll both slowly descend into madness."

"For real? Shit." Why the hell was I laughing alongside him? I'd never heard anything less funny, but there we were, giggling like we were at primary school and someone wrote BOOBIES on their calculator.

Damn.

I wanted long-term. Of course, I did. I'd never been a fuck-and-fuck-off kinda guy. I'd always hated one-night-stands. Always preferred we established a connection before smashing our genitals together. I guess now it was a case of taking things slow, trying not to scare her off, not letting her see the worst of me. That type of thing.

I would start that night.

"Look what she put her contact in as." I handed him my phone open to her details.

He smiled. Joey from Cake Dec. She'd added a peach emoji either side of her name.

"You can't tell the others."

"Fuck, no, of course not. I'll have a word with Dima as well. Keep him out of your head."

"Thanks." A thought occurred to me. Clair's advice, bouncing around in my memory. "Do you reckon being near her might trigger me? Make me relapse?" I asked, my voice quiet, as though the very idea might be enough to trigger me.

"No." No, just like that. Direct and assured. "The bond will protect her. You're worried you'll shift and claim her without consent?" I nodded, unable to agree aloud. "You won't. Uh, uh. No way."

"Oh, thank Gods." I practically melted onto the dining chair.

"But . . ."

"But?"

He rubbed his chin with his hand. "What's gonna trigger you is if she's in danger. If someone or something threatens her, your animal instincts will override like that." He snapped his fingers. "The bond, it will prioritise her safety and happiness over everything. Absolutely everything. You don't matter to the bond. Keeping yourself out of gaol won't matter. If something threatens her, you won't be in control, you'll—"

"I'll See Red," I said, finishing his sentence.

He nodded. We were quiet for a moment. "Okay, I've got it! You just need to pre-empt any danger she might be in. And stop it before it . . . escalates."

"So, I need to watch her like she's a toddler walking out into traffic, and stop bad things from happening to her before they do?" I didn't hide the sarcasm in my voice.

"You got a better idea?"

I puffed out a long stream of air. I had nothing else.

"I'm sure you'll be fine," he said. "I'm sure she's not the type of person to throw herself mindlessly into decisions before thinking them through."

Chapter 11

TAURIN - TUESDAY 5:15AM

Hey Joey from Cake Dec with two peach emojis, it's Taurin with two horn emojis (2x aubergine emojis). Just texting so you have my number as well, feels kind of unfair that I have yours

JOEY - TUESDAY 5:17AM

Hey Horns, those are not horn emojis btw (tongue-out winking emoji)

Just curious, do you operate mostly on human or vampire time?

TAURIN - TUESDAY 5:20AM

Mostly human. I have a day job which starts at 8 in the morning most days.

What about you?

JOEY - TUESDAY 5:21AM

Mostly human too

I'm getting too old for these all-nighters

TAURIN - TUESDAY 5:21AM

Same

I'll let you get your rest then

Goodnight, Peaches

JOEY - TUESDAY 5:25AM

Night, Horns

TAURIN - TUESDAY 8:45AM

Morning! Couldn't sleep. I was thinking maybe we could do a Borderlands map cross-section type thing for our cake design. What do you reckon? We could make the different landmarks from marzipan?

JOEY - TUESDAY 11:45AM

Yeah, great idea

I've just been reading the terms, we need some type of floral dec or they'll disqualify us

TAURIN - TUESDAY 11:48AM

Sorry, did I wake you?

Native Borderlands sugar paste flowers around the edges?

JOEY - TUESDAY 11:51AM

Not at all

You'll have to do the sugar paste flowers, mine was shit

I've still got yours btw, it's in my room

. . .

. . .

TAURIN - TUESDAY 12:48PM

I'll do some sketches for Monday

JOEY - TUESDAY 15:15PM

Random question, are you a lumberjack?

TAURIN - TUESDAY 15:30PM

Technically, no, but whatever helps your fantasy

JOEY - TUESDAY 15:30PM

My friend thinks you're (red-faced tongue-out sweating emoji)

He wants to know if you're single

TAURIN - TUESDAY 15:31PM

Who's your friend?

JOEY - TUESDAY 15:32PM

A 2000-year-old Summer Fae

TAURIN - TUESDAY 15:32PM

In that case, I'm single

JOEY - TUESDAY 15:33PM

I stand corrected. He's actually 1999 (face-smacking emoji)

TAURIN - TUESDAY 15:35PM

On second thoughts, I've changed my mind

JOEY - TUESDAY 15:35PM

Lol

I don't blame you. Are all Fae this thirsty?

TAURIN - TUESDAY 15:36PM

I hate to generalise, but yeah

TAURIN - TUESDAY 17:02PM

So, I have a friend, who is definitely not made up, and I am definitely not sat alone at my kitchen table, that wants to know if you're single

JOEY - TUESDAY 20:11PM

Sorry, bat died

Yes, I'm single

JOEY - TUESDAY 22.22PM

I'm off to bed now

Chat tomorrow?

TAURIN - TUESDAY 22:35PM

K, night, Peaches

TAURIN - WEDNESDAY 21.44PM

Have you had a good day?

JOEY - WEDNESDAY 21:45PM

Had a fight with Hell-Bitch

TAURIN - WEDNESDAY 21.47PM

U ok?

JOEY - WEDNESDAY 21:48PM

Am now. Just making some notes for Monday and snuggling Ludo, Hell-Bitch's Cat

Currently trying to figure out how I can sneak him with me when she kicks me out

Picture attached. (A ginger tomcat sleeps curled up between two red sweatpants clad thighs. Besides the legs, a doodle-covered notepad is just visible. A scribbled title reads: Ideas for Horny Lumberj . . .)

What are you up to?

TAURIN - WEDNESDAY 21.54PM

Just having a beer with these two.

Picture attached. (A bare chested man with pointed ears and shiny yellow hair sits on a burgundy velvet sofa. In one hand he holds a games console controller, and with the other hand he holds up his middle finger to the camera.)

Dima's there too. But, you know, vampire, so he doesn't show up on the photo. He's in the corner. For visual reference, he has shoulder length black hair, skin the colour of pissed-on snow, hellish red eyes, eerily inactive. So, completely different from every other vampire you've ever seen.

JOEY - WEDNESDAY 21:59PM

Lol. Is he naked too?

TAURIN - WEDNESDAY 22:00PM

No, Dima always wears a very fetching tunic and gilt embroidered cape

JOEY - WEDNESDAY 22:01PM

Never could pull off the look myself

Have fun

TAURIN - THURSDAY 13:09PM

Hey, u ok? Did you manage to sort things out with your flatmate?

JOEY - THURSDAY 13:14PM

No, not really, but it's fine

Might have to set Dima on her

TAURIN - THURSDAY 13:14PM

Just say the word

JOEY - THURSDAY 13:16PM

You at work?

TAURIN - THURSDAY 13:16PM

Yeah, on my lunch break

It's fucking hot today!

JOEY - THURSDAY 13:17PM

Strictly for visual purposes, does that mean you're shirtless?

TAURIN - THURSDAY 13:18PM

(Winking emoji) Yes. But try to restrain yourself, also full bullhead.

JOEY - THURSDAY 13:19PM

Pics or it didn't happen

. . .

JOEY - FRIDAY 20:04PM

I guess it didn't happen then

TAURIN - FRIDAY 20:46PM

Sorry, I'm not ready for that

JOEY - FRIDAY 20:48PM

Shit, sorry, man. That was really insensitive of me

TAURIN - FRIDAY 21:49PM

It's fine. Forget it

TAURIN - SUNDAY 18:36PM

You going to Cake Dec tom?

JOEY - SUNDAY 18:50PM

Of course. Got 5k to win

Chapter 12

Joey

Good Gods, I'd forgotten how beautiful he was.

"Still no kit?" were his first miserable words to me that day. So, he *was* pissed with me.

"I've ordered it," I lied.

"Evening, kids. Welcome back," came Horus' dulcet tones from the front of the class. "Today I will talk to each of you in your pairs and find out all about your plans for your Cakecon entry. In the meantime, I want you to make a start on it. Whether that's baking the cake itself or starting on your floral decorations using the techniques we've learned over the past few weeks. Everybody clear on that?" The class murmured their agreement. "Excellent, now pop those tails away, wash those filthy hands, and let's get busy."

"Horns, I'm so sorry about what I texted the other day. I wasn't thinking—"

"I said forget it." He had reverted to Horns version 1.0. Surly, miserable, stiff. His body angled away from mine, his brows knotted together, his massive arms folded over his chest. I wanted the sexy, easy, student bar version back.

"I don't want you to—"

"To what? Shift? See Red? Everyone is so worried that I might lose it and smash up the place. You all treat me like I'm a grenade with a loose pin." A few voices died down, but no one turned to look at us.

Without receiving instruction from my brain, I grabbed the front of his t-shirt with both hands, pushing myself between him and the desk. "Gods, that's not what I was going to say at all."

His arms fell to his sides, and he dragged his eyes down to me.

"I just wanted . . ." Now I was the one conscious of people listening in. "I was trying to make you laugh." *Because I really like you and I think your room shaking laughter might be my new favourite thing in the world.* "I didn't realise I might be pushing you into something you weren't comfortable with. That I asked you to show me a part of yourself you weren't ready for. I wasn't trying to be . . ." *Like all the others.*

"I've never met a minotaur before"—he snorted—"I don't know the . . . etiquette. Didn't realise that was a thing I couldn't ask for. Now I do." I dropped my voice to a whisper. "Horns, I'm not afraid of you." He stilled. "I get that the general consensus is to be wary of your past, but I . . . Yeah, I'm not buying it. I've seen the news reports, I know what you've done. And I also know that this guy right here," I poked him hard in the chest, "Isn't that guy. I won't be the person that pussyfoots around you." He said nothing, but I felt those blue eyes penetrate my soul. "But I'm also not going to be a prick for the sake of pushing your buttons, so I won't ask to see your bullhead again."

The classroom had gone silent, which I didn't realise until after I raised my voice and said, "Next time I'll just ask for a dick pic."

He narrowed his eyes, the corners of his mouth contradicting his irritation. "Well, if that's all you're after," he whispered right into the shell of my ear. "I can certainly help a girl out there."

"Back to work, kids," said Horus, clapping his hands together, and the cacophony resumed.

I placed my hand on the top of his, ignoring the heartburn building once again in my chest, and the sudden urge to jump on him, wrap my thighs around his hips and bury my face into his hairy neck. "Teach me about your kind. I want to learn."

He stared pensively at my hand on his and then let his eyes travel from the top of my head, right down my body, resting on my breasts for a moment longer than anywhere else. "Okay, Peaches. What do you want to know?" His tone was casual, chatty, not weary or on edge, and the ensuing relief wrapped around me like a fluffy towel fresh from the laundry, at once warm and comforting.

"How many minotaurs are there?" I said, remembering what Ash had told me.

"As far as I'm aware, I'm the only one in Borderlands. There's a large community in the East Winterlands, but they rarely move any further south than that."

"Is that where you're from?"

He nodded. "I moved away with my sister as soon as I was old enough to sign my own papers. They, my family, the herd . . ." He paused before adding, "They are true to the stereotypes, shall we say? I always knew I was different. I liked to wear both my bullhead and my human head. In my herd, it's frowned upon. Death before forward-facing eyes and all that. I realised I thought differently with my human head. You can rationalise better, think about other things, not just grass and fighting and fucking. I was a curious kid. I wanted to experience the rest of the Eight and a Half Kingdoms. I wanted to meet other species, interact with them, talk to them, kiss them." His cheeks grew pink, but he continued talking. "I've been back a few times since, but I'm not welcome in the herd anymore. No hooves." He looked down, and I followed his gaze to his massive, trainer-clad, human feet. "Too human for East Winterlands, and too minotaur for Borderlands."

I placed my hand on his tricep. I tried not to notice how hot and firm it was. *Joey don't perve on him during a moment of vulnerability.*

"Sometimes my mum will call me to tell me they've seen me on Borderlands' news, and that I'm still a disgrace to the family. I should add, not because I've smashed up another coffee shop or whatnot, but because I choose to live with"—he did air quotes—"that silage of humanoid excrement."

"Wow," was all I could manage.

It had never been about me, about him disliking me. It was about Taurin coming to terms with Taurin. Who he was underneath it all. Man, or bull? Perhaps his hatred for me wasn't really hatred at all. Perhaps he was simply too frightened to show people the real him. To let them into his life. *Too minotaur for Borderlands*. Did he expect me to treat him the same? To reject him as others had undoubtedly done.

"Thank you for telling me." I gave his muscle a soft squeeze. *My Gods*. "I won't ask you again."

He offered me a one-sided smile. "Tell me about the Human Realms. I've never been. Never had the right paperwork, or a human escort."

I didn't want to stop talking about him. I liked him open and earnest. I wanted to learn everything about him, but I got the sense that he'd reached his personal limit on the topic.

"It's nice," I said, failing to find a more evocative descriptor. "It's warmer than Borderlands. Not as built up. Mostly farms and small towns, with a couple of big cities, but they're very spaced out. My parents' house is about thirty-minutes from the beach. Have you ever been to the beach?"

He shook his head. Not surprising. There were only a handful of famous beaches in the Mythic Realms — the weather was tempestuous at best — and exactly zero in Borderlands. Only docks, at every place where the water met the land. As though the call to trade was far more compelling than the call to chill out and watch the sunset while getting your toes sandy.

"I love the beach," I continued. "But my motivations for moving are kinda similar to yours. Humans, especially humans together, can develop this . . . all-consuming sense of superiority, and I got sick of it. My father in particular. So, I came here." He didn't need to know all the reasons I left. He didn't need to know about my ex.

"Do you like it here?" The way he asked gave me the impression he was talking about more than the city of Remy, or Borderlands, but I couldn't place my finger on what.

"I love it here. I really do. I just wish I had a little more . . ."

What was I going to say? Security? Stability? Friendship? It didn't matter anyway, as that was the moment Horus chose to approach our station.

"Good evening, kids. What are we working on tonight? You ready to show me your project ideas?"

We both jumped out of our skins. Horns' face, for unfathomable reasons, flushed bright red, and he flapped as he pulled his bag onto the desk and started taking out papers.

We showed Horus — "Please, call me Russ, or I can't be held responsible for my actions" — our individual sketches of Borderlands' landmarks. They felt oddly similar, as though without knowing we had drawn the same things.

"How will you create the statues of Darren the Great, and Todd the Enigmatic?" The two founding fathers of Borderlands. One human and one fae, though I never remembered which was which.

"Marzipan," Horns said, then he explained the flavours he planned to use in the base, each with more meaning and depth than you could expect from simple cake. For example, the bottom layer would be beetroot to represent the earthen ground from which all species originated, the middle, coffee to represent the nightwalkers, and the top layer would be Borderlands' national fruit, the ohjieberry. I might have been staring opened mouthed at him. He was a man, like his cake. Of many layers.

"Great work, ingenious," said Russ, massaging the feathers on his jaw. "I've got a good feeling about you two." Horns coughed and looked at his shoes. Russ turned to face the class. "Listen up, kids! There are only two and a bit more weeks until Cakecon. I've arranged for two coaches to take us to the convention. Nightwalkers, your coach will leave Thursday at nine pm. Day-walkers, yours will be nine am Friday morning. We should arrive at about two or three in the afternoon. You'll have until nine in the evening to set up your displays. Then you will be assigned to your hotel rooms. You'll be sharing within your species. If there is only one of you"—he glanced at Horns—"congratulations, you get the room to yourself. Rooms are allocated based on your student ID and course number. You'll need to sign a form so that we can claim the cost against your UR account."

"Shit," I said under my breath.

"The coach home is at ten am Sunday. If you're not on it, you'll have to find your own way back. If you would prefer," said Russ, raising his voice a fraction as excited chatter began to break out. "You can book your own room at the hotel. Let me know either way so I can make a note on my form. And don't forget, five-thousand silvers prize money to the winning student pair, and I'm going to be extremely disappointed if it's not one of you lot. That's it. Class is over. Bugger off now."

Shit, I couldn't afford a room. And if I tried to get one assigned to me, they'd realise I hadn't paid for the course. I looked at Horns, he would be given his own room. All to himself.

Joey, don't you even dare think about it.

"Tallywhacker's?" said Taurin, piling equipment back into his bag.

Chapter 13

Taurin

"It's really good," she said, her tone at complete odds with the way she jabbed at the dish. It was the first thing she'd said since we left class. The bowl of tempeh salad she'd ordered on my recommendation sat mutilated in front of her. "I like the apple."

"Okay, but what's up with you?" I'd polished off two salads at least ten minutes ago, and she still had over two-thirds of hers remaining.

"Huh?"

"I've only known you for a few weeks, but I already know you're being uncharacteristically quiet and . . . stabby."

"Uh." She looked at me with undeniable pleading. "I'm not meant to be on this course," she whispered, casting those amber eyes over the rest of the bar as though to make sure no one overheard.

"Yeah, I know," I said.

"So, Russ won't be able to assign me a hotel room. And I can't afford to book my own."

"I'm gonna get us separate rooms anyway. The ones they give you are horrible, like prison cells. There are about eight beds in each, and there are a lot of human women in that class, so yours would be full."

She spoke as though she hadn't heard me, her voice quiet. "I could sleep in your room?"

Panic crept up my spine, and cold beads of sweat worked their way down past my collar. "They'd kick us off the course. UR has strict policies about that type of thing. And I can't . . ."

Can't what? Trust myself around her? Can't let myself fail this course? Can't afford another black-X against my record? Can't face her seeing me in my shifted form?

Yeah, actually, all those things.

Mal said I wouldn't harm her, I thought I was in full control, but I'd spent the last three hours trying to close any and every gap between our bodies. Trying to 'accidentally' touch her. She was the type of person to reach across and grab my hand without warning, but for me, those acts, those seemingly harmless gestures, didn't come naturally. I'd gotten as close as brushing my knuckles against her hair and my arm against her boob. All the while, both the bond, and my dick, screamed at me to push my tongue into her mouth, sink my fingers into the flesh on her thighs, and pin her against the filing cabinets. So no, I wouldn't trust myself with her alone in a hotel room.

And as for letting her spend the night with the other me. The larger, furrier one. Unthinkable.

"If we booked our own room together," I said, the words thick in my mouth, "They wouldn't care less, but because it's paid for by them, everything needs to be done by the book. Which means no interspecies . . . shenanigans."

"And you'd be okay with sharing the same room as me?" Her mouth pulled into what I could only describe as a horrified grimace.

Couldn't say I blamed her.

"Gods no, I'm going to book us one each. Separately."

"I can't afford to pay you back." *That's what she's worried about? Money?*

"You wanna win this five grand or what?"

She smiled then, causing the bond to purr, and I could finally make a start on my other two salads.

I was curious, though. "Question, what course are you meant to be on?"

Again, she glanced across the bar. I took the brief respite to sweep my gaze over her face. Noting the wayward curls around her temples, the way her lashes touched the skin under her brow when she opened her eyes, the defined divot above her cupid's bow that seemed like the perfect resting place for my tongue, and her lush, swollen bottom lip. I wedged my fork-free hand under my ass to stop myself from reaching over and swiping my thumb along it. That definitely couldn't be construed as a harmless gesture.

"A speed awareness course." It took me a second to pull the conversation back. "I've been known to drive a bit fast. Do everything too fast, in fact." She put on a different voice. "Typical Joey, always rushing into things." An impression, and not a very kind one. A family member maybe, or an ex? A new feeling stirred in my chest. The monster within me growled. Like a dog protecting its bowl of food, it told me to seek out whoever dared to criticise her and teach them some manners. I tipped my head back and drank the rest of my beer to steady my heartbeat. Her eyes followed the column of my throat, the breath rushing past her parted lips.

"I have another booked for next week," she said, once I set my empty flagon down. "I should get my car back then. Get my jobs back. So . . ." Her tone grew breezier. "What're you in for?"

"I, uh . . ."

She must've known. It only took a few clicks. Type my name or my species into any search engine and she'd have a chronological index of my misdemeanours. My litany of rage. My violent wake.

Note to self, both make excellent name options for a potential thrash metal band.

"You drive fast. I have a slight temper issue." Her look was all the proof I needed.

Of course she'd searched me. *I'd* have searched me. Hell, I searched her. Though, I found only social media pages with varying degrees of privacy filters. Spent a few hours poring over her pictures. Of foods comprised solely of sugar, one smush-faced ginger sack of fur, a cute little red car in various Borderlands and Human Realms locations, and occasionally, if I was lucky, a selfie captioned with some variation of *new hair choppy chop*. It'd be weird if she didn't search me. Right? She'd already know my history. I didn't need to offer further explanation.

Yet I found myself wanting to explain. Explain might not be the correct word, but I wanted to talk about it. Needed to. Perhaps partly because I'd never talked about my outbursts to anyone other than my flatmates, my lawyer, and my therapist, and perhaps partly because, I realised, I trusted her.

I trusted her.

I trusted someone outside my miniscule inner circle. She wasn't even getting paid to listen to my shit. The weirdest thing? I got the feeling she wanted to hear it. So, I pressed on.

"I Saw Red one too many times. Well, more like twelve too many times." The words came out so effortlessly. How did she have this effect on me? "I never mean to turn. When it happens. It's always because someone else is strong-arming me into it. Pushing my buttons. It sounds like I'm shifting the blame, and I'm not. I take full responsibility, but I've never turned by myself before."

Her hand was on my arm. How long had that been there? "You know who's really good at pushing my buttons? Dragons. Fuckers always know what to say to drive me wild."

She gave me an eyebrow quirk that said she understood my dragonism from personal experience. Surely not?

"My sister married a dragon," she said in response to my questioning expression. "And he's a right see you next Tuesday."

Poor girl. "The last time I Saw Red was three months ago." I left out most of the details, considering she'd probably read them all already. "The officer who arrested me forgot something crucial, so I got away on a technicality. I tricked him, basically. Poor lad, he literally pissed his pants when he questioned me. Still, they wanted me to go to therapy and to do a course at night school, because it requires commitment and patience, and being around other people."

There was zero judgement in her expression. "Is it working?"

"I think so," I said. *Because now I had a reason to stay calm.* "I haven't Seen Red in months. But I also haven't seen a dragon in months either."

"What did he do? The dragon, to make you turn?"

I lifted a shoulder. "Don't remember. I never do."

She punched me softly on the arm. "Hey, for what it's worth, I'm kinda glad you smashed up that coffee shop and they forced you to make fondant flowers."

Chapter 14

Joey

The paperback lay abandoned on Ash's coffee table, which was saying something as we'd just got to the part where Kent and Amy get stranded in Kent's surf-school hut during high tide. We had our own more pressing matters to discuss.

"He said he'd book us a room each."

Ash swilled the contents of his glass in circles.

"I can't work out if he likes me or not." I flopped out dramatically on my chair, making a wilted starfish shape. He said things like *Gods, no*, when I suggested we shared a hotel room, he told Russ to move me, that he can't stand to be around me, and yet, I keep catching him checking me out, eyes down my top, or tongue tracing his lips as he stared at mine. He paid for my food at the student bar twice, and he paid for my room at Cakecon. "Do mythics usually buy dinner for people they don't like?"

"No, we do not," said Ash, setting his empty glass back down. "But the same is true of humans, and you know it. Another martini?"

"Fuck yeah. I got the bus here today. Don't have to watch how much I drink." I supposed there *had* to be some benefits of Little Red taking annual leave.

He rang a bell and in walked Lauren, a tray ladened with champagne saucers of creamy coffee nirvana balanced in her arms. "Thank you, my lover." He turned to me. "He's vegan?"

"Yeah," I gave him a *how do you know* raise of the eyebrow.

"Ungulates."

"He doesn't actually have hooves, though."

"You should ask him how many stomachs he has." He laughed at his own joke. I didn't get it.

"I always thought minotaurs were like—"

"Carnivorous beasts that trap virgins in their labyrinth and eat them alive?" *Something like that.* "You can't believe everything you hear about other species. A lot of folks just like having something to be outraged by, even if it is completely false. It removes them from their own miserable lives. Lays the blame elsewhere. Take him to Carly's. A little street food wagon behind The Claudius Theatre. I always go there after a night out."

"Carly's, okay," I said, more to myself. I should repay him for the meals he'd already bought me. Seemed only fair. With a bit of massaging, my budget might stretch to street food, and Ash wasn't naive. The Claudius Theatre was situated next to the harbour, the pretty section of the harbour. With its piers and ancient repurposed-into-museums-and-restaurants frigates and its strings of twinkling lights stretching out over the waters. Romantic. No two ways about it.

"Best falafels this side of the Human Realms," he said, that knowing glint in his eye. "They always say the way into a man's pants is through his stomach."

"That's not quite how the saying goes—Never mind."

He took a slurping sip of his martini. "The trip is for the whole weekend?"

"Friday to Sunday."

"What hotel?"

"The Pegasus Grand."

He let out a whistle.

"I'm sure they won't be fancy rooms. He's a lumberjack, remember. I don't know if he has the money for two suites."

Ash shrugged, clearly disappointed. "And the big awards ceremony is on Saturday night?" I nodded. "What are you wearing?"

"Fuck, I have no idea."

He raised a finger, tossed his blanket aside, causing Three-Feet to jump up in shock, and toddled out of the room. When he returned five minutes later, he held a dry-cleaner's bag that stretched out taller than himself. "Close your eyes." I did. After a few moments and some rustling, he said, "Open them."

I had to clap a hand over my mouth to stop myself from squealing. For a moment I — me, Joey Silver — had nothing to say. "My Gods, it's beautiful," I eventually squeezed out.

He'd hung the dress on a room divider. Framed in such a way that the evening sun bursting through the large bay windows shone around it like a halo. It was commanding, and confident, and so sensual. A gown with personality. Or the ability to instil personality. I already wanted to be *her*. The woman who wore this dress.

"Can I touch?" I asked.

"Of course, it's yours."

Red, obviously, and old, maybe vintage. Strappy, floor length, with a scandalously low v-neck. It straddled the line between fancy evening gown and negligee. The fabric slipped through my fingers like liquid, and by the cut, I could tell it skimmed over the breasts, nipped in at the waist and hugged the hips. The almost bush-high split on the left thigh told me it was high time I shaved.

"Molly Jayne May wore it in the film *Better the Sex Demon You Know*."

An actual movie star's dress.

"And I can really borrow it?"

"It's yours to keep. Try it on. I believe it's your size. You can bequeath it back to me at the end of your pathetically short human life."

I did as instructed, nipping behind the room divider, kicking my red summer polka-dot shift aside, and wiggling into the movie star's dress.

"You'll need to zip me in," I called out.

Ash stepped behind the screen and did the gown up for me, spinning me round to see the front. His reaction was that of a mother during her daughter's first bridal fitting. He clutched his chest with one hand and fanned invisible tears away with the other.

"There's a mirror over there," he said, pointing to the other side of the room.

It was the type of dress you couldn't walk in, not because it was impractical, but because you couldn't help but strut. And boy, did I strut those ten feet across Ash's Mantacorian rugs.

"Have you got heels?"

"Mmmhmm," I said, swaying left and right, unable to tear my eyes away from the mirror.

I'd never been particularly self-conscious about my appearance. Even in the Human Realms, where fatphobia was much more rampant. I knew women my age that grew up with thinness shoved down their throats, but Mum hadn't been like that. Mostly, I think, because she was fat herself, and happy. Confident, easy to laugh, bikinis on the beach, never wearing cover-ups. That type of thing. And I couldn't see any reason, until I hit high school, why the two were often considered mutually exclusive.

Of course, when I got to Borderlands and I encountered the sheer vastness and diversity of body types, any hang-ups I may have had before vanished on the spot. Some folks have tails, or scales, or wings, or animal heads. Why, in Satan's seven testicles, would I worry about dimpled thighs, or my soft human tummy with such an array of utter, utter weirdness before me?

Also, Elvish doughnuts. A hundred percent worth the three-thousand calories apiece price tag.

Despite my lack of insecurities, I'd never truly considered myself beautiful. Until now. I looked—Sweet Mother of the Eight and a Half Kingdoms—I looked like Horns was in serious trouble.

"And you should wear your hair like it is now, pushed over one shoulder," Ash said, distantly. "You need a sparkly barrette for the other side."

"Hnnug," I said, no longer sure words were a legitimate option.

"That dress looks incredible on you, my lover." He kissed me on both cheeks. "And it's going to look even better on the carpets of the Pegasus Grand."

I still didn't tear my eyes away.

"You'd better get some condoms."

Chapter 15

Joey

I stood open-mouthed, staring at the displays in front of me. Row upon row upon row of shelves bore small, shining, colourful boxes.

In the Human Realms, choice of condoms was limited to two brands, max. Plain or flavoured, and ribbed. It was also typically a one-size fits all type deal. In Borderlands, that selection took up three entire aisles of the incredibly expansive on-campus pharmacy.

By some miracle, my bus arrived thirty minutes early for my speed course resit, so I thought I'd busy myself here until the start time. After all, it made sense to be prepared.

"Can I help you?" A Black human woman in her fifties asked. Her name tag read Elaine.

"Yeah, um, where do I even begin?" I said, gesturing towards the thousands of boxes of condoms.

"For you, or a boyfriend?"

"Oh, he's not my boyfriend, just some guy I'd like to . . ." *Shut up Joey.*

"And is he ethereal?"

I looked at her, confused for a second. "No, he's definitely corporeal. Like, *really* corporeal, if you know what I mean."

"Ah, in that case, you're in the wrong section." She led me down the aisle. I decided to shelve my potentially inappropriate questions regarding the logistics of human and ethereal mythic intercourse, protected or otherwise, until I got home. Sounded like a job for Mr Internet to me.

"Next question, human, or . . .?"

I gave a little cough, my cheeks suddenly heating. "Minotaur."

"Oh, right," she said. The widening of her eyes and the quirk of her mouth told me she knew exactly who I was talking about. Taurin wasn't lying when he said he might be the only minotaur in Borderlands, and it seemed maybe he had a reputation. Why did that make me grin like a giddy schoolgirl?

Elaine led me further down the aisle. "These should do you fine." She pointed to a brand named Ogre's, and I let out a snort of laughter. *Gods, should I be worried?*

"Thank you." I reached for the first box of non-flavoured, non-ribbed, non-singing and dancing condoms. Quite sure if anything happened between us, I could do without the additional sensory overload a bumpy, glow-in-the-dark, strawberry-scented cock might bring.

With my packet of disconcertingly large rubbers safely stashed in my backpack, I made my way to my speed course.

Three mind-numbing hours of watching a stuffy old cop on a screen explain why fast equals bad. Plus, a shit-ton of video footage of cars concertinaing into one another and creatures of all species being yanked from wreckages and stuffed in the back of ambulances, which then, rather ironically, travelled at least five times the speed limit.

Eventually I came away with a dull throbbing headache, a slight sense of achievement at having finally accomplished my goal, and a niggling sensation that perhaps I ought to become an ambulance driver.

I was going to get Little Red back. That was all that mattered. I would get my car back, get my jobs back, pay Christie what I owed her, go to a fancy cake party in a big fancy city wearing a dead movie star's fancy dress, and maybe, fingers crossed, I might at last get some ogre-sized D.

You couldn't wipe the smile from my face with a scouring pad.

Chapter 16

Taurin

"Tell me about your sexual fantasies."

I groaned and slumped down on the couch. This again! I knew her job was to find out whether I was a threat to the women of Remy, and report back to that fucker Pounder, so he could use any old excuse to lock me up, but I swear the little gnome got off on it.

"You were supposed to ask my lawyer to move her," I said, not indulging her stupid game.

"Elektra has spoken with Professor Horus and they both agree that you two working together might be the best way to prove to the courts you're in full control of your emotions," said Clair.

"What's your professional opinion?" The question had become a crutch when I didn't want to reveal my true thoughts. I didn't want to admit that I'd completely one-eightied on the decision of having Peaches moved away from me. Besides, I was pretty sure if someone tried to move her now, their life might be in danger.

She placed her notepad on her lap. "It is never important what I think." That meant she didn't agree with them. She probably thought my greatest hope lay with ignoring Peaches. But she didn't know I'd imprinted, didn't know about the bond, and how impossible it was to ignore. The longer I stayed away from her, the worse this ache in my chest became.

"You're sexually attracted to the human woman?"

"Yes." I tried to keep the desperation from my voice.

"And when you're around her, do you get any urges?" *Was she trying to give Pounder an orgasm?*

I took a deep breath. "Not any I would act on."

She nodded, apparently pleased.

"I won't do anything to her without full consent, if that's what you're getting at."

"I'm glad to hear it." She made a note on her pad.

I could control my urges. That much I'd learnt about myself. I could be near Peaches and, even though she'd send all my blood to my dick, there remained just enough in my brain to keep my wits. I now knew I wouldn't shift if I became aroused. No matter how aroused she made me.

Because, damn, those curves.

The bond needed release. Begged for it. Begged for something more than my hand and my thoughts. It had coiled itself deep within my sternum and grew tighter and tighter every day it didn't receive this. Mal said to take things slow, but if we didn't feed this thing soon, I'd likely end up on a gurney in Remy General Infirmary with some sort of aneurysm.

"And Professor Horus reports you're doing great in his class, on course for passing with distinction," she said. I sat up a little straighter, and forced myself to pay attention to Clair. Not to get caught up in my fantasies again. "Which is brilliant news. Your records are looking fantastic too. You only need to get through the next few terms without a hitch, and it will be as if this Ichor mess never happened."

Get through the course without incident. That I could do.

There were only two more classroom sessions before the big showdown at Cakecon, and Russ had us building marzipan sculptures, sugar paste flowers and icing bases. Peaches worked on making a tiny replica of the Tower of the Undead, and I continued to sculpt the highly detailed ohjieberry blossoms for the base of the cake.

She wore her hair up again today, tied with a vintage-style red bow, and a red dress with pink valentine's hearts on. The hem skimmed the bottoms of her thighs and the sleeves fluttered over her shoulders. Her tits were next-level boner inducing. I made a point of not looking directly at them since I naively grabbed my too-tight jeans from the closet before class.

"Do you happen to own any clothes that aren't red?" I asked.

"Not really, why?" And then her gaze locked onto my horns, her eyes went wide, and she burst into giggles. "Oh, my Gods! You're a—Shit! I'm so sorry. This must be getting you so worked up!" she said through gasps of laughter.

You have no idea.

"Mate." The laughter stopped, but her smile remained. "Is it true? About bulls? I just really like red. Never thought about that before. I can get new clothes for the course though if it bothers you too much."

"No, don't be ridiculous. It's not true anyway. Bulls and red. It's only a saying."

She breathed a mock 'phew' sigh, pretending to wipe sweat from her brow with the back of her hand. Instead, she treated me to the full bounce of her breasts as she angled them towards me.

"Besides, if anything is going to drive me wild, it's the cut of your dress, not the colour." That time, I allowed myself a slightly longer look at her chest. *Mother have mercy.*

"Is that so? I guess my evil plan is working."

I cocked an eyebrow. "What evil plan is this?"

"My plan to have you rav—"

"Okay, kids, listen up," called cock-blocker Russ. "There's only ten days left until the convention. Eleven for the day walkers. Some of you have been asking me about the awards ceremony, and I wanted to confirm it *is* black tie." Cheers and groans broke out in equal measure. "So, I expect you all in your fancy clobber. No jeans, no flip-flops, no sweatpants. Frocks and tuxes please, kids. I don't want my class sticking out for the wrong reasons. That's it. Lesson's over. Now get the heck out of my classroom."

"Let me guess, your dress is red?"

She wetted her lips. The subsequent smile that followed told me I was in for hell of a treat come Cakecon. "You should get a job as a psychic."

"Tallywhacker's?" I said, collecting my bag from under the desk.

"Actually, I might take you to this little place my friend mentioned. It's a street-food cart near the theatre."

"Carly's?"

"Yeah, have you been?"

"No, but I keep hearing the most amazing things about it." I picked up the white box with our cake inside. "Where should I put this?" Maybe I could ask Russ to leave it in the classroom and collect it tomorrow.

"I got my car back! You can stick it in there."

Joey's car was an extension of herself. Little, red and cute. Orange velvet fabric stretched over the seats. A ginger tom bobble-head bobbed its head on the dash, and an abundance of sweet wrappers overflowed from every storage cavity.

"My baby," she said to me, unlocking it with a *bop-beep*, and opening the rear passenger door. "Sorry about the guff stink. I deliver takeaways. Smell sort of lingers."

I placed the cake box carefully in the back seat and dropped my kit bag in too.

"If you fit," her eyes travelled once again to my horns, "I'll drop you home later."

"I live ten minutes' walk from here."

She shrugged. "Suit yourself. You should know I rarely extend very large men invitations to squeeze themselves into my little red box."

I choked out my laugh, and the bond in my chest thrummed. The briefest frown crossed her brows, and she placed a hand to her chest, as though she'd eaten something that didn't agree with her.

She felt the thrum too. The realisation that this was a shared experience crashed down around me. Was it always shared? Like, when I thought of her, did her bond vibrate at the same time? And if she thought of me, would mine?

Gods, did that mean I'd been giving her heartburn when I stroked myself at night?

She offered me an adorable smile and looped her arm through mine. Together, we walked the fifteen minutes to Carly's, talking about our cake entry, and the next steps needed to complete before the ceremony. Which were alarmingly numerous.

The street food vendor turned out to be a cutesy, hipster affair. Crammed into the back of a repurposed, forty-year-old campervan, with an orange and white striped awning and silver, candle-lit tables and chairs (all occupied) arranged off to the side. We both got falafel with every accompaniment available and took them across the plaza to a vacant bench overlooking the docks. It was beautiful, with the lanterns bouncing off the water, and the Ferris wheel on the pier in the distance. But it could have been the aurora borealis for all I was concerned. I couldn't take my eyes off Peaches.

I bit into my pitta, watching her mouth as she did the same. The food was . . . well, the word delicious would have been a terrible injustice. It was divine. Who knew deep fried chickpeas could be so transcendent?

Beside me, Peaches made a noise so explicit, so primal, it sent a tsunami of blood to my cock, and I instantly forgot about falafel.

"Gods, this is . . ." she said with her mouth full. She made the sound again. It was like stepping on the metal end of a rake. If I hadn't been wearing jeans, I was sure my boner would have smacked me in the forehead. "I never want this to finish," she whimpered, seemingly on the verge of tears.

I shifted my position on the bench, so she wouldn't notice my jeans tenting. "It's so good," I said, because I'd said nothing for a few moments, hadn't even thought about my food for the better part of a minute.

I needed to be the one drawing those noises out of her.

"Holy cow!" she said once she finished. "Ash was right. That was phenomenal." She gasped and then smacked her palm over her mouth.

"What?" I took her empty wrapper and mine, and balled them together.

"I said," she dropped her voice to a whisper, "Holy cow."

I wanted to use this quiet moment of embarrassment to reassure her, touch her cheek, or her hand as she would have done with me, but something stopped me. Why would she want a hulking monster stroking her? Instead, like an idiot, I said, "What did the mummy cow say to the baby cow?" Her brows knotted together, and she quirked a shoulder, the ghost of a *"huh?"* on her lips. "It's pasture bedtime."

She didn't laugh, obviously. It was a shit joke. "Oh, it's like that, is it? Cow jokes are acceptable."

"Only for you, though, nobody else," I said, hoping that I'd kept my tone playful.

"Ah, I see. Okay . . ." She smiled, beamed in fact. "Where do cows go on Friday nights?"

"To the mooooovies!" we both said together.

I wasn't sure if we were laughing at the joke itself, that it was so dire, or something else entirely, but she gripped my arm, leaned her forehead against my shoulder, and sighed. A sigh that said, *I'm happy and safe.* The buzz in my chest ignited like the revving engine of a motorbike. Hers did too. I felt it reverberate down her flesh, right into mine.

"Woah." She sat up straight, her laughter still etched on her face. "I need to slow down when I eat."

"Peaches . . ." She stared into my eyes, and without thinking, I lifted my palm to caress her cheek. My heart slammed itself into my rib cage. Her lips parted, tongue dipping out to wet them. The distance between our faces grew shorter. Gods, we were going to kiss. There was no other direction this could go in. I swallowed hard. Her heady, sweet perfume wrapped itself around my senses like alcohol hitting my blood stream. Peachy, of course, and something warmer, spicier, sexier, maybe ginger. Our lips were inches apart. But something, doubt, fear, panic, stopped me from closing the gap.

"Why are you not kissing me?" she whispered. "Is it your garlic breath? Because I don't mind. I have it too."

My laugh came out as a sob. I drew closer still. And again, I stalled.

"Horns?" Her eyelids fluttered closed. "Kiss me, please."

I stamped down the last little cry of self-doubt and brought our lips together. Her breath brushed my skin first, hot and sweet, not garlicky like she'd claimed. And then, before I could close my eyes, her mouth skimmed mine. Teasing, delicate. Tiny electric-like fissures, like popping candy, exploded outwards from the point of contact, and her moan filled my entire body—

"HEFF!" came a voice I recognised. A voice I knew could have me instantly relapsing. My hackles peeled themselves upwards. We pulled apart. George, the antagonistic piece-of-shit barista from my latest smash-fest, Ichor, marched towards us, dragging a blonde human woman along in his wake. His scales glowed emerald under the dockside lanterns, his crest flared like an angry green halo, and he'd spread his wings slightly open.

"Who's your girl, Heff?"

"Horns, why is that dragon calling you Heff?" Peaches lips were curled into a half-snarl, half-terrible-fart-smell.

"Motherfucker," I said under my breath. "He's calling me heifer. He thinks he's a fucking comedic genius. He's the reason I flipped out last time and got arrested," I said through clenched teeth. Like every other dragon I'd ever met, George tried his level best to push me to the edge of my control. And he always got the better of me.

"Do you know him?" she asked.

"Not really, he's just another prick dragon."

She placed her hand on my bicep. The muscle twitched under her palm. I couldn't lose it here. Could turn in front of her. She'd hate what she saw. And I could blow my only chance of staying out of gaol. I took a deep breath, held it in, counted to four.

Fuck, keep it together.

George stopped in front of us.

"Keep moving, George," I said, the words sounding as though someone else were speaking them.

"She's hot," he said, staring straight at Peaches. I sucked my breaths in through gritted teeth. "Hey Red, fancy ditching this bullshit and coming back with CeeCee and me? I have enough appendages for everyone."

Peaches' grip on my arm tightened, as though she sensed what might come next. "No thanks. I don't want to join your fucking harem."

"Pity," he said, looking at me once more.

The surrounding docks darkened. I was faintly aware of ripping sounds as my shoulders burst through the seams of my sleeves.

"I've never known any woman to choose pizzle over real dragon cocks."

Unbidden, images flashed through my mind. George dragging Peaches back to his lair, tearing her little red dress from her body, pushing her onto his haul of glittering coins, bending her in a way humans should never bend.

It happened in slow motion. Everything went black around me, and only George stood there, inviting me to tear his skin from his bones.

Gladly.

I pounced to my feet, but Joey stepped in front of me. Her ass pressed against my thighs, pushing me back onto the bench, her arms held out wide.

"Fuck off, Smokey, before I tell the police you threatened a human. And then I'll sell tickets for your execution," she said.

George mumbled something. I couldn't tell what over the pounding in my eardrums. My hands clawed out around Joey, trying to grab any part of him within reach, but something was different about this shift. For one, I was aware of my surroundings, sort of. And then George himself began to fade into the darkness, as though he weren't important enough to warrant my wrath. I stopped trying to reach him, and stared down at my hands, my claws half-unsheathed.

"Yeah, you run, you chauvinistic smog-fucker," Peaches said. I felt him — rather than saw him — and his human retreating. "And don't use sexist slurs, you piece of shit!"

The next thing I knew, she stood between my thighs, her fingers on my face.

"Horns, are you okay?" she said, over and over. "Horns? Horns? You transformed, sort of. Not all the way, I think, but you ripped your t-shirt."

Numbly, I brought my hand up to my chest, fisted the front of my shirt, and pulled it free. "Are you injured?" I squeezed out. "Did I hurt you?" My breaths came out in quick puffs, my shoulders were still tensed, and my hackles still standing to attention. I lifted my hands to my face. Human features. Did she see my bull head? Gods, that was too close. "I have to go. I have to get out of here."

"Horns, please," she said. "Don't go."

But I couldn't stay there with her. I could have hurt her, or worse. I probably would have murdered George if she hadn't been there to intervene.

"I can't. I have to." I got to my feet, pushing her aside.

"Taurin, please," she pleaded.

"I could have hurt you."

"But you didn't, you—"

"I COULD HAVE KILLED YOU!"

"Taurin, wait. Taurin!" she called after me, but I was already halfway down the street.

I was a fucking monster.

Chapter 17

Taurin

I flipped the table. Didn't even remember getting home. Remembered nothing from the ten minutes' walk. Not putting my key into the door, not who was here when I got in. I paced the kitchen, kicking over any chairs that dared get in my way.

That was so close. Too close. I'd thrown everything away.

Pounder's gonna have an orgy when he finds out about this.

Actually . . .

Fuck Pounder. I didn't give an iota of shit about him. Or my future.

But Peaches . . .

This was exactly what Mal predicted. My worst fear realised. He was right. Lust didn't cause me to turn. I knew that much now. I wouldn't touch her without permission, let alone force myself upon her. I don't know why I ever believed that I would.

"Maybe because you're a fucking animal," I said aloud.

It happened in the blink of an eye. It always did. Always will. But this time it was like lighting a match and throwing it onto petrol. I couldn't even bear one negative comment about her before the flames clouded my vision. She was more of a catalyst that I could have imagined. And I had no control over it. No way to keep it in check. As much as Clair and Elektra and everyone else wanted me to. I won't be able. Especially with her near me.

When it happens . . . I'm not me.

The monster takes over. And there's no stopping it.

I never wanted to shift in front of her, let alone See Red. And she'd seen . . .

Fuck. How much of my form did she witness?

Did it even matter? It's all disgusting. She wouldn't want me after what she saw tonight. She would get back to her flat, play the incident over and over in her mind, and come to the only conclusion available. I was a monster. A freak. I was everything the stereotypes said I was. Savage, explosive, uncontrollable, a threat to human life.

"What the fuck, mate?" said Mal, rushing into the kitchen.

She was in danger. Every moment she spent with me.

"Can you stop smashing up my tables for five minutes?"

His presence seemed to pull some sense into me. I picked the table up and stood it the correct way round. A large crack ran through the centre of the wood. I'd make him another one at work.

"George found me, at the docks, with Peach—Joey. He propositioned her. I turned. Half-turned. Fuck." I scrubbed my hands through my hair. "I've fucked up."

"Did you hurt anyone?" He cupped my shoulders. Fatherly. His wings twitching with what I knew to be anxiety.

"No." I raked through my memories. No, no injuries this time.

"Smash up anything other than my dining table?"

I shook my head.

"Well, it's not illegal to shift, so the commissioner can't pin shit against you. Where's Joey?"

"I left her at the docks. Fuck. I had to get out of there. She saw me turn, Mal."

I kept picturing her face. Shock and repulsion. Her hands on my cheeks. Tears swimming in her eyes. Lip trembling.

My phone buzzed. I took it out of my pocket and tossed it onto the table. A text from Joey from Cake Dec. I read the preview pane without opening the message.

Are you ok? Let me know when you're home.

"Are you going to respond?" Mal said, collecting a scattered chair from the ground and righting it.

I shook my head. *What's the point? She saw me turn.* "I'm too fired up. I'll scare her off forever."

He walked past me to a cupboard, took out a bowl, a spoon and a box of SpritePops, and fixed himself some cereal.

I continued to pace. What the fuck was I going to do? I've ruined everything.

Horns, kiss me, please.

I brought my hand to my mouth, as though I could trap the last traces of her against my lips. My chest burned. A growl of frustration left me.

"Where's Goldie and Dima?"

Mal sat down. "Goldie's hooked up with a water nymph, so I guess he'll be gone a couple of days, and Dima's hanging out with his blood-sucker chums." He took a noisy mouthful of SpritePops and spoke between crunches. "You remember when I told you to take it slow? I take it back. This is too slow. Glacial."

I said nothing, turning my full glare in his direction.

"I wondered if this might be the case," he said, more to himself. "Basically, if you don't *claim* her soon, you'll both go crazy."

"What?"

He lazily shifted another spoonful to his mouth. Chewed deliberately slowly and replaced the spoon in the bowl. "You need to fuck her."

"The hell, Mal?" He told me to get to know her first. "I can't just fuck her. After tonight, she'll never want to see me again."

"I said the bond would only get stronger if you fucked—"

"Yeah!" I said, at a loss for any other words.

"But, I think what's happening is that because you haven't, the ache is getting stronger, not the bond. And that's making you skittish." I wanted to bang my head against the fridge. "How quickly did you turn tonight?" He didn't let me answer before ploughing on, "I bet it was the quickest you've ever turned. Milliseconds. Am I right? I reckon because you're not giving the bond what it wants, you're placing yourself on a knife-edge. You're making it so there's no room left inside you to deal with anything else that's thrown at you. You need to make space. By fucking her." He nodded, apparently satisfied that he'd solved all my problems with one ridiculous speech.

"You're forgetting that she saw me shift. Right now, she's probably looking for places to rent in Bordalis. Why would she ever want to see me again?"

"She does." He dislodged a piece of trapped puffed rice with his tongue. "Whatever you're feeling, she's feeling too, though not as intense. You can't ignore the bond. You've already tried that and look what happened? She texted you to check you got home safe. Does that sound like something someone who never wants to see you again would do?"

In all truthfulness, I had no idea. She was . . . dammit, she was unpredictable, and I scared the ever-loving shit out of her. Even if she stuck around, even just to finish our project, why would she want anything more to do with me? She'd made it clear, several times, the only reason she wanted to work together on the project was to win the prize money and pay her flatmate back. No way she wanted me. Especially not after what she'd witnessed tonight.

Even if I could avoid all dragons for the rest of my life.

Which realistically was impossible. Dragons were fairly few in their numbers, but they were still out there. Making cappuccinos, handing out parking tickets, running police departments. Waiting to fuck up my life.

You know where there weren't any dragons? East Winterlands.

"I can't just go up to her and say, "Hey Peaches, sorry I almost pancaked you. Wanna shag?"

He shrugged. "Works for me."

"Of course it would work for you. You're a fucking incubus! Look at me, I'm a massive, angry cow."

"Gods, not this insecurity bullshit again."

I let out a snort. I knew he was tiring of me. He never truly understood. What it was like to face this discrimination. The constant belittling remarks people made as I passed them in the street. The mothers crossing the road, so their kids didn't have to share a pavement with me. The flinches. Gods, the flinches. Move too swiftly in someone's presence, or open my mouth to speak, or laugh, and up come the shoulders, eyes shuttered, faces turned away. Those flinches were the worst.

He wouldn't understand that nobody in class, except Peaches and Russ, spoke to me, or made eye contact. Too afraid to ignite the beast within.

The fucking crux of it, though, they weren't even wrong.

I proved it time and time again.

"You imprinted on her. She wants you. Just get it over with. The longer you leave it, the worse that buzzing in your chest will get. It's the bond, and it's hungry. You need to feed it, or you will both end up losing your minds."

My phone beeped again. I peered at the screen.

Joey from Cake Dec: Call me.

"So, what did George do? What did he say to make you almost turn?"

Residual anger flared in my stomachs. "He asked Joey to join his harem. Called me heifer. Told her she'd have a better time with him." I couldn't repeat all of it. Especially the bit about my . . . Gods, did he really use the word pizzle?

Mal bit down on his top lip, restraining his indignation, his wings twitching once again. Comfort briefly took the place of anger inside me. He had my back. Even if he couldn't fully empathise with me. "What did Joey say?"

"She . . ." I scrubbed a hand down my face.

Fuck off, Smokey, she'd said. She stood up for me. Like no one ever had. She placed herself in between a minotaur — mid shift — and a fucking dragon. And she showed no fear. None. In all fairness, she was probably coasting high off adrenaline, even so, nobody has ever stuck their necks out for me like that. I'd sworn to protect her. Was trying to protect her, in that moment. Was the reason I almost shifted. But she had jumped between us, stopping me from getting to him, all while yelling her own obscenities. She called him a smog-fucker, for crying out loud. I couldn't help the tiny smile that ticked the corners of my mouth.

"She told him to fuck off."

She protected *me*.

Mal held his arms out in a *you know I'm right* gesture. "Tell her how you feel."

"But how?" I growled. I hadn't meant to growl.

"Just use, I don't know what they call 'em these days, uh, words. Tell her. How you. Feel."

I ran my hands through my hair again and let out a huff of breath.

"Oh, one more thing," he said, holding up his spoon. "Don't fuck her without a rubber. Because you'll—"

"Yes, I know."

I'll marry her.

Amongst minotaurs, if a bull fucked a heifer and ejaculated inside her, he claimed her. Imprint or no. She'd belong to him, to his herd, his harem. Crude, yes, welcome to minotaur life. It was essentially a marriage contract, creating an unbreakable connection, and why I'd always been so careful to use protection in the past.

We were already irrevocably joined by the bond, but she deserved to have a say over something like marriage.

More than anything I needed to make this right. I needed her to understand I wouldn't harm her or let anyone else harm her. But how could I make her believe something I didn't believe myself? Next time I Saw Red, and there would be a next time, because there was always a next time, there was a very real chance I would destroy everything.

I needed to make this right, but I had no idea where to begin.

"I need a shower," I said. Then I left.

Chapter 18

Mal

No, no. Don't listen to the seven-hundred-year-old incubus. Nobody ever listens to the seven-hundred-year-old incubus. It wasn't like I hadn't been through the same situation myself. Wasn't like I didn't know exactly how he was feeling. But the big, dumb bull can be so single-minded sometimes.

Imprinting can be the best thing to happen to a man, and it can be the worst. It can bring about unparalleled joy, and it can ruin you. I've been through both. The ecstasy and the anguish.

Fae and demons didn't imprint the same way these animalistic mythics do, but fated mates were fated mates. No two ways about it. He loved her, even if he didn't realise yet, and she loved him. To be fair, she probably already knew. Humans were much more perceptive about these matters than most mythics give credit for. And they were lucky, both humans and minotaurs had similar lifespans. They could spend the rest of their lives together, blissful, happy, unburdened by the impending death of one half of their union. He should try imprinting on someone whose lifespan is one-twentieth of his.

If he didn't listen to me soon, and claim his woman, he'll lose it. See Red and maybe never come back. It wasn't a sexist thing either. She'd be claiming him, too.

I finished my cereal and let the spoon clunk to the bottom of the bowl. Above my head, a pipe reverberated against the floorboards, and the room filled with the ambient sounds of water running, splashing against tiles, and draining away.

His phone beeped again. I glanced over, expecting to see Joey with the ass emojis. Instead, a different message popped up.

Pegasus Grand: Your booking confirmed for 2x economy single rooms

"The fuck, Taur?" I said, looking at the ceiling. "Are you trying to give yourself a heart attack?"

I took my own phone out of my pocket, searched for the number of the hotel, and rang them.

"Pegasus Grand, how may I help?" said a disembodied feminine voice.

"Hi, yeah, I have a booking for next week. My name is Taurin. Do you want the reference?"

"Yes please, sir."

I gave them the number.

"Two economy singles for Friday until Sunday. Is that correct?" they said.

"Yes, but I'd like to make some changes, please."

"No problem, sir. What kind of changes?"

"Cancel my booking and rebook me one double room."

"Sir, I'm afraid we're fully booked that weekend for economy doubles. The only room we have left is the honeymoon suite."

"Fucking perfect!" I yelled down the phone. I shot a quick glance upward to listen out for the running water. "Yes, book that for me, please."

"Right away, sir. There is an up-charge on that room. Four-thousand silvers. Per night."

The things I did so my friends could get their leg over. "No problem. Charge the bill to a different card, though. Name, Mal Sallinbar." I gave her my credit card number.

"Absolutely, sir. Anything else I can do for you?"

"There is. Are there any sofas in the honeymoon suite?"

"Um, yes, I do believe there are."

"I want them gone before I arrive. Okay? Anything that is not a bed but could possibly be construed as a sleeping place, make it disappear." One doesn't reach the age of seven-hundred-and-five without learning a few tricks.

"Uh, sure? Can I just put you on hold for a sec?"

Pop notes filled the air before I could answer. A nasal voice sang tinnily down the line, something about getting higher and higher. I recognised the tune, though I'd be damned if I could place it—

"Hi, sir, thank you for waiting. I've made a note on your account for the housekeepers to remove the sofa."

"And if, when I arrive, I ask what's going on, you're to tell me this was the original room I booked and that there are no other rooms available. Is that clear?"

"Okaaaaay." A keyboard clacked in the background. "Will that be all?"

"Yep. Thank you so much. You've been a gem."

I hung up the phone and made myself a celebratory bowl of SpritePops.

Chapter 19

Taurin

"You left your kit bag in my car, and the cake," she half-yelled, angrily putting on her hairnet. Yup, she angrily put the hairnet on her head. I was surprised when it didn't rip.

"I know, I'm sorry." It was all I'd said for the past ten minutes. It was our last session before the big competition, and a panicked, frantic air filled the classroom as people rushed around finalising their designs. As usual, Russ floated between the desks as though he were the only customer in a department store stocked with beautiful yet reasonably priced white cotton kilts.

"You could have at least text me back and let me know you were okay. Or told me your address so I could drop your stuff off to you."

"I know, I'm sorry."

I'd had a week to think things through. A whole torturous week with only my thoughts. I hadn't contacted Peaches. Too scared I would push her over the edge. She'd sent me another two texts, one on the Tuesday and one on Wednesday, but hadn't tried to make contact after then. I took it as the confirmation I expected. That I'd never see her again. When I found her little red car in the university's carpark today my body battled the ensuing emotions of utter surprise and knee-weakening relief. Maybe things were salvageable.

"I didn't know what happened to you. I've been watching the fucking news channels all week, waiting to see if you smashed up another coffee shop or something else." At this, several people turned their heads in our direction, their eyes wide, as though stunned she showed no fear of lighting my fuse.

Wait. Add me to that list. She wasn't afraid of making me angry!

"I just needed to think. I'm sorry."

"We've only got one more class, and a few days left until Cakecon, and less than half the work done."

I didn't want to believe all she cared about was the prize money, so I shoved the thoughts aside. "I know, I'm sorry. Do you want to come to mine after the lesson and we can finish it together tonight?"

Her mouth stopped forming whatever word it was preparing to yell at me next. She paused.

"I'll explain myself. What I've been . . . What's been going through my head."

Her eyes softened. "No, I don't want to, but we don't have much other choice."

"So, is that a yes? Because I'll text Mal and see if he'll get the others to bugger off for the night."

"Yes, fine, whatever," she said, turning her body away from me so I wouldn't notice the corners of her mouth quirk up. My shoulders dropped in relief.

I rested my elbows on the table and leant my head close to hers. "Listen, Peaches, I really am sorry. I panicked. And I needed time to recover, to think about what I should do. I . . . I thought I might lose you. This . . . What we have. Uh, whatever this is."

She placed a single elbow on the desk and turned her body towards mine. It left only a few inches of distance between us. Her gaze fell on my lips for a few moments before she dragged it back up to my eyes. The imprint bond purred at me. I ignored it.

Okay, here goes, just like Mal said, use words.

I could use words. I could be honest.

But not too honest.

"It's just," I whispered, "When I'm around you I'm so frightened I might shift. That if I do shift, you wouldn't . . ." *Like what you see.* I finished the sentence in my head.

"You think I might turn you?"

"No. But I have an overwhelming sense of duty to protect you, and I worry if anyone threatens you, even in the slightest, I'll lose it. See Red. Like I almost did last week."

"It's not your duty to protect me."

Tell that to the bond.

I closed my eyes, if only to give myself an extra moment to form my next sentence. I couldn't explain the imprint. Humans didn't have these things, didn't understand them the way monsters do. Hell, even most monsters couldn't fully grasp their power. It was proper ancient magic. It had no antidote, or spell, or potion that could reverse the connection. That, in itself, was terrifying to both humans and monsters alike.

"I don't think it's something I can help," I said. "It's innate. Part of me. And you. But I want you to understand, I wouldn't be this way with any other woman."

She pursed her lips together in thought and absentmindedly rubbed her chest.

I wanted to tell her. I did. But a part of me, a large and caustic part, had me convinced if I said anything about the imprint and the bond and the pain in her chest which was because of me, she'd turn and flee, and we'd both end up going stir crazy.

"I'm just worried I will hurt you."

"You won't." She said it so matter-of-factly.

"You can't know that. I can't seem to control myself. I shift at the tiniest trigger. And . . . Next time you, I, might not be so lucky."

She looked me up and down, and despite my extra foot of height, I found her gaze intimidating. "Did you shift in front of me last week? Yes, sort of. Did you hurt me? No. Would you have completely shifted if I wasn't there and maybe hurt someone and gotten yourself arrested again? Definitely. I stopped you from Seeing Red. I brought you back from wherever it was you went. Horns, your eyes were black, and you shredded your t-shirt, which, B.T.W. I'd like to circle back to later, because wow. But it was me that brought you back to reality. If I wasn't there, would that have happened? Would anybody else have been able to do that? You need me around to stop it, before it, you, get too destructive."

Huh.

I hadn't thought about it like that, but, shit, she was right. Nobody else could have wedged themselves between me and that bastard dragon and still be standing there, able to recount the tale. She coaxed me back, rubbing my cheeks, staring me straight in the eyes, whispering my name. She showed no fear, none. Even now, confronting me, there was no fear. Even after what she'd seen, witnessed for herself, what I am capable of. What I become.

She brought her face closer to mine. If I tilted my chin our lips would have met. Gods, I wanted to do that. "I like you, Horns. Like really like you, and maybe I'm way off the mark, but I get the impression you like me too."

I'd stopped breathing a while ago.

"You want to know what I feel when I'm around you?" she said. "It's not fear. It's . . . excitement. I literally feel buzzing in my chest, whenever we're close, when you look into my eyes, or I hear your voice, or even when I'm by myself and I think about you. At first, I thought it was heartburn, but I don't think it is anymore. There's something between us. Something pulling at me, telling me not to let you be such a jackass and run away from this." She placed her hand in the centre of my chest, her fingers spreading out over my heart.

Tell her, tell her, tell her, Mal's voice echoed around in my head.

I didn't. Couldn't? She'd figured me out. She knew. Maybe not about the bond, but she knew I'd gone totally soft for her. I couldn't string together a coherent response.

Instead, my brain chose to latch onto the one tiny scrap of information she may have accidentally let slip.

Or even when I'm by myself and I think about you.

Did she picture me when she was alone? At night? When she masturbated?

"You think about me when you're by yourself?"

The wickedest smile spread over her lips, and she cocked an eyebrow. It took all my resolve not to grab her and shove my face into the curvature of her neck.

She closed the hand over my heart, fisted my t-shirt and pulled me down so my ear sat flush against her mouth. Her breath, hot and sweet, tickled the hairs on my neck. "Every night." I gulped. "But," she paused, "Do you think of me?"

My forehead fell forward onto the desk, and I let out a groan that was part frustration, and part sheer fucking glee.

Chapter 20

Joey

"Holy Mother of the Eight and a Half Kingdoms!"

Taurin's place, Mal's place, was incredible.

"I can't believe you live here! It's a penthouse apartment! Fifteenth floor! Look at the view!" Out the window, the city twinkled like strings upon strings of neon fairy lights, the moons hung like three enormous orbs in the darkness, and the office buildings across the eight-lane highway were buzzing with night-walker employees. But it was the inside of his home that had me lost for words.

I stood in the centre of the living room, if you could even call it that, with my arms held out at my sides, spinning in circles to demonstrate the vast amounts of space. Horns, well used to it and completely unfazed, kept his eyes on me, his smile caught between his teeth.

"That's what seven centuries of being the best incubus in Borderlands will afford you. Let's take this cake into the kitchen, shall we?" he said, holding up the box.

"Not going to give me the full tour?"

He thought for only a moment. "Sure, okay, everyone's out. Why not? This is the living room." He held out his free hand like a game show host.

I cast my eyes around the space. Grown-up furniture, none of the cheap faux-wood stuff Christie has. Proper tables and proper bookshelves, made from proper trees. Actual art on the walls. Massive paintings, with visible painterly brush strokes. Of waterfalls and lush, glistening landscapes somewhere far, far north of the Human Realms. One side of the room bore the only indication that the flat housed bachelors. A television screen, taller than me, hung from the wall, and columns belonging to a seriously high-tech sound system flanked either side of it. But everywhere else, on tables and surfaces and shelves, actual decor. Fresh flowers in expensive looking vases, photos in frames, bronze and ceramic sculptures. I wasn't sure why, but I had been expecting something a little more studenty. And everything was so clean. Spotless, in fact. Not a piece of rubbish littering the table, not a speck of dust on the window ledge.

"I love the sofas." My favourite part of the room by far. Massive, well, I supposed they'd have to be to accommodate Horns' hefty form, dark red, squishy, inviting. With an array of cute, old-lady patchwork blankets thrown over the backs.

"Thanks. I made them—"

"No way!"

"Well, I made the frames, and Mal had them cushioned and upholstered." He practically beamed with pride. My heart did weird floopy things. "Dima made the quilts too." At my confused look, he added, "He really likes quilting."

What an endearingly humanising hobby for a vampire to have.

He took me to the kitchen, also huge and spotless. Perhaps they had a cleaner. I let my eyes rake over the modern cupboard doors, the swimming pool sized fridge, and the homely decor pieces that continued throughout.

"What happened to your table?" I asked, fingering the massive crack in the centre of the wood. Taurin pulled a Serious Man face. "Okay, don't ask, got it."

We walked down a short corridor. He knocked on a door. No answer.

"Where are your flatmates?"

"Mal said he got them all entry to Abysm so they shouldn't be in, but just in case." He pushed the door open a fraction, peered inside, then opened it all the way, flicking on a light-switch. "Okay, this is Dima's room."

It was exactly as you'd imagine a vampire's lair to look. Wine-coloured velvet flocked walls, windows boarded up, a coffin propped up in the corner, and a black leather sofa disconcertingly covered in wipe-clean plastic sheeting. More quilts everywhere, and on the coffee table, partially drunk glasses containing ominous looking dark liquids. I shuddered. Horns laughed and closed the door.

"You wanna go upstairs?"

"Your flat has an upstairs? What the fuck? Man, I wish I was a fit-as-heck seven-hundred-year-old sex demon."

"How do you know he's fit?"

"He is though, isn't he?" I'd never met an ugly incubus.

"You're never allowed to meet him." He paused outside of a doorway. "Uh, so this is Goldie's room. You probably don't want to look in there."

"Ooh, I do. I do."

"Okay, he's a nymph, so you can't say I didn't warn you." He opened the door and the first thing that caught my attention, before he'd even turned the light on, was the slap-in-the-face stink, followed by the mess. There were clothes everywhere, empty plates, cans of beer, pizza boxes, balled up pieces of paper, bottles of toiletries. The bed sheets looked like they hadn't been changed in a century, something pink spattered against the floor length mirror, and one curtain dangled half off its pole.

"Gods, how old is he?"

"Uh, about six-hundred-and-eighty." He hurried to close the door.

"Really? It looks like a teenager's bedroom." He nodded. "Smells like one too. Smells like—"

"Don't say it."

But it was too late. The word had already left my lips, "Jizz."

Horns offered me a grim smile. "I won't show you Mal's room. He'll kill me if he finds out. He can be extremely private about stuff like that, but this is mine."

I couldn't explain the wild fluttering in my chest. He opened the door, and I stepped inside, pleasantly surprised by what I saw. The room was spacious and tastefully decorated. Translation, white walls, and little colour elsewhere. Two floor to ceiling bookshelves and a large desk sat in the corner, and the biggest bed I'd ever laid eyes on took up the rest of the space. It was easily ten feet long and the same width. He hadn't made his bed, and a couple of pieces of clothing hung over a chair, the only things out of place. It was the complete opposite of my bedroom at Christie's, which admittedly was more like a pink and red, less messy, less jizzy version of Goldie's. I wanted to sink into his bed, grab his t-shirt, and pull him on top of me.

"This bed is bigger than my entire room. You made it too?"

He nodded, his proud grin returning, tripping up the rhythm of my heartbeat. "I got the mattress from a troll homeware shop in Bordalis. I uh . . ." He twirled his nose ring. "I shift when I'm asleep. Almost nine feet." He looked away from me, as though he couldn't bear to witness my reaction. But I couldn't care less if he shifted in his sleep. Or even if he did it during the day. Of course, I'd miss his beautiful face, but I only wanted him to be comfortable. Wanted him to feel safe around me. Not to mention, a small part of me was very, very curious.

"It's not at all what I pictured," I said, suddenly needing to fill the silence.

"Did you think I slept in a barn?"

I snorted. Gods, it would be so easy to wrap my legs around him and forget entirely about the existence of time. I cleared my throat. That was when I noticed the sugar paste rose I'd created casually sitting on his bedside table. My chest gave a zap of electricity. "Maybe we should get started on our cake."

Back in the kitchen, Horns brewed us a pot of coffee while I looked around at the various framed posters and photos on the walls. In one, which I decided was my favourite, three of the flatmates stood together, relaxed arms were slung over each other, affectionate smiles on their faces. Horns was the only one wearing a shirt, and easily half a foot taller than the incubus and the mountain-nymph, who, it must be said, were both gorgeous. Someone had taken a permanent marker and drawn a cartoon vampire next to the three, complete with fangs, cape, and a hairline in the shape of an in-flight gull.

Horns stood behind me and smiled at the photo.

"You all look so happy," I said.

"We were. Are. Even Dima. I know you can't see him, but I can. Like in here." He tapped his forehead. "That was cheesey as fuck." It was, but my throat became slightly too tight.

"It must be nice to have such good friends." The words came out more pitiful than I'd meant them to be.

"You don't have many friends?" His brow furrowed, and I swear his eyes darkened.

"Not really. My flatmate is a hell-bitch, my sister hates me, my parents live three hours away. I guess I have Ash, the two-thousand-year-old fae I told you about, but that's it." I could have told him it was all my fault, that I never let anyone get close to me. Or stay close. I was thirty-four-years-old and my longest boyfriend had been six weeks. Six weeks. Not even half a percent of my life. I'd get a longer gaol term for stealing bubblegum from my local shop.

As soon as someone got to know me, they'd leave me, and if they didn't, I'd push them away.

He handed me a mug of milky coffee. "You have me now."

Heartburn fired up in my chest. He didn't seem to realise what he'd said, just walked over to the broken dining table and took a seat.

"It's a good job I like you then." I followed him, placed my coffee on the table, and gently brushed my knuckles against his jaw in a mock punch.

His gaze shot between his knees to the floor. "You don't even know me. Not the real me, anyway."

I did, though. I knew things about him I never thought I'd even care to know about a person. I knew that when he took his hair out of his topknot, it fell back into a perfect silky curtain, no irritating ridge where the band had been. I knew he saved the tempeh on his salad to be eaten last, and the apple second-last. I knew he carried a lighter around with him, but I'd never seen him smoke, though I had occasionally smelled weed. I knew the difference between his false and genuine smiles. It was his dimples, by the way. I knew the way he smelled, the gait of his walk, the little noises he made at the back of his throat when he thought I hadn't spotted him checking me out. And I knew the way he made me feel. Excited, nervous, safe, unbelievably horny.

But there was more to learn. So much more. I wanted to know what he looked like in the mornings. His favourite movie. Where he would go on holiday if he had unlimited choice. What he tasted like. What that chest felt like under my touch. What his fingers would feel like on me. What he wanted from me. What he would feel like inside me. My chest vibrated at the last thought, and he lifted his gaze to mine.

"Then show me," I whispered.

"Joey, I can't—What if . . ." He closed his eyes and was quiet for the longest time.

I said nothing. Instead, I pulled up a chair next to him, placed my elbow on the table, my chin on my hand, and watched him. I would have been happy to watch him for hours.

"Okay," he said finally.

"Okay? Really?"

"Yeah, really. You'll see it all sooner or later anyway. Might as well prepare you." He eased his t-shirt over his head, and I tried my absolute best not to gawk at his naked torso. His muscles, his ink, covering every inch of skin that had been so recently hidden. I thought about the tiny tattoo on my hip, the constellation of my birth sign, absolutely nothing compared to the level of detail now on display. There must be hours of work on him. I really wanted to imagine him under the needle, picture his pained expression, wonder how similar it was to his Oh face. But that could wait for later.

I gulped. *Did the air really get this dry?*

He undid his belt buckle and the top button and fly of his jeans but left them on. I saw the heft of his tail easing out of his waistband, and clamped my thighs together to stop the rush of warmth to that area.

He folded his shirt and placed it on the table. "Ready."

I nodded. My heart beat hard against my airways. "I'm . . . I'm not going anywhere."

He gave me one last look, somewhere between pain and an apology, rolled his shoulders back, puffed his chest out and then, poof, like a ball of static energy, he shifted.

I jumped in shock, knocking against the table, sending the coffees careening toward the lips of their mugs. He had told me what would happen, how big he would get, and I had seen it a little by the docks, but I hadn't expected the full reality of it.

Gone was his human head. In its place, an enormous, and I mean enormous, head of a bull. His fur shone the same colour as his tan skin, his horns grew twice the size, and his tiny septum piercing became a thick, bangle-sized hoop. He sat about two feet taller on the chair. I stood up and realised I was level with his eyes.

"Do I frighten you?" His voice was gravel before. Now it was nothing more than a thunderous growl.

"A little." I decided to be honest. I closed the gap between us and slowly brought my hands up to his face.

He grabbed them in his. "Not the horns. They're sensitive enough with my human head." His words rumbled through the cavity in my chest, like a tower of amps at a concert.

My heart smashed against my ribcage. Through excitement, fear, or something else, I wasn't sure. I placed my hands on either side of his face. His eyelids fluttered shut, and a puff of hot breath filled the space between us. My fingers slid into the folds of his downy, soft fur, while my eyes drank in everything.

Okay, this was weird.

Everything about him had changed, had become more. His shoulders wider, his chest deeper, more muscled. There was hair — fur? — everywhere. Across his shoulders, running right down his front and ending in a narrow point at his navel. Even his smell, that woodsy, earthen scent, was stronger. The only thing that hadn't changed, I noticed, were his eyes. They were the same brilliant cerulean-blue as the first time I'd met him. They watched me, blinking, nervous.

"It's still you," I whispered. I had the absurd urge to weep.

I leaned my face close to his and planted a soft kiss on the fleshy gap between his nostrils. He let out a small whimpering sound and brought his arms up around my back, holding me in place. And then everything shifted. Beneath me, he shrank, and I was kissing the much pointier nose of a human man, my hands still cradling his cheeks. He jerked his face upward, freeing his nose and capturing my lips with his.

I'd simply forgotten how to breathe.

His kiss was gentle at first, exploratory, butterfly soft. My fingers slipped into his hair, his palms splayed across my back, and he moaned into my mouth, sending waves of heat to my lower abdomen. He pulled me down onto his lap and kissed me like he'd been craving me. Like he was starving, and I was the last tempeh salad in the Eight and a Half Kingdoms. He parted my lips with his and his tongue dipped in, learning my curves, rubbing his teeth along my bottom lip, trading breaths.

He fisted his hand around my ponytail, the other hand gripping my nape, and withdrew enough that our lips were barely touching. Our breaths, hot and frantic, became one.

"Fuck, Peaches, you taste so good."

I wanted to stay present in the moment, catalogue everything, but his touch turned my thoughts to liquid. Could I freeze time right there? Could I keep everything the way it was in that exact moment? I knew as soon as we fucked, I would lose interest in him. Or, not lose interest, but become so terrified of things being as they always had been with me, that I'd deliberately ruin myself. Push him away. Do the typical Joey thing. The thing that I'd done with countless other guys.

Only, I didn't want that to happen with him. He was different. I actually liked him. I liked the way he made me feel.

I think, though I couldn't be sure, that maybe, *maybe*, I wanted more than I'd been promising myself all along. Maybe I wanted more than a fling.

"Gods, Peaches." His kisses became wild, desperate, his breath ragged. "You have no idea . . . How I . . ." But he never finished his thoughts, instead he pulled my head to the side by my ponytail and trailed his mouth along my neck, giving appreciative moans as he went. Beneath his unzipped jeans, movement. The end of his cock pressed into the now damp material of my knickers. Only two thin layers of fabric separated us. Heat pooled in my belly, and every part of me ached for him.

Gods, please never let this moment be over.

I tried so hard to take my time, to slow things down, but I'd lost all agency of my limbs. My hands were on him, on his naked torso, down his back, up his ribs, holding onto his shoulders as though if I let go, I might puff away like icing sugar. Perfect, simply perfect.

He took my dress strap, twisted it in his fingers and pulled it down my arm. Then his lips brushed the newly exposed skin, open mouthed kisses, tongue, heat. "Fuck, Peaches. Fuck," he whispered, the words tickling my flesh. His teeth scraped against my collarbone. The thumb of his other hand teased the underside of my breast.

My breath hitched inwards. My hips, without instruction from my brain, bucked into him, desperately searching out that friction. His cock throbbed beneath me, and the resonate growl that escaped his throat shook my whole body. It caused the pain in my chest — which, until that point, had been a constant dull ache — to surge. I pulled apart like it electrocuted me.

The look on Horns' face mirrored mine. "I feel it too," he said, pulling my hand to the centre of his chest. Gods, this man's muscles.

"What is it?" I asked. "It hurts but doesn't hurt. Does that make sense? Why do we both have this? Are we . . ." I didn't even know what I was going to ask, but I knew this thing was something mythic. That, whatever it was, was all because of him.

He opened his mouth to speak, but at that moment, the door to the kitchen swung wide open and in slunk a tall golden-haired shirtless man, with a succubus on one arm and an incubus on the other, though not the same incubus from the photos on the wall.

I leapt to my feet, moving back over to my chair.

"Hello!" The golden-haired man's eyes lit up and fell on Horns' naked chest. His tongue came out to wet his lips, and after a long second, he turned to me. "You must be Sugar Paste."

"Fuck off, Goldie. We're busy," said Horns, lipstick smeared all over his mouth and nose. I must have looked the same.

"Naw, don't be like that," Goldie said, his gaze brushing over Horns' steadily decreasing hard-on. "Let me know if you two fancy joining us. I'll go easy on the human, though I can't say the same for you." He shot a wink at Horns, and then he left, dragging the two sex demons with him.

"I'm so sorry about Goldie. He's not usually this . . . bad," Taurin said, zipping himself back up and pulling his t-shirt back over his head. He was actually putting his t-shirt back on. Why, Gods?

The moment was over. That was that. I stood up, smoothed my skirt down, and tried to steady my breaths. "It's fine." *Was it?* "We need to crack on with this cake, anyway."

He nodded. His expression unreadable.

"Can I use the bathroom first?"

He tucked his hair behind his ear. "Through that door, on the right."

So, I ran to the bathroom, slammed the door shut behind me, and then emptied the entire contents of the cold tap onto my face.

Chapter 21

Joey

Of course I was running late to catch the bus for Cakecon. It was there, idling right outside the main entrance of UR. Waiting for me, the last passenger.

Huffing, the human driver threw my hard plastic case into the hold, and I climbed aboard the coach. Horns sat about midway down, his enormous legs stretched out into the aisle.

"I saved you the window seat," he said. He watched as I stood on tiptoes to place my backpack in the overhead storage, one corner of his mouth curving upwards. Not that I was short, far from it actually, but everything in Borderlands was made to fit creatures that were, on average, half a foot taller than humans. He didn't stand to let me access my seat, he simply adjusted his legs, so I had to climb over him. The look on his face told me he enjoyed it way too much.

"Okay, folks, listen up." Russ stood at the front of the bus with a microphone in his hand. The human driver climbed into his chair, and tried, but failed, not to appear awestruck by the enormous man with the bird-of-prey's head and a well-oiled six-pack. "ETA is approximately two-thirty. We will make only one stop during the journey. Please make sure you evacuate your bladders during this time, as there will be no further bathroom breaks, and if you make a puddle on the coach, it's an eighty-silver fine that you'll be paying for."

Nervous giggles broke out.

"You laugh, but it wouldn't be the first time. Once we get there, we'll go straight to the conference centre to set up your displays. You'll find a card with your names on. You must make sure your display fits within the markings, or they will disqualify you. After you're set up, we'll meet you in the lobby of the Pegasus Grand, and we will assign you to your rooms. If you have booked your own room, you'll be free to check yourself in. Everyone clear? Great! Let's get this cake-show on the road."

The coach rumbled into life and pulled away from the uni. Even with the wider mythic-designed seats, I still found myself pressed up against the length of Taurin's extremely warm, hard body. It was going to be a long, and damp, four and a half hours.

"I thought you wouldn't make it," he said.

"I almost didn't." I had to run two red lights to get there in time. Hopefully, I don't get another ticket.

His smile disappeared quickly, leaving me bereft of those dimples. He didn't try to make conversation after that and answered all of my questions with "yeah" and "hmm". Had I done something wrong? I'd replayed our kiss a thousand times. And according to his texts, so did he.

I can't stop thinking about last night, he'd said, and then added for clarity, *The kiss, not the cake making. Though that was also nice.*

Me too, I had texted back. *Maybe we should do it again*. To which I received a massive jolt in my chest. Did it mean he'd thought about me?

Apart from his flatmate walking in, I couldn't find a flaw in the moment. Perhaps in the few days since we kissed, he'd had time to dissect it. Had we moved too quickly for him? Had he worried he would lose control? Or maybe it simply didn't mean as much to him. Maybe I was shit at kissing. He wouldn't be the first guy to tell me that.

About half an hour into the journey, I finally relented. "What's wrong? Why are you being so weird?"

He pursed his lips together, and I allowed myself a brief moment to remember the texture of them on mine, the slightly metallic zing, the bitterness from his black coffee, the soft wanting fullness of them. "I'm just trying to stay awake."

"Huh?" Okay, not what I expected. "Did you have a late night?" He probably stayed up to finish the cake.

"Not really. It's . . . when I travel, I get sleepy and when I sleep, I shift."

"So?" I said. He shook his head like I didn't get it. Maybe I didn't. I could only picture the giant, naked, sculpted torso I might rest my head on and take a nap myself. But, on second thoughts, there really wouldn't be enough space in the seats if he grew an extra two feet. He'd simply have to remain uncomfortable and awake for the journey.

But at least he didn't think my snogging skills were subpar.

We were quiet for the next couple of hours. Occasionally, Horns pointed out landmarks as we passed through, and over, other cities. It felt strange to see the real-life full-sized versions we'd only recently recreated in miniature marzipan form.

We spotted the twin statues of Darren the Great and Todd the Enigmatic. Still had no clue which was which. We saw The Palace of Gods and Mortals, The Tower of the Undead, The Obelisk of Sharon the Shy, and out the other window, through gaps in Clarke's enormous leonine body, we glimpsed The Fantastical Orbital Bridge.

The night of the kiss, after Goldie retired upstairs, and Horns had disappointingly put his clothes back on, we set to work making the little edible models. We'd been quiet and focused. I felt too awkward-slash-horny to attempt conversation, so the only sounds to be heard were the rhythmic squeak of the blonde jizz-factory's bedsprings, the incessant thump thump thump of perhaps a headboard against the wall, and a sporadic, deep throated neigh, whose owner I couldn't be sure of.

"Gods, does that man ever relent?" I'd asked. It had been amusing at first, but after thirty minutes, the novelty well and truly wore off.

"Are you kidding? He's gone in there with an incubus and a succubus. It might be a week before we see him again. He won't even come up for air until everyone in that room has at least seven orgasms. I should know. My room is right next to his."

"Seven?! Why seven?"

"He's superstitious like that, I guess."

"Have you two ever . . .?"

He'd laughed. "No, but not through his lack of trying."

"Have you been close?"

"Several times, but I can be a bit bullheaded sometimes." I must have looked confused because he'd added. "You can't tell him I told you this, but he has a creature-fuck bingo card, with minotaur very much *not* ticked off. So, I won't sleep with him out of spite."

"Fair enough. That's pretty gross, to be honest. Hey, does he have human ticked off?"

"Of course."

"Shame." He swatted my arm. "I could really go for seven orgasms right now."

Back on the coach, Horns swore loudly and slapped his face.

"I almost fell asleep then."

I looked out the window as the bus was pulling into a service station outside of Borderlands' capital city, Bordalis. "Let's get some coffee in you."

We all piled out to stretch our legs. Horns joined the Ichor queue to buy the biggest, strongest, sugariest coffees available to man and mythic. And thankfully, no dragon barista at this branch. I was about to head to the loos to, as Russ so eloquently put, evacuate my bladder, when my phone rang.

Hell-Bitch's name flashed up on the screen. I groaned before answering.

"Hi Christie."

"Joey, where's my rent money?" *Sure, don't beat around the bush*.

"I've already paid it into your account. It should be there."

"You've only given me one month, Jo. You owe another three."

"I know, but I only just got my car back. I can't afford to pay it all in one go."

"I've got bills too. I've got a mortgage. I need that money by the end of the month."

"But, Christie, that's like, three days away."

I heard a wet smacking sort of sound. Was she eating my Elvish doughnuts? "There's a girl at work, Paris. She's looking for somewhere to live."

"You're kicking me out?"

"Not yet, Jo, but if you don't get the money to me by next week, I'll have no choice."

I thought of the five thousand silvers student prize. Was I really pinning all my hopes on winning a competition? "Okay, I'll find the cash, I promise. If I don't, I'll kick myself out."

Right after Christie hung up, my phone rang again. Hell-Bitch forgot to yell something at me? But the screen read *Home*.

"Hi, Mum," I said, trying to add an air of 'I'm your happy, healthy, well-rounded daughter and there is nothing going on in my life right now that you need to worry about'.

"Flower, it's dad. Your mother's busy." I groaned inwardly. No good had ever come of parents referring to each other in the possessive terms 'your mother' or 'your father'. Also, Mum busy, ha! "She wants to know if you'll be coming home for the Harvest Festival next week. She's trying to work out numbers." *Mmmhmm, yeah of course she is.*

"Yes, I am. I already told her."

"She wants to know if you'll be bringing someone. A boyfriend maybe?"

I sighed. So bloody typical.

"Is there anyone special in your life at the moment, flower? We're both very keen to see you settled down like your sister." I could picture him, grey hairs bouncing from left to right as his body language contradicted his mouth. I knew those weren't his opinions, but Mum always found a way to voice herself through Dad.

"Well . . ." I looked over at Horns' massive form. He chose that moment to turn around and flash me a chest-purring smile. *Anyone special in your life. A boyfriend.* "There is someone. He's not my boyfriend, though."

"Great, should I tell your mother you'll be bringing him?"

"I don't know, Dad." It seemed like an awfully big risk. Given Dad's history. Given Horns' history. Given *my* history. "I'll think about it."

"I'll put him down as a yes, then."

"Dad, don't. I told you, I'm not sure."

He paused. "Is there something wrong with him? Oh, he's a monster?"

I pinched the bridge of my nose. "You can't use that word anymore."

"Fine, mythic. He's a mythic?"

"Yeah, he is." I let out a huge puff. "He's a . . . He's a . . . Dad, he's a vegan."

"Hell's teeth, flower! Your mother is going to be livid. So, he won't eat beef?"

"Gods, no, please do not cook beef. I'm not coming if you cook beef. Tell Mum I won't come."

"Okay, okay, I promise your mother won't cook beef. It's just that Wyn can get us a great deal. Does he eat salmon?"

"No, he's vegan."

"No worries, we'll work something out."

"Thanks." I let out my breath.

Not that I was worried. Was I worried? Only twice in my life had I ever seen Mum 'livid', and even that required a serious stretch of the definition. There was the one time when Tilly and I coaxed three calves from the local dairy into our living room, and another when our old neighbour, Jack, called Dad a useless waste of space at the Spring Fair raffle one year. That was it. She wasn't the type to get annoyed. Definitely not livid. Most things rolled off her back.

So why did the thought of bringing home a seven-foot, vegan, hairy as heck, minotaur make me nervous?

Dad's sigh was resigned. "You know how to pick them, flower."

I hung up the phone and watched Taurin walking towards me, an enormous plastic cup in each hand, and on his face the most adorable bounteous grin.

Chapter 22

Taurin

Peaches forgot to "evacuate" her bladder, and so by the time we arrived at the convention centre, she was pretty much at bursting point. She ran off to find a toilet, leaving me to transport the cake and its accessories and all of our luggage. It was fine; I've got big arms.

I found our names in looping black calligraphy on a table in the middle of the hall. Seeing them written like that, side by side, together, sent a sharp zap through my chest.

Did she get the buzz at the same time? I thought of all the times during the evenings when I felt it randomly thrum. So, she thought of me? That's how the bond worked, right?

Every night.

I shook my head, trying to rid myself of the delicious image of her, alone in her bed, her hand brushing over her stomach, down between her thighs. My chest vibrated again. Would she know I'd thought of her?

I set the display up as we'd talked about, pushing the little edible landmarks into their appropriate positions on the cake map, and placing the wildflowers around the edges of the board, making sure not to go over the line like Russ had told us. When Peaches finally emerged, massaging her chest, I had almost finished.

"Why are you smiling?" she said. I motioned to our cake with a *ta-da* flourish. "Shit, it looks amazing!"

I had to agree. We'd done an impressive job. Not bad for two people who had only recently begun their foray into the surprisingly over-intricate world of sugar manipulation. Not bad for a six-eleven monster and a human who got the wrong classroom.

I looked around at the other student displays, and their varying takes on the theme Unity, and a hopeful, slightly arrogant, bubble rose in my chest.

"I don't want to jinx this, but we might have a chance," I said.

"Maybe you should do this for a job." It was an offhand comment. Perhaps she didn't even realise she'd said it, but wait, did she just plant a seed?

"Only if you do it with me," I said.

We realised the innuendo at the same time. She quirked a brow, her eyes travelling down the length of me and back up. "Let's go find our rooms," she said, tugging on my arm and pulling me from my thoughts before they ventured into Filth Land again.

A shadow fae concierge checked us in. Their name tag floated in mid-air amidst a mass of black velvety wisps. It read Mia. "Names please," they said.

The lobby of the Pegasus Grand hotel was unnecessarily . . . unnecessary. Just that. Everything was too much. The space too cavernous, the marble floors and walls and pillars, too white, the pumped-in lavender perfume too pungent. It was too fancy, too echoey, too stark. I didn't belong there. This was a place for people like Mal, with proper sized bodies and proper shoes that made appropriate clip-clopping sounds. Not people like me. Lumbering, outdoorsy, steel toe cap wearing.

I felt . . . like a bull in a china shop.

To the right stood the gaping entrance of the hotel's casino. The lurid neons and jangling metallics were at total odds with the sepulchral foyer. Neither aesthetic appealed to me. I turned to my left, to Peaches, dressed in yet another fucking adorable flappy red outfit, reading a minotaur-sized sandwich board containing the Pegasus Grand's activity schedule.

"Ooh, fireworks every Saturday at midnight," she said to me, weaving her fingers into mine, and on the spot dissolving my apprehension like effervescent pain killers.

I brought you back from wherever it was you went.

As long as she was by my side, I could handle anything.

"Names please?" repeated the shadow fae, a trace of exasperation in their voice.

"Taurin, and Joey Silver. I've booked two rooms—"

They held up a wisp — hand?—to shush me. "Yep, I've got you here. Welcome to the Pegasus Grand. Here are your key cards." Two cards in the shape of Pegasus wings floated over on shadowy tendrils to Joey and me. "Take the elevator at the end of the hall. Floor thirty. All the way to the top. You'll be able to watch the fireworks from your windows tomorrow night."

"Thank you," I said. We turned towards the lifts.

"You're welcome. Have a pleasant stay. And congratulations, Mr and Mrs Taurin."

Peaches seemed too stunned by her surroundings to have heard the concierge. *Thank Gods.* Her mouth hung open as she looked around at the abstract paintings hanging in the hall, the crystal encrusted elevator mirrors, the other patrons in their fine evening clothes and befitting cloppy shoes. We'd reached the door to my room, 3003, when Peaches put her hand on my chest and said, "Wait. Did Cloudy call me—" But her jaw dropped as I opened it, and she never finished her sentence.

Because, not a room.

A fucking palatial suite.

"What the heck?!" The shadow receptionist mentioned nothing about a serious upgrade.

"Oh. My. Gods!" said Joey, stepping inside, eyes like saucers, arms outstretched as though it was snowing. "Horns, pleeeeeease can we switch rooms?" She looked at her key card. "Oh, wait, mine's the same."

"What?"

"Mine's 3003 too!"

"No, no. No, no." I booked two separate rooms. "Don't look at it Peaches. We're not keeping it." I tried to cover her eyes, but she dodged out of my way, running straight over to a huge floor to ceiling window.

I couldn't sleep in the same room as her. Shifting for five seconds in front of her was one thing. But to spend all night whilst in my bull form. No way. Not happening. Fuck that. She would hate me.

"I need to speak with reception," I said, leaving Joey running from room to room like a child looking for chocolate eggs.

Once in the elevator, I smashed the button for the ground floor. Cursing the whole situation, and the improbably lengthy ride to the bottom. How had this happened? I would never have booked one room for us to share, and surely the hotel couldn't upgrade two rooms to one single room? There must be something in the policies about that.

It was a fucking amazing room. But unless it was an upgrade, there was no way I could afford it. The two singles had cost me enough. Even still, even if it was a free upgrade, there was simply no way I could let her sleep in the same room as bull-me.

She might not mind, a small voice inside my brain told me. *She saw us once before. She kissed our nose.*

A long stream of air puffed from my mouth. Like a montage of flashing memory, I thought of everyone's reaction to my bull-form (and even my non-bull-form) over the past decade and a bit, and I shook my head. The flinching. The shuttered looks. The anxious anticipation. I couldn't let her see me like that. Couldn't let her hate me the way everyone else did.

She's not everyone else though, the voice said. *She's Peaches*.

Mia was not at the desk when I finally reached the lobby. Instead, a fresh-eyed Kitsune had taken their place, and was bobbing their head to the ambient music.

"I'm sorry, sir, but we're fully booked. It's the Inter-Realm Cake Convention this weekend, and every room is occupied. You're welcome to ask around at other hotels, but I expect you'll find a similar result," they said, not even bothering to check on their computer.

"How has this happened? I reserved two rooms. Look, I have the confirmation here. How can the booking change?" I pulled my phone out and began frantically scrolling through my texts for the one from the hotel.

This time they typed in my reference. "Again, I'm very sorry, Mr Sallinbar, but this is the room—"

I held up my hand. "Mr Sallinbar?"

"Yes, sir?"

Fucking Mal, meddlesome bastard.

"Is the cost of the room charged to Mr Sallinbar?"

The kitsune rolled their eyes. "Of course, sir. Already paid for. Plus, any charges from the mini-bar."

I couldn't help but smile at Mr Sallinbar's audacity. And stupidity. Fine, fuck it. It was a suite. A suite. There would be a sofa I could sleep on, preferably in a separate room. "Uh, I may have been confused," I said. "Sorry for the interruption." Oh, Mal's credit card was going to get it tonight. "I'll be off to my gargantuan room now."

"Not at all, sir."

"Please, please, please don't say we have to give up this room," Peaches said, rushing up to me the moment I stepped back over the threshold. "I have to show you this." She grabbed my arm and pulled me through the bedroom area into what I assumed was the bathroom. "Look!"

"It's a hot tub." A godsdamned hot tub, for crying out loud. Not a huge one, a two-person-sized thing really, the water already bubbling away like a *welcome to the hotel* gift. Two champagne flutes and a bottle on ice sat on a tiled, built-on table-ledge-thing. I glanced up to the ceiling as though Mal watched from the heavens. *Well fucking played.*

"Not just a hot tub. Look at that view!"

I did, and all my breath left involuntarily in a whoosh. The city of St. Clouds lay sprawled out before us. A superabundance of flashing neons and twinkling lights shining from the city's infamous casinos and hotels. Cars and carriages zoomed about on the ground like ants carrying disco ball tiles. And everything burned with the pink-orange hues of the sunset.

"This is amazing. Can we keep it?" she said, tugging on my arm, hugging it, tucking it between her breasts.

"Sure." Not like I had much choice in the matter. Plus, seeing her happy did weird things to my body. While one part of my anatomy grew larger, pushing against the fly of my jeans, other parts seemed to get more constricted, for instance, my throat, which felt as though it was closing over.

"Yay." She drew out the word and did a little jiggle. Damn her for being such a cute jiggler. "Which side of the bed do you want?"

She said it so casually, it almost caught me off guard. *Which side of the bed do you want?* As though I didn't shift into an animal during my sleep. As though I didn't grow by two feet. As though my horns wouldn't take up all the pillow space. As though me becoming a monster didn't bother her.

Do I scare you?

A little.

Nope. "I'm sleeping on the sofa."

"Uh." She pursed her lips together.

"There's no sofa, is there?"

She shook her head. "I think there maybe *was* a sofa. There are little dents in the carpet where, I think, a sofa would have likely been."

"Fucking Mal!"

"Mal? The incubus? What's he got to do with it?"

I marched out of the hot tub room, I refused to call it a bathroom, and into the open-plan — open-plan for fuck's sake — living-sleeping space. Gods, this place must have cost Mal a wing and a horn. An enormous four-poster wrought-iron bed pointed towards floor to ceiling, panoramic windows revealing the same infuriatingly breath-taking view of the sunset shrouded city; a small living area with a few decorative but less than practical armchairs, and a coffee table; a kitchenette and dining zone, and, well, fuck, that was it. No separate rooms. No room dividers.

"It's only for two nights," she said, appearing at my side. "I hardly take up any space on the bed." My heart churned over with the nonchalance of her words. "Okay, that's a lie. I'm kinda used to star-fishing, but I promise I'll just curl up on one side and you won't even realise I'm there."

I rubbed my chest. What I wouldn't give to have one night where I didn't shift into a fucking monster.

"No way. Peaches, I can't do it. I'll shift in my sleep. Even if I go to sleep in my human form, by the morning I'll be this massive"—hideous—"bull. I . . . What if I hurt you in the night? What if I squish you?"

What if you leave? What if by morning you hate me? Like everyone else.

She laughed. "Maybe I want you to squish me?"

"Joey, I'm being serious. I'm sleeping on one of those chairs."

"Don't be a dick. You'll flatten the chair when you shift. I'll sleep in the gods-damned chair, okay?"

"I'm not letting you sleep in the ch—"

"Stop being chivalrous. I'm sleeping in the chair and if you try to stop me, I'm gonna . . ." She looked around the room for, I don't know, something to bolster her threat with. Her eyes fell back to me. "I'm gonna touch your horns!"

"You wouldn't!"

"Watch me," she said, racing towards me, her arms outstretched.

"Okay. You win. Fuck, you're so . . . tenacious."

Chapter 23

Joey

"So, what do you want to do tonight? On the bus, I overheard a couple of sirens saying they were going to hit up the casinos?" I said it with an edge. Hopefully, he'd pick it up and realise it wasn't my idea of a fun night. Maybe under different circumstances I'd enjoy getting shitfaced and spunking a wedge of cash into a blackhole. Maybe if I weren't so poor, or in the hotel room of dreams with the very real prospect of Horns shirtless again.

"Uh . . ." His face pulled into a grimace. "If that's what you want to do?" His voice had the same edge as mine.

We had taken to sitting in the armchairs, his buckling slightly at the base, and staring, mostly open-mouthed out of the glass wall, watching the sky shift from pink and orange to searchlight-striped inky blue.

"Not really," I said. "I was just trying to be polite. When in St. Clouds, do as the St. Cloudians do. As the famous saying goes." Pretty sure I got that one from Ash.

"Thank Gods. I can't think of anything worse, to be honest. Actually, I was thinking maybe we empty the mini-bar, go for a dip in the hot tub?" He had a brand-new smile, one I'd never seen before. Was it mischievous? Not sure, but his dimples were back, and it made the weird vibrations in my chest go off like fireworks.

"Really? You thought that? You? Horns?" It was so . . . unlike him. "Doesn't the mini-bar booze cost a fortune?"

"Yeah, Mal's gonna have to take out another mortgage by the time I'm finished with it."

I understood none of that sentence.

"Ooh, room service!" he shouted, jumping to his feet. I had no idea what had gotten into him, but I liked it.

"Are you high?" I asked, but he just laughed.

He rang downstairs and ordered three vegan pizzas for himself, one margherita with extra olives for me, a portion of mushroom knucktak, and a side of seakale from the Mermish section of the menu. Then he uncorked a bottle of wine that looked as though it cost more than Little Red's turbo, and poured us each a glass.

"I don't have a swimsuit with me, and, uh, I only have this one bra. I don't want to get it wet."

He thought for a moment. "I have a t-shirt you can wear."

"Oh har-har, it's white, isn't it?"

His face flushed with colour, he spluttered on his drink. "It's grey. All my t-shirts are grey." Gods, how could someone so massive also be this adorable? I wanted to pinch his reddening cheeks.

"Wait, you own more than one of those?" I made the most Ash-est expression I could muster, rolling my eyes and turning my mouth down.

He smiled again, making my chest buzz. A comfortable silence formed between us for a few moments.

"What were you thinking about just then?" he said, almost in a whisper.

"That I might die if you ever deny me those dimples." That set the buzz into revving mode.

We ate as much of our pizza and knucktak and seakale as we could fit into our bodies while the skies darkened further. Talking about everything and nothing, skirting around the topic I knew we both wanted to discuss, but didn't want to be the one to bring up. The minotaur in the room. Us. Or whatever Us meant here.

"I miss the stars," he said, polishing off the last drops of the fourth bottle. At some point, we'd switched to champagne.

There were no stars anywhere in Borderlands. Sometimes if you stood right on the edge of the cities, it was possible to make out a few of the bigger planets. But you could see nothing from Christie's flat. If you wanted to watch the skies, properly watch them, you'd have to travel to the Human or Mythic Realms. As a kid, I spent hours upon endless hours gazing upwards. Learning the constellations, waiting for shooting stars, wishing. On nights when there was to be a meteor shower, we'd all go as a family to the beaches of Dinlow. Pack a tent, a few blankets, and a portable fire pit. And simply marvel at the beauty. Nothing like the never-ending desolation of unfathomable possibilities to make that Maths final E minus seem insignificant.

"Me too." I'd love to take him there. To Dinlow. We'd lie under the stars, my head in the dip between his arm and that great barrel chest. A blanket over us. We could live there. Could we live there? Was there a place outside of the cities of Borderlands where humans and mythics cohabited?

Woah. Wait. Okay, that was new.

Had I been daydreaming of a future, a serious future, beyond my usual six-weeks-max? My chest thrummed. He snapped his head in my direction.

His smile was unreadable. Smug, maybe. I'd never seen him smug before. He was full of surprises tonight. "What are you thinking about now?" he asked.

I feel it too. He'd said that.

What the hell was this thing in my chest?

"Were you thinking about my dimples again?" he said.

I searched his eyes. Part of me wanted to make a joke about it, but another part was yelling: *What the hecking fuck is going on?*

"Horns, what is this weird buzzing?" I whispered, wiping the smug smile from his face.

"Let's get in the tub." He shot to his feet and hurried across the room to his stuff.

Apart from my movie-star dress, which I'd hooked up, still in its dry-cleaner bag, I hadn't bothered to unpack anything from my case. Horns, however, had neatly laid everything out in the drawers, and hung all his other clothes in the wardrobe on actual hangers like a madman. He tossed me a t-shirt, grey, like he said it would be.

"I'll get in first, give me a minute, and then you can. I won't look. When you get in. I promise."

"Fine, okay." I was too excited by the prospect of *hot tub* to push him further on the tingly chest thing. He would have to tell me at some point what it meant. The vibrations were getting stronger, more intense.

I stripped off my dress and bra and chucked them over the back of an armchair. I left my knickers on and pulled Horns' t-shirt over my head. Drinking in his woodsy, earthy scent like a jilted teenager as it brushed over my skin. My chest purred again.

"I felt that!" he called out from the bathroom.

Get a grip, Joey. You have to stop doing that.

"Your fucking t-shirt smells like you, that's why," I yelled back. "Are you in yet?"

"I'm just getting in now—Ahhhhhh! Oooooohhh my Gods, Peaches!" A thrill of unadulterated excitement shot up my spine.

"Okay don't look. I'm coming in." He made a show of covering his eyes. Whether he was peeking through his fingers, I had no idea. I didn't mind at that point, in fact—

And then I felt it in my chest, the buzz, and I knew he was peeking. So, it went either way.

"Hey, I know you're looking."

He groaned and covered his face as I dropped into the tub with an orca-at-a-sealife-show splash. I thought he said something weird like, "Fucking bond." But I was beyond caring. The moment my skin hit that steaming, bubbling water, all my bones turned to butter and floated up to the surface in useless, greasy globules. Something brushed against my leg. His hand? I couldn't tell because of all the gelatinous ecstasy I was experiencing.

"Shit the hecking bed, this is magical," were the first words that came out of my mouth.

"Yeah," was all he said.

We sat in silence for a while, side by side, in front of the panoramic windows, watching the flickering signs from the casinos and hotels and brothels and shops, mingling with headlamps, and searchlights, and creatures on light up carriages. I was acutely aware of letting my thoughts drift over to the mountainous man next to me, should my chest buzz and alert him to that fact. But I desperately wanted to think about him. To look at him. At his undulating, decorated pecs, or those corded forearms spread either side of the tub. What kind of guy gets his entire chest tattooed but not a drop of ink on his arms? Gods, I wanted to look at him.

"How will you spend your two-and-a-half grand?" he asked me, and without warning, he leant out of the tub and grabbed two cans of beer.

I squeezed my eyes shut before he revealed the rest of his chiselled torso and the inevitable outline of his cock through his wet underwear.

"I guess I'll pay Hell-Bitch the rent I owe her, and I suppose with the leftover money I'll buy myself a nice sandwich from the student canteen." I opened my eyes when he pressed a cold can to my fingers.

He laughed, but rearranged his face instantly once he realised I wasn't joking. "Is it that bad?"

"It's fine," I said, not really sure why I didn't want to tell him the truth. "I don't want to live in her dingy flat, anyway. I'm going to steal her cat and move into your airing cupboard. What about you? What will you spend the money on—Oh my Gods, what is that?"

The thing that brushed my leg, brushed it again. But no, definitely not his finger, he'd draped both arms over the sides of the tub.

"Is that . . . your cock?"

He laughed so hard and loud, I swear the water parted. "It's my tail." He lifted it a little out of the bubbles and let it drop back in, as though waving hello. I'd not really seen it yet. Kinda kept forgetting he had it, actually.

He always wore it tucked into his trousers. Was that even comfortable for him? It was long and smooth, tan like his skin, with a sodden clump of hair — fur? — at the end.

"You can move it independently?"

As though to answer my question, he curled the tip around the bottom of my calf and ran it up my leg until it met my knee. A surge of heat shot straight between my legs and the buzzing in my chest exploded, threatening to split me open. I let out a gasp and practically jumped out of the tub. And I knew at that moment, this sensation was more than want. It was . . .

Something much bigger.

And it scared the shit out of me. Was I ready for it? Would I ever be ready?

I grabbed a towel, dried my face, and ran into the living space. My chest continued to throb. I wasn't sure if it was residual, because he was thinking about me, or because I was still thinking about him. I peeled his wet t-shirt off and threw it towards the kitchenette, rummaged in my suitcase until I found my kitten-print pj's and damply clawed my way into them.

Wasn't this exactly what I wanted? Hadn't this been my sole aim since sliding next to him that first lesson? For five and a half weeks, I pictured nothing except jumping his bones. So why the fuck was I freaking out now?

Horns emerged from the bathroom wearing grey jogging bottoms and no shirt, his hair dripping onto his bare shoulders. I slumped on the floor by my case, and he sat next to me.

"I shouldn't have touched you like that without consent," he said in a whisper.

Of course he'd think this freak-out was because of something he'd done, when it was all me. This was a Typical Joey issue. I could probably go ahead and chuck a ™ on the end of that.

"You have my consent," I said, too spaced out to explain what was going on inside my mind. "To touch me. However you want." I needed some time to figure it out. Needed time to think about him, and me. About us. And he couldn't be conscious because he'd know. I'd have to wait for him to fall asleep.

He scooted towards me but made no move to touch me again. His tail, which was still hanging out of his sweatpants, curled limply on the floor behind him. "There's a bond between us," he said with a sigh. "I don't really understand how it was created, but it exists. If we're too far apart, it will trigger, but it seems it will also trigger when we are close."

A bond, okay. Still explained nothing.

The alcohol and knucktak and all that cheese and the heat from the water had gotten to my head. The room span around me, my chest ached, the wet ends of my hair bled red dye onto my pj's.

I hadn't intended on ever bringing this up, but the words were already tumbling from my mouth. I needed to know. Needed clarification. My thoughts churned over each other in my head. "The second week, after class, I heard you talking to Russ about me. It . . . I heard you through the door."

His face, which already bore no hint of amusement, dropped further.

"You said . . . You can't stand to be around me. That I would drive you crazy." I wiped the wetness from my face. Salty. So, not hot tub water.

His big, callused hand came up to cradle my cheek, pausing before it made contact. He waited an eternity before answering. "Because of the bond. I thought, fuck, I thought I might hurt you. I thought I might try to . . . That the animal in me would take over and . . . I'd See Red, only I wouldn't raze a building, I would . . ." He scrubbed his hands down his face.

"I thought if I wasn't near you, I could cope with the urges, but I realised the bond wouldn't let me be apart from you. It's like a magnet pulling us together. I . . ." He paused, looking into his lap. I couldn't figure out his expression. Anxious? Resigned?

"I've done some bad stuff. You know I've done some bad stuff. I was on my last chance, and you walked in and suddenly you became everything." My heart started beating in triple time. "More important than trying to fix my wrongs. My therapist thought it might be for the best if you weren't around me for the remainder of my probation period. That maybe having you near, and me feeling . . . the way I feel about you might trigger a more dangerous monster than any I'd been before. She was worried, we both were worried. That I, Gods, that I might force myself on you. Peaches, if I'd have shifted and harmed you, like that. It would have been the end of me."

I got it now. I understood why he'd been so hot and cold.

"Mal said I wouldn't be able to harm you. That the bond," he tapped his chest, "would protect you at all costs. I trust Mal, more than anyone. A lot more than myself. Once I knew I couldn't harm you in that way, I found it impossible to stay away from you. But you saw what happened at the docks. When I . . . There will be times in the future when I See Red." He picked up the shoelace tie of his waistband and dug his nail under the metal wrap. "It's just part of me. They're getting less frequent, but it will happen again. It always does."

"And I will be there," I said, so quiet I wasn't sure if he'd heard, but his features softened. "When it happens again, I'll be at your side. I'll help you through it."

His eyes grew glassy. "I didn't ask for this to happen. The bond I mean. It just sort of did. I think, maybe, the universe wants us to be together. And I" —his breaths were shallow, his gaze tearing straight through to my soul— "I want that too." He thumbed another tear from my cheek. Was I still crying? "I really want that, but . . . I'm . . ."

Terrified. I finished his sentence in my head. Because I was too. For different reasons. Would he let me see all of him? Would I push him away? He didn't hate me. In fact, he liked me so much it made him act the way he did. He was trying to protect me. It made me like him more.

"I think I just need to go to bed. I'm sorry," I said.

"Never apologise. I'll fix you something." He walked over to the armchairs and butted two together, then he threw a couple of pillows from the bed onto the chairs, checked in the cupboards, and brought an extra blanket over. It was when he brought over the coffee table, filled up a glass with ice water and set it down next to the makeshift bed that I nearly broke down in tears again. It was so unlike me. I wasn't the careful, emotional, over-thinker girl. I was the jump headfirst, figure it out after girl. I was the grab the bull by the horns girl, and dump him two weeks later.

But maybe, I didn't want to be that girl anymore.

I clambered onto my armchair bed, and Horns tucked me in, laying a feathery soft kiss on my temple.

"Night, Peaches." He got into the huge metal bed and flicked the lamp off. Neither of us had bothered to draw the curtains, so the vibrant city night still blasted through.

"Hey, Horns," I called out.

"Yeah?"

"What happens if I touch your horns?"

A pause. "Good night, Peaches."

I waited a whole hour until I heard — surprisingly soft — snores coming from the bed before I allowed myself to think of him.

He was frightened of rejection. That was so obvious now. Hadn't he faced too much of it already? Too human for the Mythic Realms, too Unpredictable Rage Machine in Borderlands. And he was undoubtedly scared that I would treat him the same. The same as the others. Reject him because of something entirely out of his control.

I realised I'd been worrying about doing exactly the same to him. Pushing him away before he would have a chance to hurt me. Pushing him away before we got too close, too invested. Like I had pushed away every other man who'd ever shown an interest. Not because of who he was and what he became, but because of who I am. Was? Was I the same girl as before? Would I even be able to push him away now?

I knew the answer. I was already in too deep.

I wanted a relationship. For the first time since I ran away to Remy, I wanted more than just a fling. I wanted him. The whole of him. I wanted Us.

I wanted laughter, and cuddles, and fighting and making up, and cooking together, and discovering new places, and dates, and, Gods, maybe even babies?

And he wanted the same. I felt his need for it, for a relationship, stability, acceptance. Under that big grumpy hairy minotaur act, all he really wanted was someone to love him as he was. He was still nervous about letting me in. Letting me see his bull form as well as his human one. I would need to figure out a way to show him I already saw it all.

I saw all of him.

And I was obsessed.

I didn't want him to change. Didn't want him to become someone different. Didn't care that occasionally he lost his temper and destroyed buildings. As bonkers as that sounded, I really didn't care. Because it was a part of him, who he was. And I knew, not sure how I knew, but I knew he'd never hurt me. Not physically at least.

Emotionally there was always space for pain. I had been so intent on ensuring that never happened, that nothing would break my heart, I had blinkered myself to the possibility of happiness. Of a real relationship. But perhaps the time had come to take the leap and see where it went. If I pushed him away now, it would guarantee me heartbreak. The only way was forward.

It was so different to anything I'd had before, with my first boyfriend, and with each subsequent fling. My first relationship, first mythic partner, had been exciting and new, but that was where the emotions ended. I had no feelings for him beyond the novelty of dating someone outside of my species. He was fine; gentle, a little arrogant, a lot vain, but considerate, and there was passion for the short duration of our time together.

What I feel for Horns now makes what I had back then seem like nothing more than a school-girl crush.

This thing I had with Taurin wasn't novelty. It transcended novelty.

At least, I wanted it to, and I was prepared to give it a shot.

My teeth clacked together, and a ghostly chill ran down my back. We'd left the air-conditioning on too high. Down too low? I needed to stretch out my legs, and a cramp had developed in my neck. Oh, this was going to be fun in the morning. I flipped my weight onto my other side, but the neons from the hotel opposite jabbed me in the eye. I tossed around for another few minutes before deciding this was absolutely ridiculous. There was a massive bed right there. I craned my neck up over the back of the armchair. Horns wasn't even sleeping in the middle. He'd tucked himself up on one side. I could have fit three more me's next to him.

Fuck it, I was getting in.

I grabbed my pillows and tiptoed across the tiles, shutting the curtains while I was up. The room fell into near complete blackness. I crept up to the bed and lifted the covers. He was enormous, in his full bullhead, one of his horns digging right into the mattress, and even though he'd coiled his legs into a C shape, they still almost hung off the end. He had his jogging bottoms on, I think, or maybe just boxers . . . Shit, now I was squinting at his groin in the darkness. I curled up on the mattress next to him, facing him, leaving as much space between us as possible, and draped the covers over myself. His warmth slithered over to me as though it were tendrils of heat seeking me out, and I couldn't help but take a few deep inhalations of that beautiful outdoorsy male scent.

Gods, I had it bad.

In the morning, I would start over. Try again. And hopefully, convince him I wouldn't bail. And myself.

"Goodnight, Horns," I said, taking one last look at his shadowy peaceful bullhead, watching his bare chest rise and fall. "I think . . . I might be in love with you."

Chapter 24

Taurin

My Gods, this mattress was comfortable, like sleeping on a pile of freshly washed baby sheep. I would have to get the brand name before we left. If we won, I'll spend my half on that. Troll mattresses were, yeah, they were fine, comfy even, but this was next level.

The scent of her filled my nostrils. I dreamed of her. Of course, I did. I always dreamed of her.

Oh, they were going to have to pry me out of this bed.

I stretched out my toes, running them against the luxurious cotton sheets. I did the same with my tail and my fingers, and found I was holding a pillow. I gave it a squeeze. Okay, that was the weirdest textured pillow ever. I squeezed again. What sort of pillow fits in the palm of my hand? And is warm? And has a . . . button? Felt kind of like a—

I flung my eyes open, and yep, I'd been honking Peaches' boob.

"Joey!" I shot up to my knees and immediately shifted into my human form. Looking down into my lap, I bundled the covers over myself.

Her grin let me know she'd probably been awake for some time. She dragged her eyes away from my crotch. "Uh . . . Yikes," she said, almost inaudible. Her eyebrows retracted to their usual spot on her forehead, then she placed her arms above her head, curved her back, and yawned. I tried not to look at those tits I'd just fondled — could still recall the squish on my palm — or the three inches of exposed skin around her middle, or the shorts on her pyjamas that had risen right up her ass cheek.

"How long have you been—I can't believe you didn't listen—Joey, I could have hurt you."

"I was cold on that chair-bed, and my neck was getting all crumpy."

I ran my hands through my hair. I was pissed. Not Seeing Red pissed but pissed all the same. I explicitly told her she couldn't share a space with my animal form. And she fucking ignored me. She knew what I would become, and what I'm capable of, and yet she still climbed into bed with me—

. . .

Huh.

She knew what I'd become. Knew the risks, what could happen, and she still chose . . . me. And not only human me. The worst version of me. I would have been a bull when she crept in. Would have had a head as big as her torso, and horns twice the size, and a huge nose ring. Would have been hairy as fuck, and smelly, and snoring, probably.

Some of my irritation ebbed, my heart rate decreased, my shoulders de-tensed.

She was still there. Didn't run away screaming and crying. It was morning and she was still here. Still looking at me like . . . like she wanted me.

"Weren't you scared?" I asked.

"Why would I be scared?" she said, as though I was being pedantic. "You didn't hurt me. All you did was cuddle me, which was nice by the way, and then, this morning you stabbed me in the back a couple times with *that*, and then, you felt me up."

"Gods, I am so sorry." I buried my face in my hands.

She grabbed both my wrists and brought them down, kneeling on the bed a foot in front of me. "Don't apologise. I honestly don't know how clear I need to make this. I want you to touch me. Like so bad." She bit her lip and took a deep breath.

I wanted to return the sentiment, tell her I wanted the same, but she looked as though she needed to say more, so I kept quiet.

Her tongue dipped out of her mouth to wet her lips and her gaze briefly shot down to the covers that were valiantly attempting to slide off my erection. "Last night, I was just . . . I freaked out a little, and it had nothing to do with you. Well, that's stupid. It had everything to do with you. But, shit, what I'm trying to say is that I have—" She shook her head. "Had issues, with, uh, commitment, and, well, that's what you need, isn't it? Commitment . . . I—I'm not like everyone else. The people that treat you like you might turn at any second. I like you. Really like you. I want you to be exactly as you are. And, and fuck, now I'm rambling . . . And oh, Gods, here we go . . . I really want there to be an *us*."

My lungs stopped working, yet my heart beat in triple time. I couldn't seem to formulate a response.

"I want a relationship with you!" she practically yelled. "I want you as you are. Always as you are. No matter what form that is. I know you're shitting yourself about it, and, yeah, so am I if I'm being honest, but I . . . maybe we should give it a shot?"

"Okay," I said, because my throat had closed itself off to any other words.

"Okay," she repeated. Those amber eyes crinkling at the corners as she relented into relieved laughter.

The vibration in my chest had grown so intense it threatened to overwhelm me. She felt it, too.

"Horns, what happens to this . . ." She brought her palm to my chest and huffed out an ego-boosting, "holy shit" before finishing her question. "If we fuck?"

As if by answer, the bond revved its approval, and a warming sensation spread outwards from my chest. We both laughed. She didn't break eye contact.

"Maybe it will go away," I said, sort of choked out. "It's never happened to me before, so I'm not sure." Mal had said it was hungry, that we need to feed it. What I didn't mention was that I didn't want it to go away. I liked the tether we had, even if it was sometimes uncomfortable bordering painful.

"There's only one way to find out," she whispered.

My erection renewed its attempt to rob every drop of blood from the rest of my body.

She snaked her hands over my shoulders. "I've got another question. Do you shift during sex?"

Was she worried I might shift, or was she . . . hopeful?

"It's never happened before."

I let the covers drop and closed the space between us, pressing our bodies flush together. Her breath hitched and her eyes widened when the full length of me squished against her stomach. Her gorgeous, rounded, human stomach.

"You're so . . . big," she said.

"I am," was all I said back. She could take me, though. All of me. I already knew that. We were built for each other. I brushed my hands up the sides of her arms and tucked her hair behind her ear. "You're so beautiful I can't stand it."

Oh my gods, were we doing this now?

A whimper escaped her throat, and she melted into me. My lips grazed her neck, searching the soft throbbing heat of her pulse. She tasted like hot tub chemicals and her, us, the bond.

I wasn't stupid enough to have expected anything to happen last night. Hell, I wasn't expecting anything at all this weekend. I thought we'd have separate rooms. But, Gods, there she was, perfect, and practically edible and so ready for me. I could scent her arousal, feel the vibrations in my chest, the heat between her legs. I wrapped my hands around her and gently guided her onto her back, caging her with my body. She looked up at me through her lashes and bit her lip. She fucking bit her lip.

"Fuck, Peaches. Look at you. I'm already about to go off."

I placed a finger in the middle of the neckline of her strappy cat-print pyjama top and pulled it down revealing the deep V of her tits. Before I even knew what I was doing I had brought my mouth into the valley. Her skin was sweet, and warm, and softer than velvet. How many times had I imagined doing exactly this? The reality was better than anything I could have conjured. Silky, delicious, and all mine. At least for a little while. I could spend all morning between these tits. I would spend all morning there, in fact.

My open-mouthed kiss against the fleshy mound of her breast drew a noise somewhere between a toe-stub and a Carly's falafel from her, and she dug her fingernails into my shoulders. The bond sang against my lips. I dragged my tongue along it, swallowing each pulsation and tremor, greedy to please it. To give it what we all needed. My heart threw itself against my ribcage. My hips ground themselves into her pelvis, pushing out her breath, desperate for her wet warmth.

She wanted this. She wanted me. More than me, she wanted us. She accepted me for me. It wasn't a question of fucking her. I needed to make love. But first, these gods-damned cat pyjamas had to go.

KNOCK KNOCK.

"House keeping?" she said, raising an eyebrow. "Do not disturb!"

KNOCK KNOCK.

"Fuck off!" I called out.

"Good morning, you two sleepy heads." Russ' singsong cadence floated through the suite as if he were standing next to us. "Class meeting in ten minutes. Meeting room H16. I expect to see you both there and . . . decent." He didn't wait for our answer before leaving.

"Horus, the cock-blocker," she said.

"Tell me about it."

Peaches took her clothes to the bathroom and got dressed. I quickly, and I mean within seconds, rid myself of my erection. The bond seared into my chest, livid about being saddled with only my hand yet again. I came so hard, stemming the spray in yesterday's t-shirt. There was no way in hell she didn't feel that, however the only clue she gave that she had was a cheeky wink and a naughty little smile. I slung on some jeans and another grey t-shirt, identical to the one she'd worn last night.

The meeting turned out to be nothing more than signing a few forms and taking a register. Then we were free to explore Cakecon for a few hours. Sample cakes, look at the other displays, buy extra equipment for our kit bags, that sort of stuff.

"Pfft. That 'meeting' could have been done at any time," she said as soon as they released us into the main hall. "He could have at least given us an extra four and a half minutes."

"Hey, I can last longer than four and a half minutes." She cocked an eyebrow. "Yeah, okay, no, you're probably right. That was a moot point."

"Don't you mean mooooo-t point?" She fell about laughing. Literally fell to the floor, crossing her legs like she might pee herself from the mirth.

Oh, shit!

The force of the realisation hit me like a falling oak.

I loved her.

Of course I did. Why did I expect fated mates to be anything less than love?

She looked at me and rubbed her chest. "Ow! It'll go away?" I just stared at her, my brain registering her words three beats too slowly. "We really need to get this over with, huh?"

Oh. Right. She was talking about *that*.

Only, there was no way I wanted to *get it over with*. No fucking way. When it did happen. I would take my time. Savour every second. I was going to worship her. We'd need all week. It would have to wait.

"No, not yet," I said.

To which she made a noise that sounded like, "Humph," and folded her arms over her chest. But her pout soon faded when she saw signs peeking out from almost every stall reading *FREE SAMPLES.*

We meandered through the stands, taking our time, looking at all the varied, yet surprisingly similar, ways disparate creatures made, and decorated, cake. Who knew the uniting interspecies commonality was mixing sugar with eggs and flour, baking it at one-hundred-and-sixty degrees for twenty minutes and then topping it with even more sugar?

She didn't bring up sex again all morning and most of the afternoon, but I knew she was thinking of it. We both were. The buzzing in my chest had become constant. I tried to ignore it as we stuffed yet more free cake into our mouths.

"Ooh, this one's vegan too!" She would say, bounding up with a napkin full. "Look, vegan cherry pie. OH MY GODS! VEGAN MERINGUE!"

We were both having too much fun to slink off and sort out our other 'little problem' and I started to consider it our own brand of foreplay. It was incredible, intense, borderline overwhelming, knowing whenever the bond buzzed, it was because she'd thought about me. I'd just chomped down on a nice slice of vegan coffee and walnut, when it blazed ferociously.

"Will you stop thinking about my dick already?" I joked.

"I don't think I can," she said in earnest. "I'm so wet."

Oh, my gods!

"Ow!" She massaged her chest.

"Sorry, my fault that time," I said.

"Can we just go back to the room already?" The pleading in her eyes would have me stripping her bare right there in the middle of the packed conference hall C.

I pulled her over to a nearby bin. "You have to believe me when I say I want nothing more. That I've thought of nothing else for five weeks. Since the second you walked into that classroom in that fucking dress with the little peaches. Gods, that dress. You've no idea how many times I've fucked my hand to the image of that dress. You drive me wild, Peaches, and I need you. I'm desperate to be inside you."

She laughed. Warm and smooth and undeniably sexy, drawing movement under my jeans. "There's a but. Why is there a but?"

"Peaches, I don't want to squeeze in fucking you before we have to be at the awards ceremony. It won't be enough. I've not waited five weeks just to push your knickers to one side and fuck you against the wall for four and a half minutes." Though, admittedly, I was already adding those images to my bank. "I want to take my time with you. All night. All week, even." Her breath stilled. I leant closer, pushed her hair behind her ear, and whispered, "I want to ruin you. I'm going to break you. Then piece you back together. Then break you all over again. By the time I'm finished with you, you'll never be able to touch yourself without remembering that one time I completely destroyed you."

A few of the mythics with keener hearing paused their own conversations, but I didn't give a shit.

She stepped into me, pushing her breasts against my stomach. "What are you going to do to me?" she said, staring straight into my eyes, her voice breathy, her chest heaving, well aware of the effects it would have on me. Gods, she was good.

"First," I said, smoothing my hands up the sides of her bare arms, gratified when her flesh tightened into goosepimples. "I'm going to fuck you with my fingers and watch you come all over my hand." Her tongue came out to wet her lips. "Then, I'm going to split those gorgeous thighs apart and you'll ride my face. I'm going to fuck you with my tongue and suck on your pretty little clit until you're begging for release."

She managed an adorable, "Oh."

"I want to watch you fall apart over and over until the only word of English you can remember is my name. And then, when you think you can't take anymore, when you're nothing more than a puddle, that's when we'll fuck. And I'm going to fuck you how I like to fuck. Fast. And hard."

It took a moment for her to speak. "Shit, Horns, I need a shower."

"And don't even think about sorting yourself out in the shower. I want every time you come to be on me."

"Yes, sir," she said, the biggest smile on her face. "You've got a massive boner, by the way."

"I'm aware of that. I might need a minute."

She glanced around the crowded conference hall, her eyes slightly unfocused. "Shall I stand here in front of you, like this?" She placed her hands on her hips. I guessed in an attempt to make herself larger and shield more of me, but all she did was treat me to the sumptuous view plunging straight down her dress.

"I think that might be counterproductive to our goal."

With only two more hours before the awards ceremony, we retired to the room to get ready. And do nothing more. Peaches was in the bathroom for at least three quarters of that time. But from the way my chest didn't pain, I knew she hadn't touched herself in the shower and thought of me. Now I just had to stop myself from thinking about her touching herself in the shower.

I pressed my tux again; a black jacket, black trousers, black shirt (I couldn't find a white one in my size), and a black dickie-bow, and got myself dressed. Joey ran out of the bathroom, wrapped up like a burrito in her towel, her hair already perfectly curled and swept over one shoulder with a glittery pin on the other side. She had done her makeup. Bright red lips, black flicky wings above her eyes, and some other things I couldn't pinpoint but made me want to weep. In the way someone might when witnessing a particularly beautiful sunset, or when Mal brought home vegan ohjieberry ice cream for me.

She grabbed the large green dress-bag from the wardrobe and, from her little red case, another pair of knickers.

She caught me watching. "I need clean pants after the shit you whispered to me earlier." I blushed, she didn't. "And you look incredible, by the way."

I raked my hands through my hair and threw myself backwards onto the bed with a groan.

After a few more minutes, maybe ten, she called out. "Horns, can you zip me up?"

I got to my feet and almost, *almost*, made it to the bathroom before stopping dead in my tracks. There she stood, back facing me, zip hanging open all the way to the top of her ass. I knew she could feel my chest throbbing, yet she said nothing as I took in every inch of her exposed flesh. The dimples above her cheeks. The curve of her lower back. The group of stars tattooed onto her right side.

I closed the gap between us and pushed the dress open further to reveal the full constellation. I recognised that constellation. My heart stilled. I pressed my thumb to it.

"Taurus," I said.

The bull.

"My birthday's in April." She watched me in the mirror's reflection, her eyes hooded and dark. I took in the rest of her dress from the front. I had no words. Couldn't string together a coherent thought.

Fated mates.

"How are you even real?" I whispered.

Chapter 25

Taurin

The awards ceremony was in yet another cavernous hall. The glamoured night sky shrouded the walls and ceiling, so when we took our seats around a circular, satin draped table in the middle, it appeared the space was limitless. Like we were twelve-hundred people in fancy clothes perched on an icecap somewhere in the North Winterlands.

Peaches sat beside me and Russ next to her. A few other students from our class shared our table, including Clarke and his partner. They served us nibbles and pink sparkling fae wine, which crackled all the way down my oesophagus.

She looked incredible. More than incredible, but I simply couldn't summon the words. Her dress was a flimsy, silky, red masterpiece. Future generations will write dissertations on that dress. How it drove armies to war and simultaneously healed the Eight and a Half Kingdoms of all ails. The neckline split down to the top of her stomach, revealing the cutest cluster of freckles I'd somehow missed that morning, plus enough boob to keep my trousers on the just too-snug side. An entire leg protruded from the skirt, casting a little shadow over her knickers, which I knew were red, but damn, it kept them infuriatingly out of sight.

The awards themselves began without pomp, a solitary centaur stood in the middle of a white stage, reading out a long list of names. Attendees, winners, bakers they'd lost over the past year, who knew?

Horus leant across the table and quietly, which must have taken him some restraint, cleared his throat. "There are about fifty prizes to get through before they announce the big guns. Only a handful carry prize money, so there will be a lot of rosette distribution before then."

We were in it for the long haul.

I don't remember when it started, but Joey and I began a game. I thought about the dimples just above her ass. The bond thrummed.

She cocked an eyebrow, and then, a moment later, it thrummed again.

I pictured stiffly running my thumbs up her inner thighs, her flesh puckering under my fingers, and the soaked knickers I'd find when they reached the top.

Then it was her go. The bond revved. Hard.

"Dirty girl," I mouthed to her. She sipped her drink and smirked at me over her flute.

My turn. Her hands wrapping around the base of my cock, her tongue slipping out of her lip-sticked mouth and flicking over the head.

She jumped back in her seat, her hand on her chest. "Ow, Gods, what did you picture?"

"Okay, kids, the student prize is up soon," said Russ. The vibrations died instantly.

Crap, if we won, I'd have to go up on stage with a mega-chub. I tried to clear my thoughts. She looked so good. This was going to be difficult.

Distantly, the host's voice filtered through the hall. ". . . Concludes the runner-up awards. Now for the first of tonight's headliners. Here at Cakecon, we strive for innovation, for invention, and ingenuity." I centred all my energy on listening to his words, trying to dampen the raging menace under my fly with boredom. "Our focus has always been on the next generation of cake baking and decorating. For years, we've done this with our incredible series of student programmes . . ." It was great boner-killer material. I just had to avoid looking at Peaches. ". . . Fostering the future, nurturing minds. Exceptional talent. Blah blah . . ."

I ignored her repeated chest-thrumming attempts to get my attention. She took to knocking her heeled foot against my leg.

"This year's theme is unity," the centaur continued. Joey reached over and grabbed my hand, weaving her fingers into mine. "And this year's winners, we think, have captured that perfectly. What could be more unified than Borderlands itself, with its mishmash of cultures, peoples and species?" She squeezed it tighter. "Working in harmony, we prove anyone can coexist. Anyone can find commonality and hope and love, no matter their species. So, with that in mind, we'd like to announce the winners of the student prize, the recipients of five-thousand-silvers, and the first of tonight's highly coveted Cakecon trophies. From the University of Remy, with their magnificent cake in the shape of a Borderlands' map, Taurin and Joey Silver."

Russ was whooping. He got to his feet, suddenly illuminated by a huge spotlight.

"Horns, that's us!" screamed Peaches, wrapping her arms around my head, squishing my face into her boobs.

Numbly, I stood. Horus gave Peaches a hug, then me. His feathers tickled my jaw as he turned. At least, I think they tickled.

We walked to the front. Peaches' hand still woven into mine. Blurs of people were applauding. No gasps or whispered "minotaur" for a change. It wasn't until I was on the stage, and I could barely make out the sea of tables before us, that I realised we'd won. We'd won! I picked up Joey and spun her around. The audience laughed. I placed her down and kissed her mouth. They cheered and whistled. Someone handed us a trophy and an envelope and ushered us to the side of the stage. Thankfully, nobody required us to make a speech. The centaur said something about "The perfect example of unity?" Phrased like a question. I couldn't make sense of it. Didn't try to. My mind was a whirl.

"We won," Joey whispered while the host resumed announcing the awards and more and more people joined our little huddle at the side. "I can't believe it. Five thousand silvers."

"You can have my share," I said. I seemed unable to pry my hands from her.

"What? Why would you do that?"

"You're the real prize." It had sounded better in my head.

Her brow furrowed, and she stepped back, though not completely out of my touch. "I'm not something to be won."

"Fuck, Peaches, that's not what I meant. I meant seeing you happy is more than enough prize."

She didn't answer, her focus seemed preoccupied with maintaining the narrowness of her eyes.

That would have been a lot easier if you just told her you love her, said a voice in my head. I told it to fuck off.

After they announced best in show — person-sized cake sculptures of Darren the Great and Todd the Enigmatic — the doors opened to reveal a huge disco.

"Yes!" she yelled, seizing my hands again, seemingly over my earlier miscommunication. "I love dancing!"

Of course she did. Of course she loved dancing.

I went to the bar to get drinks. Beer for me, more pink fae wine for Peaches. She liked the crackling sensation, apparently. Random faces took it in turns to pat me on the back and congratulate me. Not used to such positive attention without all the flinching, I simply smiled in return and hoped my grimace was enough to say, *thank you for being nice, but please don't speak to me anymore.* I considered buying Russ a drink, but when I cast my eyes over the tops of everyone's heads, he had disappeared.

The crowds on the dancefloor immediately swallowed Peaches. A chimera stood behind the DJ booth, both headphone-clad heads bopping to the music. The base resonated right through my body, up my spine, filling my chest cavity, rivalling that of the bond. Rainbow lights flashed overhead, and the hall itself seemed to secrete sweat.

Thank the Gods for my lofty advantages. My plan was to watch the throng from the edges with the trolls and ogres. At least it had been until I spotted an Oros, with his tell-tale golden-blonde hair and pointed ears stalking Peaches. On her other side, a couple of blood-eyed vampires were attempting to muzzle in.

Nope. Not happening. Not Seeing Red tonight.

I swooped.

"What do you mean, you don't dance?" she yelled over the music as I handed her the fae wine. The Oros — who bore an uncanny resemblance to Goldie — and the vampires, scattered.

I shrugged. "I don't dance, Peaches."

"Don't or can't?"

"Same difference."

She chugged her drink in one. "Best thing to do is copy. Let's start with . . ." She looked around the dance floor. "The zombies! Just do what they do." She snapped her arms to her sides and stiffly lurched from one foot to the other. While groaning, I might add.

I gave her A Look.

"Oh, come on." She placed my beer on the nearest table and pulled my arms down to my sides. Still holding my hands, she pushed me gently left and right, and giggled so much it was impossible not to lean into her joy and zombie dance with her. After a few beats, I felt myself moving of my own volition, my own laughter rumbling the space between us. Could she make everything fun?

"Vampires now!" she yelled, motioning her head towards the two that had been eyeing her like she was a vending machine. Her mirth surrounded me like a bubble. I crossed my forearms over my chest and began swaying in a poor imitation of the listless, mournful way vampires move. I was so thankful Dima couldn't read my mind at this distance. She burst into laughter and copied me.

We did more, everyone. Gorgons with their waving, slithering arms. Sirens, and their incongruous sensual clucking. The fluid tail-swishing of the merpeople. The over-caffeinated bopping of the gnomes. Even the bounding, leg humping moves of the werewolves.

"Do the succubus," I said, glancing over to the female sex demon performing a solo dance show for a wide-eyed satyr who looked as though all his Winter Fests had come at once.

Joey raised her eyebrow. "Oh, like that, is it?"

She pulled her smile between her teeth, and I knew I was in trouble as she shimmied in her dress. Her unbound breasts bounced mesmerically, her arms caressed her hips and waist, the fabric bunching and falling across her curves.

Gods. I wetted my lips, unable to take my gaze away from her, but, because of the throbbing crowds closing around us, unfairly unable to see all of her at once. She fixed her eyes on the succubus and copied every single move she made. Spinning on the spot and leaning forward, she tipped her ass onto my lap. I made a noise like an injured animal. The bond had ignited a small bonfire in my chest, and blood rushed south, pushing my swelling cock against the waistband of my trousers.

Eventually, she turned to face me, out of breath. Her chest rising and falling, beads of sweat tracking down into the hollow between her breasts, errant curls glued to her forehead. The look on her face was utterly victorious.

It had been on my tongue for the whole dance. Until that point, I had wanted to wait to say it. Wait until I knew she'd reciprocate. But the words were already tumbling out. "Gods, Peaches, I lo—"

Before I could finish, she fisted the front of my shirt, pulled me down, and slammed my mouth into hers. And I had no choice but to yield to her kiss.

She kissed me as though she might never get the opportunity again. Soft at first. Savouring. Fluttering kisses that made the bond tingle and drew a growl from deep within me. Then fierce, desperate, like she wanted to devour me. Her hands were in my hair, sliding under the lapel of my jacket, fingers seeking the gaps between my shirt buttons. I didn't care whether people were watching, though I half expected Russ to pop up at any minute.

I ran my fingers down her back, over the silky fabric of the gown, taking it all in, cataloguing every one of her curves. That ass. My Gods. She broke away and placed both hands on my hips, pushing herself between my thighs, trapping my erection against her stomach. Her eyes grew bigger, darker, she pulled her lip in between her teeth.

I needed that dress off her. Like, now.

Wrapping her arms around my neck, she pressed her lips flush to my ear. Her breath was hot and boozy on my cheek. "Now can we go back to the room?" she said.

"Fuck, yes."

Chapter 26

Joey

I took Horns by the hand and pulled him from the dancefloor to the nearest elevators, pausing every few metres, because the buzz in my chest told me if I didn't push my curves into his plains, or suck on his bottom lip, it would make things very painful for me. If I was going to listen to this thing, now was an excellent time to start.

It was happening. Finally happening. We were giving in to this constant gnawing need. The reverberation in my chest having crescendoed to near torture. Threatening to wrap itself around my heart and cut off blood supply to all my vital organs. And at the risk of personifying the buzz, the bond, whatever, it seemed to measurably calm with Horns' tongue in my mouth. Maybe not calm, it was just as agitated, but the buzzing had changed, shifted, it became encouraging, it said, *yes good things will happen if you keep touching him, and I promise I'll stop nagging you if you get his pants off.*

I mean, who was I to argue with that?

He backed me into the elevator door. I was faintly aware of the cold metal against my shoulder blades, the light-up directional arrows pressing into my ass, the cool whoosh of the air conditioning unit overhead.

"We're gonna have to take this slow," he growled. "I—I won't last long." Not heeding his own advice, he roughly palmed the front of my dress, running his hands up my waist and filling them with my breasts. I had big tits, he had big hands, almost made-to-measure. All the bones in my legs dissolved. His hips bucked into me, pinning me up, keeping me from dropping.

"Gods, Peaches, I knew you'd be the perfect fit for me." The words sent a jolt of electricity between my thighs. Was he talking about more than my boobs?

I knotted my fingers into his hair. So freaking soft. He had worn it down to the ceremony. He looked so good with it down. And despite everything the bond, my brain, and my clit screamed at me to do, all three stopped yelling their demands to simply admire how beautiful he was. His ocean-blue eyes darkened with lust, his already full lips swollen and kiss-bloated, his face flushed, a sheen of sweat across his brow and temples.

"Why is this lift taking so long?" I said, repeatedly jamming my fingers against the up button. I couldn't wait much longer. Neither of us could. He ground his pelvis against mine, pushing his erection into my hip, creating friction the bond told me we needed. His breath left him in a trembling whimper. If we weren't careful, and we listened to this thing vibrating in our chests, we'd end up fucking in the elevator.

He twisted the strap of my dress around his fingers and ran the flat of his tongue from the freckles at the top of my stomach, right up the inside of my breast. I had to hold onto his shoulders to stop me from melting into a sticky pool and draining off down the lift shaft.

"You taste so fu—"

Someone cleared their throat next to us. It took them another two tries before we pulled apart. Eventually I regained some of my senses, the lobby music returned along with the pervasive lavender stink, my vision unclouded, and beside us stood two turtle-humanoids. They came up to my waist, had slim human bodies and some kind of shell on their backs. The instant impression I got was that they were an older married couple.

"Congratulations on your win," said the husband.

Neither Horns nor I managed a response. Our limbs still tangled, my fingers still interwoven into his hair, his on my dress. His brow furrowed, he righted his posture, opened his mouth, but no sound came out.

"Kelsey, leave them be," said the wife. "Don't you remember what it felt like to be their age and in love?" He answered his wife by sliding his hand underneath her shell and squeezing what I assumed was her ass. She giggled and batted him away.

The doors opened, and all four of us made our way inside. Horns span me around and used my body to cover the front of his.

"Twenty-eight for us," Turtle man said, cocking a brow towards the light up panel. Horns groaned and hit the button, then pressed number thirty.

"Top floor, ay? Spending your winnings already?" said Kelsey.

Horns squeezed my shoulder. In the mirrored walls I caught him rolling his eyes up to the heavens, his lips twitching with the words, "Come on, fucking hurry up." Plinky plonky piano music accompanied us upwards. In the reflection, Turtle-Wife smiled at me. A knowing sort of smile. Her gaze travelled to Horns and then back to me and she gave me an almost imperceptible nod, as if she were congratulating me on a job well done. I couldn't help but return with my own smug smile.

"Level twenty-eight," said the feminine voice recording of the elevator. It spoke in English, then in Mermish (throaty screaming) and then in another language I didn't recognise. Possibly Gobbledygook, possibly Orcish.

"This is us," said Kelsey. Because of course he did. I'd known the man for sixty seconds and I already knew he wouldn't be able to leave without announcing it.

His wife practically shoved him out onto their floor. "Enjoy your celebrations," she said, before they toddled off down the corridor.

As soon as the doors pinged shut, I crushed Horns against them, hitched my dress up by a few inches and leapt into his arms. He caught me with unsurprising ease, holding me up as though my sizeable ass weighed nothing more than an armful of laundry.

"Better," he grunted, burying his face in the curve of my neck, and pushing his tongue into the hollow at its base. His horn tangled into my hair, he nipped at my collarbone.

"Level thirty," said the voice. It screamed, and then gargled again, and we stumbled backwards out of the doors as they opened, though he never lost his grip on me.

We ricocheted down the corridor, bouncing off the walls, knocking the artwork askew, kissing and touching every part of each other within reach of our mouths and hands, until we arrived at our room. Horns pinned me against the door and fumbled in his back pocket for the key. With his hold slipping, I wrapped my legs around his hips and renewed my grip.

He hit the key card against the reader. A short angry buzz emitted, and the door stayed firmly closed. He tried again. Nothing.

"I can't think straight. Hang on a second," he said, his expression unfocused. He handed me the key card and rearranged himself. His cock, still imprisoned within his grey boxers, now pointed due north, breaking free of his trouser waistband. "So much better."

Gods, even the top half of it looked intimidating. He ground it into me, and I felt all the bones leave my body as his swollen head squished blissfully against my clit. That sweet pressure against my burning core forced out an involuntary moan, which he captured with a kiss. My back bowed and my head fell backwards against the door, any attempt to gain access to our room long forgotten. His hand found my exposed thigh and, without breaking contact with our mouths, he squeezed it and then almost painfully slid his fingers up my leg until they met the lace edge of my knickers.

He cried out and ground into me again. "Fuck, Peaches. This all for me?" He inched his whole body to my right by a fraction to allow himself access and dipped his fingers under the fabric. "Is this okay?"

"Yes," I choked out. "Gods, yes."

He gave the slightest teasing brush to my clit. "You're the most perfect peach." Dragged his finger down my slick slit. "Ripe and juicy." And then slipped it inside.

My back arched further, my pussy clenched around him, desperate to take more, force him deeper. He pulled it out and buried it again, curling the tip this time, hitting *that* spot, adding a second finger. And a third.

"You feel . . .Fuck, Peaches, so hot and tight. I have to stretch you out. Get you ready for me."

Words were no longer an option. Not anymore. My mouth hung open, pressed against his, panting into it as he pumped his fingers. I grabbed either side of the doorframe for purchase, pushing as hard as I could, and bucked my clit against the heel of his palm. Already greedily chasing my release.

His mouth was on my chest again, tongue sliding under the fabric of the neckline, achingly close to my nipples. A familiar sensation coiled in the pit of my stomach. Waves of ecstasy began building. Clouds darkening my vision. A storm brewing.

"Horns, that feels so . . ."

His lips were at the pulse on my neck. "I can feel every tremor in your gorgeous pussy."

"I'm so close."

"Let it happen, Peaches."

Gods, there was no way I could stop this. I was going to come right there in the corridor—

"Good evening, kids."

No!

No. No, no, no.

Fucking Russ!

The look Horns shared with me before turning his attention to our tutor was patently homicidal. "Dead bird walking," I think he said, pulling his fingers out, leaving me empty and bereft. He kept me pinned to the door.

"It's great to see you two celebrating your win so . . . ardently. But, as the kids will say, get a room." Russ had stopped about six-feet from us and stood with a fae man. His partner, or hook-up maybe. The fae had clamped his hand over his mouth, as though physically holding back his mirth.

I pushed the key card into Horns' hand, and he smashed it against the reader. The door didn't budge.

Russ coughed and raised his brows. "That's our room." His friend looked down at his feet, a snort burst free from his nostrils, no longer able to contain himself. "Yours is across the hall."

So it was. I'd been staring at those numbers, 3003, all that time. Fancy that. Horns' cheeks flushed as red as my dress.

"Sorry, Russ!" I called out, as Horns swivelled me around, my legs still clinging onto his waist. He tapped the card on the correct reader and opened the door.

"Have a good evening, kids. Be safe," Russ added as the light from the corridor was swallowed by the dark suite.

Inside, Horns placed me down. We shared a look, then both burst into laughter. Another thirty seconds and Horus, God of Kings, would have had front row seats to my Oh face.

"Come on," I said, tugging him by the hand over to the enormous window wall next to the bed.

He shucked his jacket, threw it in the general direction of the armchairs, and kicked off his shoes. Then he made a start on his bowtie. It struck me then that he'd chosen a proper tie on one, instead of the clip-on variety. *Odd*. If he'd have shifted, a clip-on tie would have been much safer for him. Did he know he wouldn't See Red tonight? That he could remain in full control of his emotions? Was he aware that's what it meant?

He was still fumbling with it when I intervened. He watched my face, drank it in, as I worked the too-tight knot. His expression dark, his breaths ragged.

Eventually, it fell loose, and I let it drop to the floor while I started on the buttons of his shirt. My fingers trembled. He took over. I took two steps back from him, so that I'd be able to see all of him at once as he revealed that beautiful, sculpted, tattooed torso. Fuck, he was magnificent. The sight of him flooding my entire body with a plethora of happy hormones. I wasn't really one to cry during sex, but just looking at him made me want to weep.

It was finally going to happen. We were finally going to fuck, and for the first time in a decade, it symbolised more to me than a simple release. The end to a game of chase. It was the beginning of something bigger. We had agreed to start a relationship. *I* had agreed to start a relationship. I didn't even know who I was anymore, but Gods, it all felt so right. I'd never wanted for anything as much as I'd wanted us, never wanted for anybody as much as Horns. He was irrevocably part of my life now. Part of me.

My hands found his stomach first, hard, damp with sweat, smattered with hair, before tracing each valley and peak of his abdomen, along every inked line of every tattoo. Time slowed. I watched every move my fingers made, dipping into the furrows, stopping at the juncture of every muscle, savouring every plain. Down those beautiful ridges that started at his hips and vanished into his waistband. Along each sinew and vein that disappeared with them. And he watched me watching him, through hooded eyes and staccato breaths that seemed to echo around the city-lit hotel suite. The bond practically skipped with joy.

"You are literally perfect," I whispered.

A shadow crossed his features as if he meant to contradict me, but he shook his head, tilted my face up and kissed me again, his tongue speaking without words.

I reached for his belt buckle, and he inhaled sharply through clenched teeth as though I'd poured lemon juice onto an open wound. He pushed my hands away. "Not yet." He took a few breaths to steady himself. "Let me worship you first. Turn around," he commanded. I did as he said.

He swept the hair from my back over my shoulder and caged my neck with one massive hand, then slowly, so slowly, tugged the zip down. Hot breath pooled against my exposed skin, alerting all my hairs. Fingers brushed over my tattoo again.

"Mine," he whispered, possibly to himself, and planted an open-mouthed kiss on the constellation. I didn't think I could get any wetter. I was wrong. I just needed to hear Horns' growled possessiveness. My belly cramped with want, and my sex released another wave of moisture, soaking my knickers.

He lifted my dress straps off my shoulders and dropped them down my arms, causing the gown to slither from my body like liquid, pooling at my feet, leaving me standing in nothing more than a pair of skimpy, sodden, red underpants. I stepped out of my heels.

"Fuck," he whispered. He was quiet for a few moments, and I chanced a peek at him. He'd done what I did and moved back a few steps to take it all in. In fact, he had perched himself on the side of the bed. He covered his eyes with one hand. "Okay, turn around."

Again, I did as he said. And standing nearly naked in front of him, I felt . . . comfortable. Confident. I didn't feel the need to lean my weight onto one hip to create a more pleasing silhouette, or suck in my tummy, or hide any part of me. I wanted him to see everything. Enjoy everything. Worship everything. "Okay."

He removed his hand, peeking through his fingers as he let them drop, and made a noise I could only describe as a lamentation. Could somebody lament with joy? It certainly sounded that way. His expression was pained, hungry, determined, as he cast his gaze over my breasts, my stomach, my hips, my thighs, before looking me in the eye and saying in his sex-clenching growl, "I've won the fucking lottery."

I crossed the space between us, standing over his knees. His lips found my stomach, his hands, the backs of my thighs. And then, in a movement so swift, so effortless, he grabbed my legs and span us both around, lowering me onto the bed. He hovered above me, his hair falling either side of my face, making a sanctuary for just the two of us.

A bubble of laughter escaped me, and his face lit up in a smile. My Gods, he was impossibly beautiful.

"I will murder Russ if he smashes on that door right now," he said.

"I know a place we can hide his corpse," I offered. "It's in the Human Realms. No one will ever think to look for him there."

He kissed me again. Then leaning on those massive arms, brought his lips further down my body. Down my neck, collarbone, across my breasts, taking his time with each nipple. Biting it and then sucking away the sting. All the while making little noises at the back of his throat, somewhere between growling and whimpering. He moved his kisses along my stomach, skipping over my knickers area. Kneeling on the ground next to the bed, he pushed my thighs apart, taking the sensitive, tender inner flesh into his mouth between his teeth. Straddling the perfect line between pleasure and pain. His beard both tickled and scratched. He switched to the other thigh, running the thickness of his tongue upwards to the outer frill of my underwear.

My whole body trembled with the sheer anticipation of having that gorgeous face so close to the promise land. He licked right up the centre of my knickers, through the damp gusset. By the movement his shoulder made, and the way his bicep flexed, I knew he was palming the head of his cock. He buried his nose against my entrance and dragged his face upwards until his mouth came to rest over my clit. He sucked me through the fabric. The noise that escaped my throat was entirely new.

How do I breathe again?

"These are ruined," he growled, sliding the tip of a horn between the elastic and my flesh, and moving his head upwards, shredding through my underwear as though they were made of paper. "I'm keeping these." I couldn't see, didn't have the strength to lift my eyes anymore, but I knew he had tucked them into his pocket.

Then his hands were back on my thighs, holding them open and he buried his face into my pussy. Raking his tongue up one side and down the other. Slow, languid, aching. Teasing tiny circles around my clit, before sinking it inside my entrance. My hips greedily thrust against his face, my fingers ripping into the bedsheets. He replaced his tongue with his finger, and took my clit in his mouth, between his teeth, and sucked hard.

Five seconds tops and I'd lost any control I may have had. Was I screaming? Were those slasher-pic sound effects coming from me? Yes. Yes, they were. What's more, I couldn't seem to stop them. He'd managed to unlock a mode of pleasure in me I'd previously been unaware existed. Gods, he was ludicrously good at this. And no matter how long I wanted to stretch it out for, I knew I was running dangerously fast towards release.

He moaned onto the swollen bud of my sex, the vibrations travelling right up into my belly, and before I'd even worked out what was happening, before I could tell him to slow down, I was tumbling over the edge of a magnitude eight orgasm. The exquisite explosion sending shockwaves of pleasure throughout my body, up my spine, down into each toe. Lasting longer than any climax I'd had before. Horns continued to suck me through each spasm and tremor, his fingers still gently pumping into me, not letting up for a second.

When I regained my composure, Horns knelt above me again, his hair falling forwards, his face slick with my arousal. "Fuck, Peaches. That was . . . I almost came in my pants."

His cock, still trapped in the waistband of his trousers, had shucked the top elastic of his underpants. The head, proudly poking free as if winking hello. Shining, throbbing, and copiously leaking pre-cum.

"Now can I get it out?" I asked.

Chapter 27

Joey

He bit his lip, his expression hesitant. "I didn't bring any condoms. I didn't think it would ever—"

"Oh, I did!" I yelled, ducking under his arm, and running over to my suitcase next to the wardrobe. I seized the shining yellow box and brought them over to him.

He caught sight of it, his gaze travelling to the betusked and immensely proud looking grey man illustrated on the front. His eyes momentarily grew large, and he pulled his smirk between his teeth. "Ogre-sized?"

"Is that the wrong size?" Shit, trust me to make a hideously embarrassing mistake like this. I hid my face, not sure whether I should feel ashamed or disappointed.

He took the box. His smile never faltered. "No, it's the right size. It's just . . . You're truly amazing." He cupped the back of my head and kissed me again. I could smell my arousal all over his face. So fucking hot.

"How do you want to do this?" I asked.

"Probably best if you ride me, then you can take as much of me as you want."

I nodded, but I already knew that would be all of him.

He removed his trousers and kicked them away from the bed. "Okay?" he said, hooking his fingers into the elastic waistband of his underwear, the head of his cock still eagerly breaking free.

"Wait, give me a second," I said. I realised I needed to ready myself. I'd seen the outline of it several times, felt it against me, watched it when he woke up and shot to his knees on the bed, and while the rest of his body shrank by a few feet, his morning-glory-stiffened cock remained alarmingly in proportion to his bull form. I took a few deep breaths. "Yeah, go for it."

He yanked his underwear down, and I simply forgot how to breathe. I may have even laughed. Any other man would have balked at my laughter, but no, not Horns. Right then, he had no reason to feel shy. He was big. Like, I knew he was big, but, okay, this might be painful. I stared opened mouthed at it. I mean, as far as dicks went, it was a nice-looking dick. Long, thick, vein-corded, smooth, oddly tan like his arms, like maybe he worked naked, which . . . no he wouldn't do that. Would he? No, definitely not, but maybe a visit to the timber yard was in order.

He sat himself upright against the iron railings of the headboard and rolled a condom down the entire length of his cock. Then he reached forward and lifted me onto his lap.

How was he so strong?

Right, lumberjack minotaur. He was used to lugging around logs all day.

"Uh, are we just not going to talk about how fucking massive you are?"

He smiled, his fingers winding themselves into my hair, and he pulled me down for another kiss. "I don't enter you until you're ready for me. Even if that's not today. I don't care how long I have to wait."

"Horns, I think this thing in my chest is going to kill me if I don't fuck you right this instant."

"Oh, thank Gods."

I shifted my weight up onto my knees and grabbed his cock with my fist. My fingers wouldn't meet. *Gods*. I couldn't get my thumb and finger to touch. I swallowed. He grinned. Damn him for being so adorable at a time like this.

I dragged my hand up his impressive length, squeezing the head, bringing it back down. Stroking him a few times, testing out his size. He sucked his breath in, watching my touch, his hips just barely twitching, as though he had no agency over them. I leaned up higher still and positioned the tip right at my entrance. His hands cradled my ass, massaging my cheeks, pulling them gently apart in a bid to open my sex. Then I lowered myself slowly onto him. He slid in more comfortably than I imagined he would, my pussy still dripping from my earlier orgasm, taking the sting off that first stretch.

His head lolled back onto the railings, and he let out a groan that reverberated through the entire room. I greedily drank in the unobscured view of him, staring at his body. The column of his throat, his jawline, somewhat hidden by his short beard, his collarbone, his chest, those abdominal muscles, his navel, and the veins that pointed downwards to his magnificent cock. How could one person be so unapologetically perfect?

I braced against his perfect torso, and lowered myself further, taking more and more of him until I had sheathed him to the hilt, and I had no breath left in me.

He opened his eyes partway, need clouding his vision. "Peaches, you're fucking amazing."

I was so full. Fuller than I'd ever been. Pushing all the air out of my lungs full. Rolling my eyes backwards full. Possession at a séance full. I rocked my hips forward, taking stock of the way he moved within me. The way he pressed against the walls of my pussy, against my cervix, my g-spot. A high-pitched whine escaped my lips, and I began gently grinding. Horns met each of my movements with his own languid thrusts. The pace, lazy at first, gradually built, pleasure corkscrewed in my belly.

The bond in my chest was singing. This was what it wanted. What I needed. Maybe all along it was actually my wingman, and now was simply cheering from the side-lines, no longer painful, but extremely pleasant.

Without disrupting the rhythm, he took both of my hands in his and lifted them above his head. "Now you can touch the horns."

I did, wrapping my fingers around them and stroking them softly. They were smooth and hot, not cool like bone, like I'd been imagining. His reaction was immediate. His cock jerked inside of me, his eyes rolled themselves shut and his upward thrust nearly shot me off the bed.

"Oh." So, that was what happened when you touched them.

I ran my hands over the length of them, learning, by his whimpers, and increasingly desperate rutting, how he liked it best. Rough stroking grips near the base, I decided.

"Joey, Joey," he said over and over, gasping out my real name. He was getting frantic now, his hands grabbing at my curves, fingers sinking into flesh, his breaths staccato, cock pistoning into me. "Joey, slow down. Joey." Though, he made no attempt to slow things himself.

"I can't stop," I yelled, reaching forward, and seizing the railings, because if I didn't ground myself right then I would have floated up to the ceiling like an overpriced theme park balloon.

"Get your hand down there. Play with your clit. I can't go much longer."

"I—I don't think I need to." It was already building up around me. My second orgasm. I couldn't slow down, I couldn't stop, I couldn't do anything but slam my body onto his over and over. My thighs slapping against his hips, the filthy squelching noises as he pounded into me, the muscles in his stomach spasming as he fought for self-control.

"Joey. Fuck. I'm gonna—I'm gonna—" He raked his breaths in through clenched teeth. The head of his cock swelled. The walls of my pussy tightened.

"Let it happen," I said, echoing his words from earlier.

His arms closed around me, pulling my whole body to his, while he hammered it home in a series of rapid, erratic upward thrusts. Building faster and faster. Harder and harder. Robbing me of the ability to take an inward breath.

His back curved, he stiffened and then I felt the life leave him. He growled his orgasm into my neck, shaking the bed, shaking the entire room with its resonance. His hot release ripped from his cock over and over, hitting my walls, as the pressure that had been coiled in my belly sprung free. My thighs lost their bones, while my stomach muscles seized tight, my pussy clinging to his length. I tried to bury my face in his hair, but he clamped his hands over my cheeks and pushed a gap between our bodies so that he could watch as my expression contorted with my climax.

"Oh, Peaches, baby," he whispered, waiting until the last spasm of euphoria had waned.

I collapsed beside him on the bed, pressing my palm to his sweat-slick stomach, and he wrapped his arms around me once again. Neither of us capable of words. He kissed the top of my head and trailed his finger along my hip. And we simply smiled at each other. Occasionally bubbles of laughter escaping, like neither of us could believe what had just happened. Eventually, he removed the condom, tied up the end, and dropped it down on the floor. I snuggled into his big spoon while we waited for our breaths to return to normal and the aftershocks to subside.

"Peaches?"

"Yeah?"

He paused for a few moments. "I . . . Fuck . . . Just wow."

Chapter 28

Taurin

I had no intention of letting her rest. I promised her I would break her, and I was already hard again. Nudging her in the back with my insistence.

"Too soon for round two?" she asked. The bond was already asking for more. Demanding more.

I carried her to the hot tub, got in beside her, and fucked her under the water. With my tail. Because I probably only had one more blow-out left in me before I succumbed to sexhaustion and descended into a three-hundred-year slumber, and I wasn't ready for tonight to be over. Nothing robbed my energy as much as Seeing Red or coming. I watched her from the opposite side of the tub. My own private show. Gods, she was perfect. Her fingers gripped the shaft as she pumped the bulbous head in and out. Her tits bobbed up to the surface, round and begging to be sucked. Her other hand dipping below the water to massage her clit at the same time. It was all I could do to stop myself from exploding there and then. Or from stroking myself into the next realm. And only the top half of her was visible.

When she came, she cried out my name, Taurin, not Horns. If I hadn't been sat down, I would have crumpled to my knees. I was on top of her before the second syllable, trying to swallow her benediction.

After the last tremor had ebbed and she withdrew my tail, I took her by the hand and guided her to the space between the tub and the panoramic window. All three feet of it. Hard tiled flooring, floor to ceiling windows, the neon city pulsating below us.

"On your knees. Against the glass," I commanded.

"Oh, he's bossy in the bedroom," she said, flipping her hair over her shoulder and dropping to the ground without hesitation, her ass popping out in the most delectable way as she bobbed down.

If I only had one more go left in me, I was going to do this how I wanted. How I'd pictured every night while I fucked my hand to the thought of her in that little dress with the peaches. From behind. Hard. Deep. Furious.

"Now that I know you can take me, I'm not going easy on you." I slipped into the gap behind her and with a sturdy knee, I knocked her thighs further apart, causing her balance to pitch forward, her hands to brace herself against the window and her backside to 'present' to me.

The fucking shape of her. That waist, those hips, that ass, dripping with water from the tub. For the millionth time that evening, I could have blown my load just by looking at her.

I ran a rough finger along her slit, trailing her wetness around her entrance. With my other hand, I gripped my cock and stroked it, dragging pre-cum down the length. I positioned it right at her opening. The heat from her arousal attempting to suck me in like a vacuum.

"Fuck, condoms!" I said.

"I'm on birth control. And I'm clean."

"Before you, I hadn't had sex in two years," I offered. *Why though?*

She glanced over her shoulder smirking, and looked me up and down before she said, "Fuck me, Taurin."

My knees threatened to give way at the sound of my name on her lips. "Tell me if it's too much."

"I thought you weren't going easy on me."

I didn't give another warning before I drove into her. Her half-gasp, half scream echoed across the tiles, her breath fogging on the window. Her ass slapped onto my stomach, and I was already trembling with the sweet dragging sting of my pending release.

Oh no, this was going to be over very quickly.

I grabbed her hip and pulled out, slamming back in. Out, in, out, in. Mesmerised by the places where we became one. Watching her pussy cling to my cock. Savouring the tremors along my length. That ass, Gods, that ass. I closed the gap between the top halves of our bodies, pressing my chest against her back, taking a breast in one hand, wrapping the other around the base of her neck.

She flattened her hands and forearms against the window, pushing her ass into me until I bottomed out. I couldn't refrain my hips from bucking faster and faster. My knees crunched on the tiles. They'll be bruised tomorrow. *Fucking worth it*. I was stampeding towards the climax. I had to refocus my thoughts. Stop thinking about how good it felt. About how good *she* felt. Right, cleaning the toilet. *Good.* Mal's broken table. *Oh, this was working.* Tina snapping my horn as a kid and telling me it would never grow back. Dima sucking my wrist after I'd smoked weed, then promptly throwing up all over me. *This was working—*

Fuck. I accidentally looked at the reflection in the glass and saw her. Perfect tits, perfect stomach, perfect agonised expression.

I wouldn't hold out for much longer.

"Are you close, baby? Want me to flick your clit?"

"Gods, Taurin. I'm so close. I think I'm gonna—"

Before she even finished her sentence, spasms from her sex were travelling up the length of my cock, her head falling back onto my shoulder, her cry of ecstasy filling the room, bouncing off the walls. I held her hip with one hand, braced myself against the window with the other, and fucked her. Properly fucked her. Ten, twelve more furious thrusts and my orgasm was torn from me. I cried out into her flesh, spurting my release inside her, filling her entirely, over and over, painting her thighs with the excess.

Afterwards, we sat back against the wall of the tub. Peaches nestled between my legs, my arms around her middle. Above the rooftop of the adjacent hotel, a blinding white firework detonated, followed by a rainbow of explosions. We watched the entire show, or as much of it as we could see from our cramped floor position, silent, naked, messy, and dripping.

Until the moment Peaches tilted her head up, looked me in the eye and said, "I would've had three more orgasms by now if I chose your flatmate."

It was meant as a joke, but what I actually heard was, *I chose you.*

She chose me. Of all the people in the Eight and a half Kingdoms, she chose me.

Or she didn't. The bond chose us for each other.

The bond.

. . .

Fuck! The bond. The herd!

I fucked her without a condom. I came inside of her.

What have I done?

I've accidentally married her.

I awoke with one of Peaches' hands caressing the fur on my neck and the other trailing a gentle finger against the shaft of a horn. We were in bed. Morning fervently pushed its way into the room through the open curtains. She was naked still, so was I. Hard, too. Obviously.

"Good morning, beautiful," she whispered to me.

I instantly shifted into my human form.

"You don't have to do that. I like all the versions of you."

I didn't fully register what she'd said. My stomach somersaulted, while my mind screamed at me, *You married her. The herd will consider us married. You didn't even ask her first.*

"I had four orgasms last night," she said, apparently unaware of the turmoil coursing through my head.

What do I do? What should I say?

I forced my voice into its usual baritone, scraping away any nervous squeak that might edge its way out. "Yeah, yeah. I know. You wish you picked Goldie."

She laughed. "Ew, no. That's not at all what I was going to say. I only meant isn't it time I evened out the score a little?"

"Oh." The bond, which had so far been quietly satiated, purred in excitement.

She pushed me onto my back, straddled me, and began trailing kisses across my chest, running her tongue down the ridges of my muscles, down my stomach, along my pelvis. Inching closer and closer to my cock.

I needed to tell her before she started doing *that*. Before all intelligent thought was wiped from my mind.

"I don't think I can fit all of it in my mouth," she said, inspecting my dick like a detective looking for fingerprints. "But I'll give it a good go."

Tell her now. Tell her it was an accident. Beg for forgiveness. Do anything you can to keep her. Do not scare her off. Give her oral instead. "Peaches, you don't have to—"

My sentence cut short as she wrapped her fingers around the base and ran the flat of her tongue along the seam. My lame whimper of a protestation barely made it past my lips. She dribbled saliva onto it — *she fucking spat on it, come on* — and took the entire head in her mouth, whirling her tongue around it like she was trying to stop an ice cream from dripping down its cone.

Any resolve I may have had obliterated when I looked down and saw her beautiful, soft, naked body curled between my legs, lips sheathed around my cock, face pinched into a perfect frown. And I could only marvel at her. At everything. She'd slept next to a bull for two nights, a massive disgusting bull, and she was still here, fucking me with her mouth. This was as good as it got. She liked me enough to stick around. She liked me despite my outbursts, despite my habit of shifting into a bulldozer.

A hopeful voice rose inside. *Maybe she won't mind being accidentally married to a big angry cow. Maybe she'll be happy about it.* But I squashed the thought. It was too much to hope for. The best I could aim for was that she wouldn't run miles in the other direction once she found out. Fuck, would she run back to the Human Realms? *Maybe you shouldn't tell her.*

I pulled myself back in the moment, my thoughts immediately turning to liquid, as she began suckling, her hand pumping the base. My orgasm was already building, sweet release biting at the edges, slowly consuming me. The noises she made against the length of me were sending me into a tailspin, vibrating right up my shaft, all the way into my spine.

It was when I looked down again and saw her other hand between her thighs that I knew I was past the point of no return.

"Joey. Stop. I'm gonna come," I squeezed out.

But she didn't relent. If anything, she sped up. Her moans became louder, more frequent, more resonant, and I knew she'd reached that point as well.

"Joey, I'm gonna come. Joey." I didn't know if she was the type of girl that was okay with this part of oral. "Oh, Gods, Joey."

And then she was whining her own orgasm against my cock, the head hitting the back of her oscillating throat, and I could do nothing except wrap my arms around the iron railings of the headboard, growl my release into the cavernous room, and empty myself into her mouth.

She continued to suck me through each blow, each jerk, each aftershock, finally collapsing on her back next to me, in a breathy, boneless heap.

"Did you swallow?" I asked, feeling, for the first time in a while, shy.

"Oh, whoops. Did you want some?"

I laughed. *Gods, I loved her.*

Aaaand I was instantly back to panicking about last night.

KNOCK KNOCK.

"You have got to be fucking kidding me."

As predicted, Russ' voice filled the room. "Good morning, you two lovebirds. This is your first and final warning that the bus will leave in ten minutes."

We both let out simultaneous sighs and got to our feet. I watched Peaches get dressed, red high waisted shorts, a red vest top and a red and white striped cardigan type thing, before slinging on my own clothes, jeans, and a grey t-shirt. Half of me still coasting high off my surprise morning blow job, and the other half dissolving into utter panic. Then we ran around the room flinging everything into our cases before rushing out to the lifts, chucking our key cards in the check-out box, and running full pelt across the asphalt to where twenty or so pissed-off looking creatures waited.

"Our winners have finally deigned to make an appearance," said Russ. He winked at Peaches and me, and my face grew warm. Just how long had he been stood outside that door before he knocked? "Let's give them first choice of seats, shall we? Winners' prerogative."

Everyone else groaned. The human driver tossed our cases into the hold, and we climbed aboard.

"Let's get the backseat," I said to Peaches. "I'm going to take a nap."

Of course, she knew what that would mean. She flashed me the biggest smile. I was chucking our backpacks in the overhead bins when Clarke pushed past me.

"Hey," said Peaches. "You can't sit there." He had already plonked his enormous lion backside on the bench. "My boyfriend is going to take a nap, and he needs all that space. Unless you fancy having a nine-foot minotaur squashing you up against the window."

My boyfriend.

She had said she wanted a relationship. That she wanted an Us. So I shouldn't have been surprised. But this public declaration felt like a huge step. For both of us.

"Ugh, whatever," said Clarke, looking me up and down and evidently deciding it wasn't worth the fight. Obviously. He was a gryphon, not a dragon.

I sat my ass in the middle of the back row and Peaches took the seat closest to the window, her legs bridging the back of the row in front. I removed my t-shirt.

"Damn, sir," she said, looking at my naked torso. "I'm never going to get bored with that view." I watched her greedy expression as her eyes lingered near the waistband of my jeans. "Why do you even bother wearing a shirt? Horus doesn't, your flatmates don't."

"I . . . "

I didn't know what to say. Because humans wear them? Because I only that minute realised perhaps I'd been trying to appear as close to a human as possible. It almost made me not want to shift. But I felt safe, ready to be myself in front of her. She had already accepted my bull form. This just felt as though we were cementing it. "Okay?"

She patted her lap. I took a deep breath and shifted, laying down on my back with my head on her thighs, my horn snaking round by her hip.

If she could accept my bull form, maybe she could accept the marriage thing, I told myself, trying to smother the icky feeling slithering around in my stomachs.

She smiled down at me, genuine, loving, accepting, and the ick dissolved like cotton candy in rain. "Hi," she whispered, and immediately sunk her fingers into the fur on the top of my head. My eyes closed themselves.

After a few seconds, I opened them. "Did you mean what you said earlier? That I'm your boyfriend?" I was glad she couldn't see the blush through the fur.

She placed her hand on my bare chest, and I realised she did it to feel the bond vibrating as she said, "Of course."

I slept all the way back to Remy.

Chapter 29

Taurin

Peaches drove us from the uni to my place. In my human form, I just about fit in her car. The tips of my horns brushed against the underside of the roof, but she didn't seem bothered that I might rip the fabric, even after she'd witnessed what I did to her knickers.

"Do you have to get back to your flat right away?" I asked. "Or, if you'd rather come to mine? Stay the night?"

By answer, she unbuckled her belt and practically jumped out of the car.

All the blinds and curtains were closed, which meant Dima was still up. We found all three of my flatmates in the living room. Goldie and Mal shirtless on either end of the sofa, and Dima in his usual corner, can of Blooze in his hand with a straw, because, you know, sucking.

Mal's face lit up when Peaches walked through the doors. Goldie sucked at his teeth.

"Everyone, this is Joey. My . . . girlfriend." Okay, that was weird. Good weird. Still weird though. I almost stopped myself from saying it.

"Hi," she said. And to her credit, I could smell no fear on her.

"This is Mal," I said, as the incubus leapt to his feet, ran over, and pulled her into a bear hug, his twitching wings betraying his affected unbothered expression. "Mal's the one responsible for the suite at the Pegasus Grand."

"Nice. Thanks," said Peaches, as Mal said, "Busted." Though he didn't show even a modicum of shame.

"It's great to finally meet you. You're more beautiful than Taur had alluded to."

"No." I placed a hand against his bare chest. "No incubus-ing my girlfriend."

Mal raised an eyebrow. It read *I could try, but I'd fail*.

"This is Dima," I said, as the vampire floated towards us. Fuck me, could my flatmates not even assimilate human traits for a few minutes while we got the introductions over with?

Dima lifted Peaches' hand to his lips and placed a drawn-out kiss to her knuckles. I recognised the overlong silence for what it was.

"Dima's an unregistered telepath," I said. Both he and Goldie flinched. Mal gave a bark of a laugh. "If you're going to claw around her mind uninvited, she ought to be aware so that she can try to fight it."

"I can fight it?" Peaches asked.

"Uh, probably not," I admitted. "Humans usually can't. I can't."

As if to prove a point, Dima slid into my mind. *Mate, I didn't claw around. I swear. She's practically shoving the info at me. I couldn't help it. I saw everything you did this weekend. You dirty, dirty bull. Fuck man, that was hot. I can show you from her POV later if you want?*

Stay out of her head, I replied.

Sneaky of you to hide it from us that she's your mate. I was about to swear at him when he added, *I'm really happy for you. And only a teeny bit jealous. I'll try to be good.*

Thanks, mate.

"And that's Goldie," I said, pointing to the now scowling, blonde fae on the sofa before the mind-reader could clock me on the marriage thing. He lifted his hand

and immediately let it drop. I guess that was the best we would get from him. I turned to Peaches. "Do you want some food?"

She absentmindedly rubbed her belly, neither of us had eaten anything since the measly canapés they served us during the ceremony. "And then I need a shower, if that's okay?"

Yeah, she does, said Dima. *You both stink of sex, by the way.*

I couldn't help the grin that crossed my face. We made to leave, but Mal caught my arm in his.

"I'll meet you in the kitchen in a sec," I said to Peaches. She nodded, not missing a beat, and walked out without me.

The second she was gone, Mal wrapped his arms around me and squeezed hard. I'm sure if he'd have been tall enough, he would have patted the top of my head. "What's wrong?" he said, obviously sensing my undercurrent of apprehension.

"I fucked up," I whispered.

Mal looked at Dima. Dima looked at me. "He performed his herd's marriage ritual, and now they are tied to an unbreakable bond. And she didn't give her consent."

"They're fated mates," Mal said, nonchalantly. "Of course they're tied with an unbreakable bond."

"But she's human," I said. "She didn't know what she was getting herself into. And I forgot until . . . afterwards. I got carried away."

Goldie made a disgusted sound, as if his life didn't revolve around fucking.

Mal placed his hand on my arm. "If you're worried about how she will take the news, then buy her a ring, do it the human way too."

"I can get her ring size for you," Dima offered.

A ring, yeah. Propose to her. Like humans do. And marry her the human way as well. That way she'd get the dress and the cake and . . . whatever else it was people had at weddings. Oh Gods, the dancing. But it would be both our cultures entwined. Human tradition meets minotaur. A ring. I liked it.

Goldie muttered under his breath. Pretty sure he said, "Fucking humans."

"What's up with you?" I asked.

Dima answered, "He's pissed off because now you've found your mate, you're permanently off his list of potential fucks."

"Go suck yourself, Dima," Goldie spat, getting to his feet, and marching out the room. The front door slammed behind him.

Mal shrugged. "He'll come around." He turned to me. "Congrats, bro."

I offered them both a smile. And then I left the pair of them to find my mate.

"Isn't it illegal to be an unregistered telepath?" Peaches asked later that evening.

We were sitting against the headrest of my bed, my arm over her shoulder, a bucket of popcorn between us, and a movie playing that neither of us was watching. I had made some pasta, which we ate with a glass of Mal's wine, then we took a shower together. We fucked in the shower. Her back against the tiles, her legs around my waist. Then again, on my bed. On her back, legs draped over my shoulders. She liked it deep, I was learning.

She now sat in one of my t-shirts with nothing on her legs, and I wore only sweatpants. A yin-yang of grey cotton and bare flesh.

"It's completely illegal. But Dima's never been one to follow rules. He went to gaol for a century, and still no one found out he was a telepath."

"Is there really nothing I can do to stop him raping my brain?"

"No, sorry." I tried to look apologetic. "When you're around Dima, try not to think about anything you don't want him seeing. I'm pretty sure he doesn't deliberately try to read our thoughts. Sometimes I end up projecting things into his mind, whether he wants to see it or not."

She bit her lip. "Oh. Whoops. I've been non stop thinking about last night." The bond purred and she laughed. "How much do you think he saw?"

"Uh . . ."

"Actually, I don't even care. I'm not ashamed. That was the best weekend of my life."

"Mine too," I said. Although I still had plans to make Dima shit his pants later. "There is a way to tell. When mind readers go into your thoughts. You get this feeling, like someone with minty breath is blowing into your brain."

"Sure. I know what to expect now." She grabbed a handful of popcorn and shovelled it into her mouth. "Why was Jizzy Jeff so off with me?"

"Ha, Jizzy Jeff. He's just jealous of you, I think, or maybe of us. It probably would have been easier for him if you weren't human, but . . ." I shrugged, not sure how to finish my sentence.

"Right, he hates humans."

"He thinks he does. He doesn't though. It's complicated." I wanted to tell her he'd spent six-hundred years fucking his way through life, and I knew for a fact that part of him was jealous of Mal, and now me, for finding our mates. And another part of him was terrified that, like Mal, he'd match with a human, and lose them too soon. That he uses no-strings hook-ups to avoid his biggest phobias.

"I think it's easy to blame humans," I said, instead. "Monsters like fae, and warlocks, and even my herd are so quick to claim humans the root cause of their problems. They're all obsessed with this notion that humans are out to steal magic that doesn't belong to them. What they seem too happy to overlook is that humans don't need fae magic. They have their own. It's called industry, engineering, design, whatever. They've built machines to do everything. Build skyscrapers, cure disease, provide knowledge at your fingertips. Folk like Goldie forget they use human 'magic' more than their own. Every fucking day. They drive human cars, they have human phones, they even take human medicine, and smoke human drugs. The cognitive dissonance is unreal. Without humans, there would be no Borderlands. Goldie would be up in a cave somewhere in the Kingdom of the Fae fucking his cousins. They should be thanking humans."

"That politics degree coming in handy?"

I laughed. "Sorry, sometimes I can go off on one."

"Don't ever stop," she said, looping her hand around my neck and pulling me down for a kiss.

Her phone — which was plugged into my charger next to the bed — buzzed. She broke the kiss to lean over and peer at the screen.

"Hey, you know that you're officially my boyfriend now?" She fiddled with a strand of her hair. "Is it too soon . . ."—*No, it's not too soon. Whatever it is you want, it's not too soon. You wanna get human married? Not too soon. You wanna have babies? Not too soon. Wanna put a down-payment on a three-bed lakeside cottage?*—"For you to come to the Human Realms with me and meet my parents?"

I take it back. Way too soon for that.

"Uh . . ."

"I'll just tell them no."

"What is it for?"

"It's just a small family Harvest Fest dinner with my mum and dad. Harvest Fest, it's kind of a big deal to them. Well, to Mum, anyway."

I took a deep breath. I needed to show her I would be there for her. Like she was there for me by the docks. That, above everything, I was hers. And hell, I could even make this work to my advantage. I could propose to her in the Human Realms. Get the ring this week and confess it all at once . . .

"Can you see the stars from your folks' house?"

"Of course," she said with a huge smile.

Perfect.

"I'll come. They know what I am, right?"

She pursed her lips together. "I'll tell them now."

Chapter 30

Joey

Hell-Bitch didn't even thank me when I handed her the cheque for three more months' back payment. Miserable fucking bitch.

I pressed the bell. Ash answered the door before the bing of the *bing-bong* had finished.

"Well?" he said.

"I've sent your dress to be dry-cleaned. We may have got some . . . juices on it."

He clapped his hands together in glee. "Come in. How many times?"

"Honestly, I've lost count."

Lauren brought us a tray of our usual espresso martinis.

"Tell me everything," he said, once we'd snuggled into our respective seats with our respective cats and their respective number of legs.

So, I did. Every single detail. What the hotel suite was like. How his flatmate had somehow switched the bookings. *"Ah, only one bed. My favourite trope."* What we did on that only one bed. What Horns did to me. What happened in the hot tub with his tail. And against the window. In the shower at his flat. On his bed, and every time since then. How big he was. What happened when I touched his horns. *"Oh, yes, they can be ever so sensitive. All horned creatures, in fact."* How we were officially boyfriend and girlfriend, and my real, honest feelings for him.

"Ash, I think I love him. Like, maybe I wanna spend forever with him. Fuck, this isn't me. I've never had a relationship last more than six weeks before. I've already known him longer than any of my past boyfriends. You know, the other day I was wondering if our babies would have horns." I let out a frustrated whine that made Four-Feet flinch.

"Have you told him?"

"Ha! I'm not stupid. He might not be human, but he's still a man."

"Fair enough," Ash said.

"He's coming home with me for Harvest Fest."

"To the Human Realms? To meet your parents?"

"You think it's too soon?"

"No, not at all. Not with your deplorably short human lifespans. Better to get it over and done with, I suppose. I'm sure they'll love him. He sounds like a gentleman."

"I'm sure you'll get an introduction soon, don't worry."

Ash threw his head back and laughed. "Ah, you know all my little tricks. Will your sister be there? How long are you staying?"

"No thank Gods, just my parents. And just the one night. I'm not sure it'd be fair to subject him to my dad for any longer than a few hours."

Ash seemed pensive. He ambled over to the desk by the window and rummaged in the top drawer for something. "I was wrong about him. I judged him too quickly. They say a bull never changes its spots but, in this instance, he has, or perhaps, I have." I kept my mouth shut. Didn't want to ruin the moment. "What I'm trying to tell you is, I'm sorry I assumed he was a mindless savage. I take it all back. I think he'll make you very happy. And your horned babies will be utterly adorable. But you've got to promise me you'll still visit every Thursday for our weekly literary boink-fests."

"Always."

He pressed a small metallic object into my palm. A key. "My beach house is only about an hour from your parents'."

We had moved the passenger seat as far down and back as it would go. Taurin still looked cramped, but all things considered, it wasn't too bad. The drive down to Dinlow in the Human Realms would take about three hours at my speed. Four, if I followed the letter of the law, which I would try. Like, really try.

Horns seemed nervous. His smiles only lasted seconds, his banter clipped, his swallowing audible, and every now and then he idly palmed a lump in his jeans pocket, one I knew was unequivocally too small to be his junk.

"Should I wear my tail in or out?" he asked.

"Out. I don't want you to be uncomfortable."

He responded with a nod and another swallow.

"You'll be fine. They'll love you." I placed my hand on his thigh.

"How can you know that?"

Because I do. Because it's impossible not to love you.

I wanted to tell him. It was just . . . other than my parents and, before we'd had our big fight, Tilly, there was only one other person I'd ever told I loved. My first boyfriend. And, at the time, I really thought I did. Looking back and comparing it to what I feel now, it's obvious it was never love. Not even close.

Still, it didn't remove all the sting of our breakup. Less than two weeks after I said I love you, I walked in on him balls deep in my little sister in the garage. I've not said it to another man since. Too afraid to commit, to invest.

Tilly and Wyn married six months later. I wasn't sure if that made it easier to accept, or worse.

I would tell Horns, though. I needed to. I planned to take him to Ash's beach house for a couple of nights on our way home. I'll tell him then.

"Because they love me," I said, eventually. "I've told them all about you. They know what to expect." I thought of Dad and an uneasy feeling coiled in my stomach. "A confession, though."

He snapped his head towards me.

"My dad used to be quite anti-mythic. He's . . . He's improving. But, well . . . he might say a few things that aren't exactly PC. I don't want you to think they're about you specifically. He just . . . uses the wrong terminology, or, I don't know, he might try to overcompensate, like go overboard to prove he's not a speciesist anymore."

To my surprise, Horns began smiling.

"What's so funny?"

"Nothing. You're so cute," he said. I frowned at him. I wasn't trying to be cute, I was trying to forewarn him. "Don't worry, I can handle bigots. Or ex bigots. I'm used to it." He squeezed my hand which was still resting on his thigh, and my stomach twisted. He should never have had to be used to that.

We approached Borderlands' border-crossing. Humans travelling straight through needed only to take one of the four left-hand lanes, scan their paperwork, and be on their merry ways. It felt strange, for the first time in my life, to veer off and join a queue to the right.

"Good afternoon, paperwork please," said a devastatingly gorgeous, uniformed succubus.

I handed our documents out of the window. She scanned mine with a bleepy handheld thing. "Josephina Silver. Human. Birthday, twenty-third April," she said to herself. "Very good. Any prohibited items?"

"No," I said.

"Live animals?"

"No."

"Any weapons? Knives, guns, staffs, wands?"

"No."

"Amulets? Cursed tablets?"

"No."

"Any human remains or body parts?"

"Ew, no."

"Any drugs?"

"No," I said. Horns shifted his weight.

"Either of you showing any symptoms of siren flu? Any rashes? Fevers? Unusual clucking? Any irrepressible urge to stand beside a body of water and lure sailors to their untimely deaths?"

"Nope, not in the past six months."

"Excellent." She pulled Horns' paperwork to the top and scanned it with a bleep. "Taurin. Minotaur . . ." She paused, then bent down to look at Horns through my window. "No way!" Horns looked alarmed and confused, his brows shooting up into his hairline. "I know Mal! He and I . . . go way back. Seraphina. I met you, yeah, at his seven-hundredth birthday party. What was it now, about five years ago?"

Taurin hastily schooled his features into something resembling recognition, but I knew full well he had no clue who she was. It made my heart sing that he could so easily forget this phenomenally gorgeous creature before him. With her perfect fuchsia skin, pouty as fuck lips, and those tits, which I realised she had perched on the edge of my window frame. Her succubi allure in full swing, glowing from every pore. Hell, even I wanted to lean forward and lick her. And yet, he only had eyes for me.

The thing in my chest purred. He shot me a quick glance and returned his attention to the pink goddess. "Right. Yeah, Seraphina. Nice to see you again."

"That was a night and a half, huh? And that other flatmate of yours, with the gold hair . . ." She chuckled and handed me the paperwork, evidently not requiring an answer to her musings. "Look straight ahead for your photo."

We did as she said. She pressed a button on a handheld remote. A bright flash detonated, though I'd never figured out where it originated.

"I'm supposed to ask you all these questions here, but you've already filled them out on your visas, so I'll let you and your wife be on your way." *Why does everyone keep calling me his wife?* "Tell Mal I still think about him. Oh, and happy birthday, Taurin."

I pulled away from border patrol. "It's your birthday?"

"Uh." He twisted his septum piercing.

"Why didn't you say? I didn't get you a present."

"I just hate fuss. And occasions." Right, of course he did.

"Well, I'll make it up to you after dinner," I said, wagging my eyebrows.

"Oh, yeah?" He couldn't hide his smile any longer. His eyes widened and lit up as he raked them over me.

"You can come on my back."

It had the immediate effect I was going for. My chest sung with his instant arousal.

"Wow! Simple, yet filthy."

Tits were too obvious. And I wouldn't do anything above the neckline. Not on purpose, at least. Better to surprise them. There was something primal about it. The position, the intimate privacy it offered. Animalistic even. He palmed the front of his jeans.

Bullseye.

His mood visibly brightened after that.

"Oh, shit," I said. Horns jumped in his seat, glancing at the ceiling to ensure the fabric hadn't been gouged. "That makes you a libra. Ah, it all makes so much sense."

His incredulous laughter shook the car. "To be honest, I was shitting myself that I wouldn't even be allowed over the border."

"Well, we're here now," I said. "Actually, I need to pee. Is it okay if we pull over?"

We had long since left the main highway leading to Pannor, the human capital city, and were now taking the winding country lanes that branched out to the smaller villages and hamlets and farmlands. I stopped the car in a quiet layby.

I'd already been imagining what our babies might look like, but it was still too early in our relationship to let him see me pee, so I ducked behind a bush. Horns peed openly, straight into a farmer's field. Also laughing his head off the whole time.

"What was so funny?" I asked as we got back in the car, and Horns applied hand sanitiser. *Where did he get hand sanitiser from?* It was so like him to have a secret portable stash of personal cleansing products.

"That was my first piss in the Human Realms."

I narrowed my eyes. "That still doesn't answer my question."

"I just . . . I always wanted to come to the Human Realms. Never thought in a million years I would. Thank you." He cupped my jaw with his palm and kissed me. I had to remind myself his hands were wet with sanitiser and not urine.

Gods, should I tell him now? said my stupid brain.

And spoil his happiness? I argued back. *Don't be such a bellend, Joey.*

"Hey Horns, tomorrow, after my parents' place, I was thinking I might take you to my friend's house by the beach for a couple of days?"

He squeezed the strange lump in his pocket again. "That's a lovely idea. Perfect, in fact. I'll message work and let them know I won't be in for a while."

"What is it that you keep touching?" I said. Horns' eyes grew wide. I remembered how he reacted when the succubus asked if we had drugs. "Is it weed?"

"Oh, yeah." His shoulders dropped in . . . relief? "I figured if things went badly with your folks, I would just fuck off and get high."

I laughed. "They won't. But you brought enough for me too, right?" I started the engine and pulled back onto the road. Only another hour until we hit Mum and Dad's.

Chapter 31

Taurin

Joey's house, not the house she grew up in, as she kept reminding me, but her folks' place was everything I'd imagined a human home to look like, and simultaneously, completely different. The style, I learned, was mock Tudor. The walls were painted with a pristine manila render and dark wooden beams criss-crossed through it. It had a thatched roof, for fuck's sake. Like a witch's storybook cottage.

Peaches took my hand in hers as we walked up the garden path towards the house, and the closer we got, the more I realised it was less than pristine. There were patches of plaster missing and a space near the woodshed that had been used to store bags of ready-mix cement and pallets of wood. There was a crack running the full length of the wall under a large bay window, and silver tape keeping one of the window frames in place.

Immediate panic set in. I got the feeling that an overzealous breath might bring about the building's destruction.

"Peaches, your folks' house looks kind of . . . delicate."

"It's been like this since they bought it. I keep telling them to sell it and get a new-build by the sea. It was supposed to be a doer-upper, but secretly my dad hates DIY."

And then, as though he'd heard mention of his name, the front door opened and out stepped a tall (for a human) white man with salt and pepper grey hair and an auburn beard. He stood with his arms folded across his chest. I palmed the lump burning a hole in my pocket. The ring.

Goldie, of all people, helped me pick it out.

"Hey," he had said one evening, burying both hands in his pockets. "Yeah, so, sorry I've been such a sex pest. I . . . You're . . . Mate, you're like my best friend. I should never have . . . I can't promise I won't still . . . But—"

"You wanna make it up to me?" I said, once I realised it was about as much of a complete apology as I'd get from him. He had nodded. "I need to buy Peaches a ring, a really nice one. It's a human thing. Will you help me choose? And then after, I'll make up for never letting you go down on me." His eyes lit up. "I promise you, this thing I'm thinking of is nearly as good as sex. Nearly."

We had gone to a human jewellery shop in the middle of the city. It barely seemed able to contain my oversized frame. Several glass cabinets were arranged in a horseshoe shape, and the shop smelled of window cleaner and recently vacuumed carpets.

"I'm afraid we don't carry your size," said the four-and-a-half-foot human salesperson named Gellen. They looked at Goldie. "Or your partner's."

"I'm buying for a human. Her ring size is N," I said.

"Excellent," said Gellen, their teeth pulled over their lips in an expression I couldn't decipher.

"Dima," I said to Goldie's questioning look. I had asked the vampire, just this once, to go into Joey's mind and find her ring size. Turned out, she once went ring shopping with her mum and sister about a decade ago. Dima said he thought she may have been bored in the memory, and had largely ignored her sister, busying herself instead by measuring all her fingers and toes. Conveniently only retaining the wedding finger details.

Goldie prowled around, glancing down into the cases next to the tills, before stopping short. "This one," he said, pointing to a piece in the dead centre of the cabinet.

"Sir, those are our antique pieces. They may be out of your price range."

The fae ignored the comment. "Can I try it on?"

The salesperson bumbled but unlocked the case and retrieved the ring. And as I got closer to the innocuous velvet box, I too knew that it was the one. Two narrow red stones sat on either side of a much larger pink, square-ish diamond. No, not pink, peach. Peach for Peaches. It was perfect.

He held out his pinky finger, and Gellen watched with bated breath as I slipped the ring on.

"Yes," said Goldie, fanning pretend tears with his other hand. "I'll human marry you."

And even though he wasn't Peaches, and none of the other conditions I'd imagined were present, heat prickled behind my eyes. I couldn't respond with anything other than a choked out laugh.

"We'll take it," he said on my behalf.

"Sir, that ring is twenty-eight-thousand silvers. It's antique rose gold, with an extremely rare peach diamond—"

But Gellen shut up then as Goldie threw his credit card onto the counter. "I've had a fair few years on this planet. I think I can afford it." He looked at me. "Pay me back whenever."

Afterwards, with almost my entire year's salary tucked irresponsibly into my front jeans pocket, I took my friend to Carly's and bought us both one of her famous falafel wraps with extra everything. He made the same climactic moans as Peaches did when he bit into his pitta.

"Why have I never eaten this before? I think I just got pregnant. Gods, human food. I fucking love human food."

We sat on the same bench as before and watched the sunset together.

"So, there'll be a wedding?"

"If she says yes."

"Of course she will. You're fated. And . . . You know . . . You're you."

"Thanks, mate." My throat suddenly felt too tight to swallow my food. I reached my arm out, draped it across his shoulders and dragged him into a reluctant-at-first hug.

The smile slowly blossomed across his face. He balled up his falafel wrapper and threw it with precision into the bin opposite. And before we left, I caught him slipping his business card between Carly's fingers as he grazed her knuckles with his lips.

Back in the present time, I watched open-mouthed as another Joey, thirty years older, came running out from the dilapidated building towards us, while the human man waited, pretzel-arms and brow furrowed, on the steps.

"Pudding! It's so good to see you," said older Joey, pulling my Joey into a huge hug.

"Horns, this is my mum," she said when they pulled apart. "Mum, this is Taurin."

"Oooh, pudding, he's so tall. You girls and your enormous men." And then before I knew it, she had her hand linked around my neck and had dragged me down into an uncommonly tight hug. "He smells good, too. Doesn't he smell good?" She pushed herself off me and patted my biceps. "Lovely big arms." Then she rubbed her thumb over my cheek, as though she were rubbing a fingerprint off a priceless vase and nodded to herself.

I realised this person stood in front of me was my future. Thirty years from now. She was the mirror of her daughter, or the other way around. A couple of inches shorter, and wider, but the same box-dyed red hair, the same rosy cheeks, the same slightly naughty edge to her smile. I wasn't mad about it. In fact, it pulled at something in my chest. Hope, excitement maybe, that I had my entire future with Peaches ahead of me.

"Call me Frankie, sweetie. Or mum, if you're brave enough," she said, and then linked her arm through her beaming daughter's and together they walked up the path to the house. "I love him already," I heard her whisper to Peaches.

"And this is my dad, Joe," Peaches said as we reached the front step.

He held out his hand, and I took it. I got the distinct impression he was trying to prove something with his grip, so for a second, I let him squish my hand.

"Nice to meet you, sir." He didn't return my sentiment. Or my smile. I realised how sweaty my hand had become and wiped it on my jeans. We headed inside.

The interior of the house was much the same as the outside. Panels of wallpaper missing, recently filled holes in the walls waiting to be sanded smooth. My horns scraped the ceiling, and I had to duck under the door frames.

"I've put the kettle on. Make yourself at home," Frankie said. "Good drive? Much traffic?"

"It was fine. Not much traffic," said Peaches.

There were a few moments in which everyone quietly looked at one another. Peaches eyed me in a way that was both apologetic and like she wanted nothing more than to march me into the guest bedroom and strip me bare.

"Joe, take the kids' bags to their room."

"I can do that," I said, suddenly aware that I still held both holdalls in one hand, but he practically snatched the bags from me, sagging once he succumbed to the combined weight of them.

"So, you kids met at college." It wasn't a question, but she had phrased it like one. "Pudding, you never mentioned you wanted to do cake decorating."

"I didn't—I don't—I mean, I'm not sure, really. It was a bit of an accident."

Frankie laughed. "Classic Joey. So, have you bumped uglies yet?"

My response came out as a startled cough.

"Mum!" Peaches threw me another *I'm sorry* look. "But yes, we have."

"Great! Help me make the tea and tell me all about it." She pulled her daughter by the arm out of the living room, leaving me standing there with her scowling father who had reappeared at the other end.

I made to sit in the most robust looking seat the room offered, a tall-backed, wide-cushioned armchair with a grease stain right about where Joe's head might reach—

"That's my chair," he said, pushing past me and plonking himself down. I moved to the sofa, a peeling leather chesterfield. It groaned and sagged ominously as it took my weight, and I silently lamented having to sit on the skin of my — distant — relatives.

I opened my mouth to speak, and then closed it again, tapped my fingers on my thigh, looked around the room at the framed photographs of the Silver family. Joey in her cap and gown on a fake blue-sky background. Joey, as a teenager in yet another red dress, an evening one, her hair pinned in elaborate curls, prom maybe. The sisters on the beach, cartoon-mouse patterned swimsuits and buckets and spades in hand. The whole family, around a campfire, marshmallows on sticks, smiles on faces. Happy, loved, accepted.

"So . . ."

Joe put his palm up between us, and anything I was going to say ran off and died in the corner. "It's taken quite a lot for me to get used to the idea of my daughters dating monsters. First a dragon, now a . . . minotaur?" I nodded because what else could I do? "Let's be honest with each other. You don't particularly like me, I don't particularly like you—"

"Uh—"

"Do you like me?" he asked.

"Truthfully . . . Not yet."

He smiled then. "Good, honesty. It's going to take me a while. If I can get used to one monster, I can get used to two."

Laughter echoed from the kitchen.

"I will just say this. I'm a forgiving man. But not when it comes to my daughters. If I find you've hurt my little girl, if you so much as make her cry, well . . . I happen to know the Police Commissioner of Remy, and I'm not averse to putting in a call."

I swallowed. Was he aware of my history? I doubted Peaches would have ever mentioned it. And unless he'd looked me up online, he could've only assumed that reporting me would lead to a rap on the knuckles, nothing more. He couldn't possibly know that Pounder was fuelled primarily by his vendetta against me.

"My goodness, a hot tub," said Frankie, reappearing, carrying a wooden tray bearing mugs of tea. Her naughty smile exactly mirroring her daughters. She held it out in front of me. "That one on the end is yours, dear. In the purple mug. It has oat milk. And there are some vegan biscuits on that plate. I got them off Jen From The Farm Shop this morning."

I leant forward and took the purple mug in one hand and a biscuit in the other. The sofa screamed its protestation as I shifted my weight.

"We are going to need new furniture with all these gigantic men you girls keep bringing home," said Frankie, handing a mug of tea to Joe.

"Mum," warned Peaches, sitting beside me on the couch.

"I said, *"you girls"*."

"I, uh, I could make you some," I said.

"Oh, that's right. Joey said you were very good with your wood." Peaches let out a snort that neither Frankie nor Joe picked up on, or if they did, paid attention to. "Lumberjack, right?"

"No, it's—Yeah, lumberjack is fine." Much easier than explaining what I actually did. Lifting and carrying wood, loading up lorries, shredding, plaining, building deck kits. So many deck kits. Nobody in Remy even had a garden.

"He built his own sofas," Peaches offered. "And his bed. And that's really durable." Her eyes turned to circles, and she gave me an *I don't know why I just said that* look.

"That would be wonderful. Wouldn't it, love?" Frankie said to Joe, an echo of a smile on her lips.

"Hmm," was all he said.

"So," I began, mostly to fill the awkward silence that followed the durable bed comment. "Joe, what do you do?"

Peaches froze. She gawked at me, her mouth open. The terror in her eyes telling me I had chosen the wrong lane on the conversation highway.

"Joey didn't tell you? I'm a milkman," he said, puffing his chest out in defiant pride.

"Milkman?"

Milk Man? A man that milks? A man that's milked? Never heard of it.

Peaches intervened, splodges of red blossoming on her cheeks, neck, and cleavage. "He gets up at four o'clock every morning and drives around the village at three miles per hour, dropping bottles of cows' milk to old ladies in their nighties."

"Right," I said, narrowing my eyes. Was she taking the piss, or was this really his job?

"It's how Joey met Wyn," he said.

"Dad, let's not talk about Wyn today. Please." There was an edge to her voice.

"Have you spoken to your sister recently?" Frankie asked Peaches.

"That's not changing the subject, Mum. Can we move on?"

Frankie 'zipped' her mouth shut and left me bouncing my gaze between the three, trying to decipher their expressions. Peaches, anxious. Frankie, totally at ease. Joe . . . I had no idea, bored maybe. He'd angled his body away from everyone, and rarely joined in with the conversation.

We spoke pleasantly until our teas had been drunk. Mostly about the award ceremony and our cakes.

"Have you thought about setting up a little business?" Frankie asked me.

"It's something that I've only very recently considered," I said.

Peaches took my hand in hers and the bond spread its warmth throughout my chest. The conversation moved onto her takeaway delivery jobs, and how it was going now she had her car back. In the past, I'd heard Joey say, *I'm only a takeaway driver*. Only. Like it was something to be ashamed of, but her folks never once hinted it was less than adequate. A lump swelled in my throat when I realised they really did only care about her happiness.

If she wanted to be a delivery driver, if she enjoyed it, which she did, if she was happy, who were they to push for more? They accepted her as she was because she was happy. I sat there in their living room. Horns having scraped plaster from the ceiling, vegan milk in my tea, a special trip to the farm shop to buy vegan biscuits. They accepted me — a little reluctantly, in Joe's case, but they accepted me nonetheless — because I made their daughter happy.

Absently, I thumbed over the ring. This is what I wanted, the future I wanted with Peaches. A family, our family, and nothing but unequivocal love and acceptance.

"Another tea?" Frankie said, pulling me out of whatever reflective pool I'd dunked myself in.

"I'm going to have a quick shower before dinner," Peaches said, jumping to her feet. She planted a kiss on my cheek and returned her mug to the tray.

"Taurin?" Frankie turned to me.

"Sure, thank you."

Frankie took my mug and the tray and left the room, but not before giving her husband a pointed look.

He sighed and straightened his posture. "This,"—he made a circle with his fore finger and thumb and held it up to his nose—"Is that a cultural thing? Or . . ."

I touched my septum ring. "It's . . . part of me, I guess. All bulls have them. Most heifers too. It's a coming-of-age thing. When I shift, it gets this big." I held out my hand to demonstrate the size. His gaze followed my gesture, but he showed no other signs that he'd heard me. Probably processing it all.

"Where are you from? Originally," he asked.

"East Winterlands. I grew up th—"

I stopped mid-word when my eyes landed on a framed photo of what must have been Peaches' sister, and her husband. I had known he was a dragon. Peaches had told me. Joe had told me less than an hour ago. But now that I could see him, it made it all the more real. His skin—scales—were red, like Pounder's. In the picture, which by

Ottilie's dress, I assumed was their wedding day, the dragon had his wings slightly spread. A known dragon intimidation tactic. A dominance thing. My hackles lifted. It was only a photo, and it already had this effect on me.

Frankie walked in with a freshly stocked tray and caught me staring at the picture. "Must be weird for you."

Her words echoed in my head. *Must be weird for you.* It wasn't a normal reaction to discovering your daughter's boyfriend staring at a photo of her sister and brother-in-law, but I couldn't pinpoint why.

"I mean, it took us all a while to get used to it. What with, you know," she said, placing the tray on the table and handing refilled mugs to both Joe and me.

"Because he's a dragon?" I asked, thoroughly confused.

"Oh, that never bothered *me*." She gave her husband another look. "But because of Wyn's history. With Joey."

The full mug wobbled in my hands.

Frankie, apparently not realising her mouth was full of foot, continued, "They were only together for"—she puffed out her cheeks—"Ooh, must be about six weeks, but he was her first. First mythic that is. First mythic, first true love."

The room span around me. The familiar darkness creeping across my vision.

"I mean, we all hated him at first. Didn't we, Joe? For breaking her heart like that."

Joe made a conformational sort of laugh.

"But once Tils explained this 'fated-mates' whatsit to us, well, I suppose neither of them had much choice, did they?" Her voice echoed around in my head as though she were speaking through a cardboard tube.

The dragon and Peaches had dated. She loved him. He found his mate in her sister. He broke her heart.

"When was this?" I asked, not entirely sure whether the question had left my lips.

"Ooh, about ten years ago now. Just before she left for Borderlands."

She ran to Remy to get away from him.

"Excuse me." I stood and placed my undrunk tea back on the tray. "I'm . . . I need . . ." *To calm the fuck down. To not See Red in my girlfriend's folks' house after merely looking at a photo.* "To check on Joey."

Chapter 32

Joey

I headed to the guest bedroom, my bedroom since my parents moved, and checked my phone. Two missed calls from two different numbers.

I dialled the first one.

"Good afternoon, University of Remy Admissions office. How may I help?"

"Hello, this is Joey Silver. I had a missed call from this number."

"Joey, Joey." Fingers clacked against a keyboard. "Joey, yes, here you are. Oh. Oh, dear. Joey, it's bad news, I'm afraid. There's been a suspension on your student account."

"What?" My stomach plopped next to my feet on the rug.

"It seems you're attending a course that you're not registered on, so they've suspended your details. And, oh, there was a payment due to your bank account. Prize money, it looks like."

"Yes, my half of the five-thousand silvers for the Cakecon award."

"That's the one. It's been reversed." I could barely hear them over the pounding in my ears.

"What? All of it?"

More clacking on the keyboard. "I'm sorry, I'm not at liberty to say any more than that."

"Right," I said, the word nothing more than a whisper.

"It also means you can't attend the course anymore."

"What—" I cleared my throat. "What if I pay the registration fee?"

"I'm afraid all the slots from Cake Decorating 101 are now filled. Shall I enrol you in next year's course?"

The only reason I came back was because of him. I enjoyed the course, but only because he was there. But how could the call handler possibly know that? "No," I said. "No thank you." I hung up the phone.

It wasn't like I couldn't see him outside of the cake course. We were officially boyfriend-girlfriend. We were here, together in the Human Realms, very much outside of the cake course. So why did giving up my Monday nights with him feel like such a huge bereavement?

I wanted to run back to the living room and let him hold me and stroke my hair and tell me it didn't matter, that we were strong enough to withstand it. And then I pictured him, standing in class, with his adorable, gigantic body wrapped up in electric-blue netting, icing-sugar dusting his t-shirt, another person at his desk. Who would take my spot? Who will they sit next to him, in my place? Unbidden, my brain filled in the gap with Tilly's smug face.

I shook the thought away, released my frustration with a scream, and dialled the second number.

"Hello?"

"Christie?" *Fuck.*

"Joey? Oh good, I'm glad you called. Listen, I didn't want it to be like this but—"

"You're kicking me out."

"The cheque bounced. I can't keep doing this every month. Paris has already moved her things in. We're boxing up your stuff tonight." In the background, I could detect laughter. "I want you to come and collect it tomorrow—"

"I'm in the Human Realms right now."

"Sunday then, at the latest. Or we'll dump it on the streets—"

I pressed the call end button, not prepared to listen to anything else. I scooped my feet onto the bed, wrapped my arms around my knees, and sobbed.

I cried until my face felt puffy, my sinuses were clogged with gunk, and my breaths were heaving in and out like a toddler having a tantrum.

Until a small voice inside my head piped up, *You deserve this.*

I shook the thought, but it persisted.

Christie and I were once friends. We met at uni, and we had fun. We went dancing. We cooked meals together. We talked into the night about boys, and the universe, and how we would change the Eight and a Half Kingdoms with our degrees. She'd studied law, making it somewhat more realistic to achieve this goal than me. Not sure how much change a scroll with 'Josephina Silver - Drama' written on the front might bring about. But then, perhaps that had always been my problem.

I never took anything seriously. Never made any real plans or goals. I floated through life like a pooh stick drifting down the river. Bumping into the banks, but never planting myself into solid ground and setting down roots.

She grew up, and I didn't. She got a proper job, and a mortgage, and I continued to behave like a student. Pissing my money away, bringing home fuck-boy after fuck-boy, letting my whims dictate my actions, refusing to believe I had done anything wrong.

Refusing to take responsibility for myself.

I groaned aloud again. My stomach churned, and I seriously regretted eating six of those delicious vegan cookies.

Christie, like everyone else, had given me so many chances. Month after month I failed to cough up the rent money. Sure, she would nag me for it, nag me to get a proper job, nag me to settle down. Perhaps, I don't know, she was only doing those things to look out for me. Why did I ever think it was acceptable to pay her in excuses? Gods, I let her parent me. Of course she wants me out of her fucking house. I'd want me out.

And the cake course. I'd stolen someone's rightful spot. Was that fair? I'd been so selfish, so entitled. I'd expected rewards without paying into the system. I wanted things simply because I wanted them. Without making any move to earn them.

I'd been a shitty friend, and a terrible grown-up. And everything that had happened in the past five minutes I had brought down upon my own head.

The door opened a crack, finally Horns was here to sweep me up into his massive arms and kiss the top of my head and tell me everything will be okay and none of my shameful past decisions matter a modicum now because he was beside me. I would cry, and tearfully admit my love for him and he would say, "ditto," and all would be right again.

But it wasn't Horns that walked through the bedroom door, it was Mum.

She took one look at my puffy, tear-streaked face. "Pudding, I'm so sorry. I never meant to tell him. It just sort of slipped out."

My body stiffened. "Tell him what?"

"About you and Wyn. Isn't that what you're crying about?" She sucked in a breath and wrapped her arms around me. "He, uh, didn't take it well."

I didn't answer her question, didn't want to further add to the storm clouds now hanging over her Harvest Fest. Didn't want to admit to Mum, I'd fucked up again. And again.

"Where is he?" I asked.

She hefted a shoulder. "I thought he came to check on you."

Immediately, I was on my feet, pulling my trainers back on, and heading out to the gardens. Little Red was still there, so was Mum's SUV, and Dad's clapped-out A-to-B-er. Wherever he was, he was on foot. I cast my gaze across the rolling hillside behind the house, the farmer's fields to the left, the forest to the right. No sign of fleeing flocks of birds, no tremor-inducing stomping foot fall, all was silent and still.

"Where?"

If I was a beautiful, angry minotaur, where would I have marched off to?

The top of the hill. I made a start in that direction when Mum's arm came across my waist again.

"He'll be back before dinner," she said.

"What? How do you know?" This was Horns we were talking about. Tempestuous, flighty, quick to anger. A lifelong hatred for dragons. And Mum had just told him about Wyn. I had kept it from him because I knew he'd react exactly as he had done.

"Mother's instinct." She pushed the hair from my face and tucked it behind my ear. "Come on, pudding, let's get you changed."

Mum was right. Horns turned up with precisely two minutes to spare until dinner, his hair windswept, his jaw clenched. I wanted to run to him, but something in his demeanour held me back. He caught my eye, and subtly shook his head. It was a gesture that said, *We need to talk. But we'll trudge through an awkward meal and stew some more before we can clear the air.*

I nodded. What else could I do? Hash it out if front of my parents?

"You wore this one," Horns said, touching the fabric of my red summery dress with the embroidered peaches. "I love this one."

"Horns," I whispered, "Please, let me exp—"

"Later," he said, not unkindly, but there was finality to his tone. He took my hand in his, and the bond purred at the contact.

We made it just past the guest bathroom, when the doorbell rang, and before it was physically possible for it to be answered by Mum or Dad, a familiar voice bounced across the corridor, "Surprise!"

Aerowyn. My ex-boyfriend. My sister's husband. I stopped in my tracks and shot Horns a terrified look. My heartrate snowballed. I whispered rapidly to him, "I'm so sorry. I had no idea they were coming. Gods, if I'd've known. I won't leave your side. If you want to go, just say, okay? I'm only yours."

He barely looked at me. His fingers twisted painfully in mine. "Fucking dragons."

"Joey," came Tilly's saccharine tones, as my sister's blonde balayage head bobbed into the hall. She wrapped her arms around me in a non-reciprocated hug.

"What the fuck are you doing here, Tilly?" I said.

"So great to see you too, sis." I pushed her away from me. "Mum told me you were bringing your new hunk." She gave Horns a once-over. "Um, wow."

"Girls," said Mum, entering the hall. "Be civil. It's a joyous celebration, remember?" She gave Tilly a hug. "I'm so glad you could make it, pudding. What a lovely surprise. I think introductions are in order."

Beside me, Horns stood as though he had a metal pole through his vertebrae, his eyes fixed on Wyn's silhouette framed in the front door, his free hand clenched into a fist at his side.

Mum, not sensing the tension, continued, "Tilly, Wyn, meet Taurin, Joey's boyfriend. Taurin, this is Joey's younger sister Ottilie, or Tilly if you can't be bothered with the whole thing. And her husband Aerowyn, or Wyn, if—Well, you get the picture."

"Nice to meet you," said Tilly, holding out her hand for him, one brow lost in her hairline.

Horns took it and managed a convincing smile. "You too. And, um, congratulations." He briefly gestured with our interlocked fingers towards her belly.

There was a split second when nobody registered what had been said, and then Tilly's face fell into abject shock. Everybody realised at once and began talking over one another.

"Gods, I'm so sorry. That wasn't common knowledge, was it?" said Horns.

"Am I showing already?" said Tilly.

"You're pregnant?!" screamed Mum.

"I ruined the surprise," said Horns to no one.

"I'm gonna be a grandad?" said Dad, running into the over-cramped hall.

"How did you know?" I asked Horns.

"Smelt it," was his whispered reply.

"Babe, you might as well give them their gifts," said Wyn, finally pushing his awkwardly colossal frame through the door, his wings brushing either side. He looked at Horns, and then at me, a grin slowly spreading across his human face.

Wyn had always been imposing. From his poisonous-berry-red skin, to his six-foot-nine-inches of height, literal eight-foot wingspan, and swirling horns that curved up and backwards in a loop from the top of his head. And this was just his human form.

"We were going to tell you all today," said Tilly. She handed Mum, Dad, and me a white box each. "We had these made." Inside was a plain mug with the words BEST AUNTIE EVER printed on the front. Mum and Dad had similarly appropriate ones. Something icky stirred in my stomach. Guilt? Anger? Shame?

Mum wiped her tears away on the back of her hand and there was pandemonium as both my parents tried to pull Tilly and Wyn into hugs. Followed by a slew of questions. "How many weeks are you?" Mum. "Have you had any scans yet?" Mum again. "Is it human or dragon?" Dad.

We made our way into the kitchen, the earlier animosity between Tilly and me, and Horn's accidental slip-up brushed under the rug, though not entirely forgotten. Wyn had switched up lurking at the front door to lurking beside the kitchen doorway.

"I really wish you'd told us you were coming," said Mum, frantically pulling extra crockery out of the cupboards and setting it down on the table. Dad dove into the cupboard under the stairs to find the spare fold out chairs. "Wyn, I've made a vegan roast." She placed her hand on her hip and gave him a helpless sort of look.

"You vegan now? Typical." said Tilly, looking straight at me.

"I am," corrected Horns. He squeezed my hand, yet his tone remained completely impassive. Mum, Dad, Wyn, and Tilly all shared knowing looks. Wyn's face slowly mutated itself into another smarmy grin.

"That's okay, Frankie," he said. "I've brought my own lunch." My stomach dropped. *Oh. Fuck.* "And Tils isn't really eating that much at the moment."

"Morning sickness," she clarified, pointlessly pulling a barfing face.

"Pudding," said Mum, placing her hand on Wyn's chest. "I might have to ask you to eat separately."

Everybody looked at Horns. He didn't outwardly sigh or make any movement, but I felt his resignation. Through the bond. A strange new, slightly ominous, buzz struck up.

"I'm assuming you've brought steak? And honestly, it's fine," he said, though his fingers wound themselves more tightly around mine. "I understand everyone has different diets. I have a flatmate who's a vampire." It was the same line he'd given me that first time we had lunch in Tallywhacker's. Only now I saw it for what it was; a soundbite designed to make others feel more comfortable in his presence.

Everyone's — apart from Wyn's — jaw fell open.

"What does your flatmate eat?" said Tilly.

"What do you think vampires eat?" I said, like the petulant teenager I was.

"How? Have they ever eaten p. . ." Dad began, but never finished.

Horns twisted his septum piercing, a nervous smile twitching at his lips. "Uh, there are banks. Humans and other species can donate blood in exchange for cash. So mostly he drinks it from cans or bottles. You know, like a beer. And about the last question, which you didn't finish, but I'm guessing was, have they ever eaten people? The answer is yes, two. It was a very long time ago. Long before the death penalty was brought back. And he's served his time in gaol for it. A hundred years, actually."

Nobody said anything. The atmosphere in the kitchen was thicker than royal icing. Wyn's shit-eating grin was still firmly fixed on his face as his eyes swept over the dumbstruck faces of his in-laws and wife. The absurd urge to laugh bubbled in my chest. Horns turned to me, his lips pursed so tightly they'd disappeared, and regret shone in his eyes.

"I think," said Mum, at about four-hundred decibels louder than her usual voice, "That means you're forgiven?" She shot nervous glances between Wyn and Horns and laughed in the most un-Mum-like way possible. "Well, everyone sit down, please."

A sinking sensation blossomed in my stomach. If Mum was on edge, well, that said a lot. Mum could be on a desert island during a hurricane, and still insist on finishing her pina colada, and tipping the waitstaff.

"This is why I never talk to people I don't know," Horns whispered, as we took our seats.

Mum had placed Taurin and Wyn on either end of the table, most likely due to the size of each of them. I wanted to reassure him but reaching for his hand would have felt too exposed and I didn't want to embarrass him any further. So, I did the only thing that would let him know I was thinking of him. That I was with him, and I was his. I thought of last Sunday morning in the Pegasus Grand. I pictured his hard cock in my mouth, his beautiful, agonised face as he came, and his roar of pleasure that shook the entire suite. My chest vibrated with my sudden arousal. He caught his smile between his teeth, and under the table, his foot knocked against mine.

Relief flooded my body. If we could get through dinner with a dragon, it was salvageable.

Mum and Dad dished up the soups (pumpkin) and the starters. Usually, we'd have prawn cocktails. Not sure what prawns had to do with Harvest, but this time Mum had made some sort of pastry boat thing with mushrooms and thyme. It was meh. Mum's cooking had never been astronomical. I wouldn't tell her that in my nightmares, though. Guaranteed, it would be the one thing she'd lose her cool about.

The first courses passed without incident, and generally pleasant conversation. Mum asked if Tilly and Wyn had any baby names in mind. Tilly confirmed they did but aren't revealing yet what they were. Dad asked Wyn how business was, and thankfully Wyn managed to answer his questions without delving into any detailed logistics of his job.

All the while, my thoughts flip-flopped between, *How can I make him see that Wyn means nothing to me? That what I feel for him is a thousand-fold what I ever had with the dragon?* And, *How can I tell him that I've fucked up the course, lost all our prize money, and gotten myself kicked out of my flat?*

I was homeless.

Shit, I'm homeless.

I swallowed down the ominous buzzing in my chest and pulled my focus onto the conversation as the topic switched to Horns. Of course, Mum wanted to know everything.

What it was like in the East Winterlands. What his parents were like. What his work involved. What other things he could make out of wood. He answered all the questions without bringing up his people-eating roommates again, and I could tell Mum had already fallen in love with him. She perched her chin on her palm when she listened to him, and often shot glances at Dad. Her way of saying, *Isn't he wonderful?* I tried not to let my own smugness show on my face. *Have that, Tilly.*

Dad was taking it all so much better than I would have first thought possible. His brow was still firmly set into a frown, but it always had been. Mum said it was because his eyesight was on the blink, and he refused to get new glasses. His old ones worked just fine, thank you. But I knew the real reason, and I was thankful he was at least trying. In his own way.

Occasionally Tilly caught my eye, and I couldn't quite be sure, but her expression was almost apologetic, or cautionary. Though it could have been the weird pregnancy hormones.

Only Wyn refused to hide his eye-rolls and brow wagging whenever Horns spoke. And it was really beginning to piss me off. Old Joey would have thrown her napkin onto the table, caused a scene, and demanded he explain his shitty behaviour. But I couldn't risk it. Not then. Not with Horns' history around dragons. Not with my history around Wyn. Not with the current tightrope I was walking between maintaining a calm, unaffected mien, and breaking down into a full menty-B over my living arrangements, financial problems and boyfriend sitch.

"Thank you. For going to so much trouble for me," Horns said, after polishing off everything from both courses, including the leafy garnish, and taking the higher road of totally ignoring the crabby, huffy dragon opposite him. Wyn sat, arms folded, with his plate inauspiciously empty.

Mum beamed. This was exactly the sort of thing she loved to hear. *Manners are everything*, she used to say. "You are very welcome."

The main course was a normal roast dinner — potatoes, veg, Yorkshire puddings, gravy — but with the meat switched out to a fruity nut roast thing. Even Dad accepted the vegan replacement without complaint.

But, and there was always going to be a but, it was at this point that Wyn, without warning, upended his carrier bag of raw meat and all its juices onto his plate. The steak, if you could even call it that, slapped onto the china like a giant turd hitting the bowl. Gods, the slab of meat still had a fucking hide. It was cow fur, brown and white. Unmistakable. I pushed my foot out of my high-top and wound it around Horns' leg.

"Babe, you just splatted me," said Tilly, fetching a dishcloth and wiping up the rogue puddles of cow blood.

He didn't apologise. He merely laughed and leaned closer to Dad. "Killed her this morning."

Horns' fork clanged against his plate.

Oh Gods, perhaps we should excuse ourselves and leave now.

Mum face-palmed and grabbed Horns' bicep. "I'm so sorry. Are you sure this is okay? Wyn's a dairy farmer."

"Sometimes beef too. When the heifers get too old," Wyn added, his eyes locked on Horns. "And the bulls. No use keeping more than one male around."

Tilly's tone was warning. "Babe."

The strange thrumming began again in my chest. Deeper, edgier, more dangerous than the usual motorbike-race excitement of the bond. I realised I'd felt it before. At the docks, when the dragon barista got up in Horns' face.

Horns' eyes had clouded, were darker, but then he looked at me, blinked, and they were blue again. The thrumming stopped. Wyn knew exactly what he was doing. The piece of shit. After tonight, I was going to kill him.

He stabbed his fork into his hunk of meat and, without bothering to take his knife to it, he brought the entire thing to his mouth. It made a plunger-like sound as it left the plate. "How long have you two known each other?"

"About six weeks, nearly seven." I answered, to save Horns from doing so.

He raised his eyebrows. The atmosphere had shifted. It was no longer the pleasant chatter of a family catching up, but heavy, stormy.

Mum made an unsuccessful attempt to change the subject. "I heard on the news there might be a meteor shower tonight—"

"How long since you've been officially mated?" he asked, ignoring Mum. He took a bite from the steak like it was a fucking cake-pop. Juices grotesquely rushed down his chin.

"Are you seriously asking us about sex in front of my parents? In front of your in-laws?" I said. It was the second thing mum had wanted to know, but coming from Wyn's mouth with Dad around felt all kinds of wrong.

He looked at Horns, one of his eyebrows raised. "I don't know, am I?"

Horns stiffened beside me, and the dangerous thrum kicked up a gear.

Ignoring Wyn, and the strange new sensation, I leaned forward and grabbed my boyfriend's forearm. "Do you want to leave?"

He closed his eyes, as though praying for patience.

"Don't leave," pleaded Tilly. There were tears in her eyes. "My mate is going to behave himself now. Aren't you?"

Wyn gave a large puff of air. He looked at his wife in the same way a teenager caught passing notes in class might look at the teacher who confiscated them. Mum nervously cleared her throat, and Dad mouthed to her, "See?"

Oh Gods, time to deploy the big guns.

"So, Tils, how does maternity leave work at FaeCare?" Everyone cocked their brows at me. Tilly, being the smart little Silver kid she'd always been, latched onto my sudden change of demeanour.

If her eyes alone could speak, they'd have said *thank you*. "I get up to a year, but there's a very interesting clause where, if the baby isn't human, or if they're part human, I may get longer depending on its needs. So, if the baby is more dragon than human, I could get up to thirteen years."

Mum was nodding enthusiastically, as though this conversation alone could save the entire dinner. I rubbed my socked foot against Horns' calf, just to remind him I was right beside him.

"For your sake, I hope it's human," said Dad. Setting down his knife and fork at the edge of his plate.

Gods, not him too now.

Tilly ignored Dad's comment. "And Wyn's self-employed, obviously, so any time he takes off work ends up costing us more. Once we hire the farm hands and whatnot. We've already begun looking for extra help around the farm, though. Had interviews last week. One guy—you'd really like him, Mum, he's a redhead—we're thinking of trialling." I realised she was speaking simply to fill the void. Or to keep everyone's mind off how aggressively weird her husband was being. It seemed to be working.

He'd always been a bit of a prick. Wyn. No revelations there. Ten years since I met him, and he hasn't changed a modicum. At the time, Dad had been desperately trying to get me to take an interest in finding a proper job and had the harebrained idea to combine my love of driving with my need for income. So, he asked me to trial a shift with him.

My dad.

Thought I would enjoy driving a milk float.

With a top speed of six miles an hour.

Yeah.

To be fair, it was pretty fun at first, but the novelty wore off quickly when every day started at four am and I could run faster than that bloody float.

Pedal to the metal. That thing was excruciating.

Abandoning the milk-woman idea, Dad thought, perhaps delivery driver. Now, those tankers can rack up some decent speeds, and could flatten a barn, given the right trajectory. I'd need a special license and years of training, however, never deterred by technicalities, Dad took me to visit the local farms that supplied the dairy.

And that was when I met Wyn. The first dragon I had ever seen in real life. Tall, young (about three hundred, so, young for a dragon), and handsome. He leant against the entrance to his milking shed, his wings spread impressively at his sides. He offered me a bunch of hand-picked and hand-tied wildflowers, and twenty-three-year-old me was besotted. Four weeks later, I lost my dragon virginity, and two weeks after that, I caught him with his dicks inside my sister.

"Will you be extending the farmhouse?" Mum asked, her voice uncharacteristically squeaky.

"Maybe. It depends on whether we need to fireproof the nursery."

Dad dropped his wine, the glass toppled over onto its side, and the dregs of his drink gushed over the cloth. He stood and grabbed a tea towel.

"It's okay, Dad," Tilly whispered taking the towel sopping up the spills. I knew she wasn't talking about the wine or ruined tablecloth.

"How tall are you?" The question came out of nowhere. So much so, everyone, already on edge, seemed to duck for cover. Wyn folded his arms, clearly waiting for the answer to his surprise interrogation.

"Uh . . ." Horns glanced at me, a *what the fuck* expression on his face. "Six-eleven?"

"In your shifted form." Wyn said, in the way someone might add *duh*.

"Almost nine feet."

Wyn smiled and sat back in his seat, knowing that he'd won whatever stupid pissing contest he was playing in his head. In his dragon form, he was easily quadruple that. For the brief span of our relationship, I saw the shifted Wyn relatively frequently. Unlike Horns, he seemed to have no qualms with people accepting his non-humanness. Wanted them to see it, even.

"What car do you drive?"

"Aerowyn," said Tilly, using his full name. "Do not even dare to start this again."

"I can drive, but I don't have a car. Don't really need one in the city," said Horns. His voice was calm, but he spoke through gritted teeth. His eyes darkened, and the thrumming in my chest grew.

Wyn sat back in his chair and sucked his teeth, evidently realising he couldn't win a game if the other party had no interest in playing. "You own a house? What's that like?"

"Why the fuck are you doing this again?" asked Tilly, giving her husband a sharp shove to the centre of his chest, as Horns said, "I don't. I live with friends."

"Has Joey told you she loves you yet?" Wyn looked at me. "It took you what, like a month to confess that to me? Never said it back though, did I?"

This got the exact response he'd been looking for. I watched in horror as the seams along Horns' shoulders popped open like tearaway paper. I stood abruptly, putting my hands on his chest.

"We're leaving. Now," I said. Horns stood too, and as his face passed mine, I saw his eyes were black, his chest heaving.

"It's nice knowing I took both sisters' mythic virginities."

Time slowed. Tilly was the first to respond, leaping from her chair and grabbing Mum by the arms, she yelled, "Get out of the house! NOW!"

Chapter 33

Joey

Taurin's shirt peeled away from him like a snake shedding its skin, as the man under my arms grew by at least two feet. His head burst through the ceiling. Plaster and dust rained down onto the table, sprinkling over the half-eaten roast dinners.

"Taurin!" Unable to reach his shoulders, I tried pulling at the fur on his chest.

Mum and Dad were already out the back door, in the garden, Tilly in the doorway.

"Joey, come—" But my sister's face froze as she took one look at her husband, her arm outstretched as though she could possibly stop what would happen next.

I turned, just in time to see Wyn smile triumphantly, then shift into his dragon form. His red scales overfilling every available space in the kitchen and then some. His head smashing through the external wall, his tail through the fireplace, and his left wing shooting out and practically cleaving the house horizontally in two. I had milliseconds to duck my head pathetically under my arms and wait for the debris of the upper floor of my parents' home, and the contents of each room, to crush me like a beetle.

This was how I would die.

Probably smushed to death by Mum's claw-foot tub.

And I hadn't told him I loved him.

The smushing never came. A few pieces of shrapnel hit my shins and sides, but the death blow never arrived. Gingerly I pulled my arms away from my head and Taurin — massive bull Taurin — had shielded me from the impact with his enormous body. He had stepped himself between me and Wyn, who opened his six-foot maw and roared.

In his human form Wyn was intimidating. In his dragon form he was downright terrifying. His red scaly body was now easily thirty-five, forty feet long with his tail. His four tree-trunk legs ended in huge curved, taloned claws. His leathery wings spread overhead like a sail canopy at a beer garden and his tail lashed about behind him, literally levelling what was left of the house.

Flames shot from his mouth into the sky. The severed gas-pipe in the kitchen must have thought, *why the hell not* and decided to join in on the fun with its own fireworks display, sending me flying through the air.

No, it wasn't the explosion that had sent me backwards but Taurin lifting me with one hand and throwing me like a ragdoll out of the blast zone. He saved my life. The area where I stood only seconds ago, now resembled a toddler's art project. If said toddler had only charcoal paint and chunky glitter at their disposal.

I landed in a heap on the guest bed mattress, now blackened and half propped up against the upturned Welsh dresser. My head span. But I wasn't hurt. I didn't think. I ran my hands up and down myself, checking for blood, broken bones, burns, sharp pains, bits of glass sticking out of me, missing appendages. Nothing. Though if I did have any injuries, they'd probably become evident as soon as the adrenaline wore off.

Stars twinkled above me. I was still inside the house, yet I was looking at the night sky. Gone were all the walls. Only mounds of . . . rubble and flaming thatch. I couldn't make out what used to be part of what room.

Ahead of me, almost totally unscathed, was Taurin. His arms held in front of him, as he let out an earthshaking warcry, turned and leapt onto Wyn's neck, tearing at his scales with his claws.

Wait, he has claws? And his muscles. I've seen him shift before, of course. *But . . . What the actual fuck?* He was so big. Bigger, maybe, than ever. This wasn't his prone, sleeping, shifted form, this was so much more. Each of his arms were the length and thickness of my entire body. His fur covered his massive shoulders and head, his nose ring was now the size of a handcuff, and his horns jutted two feet in front of his face.

Just beyond the immediate blast zone, Tilly was getting to her feet, yelling at her husband, words I couldn't hear over the ringing and pounding blood in my ears. Mum stood on the other side of the road watching her house crumble and burn, her back against the Victorian style lamppost, the reflection of the flames bouncing off her spectacles. Dad was nowhere to be seen.

There was my parents' claw-foot tub, on its side across the street, a tiled section of the bathroom wall draped like a blanket over it. The splintered remains of the wooden guest bed scattered like matchsticks over the drive. Dad's armchair, sticking ass-end out of the rubble. My high-top! Still impossibly under the now topless dining table. My head span again, and smoke seared my lungs.

Wyn, with his smoking rictus hanging open, hissing words from an ancient language, stretched himself up onto his hind legs and launched himself into the sky. Taurin dropped from his neck, gave another bellow, and began firing chunks of house towards the dragon.

"Joey! Get out of there!" my sister yelled, tinnily, in the distance.

But I couldn't. I knew what I needed to do. I was the only person in the world that could affect Taurin when he was like this. I knew it. I ran to him, dodging under his hefty limbs as he stalked what was the kitchen, and sent an entire piece of drywall streaming through the air.

I was terrified of course, but *for* him, not of him.

"Taurin!" I grabbed at his chest, his arms. Slapping him hard with flattened palms. Nothing. "Taurin, stop.

Taurin! Horns!" At this, he paused. "Horns, it's me, Joey. Peaches."

He turned his gaze down to me, his back stooped, his eyes black as the sky above, his breath clouding in puffs between us. Blood trickled from his scalp, running in rivulets past his eye and down the bridge of his nose. I wound my fists into the fur on his chest and pulled, as hard as I could, but still only guiding him until his head became level with mine. It was as big as my entire torso.

"It's me. Horns, come back to me. Come back." My fingers were on his face. He flinched. His eyes, still dark, locked onto mine. I had no idea if he understood me, or could speak while he was in this state, but something had shifted. Not him, he stayed in his mountainous bull-form, and his eyes — the only difference between his voluntarily shifted form and Seeing Red — were still black. Not even a ring of blue there. Yet, I felt it, like the ground had moved. He was in there. Somewhere.

It was the bond.

Without taking his eyes off me, he lifted his hand to my dress, which had torn right down the front to my navel and hung open, revealing my ash-ruined bra. He passed the fabric through his clawed fingers, taking in the embroidered peach design. Then he flattened his palm against my chest.

"Mine!" The word burst from him like thunder detonating directly overhead. Loud, long, and low. Shaking the ground, reverberating through the trees around us, travelling straight up my spine. There was no excuse for the surge of arousal I felt at his primal possessiveness.

"I'm yours," I said in a whisper, the wobble in my voice coming from something other than fear.

Above us, Wyn filled the sky with flames. I saw it reflected in every shard of broken glass and felt its unwelcome warmth against my neck and shoulders, but I wouldn't give him the satisfaction of my attention.

"Can you hear me? Do you understand me?" I asked Horns.

He said nothing. Didn't nod or shake his head. But his eyes never left mine, and my fingers never left his cheeks.

"Can you change back?"

Again, nothing.

"Please, Horns. I need to help you."

He blinked. Did it mean anything? Was I reading into it?

Wyn roared again, setting a blanket of heat across me, and Horns shifted his attention to the dragon. His back straightened, his chest puffed out, and a guttural scream shook the ground beneath my feet.

I renewed my grip on his fur and pulled him towards me with greater effort. I needed for him not to be at the scene when the fire engines and probably police arrived. If I somehow had to take all the blame for the mess, then that is something I was prepared to do, and the consequences of such dealt with later. But if he were to be discovered, shifted, amongst the rubble, he'll be put away for longer than either of us could bear. I'd never see him again. Not without the presence of an armed guard and a prebooked visitors' appointment.

I didn't realise I was crying until I saw the tears hitting the charred fabric of my dress. "You need to get out of here. If you can understand me, take my car. Go to the border. There's a hotel, it's called The Barn. It's big and red. Get a room. I will come and meet you there as soon as I've sorted everything here. Okay?"

Slowly, so slowly, Horns closed his eyes.

I knew he understood me because the thing in my chest told me he had. I let go of him and retrieved my lost high-top, then emptied the detritus from it, and pulled it on. And together we crunched our way down the glittering garden path to my little red car, which now seemed absurdly too small.

I wanted to kiss him. But . . . where? I pulled his head down, wrapped my hands around his jaw, and planted my face against the bridge of his nose.

"I love you."

Taurin's eyes closed, and he pushed his fleshy nostrils into my chest with a forceful billow of breath.

"Gods, I love you."

He got in the car, instantly overfiling the space, his nose almost touching the windscreen, his horns cutting rivets into the metalwork of the roof. Through the passenger window, he simply stared at me. Wait, he did know how to drive, didn't he? Or perhaps he couldn't drive while Seeing Red? Was he technically still Seeing Red? He was so much calmer.

As I watched him, his body seemed to shrink a little, as though moulding itself to the vehicle. Was he shifting back to his human form? No, he was—

He hit the gas. Little Red's engine roared into life, and before I could collect my thoughts, Horns careened off into the night at a velocity Past Joey was secretly high fiving him for. Giving me distinct adult driving a child's go-kart vibes. I would have laughed at the absurdity of it all had the situation been different.

I watched Wyn, poised, my breath held. Wondering if he'd go after Horns. My hand twitching ready to jump into Mum's SUV and follow them both, but Horns must have rounded off Wyn's scope because the next moment the dragon lifted his head and roared, filling the air above us with flames once again. He didn't give chase, he simply continued making broody circles in the sky, and I let out a breath of relief.

As I got closer to the house, or what was the house, things started sliding into focus, and the things I saw made my head hurt. Mum was sitting on the grass. She'd spread a picnic blanket—an actual picnic blanket for crying out loud—and was smoking a joint. Since when did Mum smoke weed? And where did she get a minotaur sized—*Oh. Duh*.

"I found it in the guest room . . . area," she said, motioning her hand to indicate towards a particular patch of rubble. "Yours, I presume?"

At that moment, Tilly, flapping her arms, screamed, "Aerowyn Robert Pounder you get down here this instant! You are in so much fucking trouble! I can't even with you right now!" To which, Wyn responded by soaring even higher into the sky.

I sat next to Mum on the blanket. "Taur's, but yeah. Mum, do not smoke that entire thing. You'll be sick." She shrugged. "How's Dad?" I knew from the joint in her hand and her demeanour that Dad was probably unharmed, but I hadn't seen him since the house stood intact.

"Your father's on the phone. He has a lot of things to sort out. Like somewhere for us all to stay tonight. Fire engines are on their way. Might take a while. We're out in the sticks here."

That wasn't what I'd asked, though I was glad to hear all of it. "But how is he?"

She exhaled the lungful of smoke she'd been holding, then rolled the tip of the joint on the grass, extinguishing the glowing cherry, evidently deciding that the two or three puffs she'd had would be enough to muddy the edges of the utter calamity that was this evening's Harvest Fest celebrations. "He . . . He'll . . . It might take a while. Between you and me, he always hated this house. You were right, should've got a new-build by the sea."

"Mum," I said, placing my hand on her arm. Tears popped at the corners of her eyes. "I'm so sorry. About all of this. If we hadn't come, you'd still have . . ."

She shook her head. "Don't. You're not allowed to fall apart. Not right now."

Mum had always been the laid-back type. When I was eight, I snapped my wrist roller-skating down the drive, she told me to sleep it off. Obviously, it was still broken in the morning, and we had to go to A and E. She packed a picnic, even baked cupcakes, so that we could make a day of it. Another time, our car broke down during the one solitary snowstorm Pannor had ever seen. Mum didn't even bother to get out of her seat. She simply assigned places to sleep, should we need to camp the night. I was going to have the boot, and to be honest, I'm still disappointed the repair guy made it out to us.

But this.

It was ridiculous even by Mum standards. I wanted to shake her by the shoulders.

"Why are you so calm? Why are you not more freaked out?"

She actually laughed. "Sure, I'm upset. Is that what you want to hear? Of course, I care. That dining table was a wedding gift from your grandparents. But here's the thing. When you get to be a sixty-four-year-old woman with two beautiful, successful daughters, and a grand-baby on the way, sitting on a blanket outside the ruins of her house smoking a, frankly comical, spliff — which I'm keeping by the way — you learn to realise there are much more important things in life than . . . stuff. Things. Belongings. All of this,"—she waved a vague hand towards the carnage, her eyes briefly slipping out of focus—"Can be replaced. We have excellent insurance. Your father made sure of that, and it gives me the chance to buy the new things, like a dishwasher, that he said I wasn't allowed because they were still working fine." She gave a chuckle and brushed my cheek with her weed-fragranced fingers. "Stuff isn't what matters. What matters, pudding, are the relationships we build. This. This is what matters. Love. Family. Friends. *Mates*. What connects us. These are the "things" we shouldn't let go. That we must protect from ruin."

She placed her palm across my chest, right where my heart is. Right where the bond, which had now become eerily silent, led. "I'm just thankful that you're both okay. That we're all okay. Tilly said the baby will be fine. In fact, the doctors encourage a little smoke inhalation for half-dragons. Your father will be fine. He was only telling me the other day about how happy you seemed. And yours and Til's happiness are the only things that matter to us. Always has been. A wrecked house won't change that. Besides, I'm quite sure the tub is salvageable, and you know that all your old drawings and photos from when you were girls are still in boxes at Nan's house. Nothing was destroyed today that cannot be repaired. Especially your friendship with your sister."

"I'm so sorry. All of this is my fault."

If I had never met Wyn, I'd never have inadvertently introduced him to Tilly. I'd never have run off to Borderlands, never taken a job as a takeaway driver, never have pushed my luck with the speed limits, and never have met Horns.

But those things, all those things, led me to him.

"If we can forgive Wyn for tearing apart our house, we can forgive your bloke for trying to defend us."

Huh. It was like another, very small, gas pipe exploded over my head.

Wyn had started it all.

He goaded Horns. He was being a prick. He knew he'd shift if he pushed him hard enough.

Taurin may have thrown sections of Mum and Dad's house into the night sky, but he wasn't the one who caused the chaos. And Wyn was responsible for ninety-nine percent of the destruction. Horns wasn't at fault. I wasn't at fault. Though, it still didn't stop the nagging feeling that the damage went beyond a ruined house, and a lifetime of memories.

Mum laughed, seemingly out of nowhere. "I like him, pudding. He's spunky. You know I like that. He stuck up for you when Wyn was being an A-hole. And it's obvious you love each other very much."

"Is it?"

She sighed, a lovestruck kind of sigh. "The way he looks at you, it's like . . . you're the rain after a thousand years of drought." She laughed again and swatted my arm. "I gotta stop smoking things I find in the garden."

Right then, Tilly plopped herself onto the blanket next to Mum and me. "I'm going to kill that scaly motherfucker. I swear to the gods. This is the third time he's done this." She released a breath that could rival one of Horns' and rubbed her non-existent bump. "The soot's good for baby apparently," she said, rolling her eyes up to her fuming husband.

"I'm going to check on your father," Mum said, pushing herself to her feet. She kissed the top of my head and then Tilly's. "Love you, girls."

"Love you, too, Mum," we both said in automatic unison.

"It's a dragon thing," said Tilly, as we watched Mum toddle off. Not that I'd asked. "Joey, I'm so sorry. I'm sorry about all of it."

I figured she was talking about more than the house. She was apologising for everything that came after I met Wyn. Finding them together in the garage, the non-stop arguments about his character, losing our friendship. And I was sorry too. I lost my best friend the day I lost my boyfriend, and only one of those still hurt.

"I never blamed you. You didn't know we were a thing. How could you? I never told anyone about us. It was so new and exciting, and I was so worried what Dad would think, or say, or do." I cast my eyes into my sooty lap. "I really thought I loved him. I had no idea what love was. Not until recently."

"He's the one?" She'd switched the conversation to Horns.

"I think so. I just get this . . . ache in my—"

"Chest?"

"Yeah."

She smiled and nodded. "That's what I have too. With the dead-man-flying up there. Now you know why I couldn't simply walk away from him. There's a bond."

"A bond, yeah."

It was what we had fought about. Originally, and in every argument since. I wanted Tilly to see that he was a useless, waste of space, dragon-player. That, if he could so easily cheat on me, he would do the same to her. I was trying to spare her heart, but she was adamant he wouldn't break it. *"How do you know?"* I would yell. *"I just do,"* she would say. *"You're being an idiot." "Then you'll have to accept me for that." "I can't do that. He'll destroy you." "He won't."* And thus, it would repeat itself, over and over with only brief pauses. A month's ceasefire here or there to pretend to Mum and Dad we were friendly again, for holidays and gatherings, but nothing longevous.

I got it now. Why she couldn't leave him. Even if she'd have wanted to, she couldn't. It was exactly how I felt about Horns.

"You have to go to him," she said. "At least *he* didn't destroy Mum and Dad's house."

I laughed, because maybe all the toxins from the burning plastics had gotten to me, but because really, what else was there left right now? "I'll get Mum, or Dad"—I thought of Mum's current inebriated state—"definitely Dad, to drive me to the border soon."

"Don't worry about any of this. Wyn's going to clear up his own mess this time."

I managed a half nod. "So . . . It's a dragon thing?"

She laughed a humourless laugh and rolled her eyes up to the sky where Wyn still beat circles with his wings and occasionally let off angry little bonfires. "When a dragon's mate,"—I cringed. I always found it weird when Tilly referred to herself as his mate and not his wife—"Is pregnant, sometimes . . ." She closed her eyes and shook her head. "No, he *will* challenge any alpha male he comes into contact with. Or at least, anyone he feels personally intimidated by." She let out a breath.

"There are maybe a handful of creatures that dragons feel threatened by. Other dragons, namely, but also minotaurs." She genuinely laughed then. "A fucking minotaur Jo, I shouldn't find it funny but, Gods, it's brilliant. Mum said you might be bringing a boyfriend, but in all the variations of that in my head, he was either human, or . . . uh, not actually present. I'm sorry, I honestly didn't expect you to bring anyone, especially not a fuck-off, gigantic, brick-wall of a man."

And then we were both laughing. So hard that tears popped out from the corners of our eyes, tracking pink lines through our soot-covered faces.

"I'm so glad you found someone that can give Wyn a run for his money. Fucker's been prancing around like he's infallible for far too long."

I chanced a peek at the blood-streak against the sky. Would I ever be able to forgive Wyn? For tonight? For the past? Did it matter? If Mum and Dad could accept he was half of Tilly, then I supposed I ought to join them. For the most part, he made her happy. And that really was everything. I should care more about my sister's happiness than being vindicated. Perhaps if there were another family get together, we could make more of an effort to get along. Or make sure we're not in or near any already-halfway-to-collapsing buildings. The beach maybe. The two of them could hash out whatever it was giant men fought over on the sand dunes.

"So," I said, "The horns, are they always that sensitive?"

She laughed so hard she had to cross her legs, probably to stop peeing herself. "One time," she said, between gasps, "I put it in my mouth, and he came in his pants."

"I'm definitely going to try that."

In the distance, flashing lights illuminated the treetops as two, wait three, fire engines barrelled down the country lanes.

"Girls." The blanket shifted under my splayed palms and Dad dropped to his knees on the other end. His face was blank, ghostly, his skin paler than usual.

"Where's Mum?" asked Tilly. "She just went to find you?"

"She's fine. Girls—Flower," he said, looking at me, "I think I've done something terrible."

Chapter 34

Taurin

The strip of peach embroidered material sandwiched between my fist and the steering wheel was the first thing I saw when I came to. Without pulling over or slowing, I shifted into my human form. If anything, it gave me more space in the cramped car. I glanced around. Peaches' car. It was . . . fucked. No doubt entirely my fault. The passenger's side window had blown out. A crack ran up the centre of the windscreen. The backrest of the driver's seat now lay pathetically in the rear footwell. And there was a sunroof above my head, where there was once solid metal and fabric.

Fuck. What did I do?

My memories of the past few hours were hazy at best. I remembered the dragon and his mate. His fucking half a cow that he insisted on dribbling down his bran-flake chest. Peaches' parents, the terrified looks on their faces. Peaches winding her foot around my ankle, letting me know she was beside me.

I didn't remember getting in the car, but I must have at some point. I didn't remember crossing the border, but the dawn-painted cityscape of Remy lay ahead of me, so, again, I must have. How in the Eight and a half Kingdoms did I cross the border without papers?

But what was I missing? What led me to See Red? What did I do? Or, more importantly, what did I destroy? I scraped at the recesses of my mind. The dragon had wanted a fight. Of course he did, how fucking typically dragon of him. He'd said . . . Gods, what was it he'd said?

It came to me in a lightning flash of memory.

He'd said he took both sisters' mythic virginities.

My fingers clamped tighter around the wheel. My jaw locked itself shut. I let out a breath and shook my head. I couldn't allow the anger to bubble over again, not when I was so close to home. Not when I was entering Pounder's jurisdiction.

But what happened after that?

Images began popping up. Darkness, columns of smoke, flames, broken glass, and splintered furniture. *Fuck.* Frankie and Joe's cottage razed to its very bones. *Double fuck*. Me launching actual fucking pieces of their house into the sky like grenades.

Oh, this was very, very bad.

And Joey. Holding my face. Her dress ripped. Her fingers in my fur, and her lips on my head.

She said . . .

She'd said she loved me.

I almost skidded the car to a stop.

The first time she'd told me she loved me, I was full bull. And I couldn't say it back.

I pulled into my building's underground car park. Mal's vintage convertible was there, and Goldies' ridiculous sports car. Of course they were. It must have been six, seven am. Dima would be home too. The thought of seeing those three filled me with so much relief an involuntary sob escaped my throat.

I thought of Peaches' parents, and the many framed photos that had stuffed their ramshackle living room. How much they loved their daughters, how accepting they were of them, and their monstrous partners. I compared them to my parents. My herd. Remembering the time Tina and I ran south, to Borderlands, away from all the misery the herd brought us. The constant criticism of our human traits.

But the discrimination was worse for her in Remy. As an eight-foot human woman (twelve as a cow), she didn't experience the fun, peaceful time we'd stayed up late every night discussing. The one we'd imagined. The one we'd dreamed of. She'd started a relationship, which had ended, as was the way with most minotaurs, in violence. Though she never gave me any further details on the topic before Pounder chased her north again.

"Taur, I'm going back. I'm going home," she had told me. I'd reminded her of why we left in the first place. "I'll take that over what we can have here. They'll never accept us here. We can never be what they want us to."

She was wrong, of course. I had found acceptance. Namely, with a misanthropic, philandering fae, an entrepreneurial bloodsucker, and a paternal incubus. They were my home. My family.

And now Peaches.

My Peaches.

Gods, I missed her.

After ten minutes of pressing my forehead against the steering wheel and Peaches' scrap of fabric bunched under my nose, I had somewhat composed myself. Who am I kidding? I still had no clue what my next move would be, other than calling her and grovelling profusely for forgiveness.

A thought occurred to me.

She'd said she loved me after I'd bulldozed her folks' house. She must have at least begun to forgive me.

Hopefully.

I jimmied the car door. It helpfully relinquished itself from the burden of staying attached to the body, and crashed to the asphalt with a tinnitus-triggering flourish. *Well, shit.*

My phone buzzed in my back pocket. The screen had cracked, but the thing still miraculously worked. There were seventeen missed calls from Joey from Cake Dec with two peach emojis, and two texts. Nerves, or acid, flared up my throat. I opened the texts as I scanned my entry card to the building's elevator.

Where are you?

and

I love you.

I fired a text back.

Just got home. I'm sorry. I will fix this. Call you soon.

I wanted to tell her I loved her. But I simply couldn't do it by text. Not the first time. The first time I told her would have to be to her face. I needed to see it reflecting back in her eyes. I also needed to explain a few things, why I had run off before dinner, that it didn't matter who she was with before me. It was none of my business, even if it was a dragon.

I ran my hand through my hair, pulled my shoulders back, and stuck my key in the hole. She loved me. We could get through this. My phone pinged with a third message. This time from Goldie. As I crossed the threshold and stepped into the living room, I found all three of my flatmates staring up at me, and another, undoubtedly uninvited guest. He leant against Goldie's precious sound stack, beaming from ear to ear.

My stomachs dropped somewhere below my knees, sweat instantly beaded on my forehead, and my phone fell to the floor. The ghost of Goldie's text still burned into my retinas.

Don't come home. Pounder here.

Chapter 35

Joey

"Big guy. Like seven feet. Long hair. Naked from the waist up. Huge white horns. Possibly a cow's head. Ringing any bells?"

"Sorry no, haven't seen him," the black-haired receptionist of The Barn said, cracking her gum. "And we're not actually meant to take bookings from lone mythics. It's part of the Mythic Human Travel Act of '932."

"Right, of course," I said, failing to hold back the sting of tears. I got into Mum's car, Dad at the wheel, his face pale, and brows still knotted together.

In a moment of panic and relapsed rage, he had phoned Remy Police station as the house was crumbling. Minutes later, he realised he'd made a mistake. Taurin wasn't to blame. His son-in-law had been. He called the station back, retracted his statement, gave a new one. As easy as that.

It did nothing to dampen the rising fear that it was all too late.

I pulled out my phone and rang Horns' number once again. Straight to voicemail. I text him. *Where are you?* Immediately followed by *I love you.* Because I did.

Because, I understood, that we could go through things like this, and I still needed him next to me. It had only been a few hours, but I missed him. So fucking much. I missed his face, his voice, his rumbling thunder-crack laughter. I needed, desperately, to feel it in my chest.

And that was the other thing. The bond had gone quiet. Not a buzz, or even a tiny hum. Did this mean it had been severed? Were we still bonded? I couldn't think about it. Every time I did, I started to hyperventilate.

"We'll find him, flower," Dad said, placing his hand on my forearm, right before I shut down completely into a quaking, snotty, bawling mess.

Through uncontrollable sobs, I gave Dad Horns' address, and he drove me across the border into the city, while I periodically dialled his number.

Mum's SUV rumbled onto the Remy Flyover. Behind us the sky was grey and lavender, and ahead, pink and orange. My colours. It should have felt like driving home. My phone pinged.

Just got home. I'm sorry. I will fix this. Call you soon.

I laughed and then broke down into renewed tears. "He's home now."

Dad smiled and snapped down the indicator. Twenty minutes. Twenty minutes until I saw him again. Until I was in his arms.

Chapter 36

Taurin

"Taurin, Taurin, Taurin. I knew it was only a matter of time," Pounder said, no attempt to hide his euphoria. "You won't be getting out of this one so easily."

"What did you do?" asked Mal. There was no judgement in his voice. Only curiosity.

Dima said nothing. He wouldn't have risked it in front of Pounder, but I felt his minty presence. The vampire's jaw dropped.

"Your main bull here only went and pancaked his girlfriend's parents' house," the commissioner offered.

Goldie and Mal froze, my silence only confirming the accusations, and Pounder's gloating smile slid further across his stupid, scaly, red face.

"Taurin the minotaur," he said, uncrossing his legs with a flared kick, and stepping up to me. "I'm arresting you on suspicion of causing gross damage to human property. Of endangering human life, and of causing injury with serious intent to harm a non-human."

And the fucker read every single one of my rights, while smiling the whole time.

I rolled my shoulders back and shifted into my bull form. Pounder didn't flinch. Not that I'd have expected him to. He finally had what he wanted. I had committed a crime I couldn't 'technicality' my way out of. I was guilty. For everything he accused me of. A house was flattened, lives uprooted, memories destroyed. I tried to kill that dragon. I would have if the bastard hadn't fled upwards.

"Any last words before I take you in?"

I held my wrists out, and Pounder slapped the size zero-zero-B cuffs on me. They fit, only just, biting into my skin, falling this side of being circulation-stoppingly too tight. I didn't have anything to say. Or maybe I had too much to say and didn't know where to begin.

I kept thinking of Peaches' texts. *Where are you?* And, *I love you*.

She had sent them after everything.

Would she still love me after twenty, thirty years behind bars?

Would she still—No, it was unfair of me to expect her to wait.

Besides, we'd probably both end up losing our minds before we reached that point. I've condemned her to madness.

I was a monster.

"Hey, mate, we still love you," said Goldie, as Pounder nudged me towards the front door. Mal nodded.

We'll do whatever we can, said Dima.

I don't deserve it, I replied, and then I was outside, being pushed into the back of Pounder's cruiser.

I was photographed, dunked in ink, stripped, and made to wear a flattering acid-green Remy City Gaol boilersuit. They assigned me basic supplies, gave me an ID wristband, microchipped me, locked me in my cell, and pointed towards the top right bunk. Potentially my home for the next — if Pounder had any say in it — fifty years of my life.

Two of my new cellmates hunched together playing cards. I didn't spare them any attention. There would be enough time for that later, I was sure. The third cellmate, a scrawny-looking gorgon, sat up on his mattress.

"I'm taking the bottom bunk," I said.

He said nothing, slowly raking his eyes up the entire length of my body, all nine feet of it, and moved his pillow and paperback to the top bed.

One of the cards playing guys introduced everyone. I didn't bother to listen to their names, I simply sat down, puffed out all the tension, and let my head fall backwards onto the too-thin mattress.

I would not think about her. I couldn't bear it.

I was beginning to believe Elektra's forefinger and thumb had been glued to the bridge of her nose.

"Let me see if I'm on your page, here," she said, without looking up at me, her elbow wedged on the white Formica tabletop in the interview-slash-private visitor's room, her face still cradled between two fingers. I hadn't shifted back to my human form in the few hours I'd been there, and it was the first time my lawyer had seen me full bull. To her credit, she showed no signs of nerves. "You don't remember what happened?"

I mean, sure, by that point I must have told her at least a hundred and fifty times. I bit back my exasperation. "I remember the dragon goading me. I remember standing in a burning pile of house. I remember hauling chunks of aforementioned house at the fucking dragon—"

"Taurin, please, language."

"I remember Joey walking me to her car. I remember 'coming to' just outside of Remy." I left out the part where Joey told me she loved me. That was for me alone.

"And who shifted first?"

"I don't remember. Me, I think."

"Who smashed up the house?"

"No idea."

"What injuries did the dragon suffer?"

"Come on! I don't remember. How many times do I need to tell you?"

What I did recall was the black dragon blood all over my hands. The fingerprinting guy had to scrub it from under my claws before dunking my hands in ink. I hope I really fucked him up.

Her palms dropped to the table with a slap. "Honestly, it just feels like we're going round in circles."

"Because you've asked me the same fucking questions about three-hundred times."

"Taurin, I'm running out of angles to fight this. We can't keep doing this back and forth, you smash up a place, I find a hole in the system to wiggle you through. Eventually, you deplete all holes."

She was right, of course. I had run this race so many times, I knew there was no other way out. I was screwed. Beyond screwed. I'd fucked everything up. And now my only option was to jump at whatever sliver of hope Elektra could concoct from nothing. If, indeed, she could.

"I need to gather some witness statements, talk to Joey, and her family. Especially this dragon. Hopefully, we can get to him before he can make an official statement or even press charges. Do you have any contact details for Joey? Her number? Address?"

"My phone's at my flat, and . . . I don't know where she lives." I'd never asked her about where she lived, all this time she was having problems with her accommodation, and I never bothered to find out more. Her flatmate was called Christie, but I didn't even know what part of town she lived in. I was a terrible boyfriend. "Try Mal, he knows the passcode to my phone, he could call her."

Elektra nodded. "Anywhere else you think she might be? Or her family? Would they have stayed with a relative, or neighbour? Or gone to a hotel, perhaps?"

"Joey has a friend. A two-thousand-year-old fae, Ash, I think his name is." I couldn't think of anywhere else she might have gone.

"Ash Lavandou? Summer fae?"

"Sounds familiar. He lives in Eastside."

She leant back in her chair, and finally permitted herself a solitary smile. "Friends in high places."

"She'll visit me soon." I realised as I said it, I didn't believe it. I was trying to convince us both. But she had to. She had to visit. I couldn't bear to think of not seeing her again, not to mention what it would do to the bond. "I'll ask her then."

Elektra pursed her lips together and placed both palms faced down on the white vinyl. "Unfortunately,"*—no, no, no, anything but that fucking word—*"Pounder has already spoken with Dr Landyn and Clair may have mentioned Joey being a person likely to stimulate a triggering response in you. He's signed an M-77 injunction against her, prohibiting her from visiting you."

"What?! Forever?" Tears — my tears — splashed on the tabletop. I didn't bother to wipe them away.

"I'm sorry, Taurin. We'll do everything we can to make this as comfortable as possible."

As comfortable as possible, she was speaking as though I was dying. Oh, he knew what he was doing, the sadistic asshole. He would have me rot in here, with no contact from my mate. I would lose my mind. Just to prove his point about minotaurs.

"There haven't been any charges made against you, not yet. It's a race to collect evidence. But Pounder . . . seems committed to the cause." *Of course he fucking did.* "It's not looking good, Taur. He has a statement from Joey's father, damages that need paying on the property, on-scene police and fire reports, and time stamps of you crossing the border. Into the Human Realms and fleeing it. Not to mention the mess you caused when you drove straight through the barrier to Borderlands."

That would explain some of the wreckage to the car. Another pang of guilt bubbled in my stomachs. She loved that little car.

When I said nothing, Elektra added, "Let me guess, you don't remember that either? It's going to be a difficult one to fight. Pounder's gunning for a fifty-percent term. The best we can hope for is a reduction." She ran her hands down her face as though she was the one facing fifty years in this shithole without her mate.

I banged the table with my fists. Not hard enough to break it, but enough to cause Elektra to jump in her seat. And let me tell you, it takes a lot to make a fully grown Orc woman flinch.

Fifty years. Without Joey.

But I wouldn't allow myself to wallow. Not until Pounder charged me and took me to trial. And then, if all else failed, I will break out of this hellhole.

Raze the entire gaol.

The tuning-fork metal-on-metal clang rang throughout the cell. The guards made a big show of puffing out their chests and pretending they weren't about to piss their pants in my company. But I could always smell their fear seeping out of their pores.

"Visitor. Minotaur."

A tiny ray of hope filled my chest. Had she found a way round Pounder's injunction? That ray of hope died instantly when I saw Mal's white-blonde hair, onyx skin and six-five frame sitting opposite the table. Great, guilt as well as grief.

I shifted into my human form, my coveralls sagged down my back. Mal didn't deserve to see me at my worst. He pulled me into a hug. Gods, how much have I missed this man's hugs? Eventually, the guard cleared his throat and Mal pulled away.

"Stupid question. How are you?" he said.

I couldn't muster an answer.

"You've had a shower. That's good. Have you eaten? Slept?"

The absurd urge to laugh struck me. Mother-hen Mal. Always looking out for us. Even if we were trapped in a lifetime of hell.

"Dima showed me what happened. Or at least what you can remember. You've . . . Mate, the dragon shifted with you. That's never happened before, right?"

"Have you seen Joey?"

Mal paused, the briefest hint of something, perhaps annoyance, flashing over his face. "No, not yet."

My shoulders sagged. He would understand, he'd been mated before, he knows how all-consuming this feeling was. "Pounder's signed an injunction forbidding her from visiting me."

He never broke eye contact. "I know, mate. He dropped the letter off with us when he came to arrest you." My face found my hand. "We're going to fight this. We're not giving up on you."

But what could they do if Pounder was this determined? And the evidence mounting up?

I told Mal everything I knew, everything Pounder had against me. When I mentioned Seraphina, he smiled, but for the rest of my oratory, his brow had set into a firm line. He'd told me over and over he would do everything possible to get me out. Legal or otherwise, but my nerves never settled.

"The house," I said. "I'll need to pay damages." It wasn't a question. I hated myself a little for it, but what other choice did I have?

"No," Mal said, flatly. "That's the one thing I can't do. I can't pay your damages anymore, Taur. You owe me like two-hundred-grand already. You've wiped me out. There's nothing left in my savings." A small pang of guilt hit me in the stomachs, but I stomped it down. "Ask Goldie or Dima for once. Why's it always gotta be me?"

Because Goldie and Dima aren't you. Because I'm more myself with you than either of them.

But, like the idiot I was, I didn't voice either of these thoughts. Instead, I said, "Can't you just go on one of your medicine rounds and whore yourself out for the money?"

"Really, man?" He sat upright and stared down at me for a beat, and when I failed to respond, or apologise, he stood, shaking his head. The chair legs scraped painfully against the linoleum flooring, and without looking over his shoulder at me, Mal signed the visitor register and left through the opposite exit.

Stiff fingers closed around my tricep and guided me to my feet, and I shifted back to my bull form. I definitely didn't take any pleasure in the way the guard's grip flexed, or the way his heartbeat revved, or the trickle of sweat that ran down his temple.

Chapter 37

Joey

Eight hours earlier

I promised Dad I'd ring him later. He apologised for everything. Not only for calling the police last night, but for every time he'd made a derogatory comment about a mythic, for using the term monster, for pointing out obvious differences between species, for ever making either Tilly or me believe we shouldn't love who we loved.

"I still don't understand this whole bond thing," he'd said. "But you deserve happiness. Your mother and I love you as you are. We never wanted to change our girls. Our worry was that you'd fall in love with someone who didn't appreciate the real you. That they'd try to turn you into someone you're not. Take our bright, smiling Joey and put shadows in your heart." He laughed and thumbed my cheek, and I realised he was finally speaking his own words. Not Mum's. Mum had always simply wanted me to settle down. Dad hadn't. There had always been an undercurrent of trepidation from him. Now I knew why. "He's not like that. That's plain to see. He loves you as you are. He's . . . like us."

We hugged, tearfully, for a good five minutes. Then I kissed him on the cheek, and he drove off, back to Mum, and Tilly and Wyn, and the mess left behind in Dinlow.

It wasn't until I was ringing the bell that I considered what I must look like. My dress blackened and ripped down to my belly button. My hair scraped haphazardly into some sort of imploding beehive, make up — was there any still left on my face? Or was it as sooty as the rest of me?

The door opened, and behind it stood the gold-haired, shirtless flatmate. His eyes travelled over my exposed bra, one brow quirking in a greeting. "Sugar Paste?"

"Who is it?" called a voice, not Horns, from inside. The vampire, I think.

"It's Taur's mate," said Goldie. Something in his tone forced the hairs on my neck to prickle.

"Where is he?"

He didn't answer, just stood to one side, so that I had to squeeze past him to get in the apartment. Darkness shrouded the living room, the blinds drawn, the cosy evening lamps still lit, and the vampire, Dima, hovered in the corner. He cocked his head to the side, taking in my dishevelled appearance.

"He's been arrested. The commissioner took him to the gaol about thirty minutes ago," said Goldie, plonking himself down on the sofa.

"But . . ." Surely my brain had bottomed out. How can he be arrested for something he wasn't at fault for? "My dad was the one that called the police to begin with, but he's already rang and retracted his statement. Told them he got it all wrong."

"What happened?" said Goldie. "He didn't remember it, only patches of the night."

I threw myself down onto the opposite sofa, and opened my mouth to speak, but Dima interrupted.

"May I?"

Assuming he meant scrape around inside my memories, I nodded. The sheer exhaustion from the previous day and night had crept up to me and robbed me of the ability to give a damn about being invaded in that way. A gentle cool breeze passed through my mind. Horns was right, it did feel like someone with minty breath was blowing into my skull. There were a few moments where Dima stared into Goldie's eyes, and I realised he was showing the information to him, too.

"He's innocent!" Goldie said, leaping to his feet. "It was self-defence. He saved Sugar Paste's life."

"We need to tell Mal," said Dima.

"Where is he?"

"He's gone to speak with their lawyer." *Their lawyer?*

"Oh," I said. And despite everything, I felt my shoulders sagging in relief, my breath leaving me in a whoosh, calming hormones flooding my system. Okay, Horns was behind bars. But he was innocent. Well, innocent in the grand scheme of things. Innocent compared to Wyn. They couldn't hold him indefinitely, and they certainly couldn't charge him.

I stood up. "I am going to go down to the station to see what I can do. Or wait for him to get let free. Or whatever."

Goldie and Dima shared an *uh-oh* kind of glance.

"They've taken him to the gaol, not the station," said Goldie.

"And the commissioner left this for you," Dima said. A brown envelope hovered from a side table and floated over to me. So, a telekinetic as well as a telepath. Handy. "I read the commissioner's mind. It's an injunction preventing you from visiting him. On the grounds that you might trigger another burst of rage."

"What the fuck?!" I snatched the envelope from the air and tore it open. Sure enough, all those shitty words were there. I wouldn't even be able to look at him through the glass. "Well, bollocks. What am I supposed to do now?"

"Maybe have a shower?" Goldie said, his expression lightly mocking. "Put some, ah, whole clothes on? Have a sandwich and or a nap? Mal will be home soon. We can tell him everything we know. It'll get sorted."

I didn't want to do any of those things, especially nap. I was exhausted. Fucking exhausted. But there was no way I could sleep right now. I wanted to go to the gaol, kick and scream and pound on the doors until they let him go, but it was here in black and white. If I tried to make contact, I would risk arrest myself. He will be let out soon. And what would happen if he walked free only to find I'd been arrested instead?

And I supposed there were helpful things I could do here to speed up the release process. "Okay, yeah," I said, trying not to yawn. "Do you mind if I shower here?"

"I'll find you something to wear," he said.

"I'll just get something from Horns' room."

"My clothes will fit you better."

I couldn't really argue with that, so I nodded. I didn't much fancy wearing sweatpants I'd have to roll the hems over at least six times on. I offered the boys a small smile, one that hopefully conveyed my thanks, and headed up to the bathroom.

Thirty, forty minutes passed as I stood under the blistering super jet stream of the showerhead, scrubbing the accumulated soot and grime from my skin, and inhaling the woodsy scent of Horns' soap. He used bar soap, and bar shampoo and I didn't know why, but those facts brought me to actual tears. Underneath all the building-smashing outbursts, he really was such a quiet, considerate, tender person. And despite how everyone treated him, how they held him at arms' length as though he might explode at any moment, he only wanted good things. To help people, to save the planet, to be loved.

Because he was a good man. My good man.

I missed him. I owed him an apology. For everything. For storming into his life and refusing to leave him alone. For denying to take his taciturn, monosyllabic responses as the less than subtle fuck-offs that they were. All I wanted was a fumble.

I laughed out loud, letting the shower water flood my mouth.

Typical, selfish Joey. I never meant to fall in love, never meant to upside-down someone else's life so irrevocably. And now look at me, crying over a bar of vegan, sea-salt infused, pine-scented, hair-body-and-face scrub.

With Horns' disappointingly regular sized towel wrapped around my midsection, I waddled across the hall to his bedroom. Everything was so neat and ordered. The bed made, the curtains drawn, the Nikki Star paperback that I'd left the last time I was there on his nightstand. Goldie had placed some clothes for me at the foot of the bed. A pair of jeans, and a black t-shirt with the FaeGames' crossed controllers screen-printed logo on the front. No underwear, which was somewhat of a relief. Not sure how I felt about wearing a sex addict's pants.

The jeans were a troublingly decent fit. High-waisted on me, but, actually kinda cute, especially once I tucked the t-shirt in. I towel dried and finger combed my hair, then I made my way back downstairs.

All the curtains and blinds had been opened, which I guessed meant Dima had gone to bed.

"You want a sandwich?" Goldie yelled from the kitchen.

I floated, like a cartoon dog sniffing visible ribbons of t-bone aromas, to the plate waiting for me on the table. Goldie sat in the adjacent seat, chewing down on his own food.

"That's not a sandwich, that's a burger." A chicken burger the size of Horns' hand nestled in an overlarge sheeny brioche bun. Cheese, lettuce, tomato, onion rings, something white and dripping — hopefully mayo — the works.

"It's in bread, isn't it?"

I bit into it. "Oh, my gods!"

"I make a great vegan burger, too."

And then, I don't know what came over me. Maybe it was the exhaustion, maybe the orgasmic burger, maybe it was that I'd simply reached emotional overflow, but I said, "Horns is really lucky to have you. All of you."

Goldie smiled. "Ditto."

A thought occurred to me. "Earlier, you called me Taur's mate?"

Mate. Like the same word Ottilie used to describe her and Wyn. Mate, not wife. Mate, not girlfriend.

"Yeah," he said, taking another enormous mouthful of food. He studied my confusion. "You know like . . ." He swallowed. "Fated mates, uh," he puffed out his cheeks, "like the mythic equivalent to human marriage."

"What?" *Fated mates? Human marriage?* Did that mean . . . "We're technically married? But, how?—When?—Huh?"

"Not to put you off my delicious cooking, but I believe it happened when he released his hot minotaur seed in you." I must have still looked confused because he clarified, "When he rearranged your insides without a rubber."

I leant forward in my chair and slapped a hand over my mouth. Mostly to hide the laughter forming. "Wow. But still, how?"

He shrugged. "Minotaur thing. It's actually quite common in animalistic shifters. They can imprint. You ever heard of that?" I nodded. "If that happens and then they go in bare-back, it essentially seals the bond. Permanently." He added a lot of emphasis to the word permanently, before shoving the last of his burger into his mouth.

I was silent for a few moments, trying to process it. I wasn't mad. Should I have been mad? Horns most likely knew it would happen, even if he, in the moment, had been so carried away he'd forgotten. He'd married me without asking if it was something I wanted. I probably should have been upset, even a weensy bit affronted, but the only emotion I could summon was relief. We belonged together. I couldn't think of anything truer.

And I couldn't push him away.

Even if I tried.

Old Joey can fuck right off.

"So, we're married?"

"Congrats. Sorry we all missed the big ceremony. I'd have loved to have been there. But you still have your human wedding to look forward to." His eyes darted over my hand. "Forget I said that."

After we ate our mega burgers, I spent a few hours chatting on the phone to everyone and anyone, trying to sort out as much as I could from the comfort of Horns' handcrafted sofas. Despite it now being in excess of twenty-four hours since I'd last slept, I wasn't in the slightest bit tired.

I video-called Mum first. She assured me she and Dad were fine. They were going to stay with Jen and Nige From The Farm Shop. Mum was excited because Jen asked her to help out in the shop and, as it turned out, Mum had always wanted a part-time job to keep her busy. Dad had called the insurance company. He was over the moon. The five-hundred hours plus he'd pored over the policies, scrutinising every bullet point, had actually paid off. They were due to receive a full pay-out of the house's value (which had risen twenty-four percent since they purchased five years ago) plus the estimated value of the contents. "We're so rich now, flower. We could live anywhere," he had said on the video-call, while Mum held the phone in such a way only her forehead and bright red curls were visible. "We're going to get somewhere with really high ceilings this time, and no DIY necessary."

I called the police station next, and put in my official eyewitness report, after Mum told me she did the same.

Then a video-call to Tilly, who, for someone whose husband had recently destroyed her parents' house, was in an extremely chipper mood. "He's doing anything I tell him to, now," she said. The mini-Tilly on the screen chewed on her thumbnail, her eyes wide with mischief and glee. An expression I both recognised from our childhoods and missed wholeheartedly. "I've just asked him to extend the kitchen and garage. And I told him we need a playroom too, because I don't want the baby's junk taking up all the space in the living room. He's going to sell off some of his hoard to pay for it."

Apparently, after Dad and I left, Wyn finally gave up his incessant brooding and came down with his proverbial, and literal, tail between his legs. He, too, called the station and submitted a full, unabridged confession. In his words, "Taking responsibility for eliciting an incendiary response in a being known to present volatile traits." He had said Taurin was not at fault, that a recent change in his circumstances had led him to behave like a jealous, irrational fledgling. That he was sorry for the destruction and pain caused, and that he would make amends to all involved, including accidentally almost killing me.

And one day I might find the strength to forgive him. For everything. Though I still reserved the right to hold an indefinite grudge.

After that I made one last phone call.

"Hey, uh, good afternoon, Officer Ozwald. I don't know if you remember me, Joey Silver?"

Oz laughed. "Knucktak! How are you?" he yelled down the receiver. "Been keeping yourself out of trouble I see. What can I do for you?"

It was a long shot, but the last I had. "My boyfr—mate has been wrongly arrested and, well, I was just wondering if there was anything you could do from, you know, your end to help speed up his release. He's innocent."

"Mmhmm." It sounded like his mouth was full. "Do you know when he was arrested? And who by? I can look into it for you. Can't make any promises, though."

"This morning about seven o'clock by the commissioner."

"The commissioner arrested him personally? Chief? Oh, Gods, this is brilliant. Your mate is the minotaur?" I could hear the smile in his voice.

"Yes," I said. "It's been a big misunderstanding, and basically he shouldn't have been arrested."

There was muffled talking, like Oz had covered the mouthpiece. When he came back to me, he was laughing. "Okay, Joey, I can't say anymore on the phone, but leave this with me."

"That's it?"

"That's it. Someone will be in touch. Thanks for the knucktak and the chat last time. It honestly meant a lot. Let's just say this'll make us even." He ended the call abruptly. I assumed because the line was recorded or monitored in some way, and he wasn't able to speak freely.

So now with all my calls made, and my contacts contacted, it was a case of waiting until they either released Horns, considering they had no evidence or reason to keep him there, or waiting for Mal to badger their lawyer.

I let out my breath of relief, and on the screen, I aligned the view finder, pointing the automatic crossbow at the human man's chest. It seemed harsh. He was only reading a book, minding his business, probably waiting for a train or something. The sun shone in the game, and the faux bird song triggered all manner of disassociated serotonin.

"No, line it up between his eyes," Goldie said. "It makes a really satisfying sshdunk sound when it hits. We did studies on the cognitive rewards of euphonious sounds."

I blinked at him. What a multi-faceted little fertility-fae he was. "I'm not going to shoot him in the face. That just seems gross."

Mal got home before Oz could call me back. He threw his key against the table and snarled. "The things I do for that gigantic motherfucking bull. Pay his fucking lawyer's fees. Fuck me, she's not cheap, she's—" He spotted me and stopped in his tracks.

"Hi," I offered.

"He's innocent. I've just called for Dima. You have to see this," said Goldie.

All the curtains and blinds simultaneously drew themselves, and the vampire floated in a few minutes later, rubbing his forehead, where it looked like a large angry lump was blossoming. Perhaps Goldie had yelled his name internally, and he'd smashed his head into the underside of his coffin.

That's exactly what happened, he said into my mind.

He showed Mal my memories of the previous night, and we told him everything that had happened while he was away. All the formal statements that had been submitted. Wyn's confession.

"So, why is he still there?" asked Dima.

"The commissioner's always been out to get him. It wouldn't surprise me if he's pretending there aren't any eyewitness statements," said Goldie.

"It wouldn't surprise me either," said Mal. "The evidence that he's keeping him on is flimsy at best. Apparently, a disputed claim and a report of him passing over the border. But I've just got off speaking with Seraphina." Goldie shifted in his seat, his eyes momentarily growing large. "She tells me she's dealt with it. No evidence now of either of you crossing the border, so if the commissioner tries to pin a time and location on Taur, he's going to have *a right fucking 'mare*." He laughed. "Seraphina's words."

"How is she?" Goldie asked, apparently unable to go without thinking about sex for fifteen seconds. Mal cocked his eyebrow but didn't bother to respond.

"I'll call Elektra now and let her know the latest." He puffed out a long sigh. "It's just . . . I don't think the commissioner will be happy until Taur is permanently behind bars. Like, what'll make him back off?"

"I've got no clue what Pounder's problem is," Goldie said.

Hold up.

"Did you just say Pounder?" I said, jumping to my feet.

"Yeah, Commissioner Ball-Sack Pounder."

"Oh. My. Gods! Where's my phone?" Goldie handed it to me. I pulled up the relevant contact details and pressed dial. "Tilly! Hi. Put your gods-damned mate on the phone!"

Chapter 38

Commissioner Pounder

I hummed as I sipped my coffee. Damn, even that was perfect today. Piping hot, not too watery, not over-brewed, and in my favourite mug. The one with MINOTAUR TEARS written on the front. The sky was a cloudless blue, the sun high, a rainbow-jay nesting in my window-box chirped sweetly at me, and Taurin, the bastard Minotaur — the only minotaur left in Borderlands — was behind bars. Hopefully, for the rest of his miserable human-length life.

I pushed the binoculars into the craters of my sockets and pointed them towards the stark building opposite the station. The main wing of Remy City Gaol. To Taurin, flat on his back on the bottom bunk. I chose that exact cell for him. I'd been congratulating myself ever since. Now I could watch exactly how miserable I was making him. My own twenty-four-seven, five-star streaming service. I would see everything. Every tear, every angry outburst, every threat he'd issue to his cellmates. He couldn't beat off without me knowing about it.

This whole circus was made so much sweeter once I scented him and figured out he'd imprinted. And there I was, thinking she was simply a girlfriend. As soon as I got the call to say he was involved in a major criminal damage case, I put in a phone call to his therapist. Squeaky, stubborn and reluctant to part with the info she was. Still I got what I wanted. Got the name of his mate. I may have bended a few truths, told her without that name people may get harmed. But then again, the truth is a subjective little mistress.

Did he deserve my borderline obsessive stalking? *Meh*. The guy was a minotaur. What other reason did I need?

The fact of the matter was, if it weren't for him, I'd never have met that deranged sister of his. Tina. What a piece of work she was. You think you know someone. Think you've found your mate. And then she goes and tells your wife. But she wasn't around anymore. Typical. You lose your temper eight times, and they turn on their tails and fucking run to the hills.

So where did that leave me? I've got to take my frustrations out on someone.

I was only annoyed they didn't let me keep that pretty pink engagement ring he had on him. It would have made the most delicious addition to my hoard. Still, I would wait until after the trial, let myself into the inmates possessions lock-up and help myself. Like I always did.

My computer did that hellish blooping noise, and I instinctively glanced down at the notification flashing up on the bottom right of the screen.

Eyewitness Statement and Full Confession Received from Aerowyn R. Pounder

I read the heading twice. Blinked. Massaged my temples. Closed the notification. I could still make it work. I hadn't come this far to throw it away now. Hadn't spent this long chasing one man, only for him to walk free again.

Knuckles rapped on the door, which opened without invitation, and Clive stepped in. I held up a palm to stop him before he even began.

He spoke around it. The insubordination in this place was the first thing I would address in tomorrow's debrief. "Chief, we need to let the minotaur go—"

"No."

"Another statement has come through. That makes five in total. And a full confession."

"They're covering for him."

"They've signed waivers to undergo Telepathic Memory Mapping. All of them. Including the dragon."

I swore. "What about the dragon's injuries?"

"Hospital's treated him, Chief. Few scratches, couple of missing scales." I winced. Missing scales could sting like a bitch, but they were hardly life threatening. Shame. "The dragon's saying he initiated the fight, and the injuries he received were in self-defence."

I swore twice. "I have a timestamp with the minotaur crossing the border. I can still pin him to the location of the destruction."

His gaze settled on my favourite mug, and that was where it stayed for the duration of our discussion. "There's been a problem with that particular piece of evidence. It's . . . it's gone missing. Vanished from the system. Disappeared."

"How?!"

"Not our end, Chief. Border patrol's end. No copies were kept since we share a database."

"Shit!" My free hand shot to my crest. I'd have to start all over. Wait for the bastard to lose it again. And I wasn't prepared for that.

An idea blossomed. I'd spent hours, days, collectively weeks, poring over his records. His problem was with dragons, and only dragons. Almost every time the big bull lost it over the last decade, a dragon was involved. Fucking minotaurs can be so speciesist. Can't seem to control himself around my kind. Good job I know a patient, persistent, and really fucking irritating dragon, ay?

I was going in.

Pay him a visit. Prod his buttons a little. Wait for the explosion. Wait for the thirteen floors of Remy City Gaol to crumble around us. There'll be casualties. Maybe fatalities. Even better.

"Uh, Chief, there's something else," said Clive, interrupting my blissful itinerary. "The dragon, he's your nephew?" My heart dropped into my tail. "There have been a few allegations made . . . about you. They've come from inside and outside the department. They're, uh—"

"What are the allegations?"

"They're sending the commissioner from Bordalis and a team to—"

"What are the allegations?!"

"Chief?" I cocked a brow. He swallowed. "Harassment,"*—okay, manageable—*"coercion,"*—could be worse—*"falsifying evidence,"*—hard to prove—*"speciesism,"*—who isn't a little speciesist?—*"and serious conflict of interest."

Well, fuck.

"They're saying that you had an extra-marital affair with the minotaur's sister and that your wife has copies of missing complaints against you dating back over a dozen years. There have been several reports submitted by officers in your department, as well. You're . . . shit, Chief, you're being placed under suspension while they investigate."

Clive barely flinched as my MINOTAUR TEARS mug exploded against the window.

Chapter 39

Taurin

I swear they waited until you were just about to drift off before slamming their metal batons against the metal of the door. It wouldn't even surprise me if they'd taped a cymbal on their side for extra shits and giggles. I'd barely slept all night, and there was only half an hour before they'd serve us breakfast.

"Minotaur, up, out!"

What now? Visitor? One more sermon from Elektra detailing how I was going to rot in this sweaty, dank arsehole? Mal demanding an apology? Pounder come to rub salt in his M-77 injunction?

They took me to an empty room. Another nondescript space with a white Formica table in the centre and two plastic backed chairs that would barely take my human weight.

"Strip," said the guard. I did as he ordered, while he stood in the corner supervising but pointedly not looking.

"Pounder's watching this, isn't he? He's probably behind that mirror now whacking off."

The guard said nothing but pursed his lips together.

I readied myself for the intimate search. Slow breaths, relaxed muscles. Not my first rodeo. But the gloves never went on. Instead, he handed a paper bag to me and pushed a tray across the table. In the bag, my jeans. My dirty, ripped, soot-blackened jeans. And my trainers. In the tray, a lighter, my wallet, a scrap of peach embroidered red fabric, and a deceptively plain black velvet box.

"I'm . . ." I turned to the guard. "I'm being released?"

He nodded once. I could have hugged him, but I was still naked, and I didn't fancy being pointed around and marched straight back to my cell for sexual assault. I shifted to my human form and shot into my jeans, stuffing my pockets with my things. The guard opened the door and together we walked, skipped more like, to reception to sign my release forms.

"—Holding him under false pretences. It's gross misconduct. When I'm through with the commissioner you'll be mopping him up off the—Taurin! You're free!"

"Elektra!" I hugged her. Lifted her off the ground, in fact.

"Oh, wow. Okay, you are strong," she said, awkwardly patting my shoulders. When I set her down, blush blossomed in those green cheeks of hers.

"Thank you so much. However you did this."

"Nope, not me. It was your mate." She smiled. "And your good friend, Mal, that orchestrated it all. I'm just doing my job."

The bond in my chest roared like it had been kick-started. "My mate?"

Elektra motioned a hand towards the glass double doors. Beyond them, idling in the street, was Mal's spearmint-coloured, classic convertible. Mal in the driver's seat, Goldie in the back chatting on a video-call, and Peaches . . .

Leaning against the passenger door, one hand on her hip, one hand shielding her eyes from the morning sun.

My body was already carrying me towards her.

"Sir, you need to sign—"

Distantly, Elektra spoke, "I can sign them. I'm his lawyer . . ."

The doors slid open, and I stepped outside. Peaches pushed herself off the car. Goldie and Mal's heads shot up.

I was running to her. And she was running to me. Leaping into my arms. Wrapping her legs around my waist, and her arms around my head. Her fingers sank into my hair, her face tucked under my horn, breathing me in.

Had I really only been in gaol for twenty-four hours? It felt so much longer. She wiped the tears from both of our faces.

"You're here," I said.

"You're free," she said.

"Every second away from you was an eternity."

"I'm sorry I couldn't come to see you yesterday."

"That fucking dragon," we both said together.

"I've got so much to tell you." She trailed kisses along my jaw. "You're innocent. Wyn's confessed to it all." Her kisses moved to my mouth. "Pounder's under investigation. They might sack him. Wyn's his nephew. He told them everything." More kisses. Hands moving across the plains of my bare shoulder blades. "Do you remember the last time you got arrested? The human police officer? I called him, asked for a favour. He liked me because I gave him knucktak and listened to his rants. Turns out over the years the commissioner has built up quite a few enemies over the force, and they all have been waiting for the perfect opportunity to submit their complaints. I never want to be apart from you again."

"Tell me more," I said, returning the butterfly kisses along her neck, and the neckline of her t-shirt.

"About Pounder?"

"No, that can wait." And it could. It could wait a lifetime. "Tell me more about us." I thought I'd never see her again. Really thought I'd lost everything.

"We're fated," she said, and my heartbeat tumbled over itself. Whatever I had been expecting her to say, it wasn't that. "Fated mates, right? We belong together. You're mine." She laughed and ran her hands over my shoulders. "This entire mountain is mine."

"That's your little flag there at the top of my head."

"And I'm wholly yours. And I'll always be yours. I want to get old with you, and eat falafel by the docks, and serve pasta at your broken table, and drink Mal's wine, and fuck you in the shower. And I want to kiss you in the mornings before you go to work, and sniff your disgusting sweaty, log-lugging, man smells when you get home, and I want to be there when you start your own cake decorating business."

A sob escaped my throat. I was sobbing. A six-eleven minotaur openly sobbing, and not giving a single fuck.

"I want to spend forever with you," she said, her voice cracking. "Is that okay?"

I kissed her. No time for build-up, I went straight in there. Tongue on tongue. Heavy, needy. My hands splayed against her back, pressing our bodies as close as they could be, leaving not a millimetre's gap between us.

Eventually, I broke the kiss. "I love you."

She didn't return the sentiment, instead she said, "Do you think our babies will have horns?"

"Fuck, I love you." I kissed her again, dropping her weight just a little so that I could rub the seam of her jeans over the bulging fly of mine. "You are so going to get it."

She beamed at me. "Yes please, but not in front of these three."

"Three?"

At that exact moment, Goldie held up his phone and said, "Yeah, he's out. Look."

The velour interior of Dima's coffin filled the screen. That was the trouble with video-calling vampires. "Yes, mate!" he crackled.

With a final kiss and a final whispered, "I love you," Peaches swung her legs free, and Mal instantly pulled me into a one-armed hug.

"Mate," he said, cupping my nape and bringing our foreheads together.

"Thank you," I said. He shook his head. "And sorry. I'm really sorry. About what I said yesterday. I . . . I was so scared I'd lost everything. I was out of line."

"It's under the bridge."

"I love you, man."

Goldie hopped out and wrapped his arms around me, Dima's coffin still visible in his hand. He didn't even try to grope me or rub his dick on me. Maybe he was growing up. "Pounder's going down for good this time."

We got in the car, Goldie in the front, now arguing with his phone about whether Dima could read minds through video-call. I took the backseat with Peaches, her lap in mine, our legs across the seat.

Mal spent the entire journey home explaining exactly how they'd wangled my release and outmanoeuvred Pounder. Not that I heard much of his speech. Between the rushing of city air against my ears, and my fingers teasing their way up and under Peaches' t-shirt, it was very hard to focus.

"Wait, are you wearing Goldie's clothes?"

"She looks cute, don't she?" Goldie said, then immediately turned back to Dima. "But how did you know I'm not wearing underwear? I never said that out loud . . ."

She looked more than cute.

Joey looked like home.

I had to at least say hello to Dima before I whisked Peaches up to my bedroom.

"You had me worried there," he said, pulling me chest to chest and wrapping his arm around my back. "I hated that place when I was there."

"Shit!" said Peaches. Everyone flinched. "Shit, I totally forgot."

"Forgot what?"

She read out a text from her phone. "Joey, your crap is boxed up in my hallway. Pick it up today or I'm tossing it onto the street." She looked at me, her eyes pleading. "I, uh, I kind of got myself kicked out of my flat. And I lost the prize money too."

"I couldn't care less about the prize money." I pulled her tight to my body, and turned to my landlord. "Hey Mal, can Peaches move in for a little while?"

"Like I would try to separate fated mates." He leaned forward and peered down at her phone, a smile spreading across his face. "Why don't Goldie and I go get your stuff while you two catch up?"

"Yes!" said Goldie, leaping to his feet as though the most exciting adventure lay ahead of him.

"Gods, I would love to see Hell-Bitch's face when a fae and an incubus rock up to collect my stuff," said Peaches. She gave the address to my flatmates.

Dima piped up. "I can show you later. So, I'm probably going to hit the velour . . ."

"I'm driving," said Goldie, snatching up Mal's keys from the side table.

"Not happening," said Mal, and they both made for the door.

"Hey Goldie," said Dima. Goldie turned. "Don't forget the cat."

Peaches' shirt hit the carpet before we had crossed the threshold to my bedroom. My face found the valley between her breasts. Her bra still smelled of smoke. She reached a hand behind her and pinged it off.

"Wait, are those his jeans too?" Why did they fit her so well? She slid out of them and kicked them aside. My jeans fell to the floor with a muffled thud. Neither of us had on underpants. I laid her down on top of my messy bed covers — she must have slept there last night — and caged her body with mine.

And for a moment that felt like hours, and at the same time, fractions of a second, I simply stared at her. Not a stitch of clothing or makeup on. Her curls, wilder than usual, fanned out over the pillow. She smelt of herself and my soap, and the mix of the two was doing funny things to my insides. Had I really forgotten how beautiful Joey was? Or did she get more beautiful?

I thumbed down her nose and across her cheek, bringing my lips to hers. If I didn't remember her accurately when I was in gaol, I damned would now.

"I missed these lips," I said. "And these freckles." I kissed the space under her ribs where the vulnerable soft flesh of her stomach began. "And these tits. I love these tits." She laughed, and I took one in my mouth, sucking the nipple to a hard bud.

Her breath hitched, and the bond buzzed. Gods, I missed that buzzing.

"I thought I'd never see you again," I said.

"Talk later," Joey replied, and opened her thighs to me.

I didn't need to be told twice. I lowered myself to her and, without preamble, slipped inside. Just the tip, barely inside, but I wanted to kiss her as we fucked. I wanted to watch her. I didn't want her with a face full of shoulder. She arched her back, and bucked onto me, trying to swallow more of me. Trying to sink down, but I had her pinned.

Slowly, in and out. My thrusts were unhurried, deliberate. There would be another time to brace against the wall and pound her senseless, but now was not it. I needed to feel, see, hear, smell everything. Every skipped heartbeat, every flutter of her sex, every time she moaned my name. Every quiver of her lip, every soft exhale, every time her grip tightened.

"Give me more, Taurin."

I shook my head, not ready for it to be over. I didn't think I ever would be. I took her hands and pinned them above her head with one of mine. Her eyelids fluttered closed, her breaths escaping in pants against my hair.

Every thrust was an apology. I was sorry for letting my animal instincts take over. For her folks' house, the coffee-shop, all the places I'd razed before I even knew her, everywhere. For putting people in danger. I was sorry for letting it control the type of person I was. I was closed off and frightened. Frightened to get close, experience life, be myself. I was a miserable, grumpy bastard, and I was sorry I didn't let her in sooner. She found the real me, even though I tried to hide everything, and spoiler alert, the real me was me all along. I'll still always be a miserable, grumpy bastard, but at least now I know she loved me as I was. Accepted that about me. And I was beginning to accept that in myself.

It didn't matter what others thought of me. People will always be prejudiced about my kind. What mattered was family. Mal, and Dima, and Goldie.

And Joey. They all loved me. Unconditionally.

Beneath me, Peaches became frantic. She had worked a hand free and slapped at my shoulder, pushing my head up from the crook of her neck.

"Are you close?" she asked.

"I'm just enjoying you."

She smiled. That naughty, knowing smile. "I'm so close. I'm going to come any second. And then . . ." Her breaths were catching, she spoke between whines. "You're going to . . . fuck me. Hard. Wearing your bull head."

"Oh, Gods," was all I could manage. My knees turned to liquid.

It had been a fantasy since—Who was I kidding? Since coming to Borderlands. It was the ultimate fantasy. To find a woman so accepting of me she'd let me fuck her in my shifted form. I might be able to think better with my human head, but with my bull form, I could *feel* everything one thousand-fold.

Peaches slipped one hand between our bodies and roughly massaged her clit. Her back lifted her off the bed. With her other hand she pulled me by the horns to her chest so that I could hear the buzz of the bond as she came hard around me, clenching my length with her sex.

After the buzzing had finished, she looked up at me through heavy lidded eyes. "How do you want me?"

With one movement, I scooped her up and flipped her onto her knees. I wanted this. Fantasised about it since leaving the Winterlands. I just didn't want her to see me. At least not the first time. Baby steps. She understood. I knew she did. The bond told me.

She placed her palms against the headboard and tossed a quick look over her shoulder. "Give me everything you've got."

I shifted — Gods, this felt weird — and slipped inside her again. And I lost everything. All sense of control. My slow, methodical rhythm turned into a frenzied pursuit. It was intense, like nothing I'd ever experienced before. Each stroke of her pussy against me was like a mini climax. The only time my dick got attention while in my shifted form was from my own hand, but this . . . This . . .

Made to fit. Fated mates.

My hands sealed themselves around her hips. Hers gripped the headboard. There was no way I could make this last more than five minutes. Four and a half. At a push. Everything was too delicious. The filthy wet slapping sounds, the sight of her white knuckles, her soundless screams, as though each thrust had knocked all the air from her lungs.

The fucking shape of her. Where her waist dipped in and curved back out. Her ass smacking against me. I watched, ravenously, the juncture of us. Watched her sex clinging to me as I pulled out. Watched her tremble as I pushed back in.

All too soon, I had reached the point of no return. I braced my hands over hers and furiously drove it home, fucking her hard, until I tossed back my head and roared my ecstasy, rattling the entire room. Filling her, overfilling her, with my release.

Afterwards, we collapsed beside each other, one gelatinous pool of boneless limbs. I didn't immediately shift back. She just fit so well into my form. I draped my arm around her shoulder, and her fingers traced lazy circles in the fur on my stomach.

I didn't have any words to fill the silence. Thank you didn't seem enough. She loved me as I was, in whichever form I took. She let me fuck her wearing my bullhead, and she folded into my arms without flinching.

"So." Peaches lifted her gaze to me, her face sweaty, baby hairs glued to her forehead, lips kiss-swollen. I'd never seen her more beautiful. "We're married?"

I froze. How did she know? "I . . . I never meant it to be a thing you didn't have a say in. We . . . I got carried away and—"

"I'm not mad about it."

"You're not?"

"I don't think either of us had a choice in it. Not if we're fated mates."

Someone told her. "Mal or Goldie?"

"Goldie. He cooked me a chicken burger and made me shoot humans in the face."

I laughed and pulled her tighter into the cuddle. "I think that's his way of welcoming you to the family."

And then I remembered something. Abruptly I dropped her, hopped over her naked body, and groped around on the floor for my jeans. Digging in the pockets, my hands closed around the ring box. Now was it one or two knees I was supposed to kneel on?

It's one knee, Dima said into my head.

Get out of my head, Dima. And thanks, I said back to him.

You're welcome, and stop thinking so loudly, I'm trying to sleep.

Peaches watched the silent exchange, her head cocked to the side, her tongue peeking out from the corner of her mouth. Since I was already kneeling on the floor, I brought one knee up, and wobbling, put my foot down. Her expression slid from intrigue, to recognition, to perhaps excitement. I realised how completely naked I was, and that I still had my bullhead on. And, well, if she said yes to me like this, we really were meant to be.

Mal had told me to give a grand, romantic speech, declare my all-consuming love for her, but in that moment, I couldn't string together just how much she meant to me, everything she'd done for me. Standing by me, expecting nothing more than simply letting her in.

It was too much, the things I felt for this woman.

The overwhelming love I had for her.

In the end I went with, "I really fucking love you. Will you human marry me?"

Chapter 40

Joey

Two months later

She purred. Like a cheetah that was also a professional opera singer. I dropped my foot to the gas and felt her notes travel up through my spine, mutating into endorphins on their way, as I pulled onto the highway leading to the main gates of UR.

Big Red. My nearly new, bright red, 4x4 baby. An engagement gift from Horns. Only four-thousand miles on the clock. Boxy, red faux-suede interior, round headlamps, super fucking cute. With a top speed of one-eighty. One-fucking-eighty. Ha, take that milk float!

Taurin smiled at me from the passenger seat. There was so much room in this car he only had to hunch his shoulders the tiniest amount.

His lawyer — and Mal's lawyer, their family lawyer? — had wangled an out-of-court settlement from Aerowyn for damages and trauma.

Tilly spent the entire mediated appointment in Elektra's boardroom laughing her head off, insisting her husband's hoard could pay the agreement twice over and, *"That'll teach the fiery bastard."*

Horns paid off his secret debts to Mal and Goldie, and with the extra, he bought a new (to me) car. I loved her. I gripped the steering wheel with both hands, enjoying the way my ring threw glowing peach and red fractals onto the ceiling. Between my delivery jobs — I took on a new restaurant, Carly's, keeping Remy in a never-ending supply of falafel — and zooming to and from wedding planning appointments, I was never out of her.

Ash said we could marry at his beach house, so long as we invited him. Which we did. And Lauren too. Also, Russ, because he really held a large majority in the architecture of our relationship. Horns' sister, Tina promised to come for the big day, though somebody would have to meet her at the border.

In terms of vendors, so far, we had Carly's booked for the catering. Goldie asked if he could bake the cake, and Horns would decorate it with sugar paste roses. I didn't have a dress picked out yet, but I had a sneaking suspicion it would be red.

Mum and Dad finally moved into their new build by the sea. A bungalow, about eight miles from their ruined house, only a short commute from Dad's depot, and Mum's new farm shop job. It was idyllic. High vaulted ceilings, open plan living-dining-kitchen area, log burner, panoramic sea-scape windows, a fucking reading nook. And Horns was mid-crafting their bespoke furniture, with only the guest bed left to complete. After that, he'd promised them a log store and a chicken coop. The claw foot tub was unfortunately not salvageable, but it now sat in the garden overlooking the lapping waves of the ocean. "I might plant it up," said Mum. "Or I might find somebody to fix the cracks and plumb it in right here. How wonderful would that be?"

Dad put his incomparable insurance finagling skills to the metal and conjured Horns an airtight policy, should he ever See Red again and destroy anything. Meaning no matter what future damage he might cause, he shouldn't ever need to borrow money from Mal to pay for it again.

"Because allowances should be made for innate species idiosyncrasies. They wouldn't punish a werewolf for turning at the full moon, so why should they penalise a minotaur for being a minotaur. Especially if he had been goaded into such a state," Dad said, when Horns and I delivered his newly crafted and upholstered armchair. I was so shocked I dropped my glass, and Horns surprised everyone by swooping in and hugging him, lifting him from the ground.

They sacked Pounder. Though the investigation was still ongoing, so Elektra never had much to update us on, but we all submitted formal statements. Of course, Horns' concerns with the ex-commissioner stretched back over twelve, thirteen years, so he frequently dipped in and out of his lawyer's office to add more info to the pile. And Ash, being the absolute shit-stirrer he was, decided to throw the weight of his lawyers behind the case as well. Between his solicitors and Elektra, they were fairly certain Pounder was looking at considerable gaol time.

"He'll be in a special wing," Ash said. "Can you imagine the number of men and mythics that dragon has put there? They'd certainly be pleased to see his face in the exercise yard. Don't you think? And don't worry, by the time he's released, both of your insignificant human-length lives would have reached their natural conclusions."

"Jeepers, thanks," I replied.

And Horns had continued with his therapy. He'd even started hypnotherapy to help him stay present and calm should he get so enraged that Seeing Red was an inevitability. A sort of self-intervention type thing. So far, during his sessions, he'd only smashed up two side tables, a standard lamp, and burst seven inflatable dragons. All in all, I think we could call that a win.

I parked Big Red as close to the entrance as I could get, and together we walked into the university.

"Good luck today. Not that you'll need it," Horns said to me, pushing an errant spray of hair behind my ear and pulling me into a kiss so deep and passionate, Ben, the merman receptionist had to clear his throat to bring us back to our senses.

"Enjoy your few hours with Russ, and I'll meet you in Tallywhacker's for lunch."

He kissed me again, and I watched my fiancé walk towards, and disappear into, the elevators, on his way to Cake Decorating 101.

I approached the desk. "Joey Silver." I gave a sheepish smile. "Here to start an Emergency Response Vehicular Driver Training course."

Tapping the edge of his papers against the countertop, Ben said, "Welcome back, Joey."

The end.

About the author

Jemma is a regular human author living in Bristol, UK, with her husband, daughters and an anxiety-ridden Brussels Griffon.

She writes funny, smutty, very British stories about humans falling in love with non humans.
She loves dick jokes, foods where sugar is the first listed ingredient, and ignoring all her grown up problems.

You can find her on Instagram @jemma_croft
On tiktok (if she can figure it out) @jemma_croft
On her newsletter www.jemmacroft.com (cool free stuff)
Or by email jemmacroftauthor@gmail.com

She would love to hear from you.

COMING SOON...

By the Fae

Dream job – check.
Dream apartment – nearly check.
Super-hot fae boyfriend – Uh, she'll have to get back to you on that one.

At age 29, technically-not-a-virgin, **Holly Briar**, thought she'd have it all by now. After all, everything else on her metaphorical (and physical) list is checked off, but she's still very much lacking in the love dept. When her crush makes it clear he's looking for a partner with more bedroom experience, Holly embarks on a mission to find someone willing to teach her exactly what fae men are into.

Borderlands' most notorious rake has a problem. **Goldie** needs to design a new video game that will appeal to humans, or risk losing his job. The trouble is, he hates humans. Everything about them. Especially their incessant need for love and their stiflingly short lifespans. But there's a new girl at work. She's human, and she knows what will sell a game to her kind. And she has a little problem that only Goldie can solve.

Reluctantly the pair come to an agreement to help each other out. But on one condition . . .
Under no circumstances, whatsoever, are either of them allowed to fall in love.

Available to pre-order now!

Printed in Great Britain
by Amazon

23518705R00175